The Key to the Pit: Resurrection

JOSEPH BUSA

Copyright © 2018 Joseph Busa

All rights reserved.

josephbusa.com

ISBN: 1981879870
ISBN-13: 978-1981879878

To Michelle

JOSEPH BUSA

PROLOGUE
Monday, 25 November 1963, Texas

Qarinah Pirez was driving south out of Waco along Interstate 35 at over a hundred miles per hour, she thought her jaw might be broken and she was at risk of going into shock. She had never been badly injured in her life and vowed to never repeat the experience. She deeply regretted not taking a head shot, but then how was she to have known that the Soviet agent would wear a bullet-proof vest, an item of personal protective clothing that nobody in the World had seen before?

None of that mattered now. No, what mattered was that the American president was dead and that a man named Jack Ruby had saved her the trouble of having the patsy, Oswald, killed. The Russian was a loose end, albeit a highly dangerous one, who could be dealt with at her leisure. With Kennedy gone, Pirez was certain that the costly moon project and the war in Indochina would both wither on the vine without him.

൫൫൫൫

Two days later Pirez's hopes for the future were dashed, when President Lyndon B. Johnson used his address before Joint Session of Congress, to reaffirm Kennedy's pledge to put a man on the moon. In the weeks and months that followed, Pirez was dismayed to hear that the war in Vietnam was escalating. It would finally reach the point of no return on March 8th, 1965, when the 9th Marine Expeditionary Brigade waded ashore at China Beach.

ONE
Present day, Geneva, Switzerland

It was a hot cloudless summer evening in Geneva. Not that the CERN professor knew, or cared, what the weather was like above the subterranean complex that was home to the world's largest machine, the Large Hadron Collider. The professor had been given the honour of flicking the switch which would send massive quantities of electrical power pulsing through the giant superconducting magnets, causing two opposing particle beams to accelerate to world record speeds. But as the Protons traversed the subterranean ring at speeds close to the speed of light, huge dark clouds started condensing out of the seemingly dry air hovering above the city. Then, as the thousands of millions of particle collisions produced the first of the micro black holes, the lightning began.

It didn't take much to upset Geneva's cossetted multi-millionaires, but they'd have been right to be worried about the bizarre bolts of lightning, as all was not right in the subterranean complex below their feet. But one of their number had been expecting the storm, having invested billions of dollars and years of her life, in the hope that humankind might, one day, create the conditions on planet Earth that had hitherto been the preserve of the gods. Her name was Lilith Namdar.

'Is there a problem, Fyodor?' asked Namdar, beads of sweat visible on her forehead. 'The screen is blank. You assured me that the satellites were in the correct positions!'

Fyodor Maknov's heart was racing, he had never seen the mistress flustered before and it was making him nervous. He had been assured that the satellites were fully operational, ready, and waiting to record electromagnetic pulses generated anywhere upon the surface of the earth.

But without visual proof, neither he nor Lilith Namdar knew what to believe.

'Don't worry madam, everything is in place, every detail is being recorded,' said Maknov, lying. 'The storm is most likely disrupting the uplink.'

'You know how important it is that –'

'The link has been established, the images will be directed to the monitors at any moment,' interrupted Maknov. In all the years that he had worked for Namdar he'd never once dared interrupt her, but today, the stakes so high, he'd forgotten himself.

'Thank you, Fyodor' replied Namdar as she studied the images on the giant plasma screen. In a few moments she would know whether she had interpreted the ancient texts correctly. Then, to her relief, whilst the lightning bolts lit up the skies over Geneva, an electromagnetic field was detected over the ancient stone circle of Stonehenge. The invisible field, coloured pale blue by the software, started flowing, like a river, down through England, across the English Channel, through France and Switzerland, passing through CERN, before coming to a halt at Egypt's Great Pyramid on the Giza plateau. That had been a marvel to behold, but it was only the beginning. Namdar held her breath as the river of primal energy split into multiple streams; each one connecting the Great Pyramid with every other ancient pyramid on planet earth.

Namdar rose from the mat she had been sitting on. She was an imposing figure for a lady, standing close to six feet tall in her stockinged feet. Maknov thought she looked fifty-five years old, but then he'd thought that she'd looked exactly the same age when he'd first met her, seven long years ago. She had dark brown eyes, with streaks of grey running through her ginger brown hair. But just like most other women, Namdar kept her chronological age a closely guarded secret. Nobody, not even her personal physician, knew how old she really was.

'I hope that everything is to your satisfaction?' asked a relieved Maknov.

'Yes, Fyodor, we have done well, very well indeed,' she said as she wiped tears from her eyes. 'Are arrangements in place for the final meeting of the Grand Council?'

'Yes, mistress.'

'And what of our plumbing problem?'

Maknov looked worried again. 'The problem is more complicated than initial reports suggested. Multiple leaks have been detected, but rest assured they are being plugged as we speak.'

'Then a celebration is in order, Fyodor. Please join me in a glass of Artsakh.'

A few minutes later, Namdar and her faithful manservant were standing, glasses in hand, facing the giant plasma screen.

'A toast, Fyodor. Santé, grands fruits, joye and temps mellifique,' said Namdar.

'Santé, grands fruits, joye and temps mellifique!' repeated the two of them raising their glasses.

TWO

Harry Windsor had arrived at the Parisian Cafe half an hour before his target, Shahram Abbasi, an Iranian nuclear scientist and professor at Shahid Besheshti University. Abbasi was in Paris for discussions with his peers from the budding Syrian nuclear industry. The Syrian government, reeling after years of civil war was very keen to make strides in its nuclear programme. The regime having taken the view that they could only remain in power if they possessed *real* weapons of mass destruction. Poison gas and chemical weapons had their place, but the footage of the very public executions of other middle eastern dictators had unified them in their belief that such weapons were never going to deter the foreigners from trying to remove them from power.

Windsor had been an assassin for many years, having been approached to work for Her Majesty's Secret Intelligence Service on a contractual basis shortly after retiring from a long and distinguished career in the Special Boat Service, the SBS. His peripheral vision was excellent and now, out of the corner of his eye, he noted that two bodyguards were accompanying the nuclear scientists - one minding Abbasi, the other one shadowing the Syrian delegation. He wasn't one to suffer nerves, but now, sat in the presence of Abbasi he was feeling nauseous, a feeling he hadn't experienced for thirty years. He tried to take his mind off Abbasi by focusing his attention on the bodyguards, who were sitting on separate tables on either side of the scientists' table.

In addition to the scientists and bodyguards, were two men Windsor assumed to be facilitators from each country's diplomatic services. Just like the scientists, they were lean, intelligent looking men, but unlike the scientists they looked relaxed and comfortable in their own skins.

Most of the scientists' real work had already been done, Abassi having already spent three long and exhaustive days with his Syrian peers. Today was a semi-informal day, included in his schedule on the behest of the diplomatic corps, in the hope of fostering real and lasting friendships between the scientists of the two countries.

The bodyguards had been quick to note Windsor's physicality underneath his tailor-made clothes. Middle-aged he might be, but the years had been kind to him - his fifteen and a half stones of muscle, bone and sinew made him a highly capable killing machine. Windsor was listening intently as the waiter took the scientists' order, he had been told that Abbasi always drank green tea with a single teaspoonful of honey. He wasn't completely fluent in Arabic but understood it well enough to know that everyone, except the mark, had ordered strong black coffee; Abbasi opting, as expected, for a cup of green tea.

Windsor made his move when he saw the waiter returning from the bar with a tray containing the scientists' refreshments. He stood up from his table and started walking slowly in the direction of the restroom. The bodyguard sitting closet to Windsor shifted his gaze to the man bag lying unattended under Windsor's table. Whilst the bodyguard's attention was drawn to the unattended bag, Windsor purposely blocked the path of the waiter. As Windsor and the waiter stood facing one another, a beeping tone could be heard coming from the bag lying under the vacant table, the tone capturing both bodyguards' attention as Windsor had intended.

It was now, whilst the bodyguards' eyes were fixed on the unattended bag, that Windsor stepped across the waiter's path, trapping him between two tables. The waiter tried to move to the side to let Windsor pass, but he had nowhere to go. Windsor complimented the waiter, in perfect French, on the establishment's excellent English Breakfast Tea, touching the waiter's wrist as he did so. The waiter instinctively looked down at his wrist, only to see the customer staring over his right shoulder when he looked up again. The waiter couldn't help himself and turned his head to look at what had caught the patron's attention. In those few moments, which passed in a flash to the waiter, Windsor waved his left hand over the serving tray and squirted a few droplets of clear liquid into the cup of green tea, from a flesh-coloured syringe concealed within the palm of his hand. The act completed; Windsor nodded his appreciation at the waiter, before continuing on his way to the toilets.

The bodyguards, having missed the seemingly innocuous exchange between Windsor and the waiter, were starting to relax, as they sensed the danger of being blown to pieces by an improved explosive device had passed. They resumed scanning the room whilst the waiter served the refreshments. The scientists, who had been oblivious to any danger that they might have been in, continued their highly technical conversation about uranium enrichment and centrifuges, the moment the waiter left their table.

On his return, Windsor made a show of taking a mobile phone out of his man bag and reading a text message from it. Then, feigning urgency, he placed a twenty euro note on the table before hastily collecting his belongings and walking briskly towards the exit. One of the bodyguards smiled at the performance, satisfied that Windsor was just another businessman running late for a meeting.

Later that evening Shahram Abbasi was taken ill with suspected food poisoning. The next morning, he was rushed to Paris' famous Pitié-Salpêtrière Hospital where he underwent extensive tests for his mystery illness. Many famous people had been treated in the hospital over the years, including former president Jacques Chirac who had a pacemaker fitted there in 2008 and the late, Diana, Princess of Wales whose dead body was taken there in 1997. For Abbasi the prognosis was not good and within a few days the Iranian nuclear scientist would be dead.

THREE

Sanda Osmond started her day hoping that she was still in the throes of a nightmare, having seemingly opened her eyes to see her bed surrounded by large black dogs. She had just started to convince herself that she might actually be awake when the dogs vanished and people, purporting to be the police, started hammering on the front door of her one-bedroomed apartment. An hour later the little-known eco-blogger had been fingerprinted, had a DNA sample taken, and issued with a rough blue blanket as she was locked-up in a cold police cell.

Osmond, who had never been arrested before in her life, now found herself detained under section 44 of the Terrorism Act. She didn't yet know it, but her arrest had followed that of nine eco-activists who had attempted to destroy a genetically modified crop trial, stabbing a security guard in the process. Osmond knew nothing about the raid on the farm but had been arrested because four of the nine activists were wearing badges containing the logo of her website, MutantRainbow.net.

The police had seized all Osmond's communication equipment, telling her that copy images of her computer's hard drives would be analyzed by a Metropolitan Police computer forensics team. Knowing that she hadn't done anything wrong, Osmond had declined, probably unwisely, the services of a solicitor and was now well into the second hour of questioning.

'Miss Osmond, I'll ask you again. What do you know about the break-in at Wakefield farm?' asked Detective Inspector Barnes.

'I've already told you, I've read about the crop trial, like thousands of others, but that's all I know about the place?'

'We've got your phone records and have recorded

images of your computer hard drives. Soon we'll know everything there is to know about you. So why don't you do yourself a favour and start telling us the truth?'

'Look, Inspector. I declined the services of a solicitor because I've done nothing wrong. You can ask me the same questions a hundred times, but I can't tell you what I don't know.'

'And I've told you that a security guard has been stabbed. A very serious crime has been committed, and we have every reason to believe that you are responsible for inciting others, through articles posted on your website, into destroying a GMO crop trial.'

'So, I've written a few articles about GMO crops, what of it? I've never written or recorded anything that might encourage anyone to destroy anything... not illegally at least.'

'Several of your blogs ask for a "call to arms" saying that "GMO trials must be stopped". Some of your language could be construed as inflammatory'.

'And as I've said, several times already, I might not like GMO foods, and I might think that they have the potential to do harm on a massive scale, but my main concern relates to what are known as the Regenisists - the Synthetic Biologists. Sure, I'm not happy at the prospect of eating genetically modified food, but the reason I do what I do is because I've taken the trouble to research what the corporations are doing with our food. The authorities might not like the Dark Web, but I use it to source stories about mutant babies being born in illegal laboratories, as scientists race against each other to create what they are calling "perfect human specimens". People are being forced into posting things on the Dark Web because they don't feel safe doing so on the mainstream internet. I've met activists who claim that scientists in unlicensed laboratories are trying to recreate mythical beasts, such as Monitors, Mermaids and Unicorns. Now Unicorns, I can just about live with, but half-human half-animal hybrids; if any of that stuff is true, it's got to be stopped! All I'm trying to do is help keep humankind safe. People are fragile, the planet can look after itself.'

'Are you saying that you consider yourself to be a saviour of mankind?'

'What? No of course not. I'm not delusional or anything like that. I'm just a blogger, a self-published anti-establishment journalist, trying to make people aware of what's happening out in the world before it's too late to do anything about it.'

'And it doesn't concern you that four of the nine individuals arrested at Wakefield farm were wearing MutantRainbow badges?'

'I've already told you - I don't sell badges! I don't know where they would have gotten them from. I haven't got copyright over my logo. If somebody is making money advertising my website, then fair play to them!'

'A security guard is in intensive care. He might die of his injuries. Doesn't that concern you?'

'What I think, has no bearing on the matter, because I don't know anything about it.'

'Very well Miss Osmond, I'm going to conclude our interview there. You haven't been charged with anything, but your computer equipment stays with us until the forensic inspection has been completed. It goes without saying that you will be rearrested should we discover any information that contradicts your statement.'

Another half hour passed before Osmond finally had her freedom. She was angry at having her computers confiscated, but her mobile phone had been returned to her. She had been through a very stressful sixteen hours, but her main concern on leaving the police station was that she hadn't thought to copyright the logo of her website.

FOUR

Osmond was standing in the window of a charity shop across the road from the cafe where she planned to meet a grey-hatted hacker known, to the activist community, as Loki. She had no practical experience of counter-surveillance measures, but had read somewhere that looking out through shop windows provided good protection from prying eyes. She wasn't sure exactly who she was hiding from, it just felt like the right thing to do.

She'd had a good night's sleep, which surprised her. There had been no repeat of the early morning call by Her Majesty's constabulary or nightmares about large black dogs. She couldn't wait to get her computers back from the police, having been forced to spend the previous day viewing the internet through her smart phone. She knew a lot about computers and owned a lot of aging, high end IT equipment. Her systems might be old, but they allowed her to run encryption programs of sufficient complexity to keep out most agents of the surveillance superstate. She used a proxy server to access the internet but it was her use of TOR, The Onion Router, that made her and techies like her a thorn in the side of the authorities who couldn't easily track her movements through the Dark Web. Not that that seemed to count for much when the police had taken her computers from her.

Osmond had been prompted to buy an anti-spyware program from Loki because she had a feeling that the police might load a tracking program onto her computers, before returning them to her. She'd been standing close to the charity shop window for over twenty-five minutes and there was no sign of him, which was unusual as he had been early for all their previous meetings. Under normal circumstances she would never have contemplated buying a copy of Dion Fortune's Psychic Self-Defense. She'd randomly selected it to stop the suspicious glances she'd started receiving from the shop staff.

Eventually she gave up waiting on Loki to arrive. Feeling more than a little pissed-off at having wasted her time she walked across the road to the cafe and bought herself a cappuccino. Poor and unemployed she might be, but she always found the money to buy books and coffee. She was skimming through a chapter entitled Projection of the Etheric Body when she spotted Loki in the queue. It was clear to Osmond, the instant they made eye contact, that something was troubling the cyber-hacker.

Osmond watched as Loki sat down at a separate table, something he had never done before. She started to wonder if news of her arrest had spread amongst the activist community. But even if it had done, she couldn't think why Loki would care about it, as he was a computer hacker with no obvious interest in eco-activism. She spent her time scanning the pages of her book hoping that Loki would give her a sign. Finally, he finished his coffee and dropped a folded-up piece of paper on her table as he made his way to the exit. She waited for him to leave before opening and reading his note, which read "The police have you under surveillance. Meet me across the road in the charity shop in five minutes or the deal's off."

Osmond waited four minutes before leaving the café and walking across the road to the charity shop.

'I don't know what you've done, but I'm as sure as I can be that you are being followed,' said Loki.

'What makes you think that?'

'I was keeping a look out when you arrived and couldn't believe it when I noticed them following you. There are at least two of them, a man and woman.'

'You're certain of that?'

'Surveillance is part of how I make a living. You set my spider sense off when you came in here instead of heading straight to the café. Trust me, somebody is definitely following you. I'll give it to them, they're good. They'll be invisible to you, but there's no hiding from a third party who knows what to look out for.'

'Are they the police?'

'Who knows? I hope for your sake that they are.'

'What do you mean by that?'

'I don't know. All I know was that I was tempted to walk away when I spotted them.'

'You've got the app with you?'

'Yes, you can have it, but chances are the people following you will know what you've come here to buy from me.'

'Will it still work?'

'It will work fine for a day or two. But if these people have already gained access to your computer, it won't take them long to exploit it. If I were you, I'd save it for a rainy day.'

'Why's that?'

'The program will load on most any operating system. You can use it to search and destroy any program you like. So why waste it?'

'Do you still want a hundred quid for it?'

'No, I've changed my mind, you can have it gratis. You're obviously doing something that somebody doesn't like, and I like that.'

Loki passed Osmond a clear plastic bag containing a green memory stick. She took a quick look at it before placing it in the small front pocket of her blue jeans.

'Thanks, I owe you one,' said Osmond.

'Keep an eye out for a guy in grey hooded sweatshirt. He's about five ten with blonde hair. The woman's a brunette, wearing pale blue cloths. Be lucky,' said Loki as he left the charity shop.

Osmond's heart was pounding. She picked up a china cup and held it up to the light streaming through the large shop window, but her eyes weren't focused on the cup, they were looking passed it into the street. Finally, she thought she saw one of them, a man in a grey hoodie staring back at her from inside the coffee shop. Osmond watched as the hoodie vacated his seat, which was immediately taken by a brunette, dressed in blue.

The man wearing the hoodie left the café and started jogging along the road in the same direction as Loki. Osmond, worried about what might happen to the hacker, left the charity shop, and started running after the hoodie. He stopped suddenly, raising his left hand to his ear, forcing Osmond to run straight passed him. She didn't stop running until she came to another coffee shop, about one hundred metres further along the road. Osmond walked into the coffee shop, bought herself a hot chocolate, found herself a seat, and pretended to read her book. She was hoping that the hoodie would chose to follow her instead of the hacker.

Osmond was trying to get her head around what was happening around her. Sure, a security guard had been stabbed, but incidents like that happened all the time. Nobody had been murdered, so why would anyone, especially the police, bother putting so much time and effort into following an unknown blogger's movements?

That was a question that she didn't have an answer for.

FIVE

MI6 analyst, Ian Moore, was sat opposite his line manager, Elizabeth Middleton, in a meeting room buried deep in the heart of the Secret Intelligence Service's headquarters located on the south bank of London's River Thames. They had waited twenty minutes before an LED on the digital monitoring equipment started flashing green, informing them that they were finally at liberty to speak candidly about the things that really mattered to them.

'What is it that you want discuss, mistress?' asked Moore.

'The Black Knight has been compromised.'

'But I thought his last commission went perfectly.'

'It did, but there has been an unforeseen development – familial DNA.'

'What? How? He has no children.'

'Maybe he lied to you, maybe he doesn't know it, but he has fathered a daughter. His DNA is flashing red on several police databases.'

'How is that possible?'

'As I said, familial DNA.'

'I am sorry, mistress, but I don't understand.'

'His daughter was arrested a few days ago and a DNA sample collected from her. Her sample has been matched, indirectly, to a number of sites where the Black Knight completed commissions for us.'

'Who is she?'

'A thirty-year-old unemployed eco-activist living in London.'

'What did she do?'

'As far as I can tell, nothing.'

'Then why was she arrested?'

'She has a website that could be construed as promoting eco-terrorism. There was an incident at a farm trialing GMO crops, a security guard was stabbed.'

'Will MI5 sit on their hands?'

'What do you think?'

'And what about Dobrynya?'

'We must assume that sooner or later he will learn of this woman's existence.'

'In that case, it would be prudent to assume that he will make arrangements to eliminate her.'

'That is a possibility.'

'Wouldn't it be expedient to make our own arrangements? There will be fewer complications.'

'I agree, but they don't want that.'

'What do they want?'

'You are to inform Windsor that he may have fathered a child and collect a sample of DNA from him. They want to rule out the possibility of a false positive. All being well they want to use the woman to lure Dobrynya out from the shadows. If we are lucky, Windsor might be used to eliminate him for us.'

'That's a risky strategy.'

'It is what they have instructed us to do.'

'I'll make the necessary arrangements, mistress.'

'Our time is up,' said deputy director Middleton, noticing that the LED had started flashing amber.

The two spies sat in silence until the LED flashed red, after which they returned to discussing mundane matters, such as terrorist threats to the United Kingdom and her dominions.

SIX

Ian Moore was joined in the queue for the Thames cable car service behind a baseball-hatted, sunglasses wearing, Harry Windsor at 3.25 p.m. The two men purposely made a hash of boarding their carriage in the manner of a couple of clumsy tourists, stopping anyone else from boarding in the process.

'What's so important that you couldn't write it in a message, Michael?' asked Windsor getting straight down to business.

'An awkward situation has developed, Harry,' said Moore, who had grown used, over many years, to Windsor referring to him by the name he used out in the field.

'Such as?'

'I'll get straight to the point. We think you might have fathered a child, a daughter.'

'What?'

'A woman was arrested a few days ago and a DNA sample collected from her. The upshot is that familial DNA matches have been made to several locations where you have executed commissions for us. The balance of probabilities indicates that the woman is very likely to be your daughter.'

Windsor said nothing for a few moments as he looked out of the capsule with its views of the O2 as it soared high above the Thames. 'So, I might have inadvertently fathered a child, what of it?'

'As things stand, it is only a matter of time before MI5, and several European police forces, start making enquiries into your identity. We would like to nip any such activity in the bud. Your providing us with a sample of DNA will allow us to be absolutely certain that it's your DNA we are deleting from national crime database.'

'And say I refuse to provide you with one, what then?'

Moore gave Windsor a wry smile. 'That would place me in a very awkward position, Harry.'

'What you're telling me, Skip, is that either I willingly provide you with one or you'll arrange for one to be taken from me,' said a visibly irritated looking Windsor behind his sunglasses.

'We need a sample from you, Harry, it is as simple as that,' said an agitated looking Moore, noticing that the pod had just passed the halfway point. Meaning that they would shortly be arriving on the other side of the river. 'As you can appreciate, Harry, we are a little pushed for time. So will you do the honours?'

'Okay, get on with it.'

Moore produced a clear plastic tube containing a cotton bud. 'Can you scrap this across the inside of one of your cheeks and drop it back inside the holder? They use some modern wizardry called Low Copy Number DNA Profiling to produce your entire genome from the few thousand cells collected off the cotton bud. It's all very interesting, a polymerase chain reaction -'

'I'm not going to swab my arse cheeks for you, if that's what you were hoping' said Windsor before bursting out laughing. 'I don't care what the science is behind it.'

'Don't be facetious, Harry, you know that's not what I meant,' said Moore, his agitation turning to irritation.

Ten seconds later it was done.

'Is there anything else that I need to know?' asked Windsor.

'No. I'll be back in contact as soon as the chaps in the lab have done their stuff. I think that they can turn this stuff around in as few as nine hours, so you might make a point of regularly accessing the message base.'

'I don't like logging into the system when I'm on the move, but I'll keep an eye out for you.'

'Okay, that will have to do then. Thank you for being so cooperative, Harry.'

'Well, you had two things going for you.'

'And what might they have been?'

'Firstly, I can see the necessity of it; and secondly, the idea that I might have fathered a child or three, without knowing about it, interests me. Can you tell me anything about her? Like how old she is and what she does for a living?'

'We don't know definitively that she is your daughter yet.'

'You wouldn't be here if you had any doubts. At least tell me her name.'

'I'm sorry, Harry, no can do. Be sure to check the message base. Oh, I nearly forgot, that was a bloody good job you did in Paris.'

'I try to do my best for Queen and Country, Michael,' said Windsor as he stepped out of the pod onto the northern shore of the Thames, leaving Moore to make the return journey back to the south side of the river in the company of a couple of loud, gesticulating Italian tourists.

The middle-aged assassin decided to take a leisurely stroll around the Victoria Dock before returning home. He climbed a footbridge that afforded a good view of City Airport and stopped to watch a plane take off. He imagined where the plane might be travelling to, thinking about all the places he'd visited in the world. He'd taken many lives in many countries and now he wondered if it was possible if he'd accidentally given one back to planet earth. He'd given a lot of thought to having children but had always reached the same conclusion - that his wasn't a life that would allow for a wife and family.

Windsor thought that he and his daughter might share the same DNA, but they were perfect strangers to each other. He'd not seen the girl grow up and didn't know the first thing about her. That thought hurt him, but he knew that it had been better that way. Having a family to think about would have blunted his edge. He'd killed many people in the service of his country, almost always placing himself in harm's way. No, the life of an assassin was no life for a family man.

SEVEN

Tatjana Umansky was in the final year of her Cybernetics degree at the Taras Shevchenko National University in the Ukrainian capital city of Kiev. She was a brilliant student, with looks that set her apart from most of the Ukraine's rising smart set. She was slim and tall, standing five feet nine in her stockinged feet, with chiseled features and short blonde hair. She had chosen to study cybernetics after getting hooked on the Terminator films as a young girl, and still had difficulty dissociating the image of Arnold Schwarzenegger from the machines in the university's research laboratories. She knew that she was probably decades away from creating her own cybernetic organisms, but all her studies were taking her in the right direction. Having spent the last few years studying such dry topics as cognition, adaptation, social control, emergence, communications and biology.

In between studying and socializing, she liked to communicate with like-minded individuals through the Darknet. The idea of sharing a medium of communication favoured by criminals and perverts intrigued her, and she spent many hours communicating with individuals from a shadowy group who called themselves The GreyFriars. She liked this particular group for two reasons: firstly, one of her ongoing boyfriends, a particle physicist named Solomon Biratu, was always raving on about them; and secondly, because the organisation seemed impossible to join, it seemingly having only one official member, a blogger going by the name of Matthew5:5. Solomon, whom she called her African Prince, had warned her to be careful when communicating with the GreyFriars, as rumour had it that a number of its followers had died suspicious deaths. Umansky didn't care for such rumours as she knew Solomon to have a paranoid streak.

The GreyFriars's blog posts came straight out of a computer virtual world, its quasi-members obsessed with the age-old battle of good against evil. Solomon had told her that the GreyFriars were a splinter group formed from the apocalyptic movements of thirteenth century Italy, the original organisation, the Apostolic Brethren, founded by a man named Fra Dolcino. Solomon had said that the AB had hidden in the shadows for centuries, its members resurfacing in the mid-twentieth century to do battle against a modern-day witchcraft cult, named The Church of the Six Salems. Ordinarily Umansky wouldn't have given anyone harbouring such views the time of day, but Solomon wasn't your everyday paranoid conspiracist. His adopted mother, Lilith Namdar, was reputed to be the world's richest women and, according to GreyFriars's blogposts, was also the leader of the evil Church of the Six Salems.

Umansky was too busy living in the fast lane to care much about the GreyFriars's stories of imminent apocalypse. She had her studies, her boyfriends, and although she personally saw little evidence of it, she was living in a country divided by civil war. She and her intellectual friends were fully aware of the propaganda battles waged by the East and West. Much of it being fought through the sphere of social media, the porthole that had done so much to capture the hearts and minds of the young.

Solomon had returned to his studies in America but the two of them kept in regular contact, spending many hours dissecting the posts uploaded by Matthew5:5. Just over a week ago the blogger had posted links to hundreds of encrypted files that he said had been hacked from the servers of a non-government organisation called the Faithless Freedom Foundation, an organisation founded by Solomon's adopted mother. Matthew5:5 had challenged GreyFriars's followers to use a bespoke decryption program to convert the files back into plain text, so that they could be uploaded onto the internet for all the world to see. Umansky had spent many hours trying to crack the files without success. That was until this morning, when she'd found ten plain text documents sitting on her computer's hard drive waiting to be read. She was in a hurry to get to her morning lectures, so only had time to scan the contents of the files between mouthfuls of cereal.

What she read made her think that Matthew5:5 might actually be a Russian propagandist, as the text in first file implied that the Ukrainians (her people) were the bloodline of Japheth, a grandchild of the Biblical Noah, and would be responsible for the coming apocalypse. All but one of the documents were written in English. The odd one out was written in what Umansky thought might be French. It consisted of a single paragraph made up of four lines. Not being able to read French she decided to print out a hard copy on her wireless printer, but it didn't print because the machine was out of paper.

What Umansky found odd about documents supposedly hacked by Matthew5:5 was that none of them mentioned the secretive Church of the Six Salems, instead they were peppered with references to *Hidden Masters* and an organisation called the *Revelati*. She would have liked to have read all of the documents at a leisurely pace, but she was running late, so she rushed off to her morning lectures with her mind filled with gobbledygook.

֍ ֍ ֍ ֍

Osmond had finally received her computer equipment back from the police. They hadn't found anything incriminating on the hard drives, so as far as she was concerned, she was free to get back on with her life. She didn't like the thought of living in an Orwellian world, where an individual's opinions on the environment and gene technology could be construed as inciting others to violence. The experience had left her more determined than ever to try and save the planet.

Osmond hadn't seen any sign of the police surveillance team and hoped that, now her computers had been checked, they would be reassigned to another investigation. She had been tempted to load the anti-spyware program she'd purchased from Loki onto her computers but decided to take his advice and save the intrusion detection program for a rainy day. If that meant that the police might have a backdoor into her personal space, then so be it. That didn't stop her from initiating computer programs she already owned to test the cleanliness of her systems, and she spent the next few hours checking registry files for any changes in the configuration of her systems.

Having assured herself that everything was in order, she started a full system scan, and with nothing useful left to do, she decided to go out for a run. She hadn't run further than 10k in ages and hoped that a long slow run would help clear her mind and recharge her batteries.

꾸꾸꾸꾸

When Umansky returned to her dorm, she didn't notice the small but sturdy metal hook embedded into the ceiling adjacent to the light fitting. She made herself a cup of tea and opened her notebook to a fresh page, entitling it The Revelati. Then she started drawing mind maps from keywords contained in the texts. There were references to: two solar eclipses; six North American towns named Salem and one called Carbondale; the secret society she already knew to be the Relevati; and an island named Kish. She studied her mind maps and making no sense of them, opened Google Maps on her computer and searched for the island of Kish, discovering that it was situated off the south-western Iran province of Hormozgan. She checked the time, it was 12.30pm, and as Kiev was seven hours ahead of the American East Coast, she knew that she'd have to wait at least three hours before skyping Solomon.

Having already failed to notice the hook in the ceiling, Umansky also failed to notice the heavily built man who'd crept out of the en-suite bathroom and was now standing behind her. She did see the noose as it passed over her head, but even her sharp mind and quick reflexes didn't allow her to react before the man had pulled it tight into her throat, before hauling her backwards, up and out of her chair. Her assassin wasn't the tallest of men, but his six-foot frame was plenty enough hold Umansky on his broad back so that her feet lost contact with the carpeted floor. Her lithe ten-stone frame was working against her now, gravity pulling the cord deeper and deeper into her slim neck, blocking the supply of blood and oxygen to her brain. Seconds later she stopped struggling as the darkness of unconsciousness overtook her.

Her murderer didn't wait for her heart to stop beating before lowering her body gently onto the carpeted floor. He threaded the open end of the cord through the hook in the ceiling and hoisted her unconscious body off the ground until her feet were just an inch from the floor. Whilst the last remnants of life were leaving Tatjana's body the assassin got to work on her computers, loading a crawler program that quickly located the folder she'd used to store Matthew5:5's encrypted files. Then, when he was certain that the computers were clean, the assassin uploaded Tatjana's suicide note onto her Facebook page. His work done; he spoke quietly into his transponder informing his accomplice that he was ready to leave the dorm. A few seconds later a female voice gave him the code word, and safe in the knowledge that the coast was clear, he opened the door to the dead girl's room and walked calmly out into the corridor and safety.

EIGHT

The hipster activists arrived at the house party in groups of twos and threes. Most of them had travelled around the city for hours, jumping in and out of cars along the way, in an attempt to lose anyone who might be minded to follow them. House parties were a boon to the social justice movements and usually included the viewing of banned films and documentaries, information communication technology training, drink, drugs, and sex. The obstacle to be avoided by participants, at all costs, were the Gopniks - ultra-conservative, ultra-aggressive, homophobic, nationalist, tracksuit wearing, Jaguar drinking inhabitants of the run-down housing estates. The Hipsters were anathema to the Gopniks, whom they tended to give a wider berth too than the security police.

The party's main event was a seminar detailing best practise in the use of social media - a euphemism for the latest encryption techniques used to keep their identities safe from the Russian security services. The principal speaker/come trainer was William Meek, an Englishman from the village of Barley, close to Lancashire's the Forest of Bowland and Pendle Hill. Meek looked the archetypal computer geek, a dumpy man of average height. But as a salaried member of the Faithless Freedom Foundation, he was something of an anti-hero to the hipsters of the Russian youth movements. Meek and others like him were helping the Muscovite Hipsters' hone their hacking skills, and more importantly, providing them with technology enabling them to keep one step ahead of the Russian authorities. Tonight's delegates were some of Moscow's most influential bloggers, critical mouthpieces in much vaunted transition to a true and open democracy. Navalny had taken them so far, and they were now pinning their hopes on the Paris Hilton of Russian politics being able to smash the regime of liars and thieves.

The Hipsters and the Gopniks had equal contempt for each other. Unlike the Hipsters, the Gopniks weren't particularly discerning in their hatred, hating everything and everyone outside of their insular world. Whereas the educated, moneyed, well-travelled, Hipsters, tended to hate all things Soviet and viewed the Gopniks as the nearest human equivalent to H. G. Wells's underground-dwelling Morlocks - throwbacks to a bygone age of repression and darkness.

The Hipsters had no understanding of the Gopnik fear and hatred of the neo-platonic West, as their friends in the West were providing them with money, technology, and the fruits of enlightenment. The Hipsters believed that once true democracy was established, there would be plenty of money and leisure time for all, even for the undeserving Gopniks. But the Muscovite Hipsters were nobody's fools and had the good sense to know that there would be a few sticks hidden amongst the Western carrots. However, for the time being at least, they were intent on enjoying life funded in part by agents of the Western democracies.

Meek wasn't in Russia to preach to the converted, it was the job of others to do that. No, his job was to help keep the pro-Western bloggers safe from the heavy hand of the Russian security services, with their SORM boxes and deep packet inspection hardware. He ran numerous websites for the FFF promoting social media techniques, but neither he nor his employer allowed anyone unlimited access to their encryption software. No, to do that would undermine their efforts to facilitate communications channels that even GCHQ and the NSA had trouble cracking. In fact, unbeknown to the Muscovite Hipsters, Meek's encryption algorithms were detested by security agencies the world over, as it wasn't only the authoritarian regimes of Russian and China who liked to keep an eye on what the chattering classes were discussing over the information superhighways.

Meek was no oil painting, but he thought he knew the way into a woman's heart. Female activists who wouldn't normally give him second glance, were all over the maverick genius at Hipster parties. After all, wasn't he willing to risk his own life to keep the internet safe for the members of the world's pro-democracy movements? Meek used his elevated status to bed women from all the nation states that had participated in the Seasonal revolutions of the Middle East, and Colour revolutions of Eastern Europe. He'd cut his teeth in the Iranian Green revolution, and in recent years had focused his efforts on the Ukraine, finding the young women of Kiev very grateful for his technical assistance and internet wizardry. Now his paymasters were zeroing-in on Russia and he was intent on exploiting his first visit to Moscow to the full. Meek doubted that the young Russian girls would have been so keen to make his acquaintance if they had known that he'd spent the last few weeks spying on them through the webcam cameras embedded in their smart phones and tablet computers. Meek's encryption algorithms made sure that the young activists could correspond with each other in total privacy. Private that is, apart from himself and his colleagues at the FFF.

Better me perving over you darling than the FSB, thought Meek as he eyed a tall, toned Russian pro-democracy activist named Aglaya.

Later that evening whilst most of the hipsters were testing their new encryption software, Meek was shagging Aglaya back at her Moscow apartment. He in no way matched the men that Aglaya fantasised about, but she sensed that the British man knew instinctively how to touch and kiss her. Somehow, the overweight Englishman knew exactly what she wanted in the bedroom. What she wasn't to know was that Meek had viewed the inside of her bedroom many times in recent weeks and had learned a lot about her sexual fantasies from the pages of the ebooks and e-magazines she'd read.

NINE

MI6 Director of Cyber-Terrorism, Richard Thomas, was feeling tired. He had been invited to Puzzle Palace, known formerly as Fort Meade, to attend a series of meetings to be chaired by Ronald Patterson, the Deputy Director of the National Security Agency. Also in attendance were Majors, George Kerry and Richard Weinstock, respective heads of the NSA's A-Group (Russia) and G-Group (Middle East). Unknown to the American intelligence community, Director Thomas knew the two generals far more intimately than their official engagements might suggest, the three men having vowed allegiance to Lilith Namdar, above President, Queen, Flag, or Country.

Director Thomas had been sitting watching Patterson as the other delegates made their introductions around the meeting table. Thomas already knew that Patterson was in his mid-fifties, but he didn't think that the man, with his full head of greying hair, parted to one side, and cold dead grey eyes that betrayed no emotion, had the look of a cryptographical genius. The MI6 director had not met the Deputy Director of the NSA before and was keen to make a good and lasting impression on the man rumoured to have thrown massive fits of temper in response to recent inter-agency leaks to the media. When it was his time to speak, Director Thomas provided a summary of the Secret Intelligence Service's social media operations in Syria, Iran, Russia and the Ukraine; deliberately referring to the ever-increasing problem of media leaks being perpetrated by a growing underground army of whistle blowers.

'Tell us, Richard, how have you been so successful in containing media leaks in your country?' asked Patterson.

'To be honest with you, we don't really know. I think that most people in the UK trust the police and security services to look after them. This feeling of trust emanates from how we handled the troubles we used to have with the IRA. Their bombing campaigns have given the British people, the older generation at least, experience of a clear and prolonged terrorist threat. Our research suggests that most of our citizens feel that our surveillance measures are a necessary evil required to defend the British way of life.'

'So, you think that this is a trust issue?'

'Obviously there must be more to it than that, as nothing is ever that simple. Your security infrastructure is far larger than ours. If I were to hazard a guess, I'd say that your problems might simply emanate from the huge volume of people with access to secret information.'

'I concur with your assessment Richard. Here in the U.S. we've suffered the catastrophe of 9/11, but barring the acts of a few random lunatics we haven't experienced a sustained campaign of terrorist action. This lack of a perceived threat seems to lie behind the actions of Snowden's and Manning's of this world,' responded the DD, his dead eyes momentarily showing a hint of emotion. 'I sometimes wonder whether the proprietors of news media organisations, and their employees, prefer the destructive tools of regime change: sanctions, tanks, missiles, and boots on the ground; to internet soft power influence. Surely, it's better to overthrow a regime from within, rather than to have a new one visibly imposed upon it from above, with all the collateral damage that goes with it?'

'I very much agree with you,' said Director Thomas.

Then Patterson paused, taking a breath before asking his next question. 'Tell us Richard, do you or the people in your security agencies have any reservations about our foreign policy or should I say more correctly, our lack of foreign policy?'

Director Thomas pondered the question, taking a sip of water whilst he considered his options. He knew that the answer he had to give was a resounding no, but he wanted to frame a cryptic response in the hope of discovering the reason for Patterson's question. 'The massive shift in emphasis to the soft power apparatus of social media has been good for us. By this, I mean that our Ministry of Defence has been able to make significant cost savings in the annual defence budget. As for departments such as my own, we have seen budget increases, even in these times of austerity... but I suppose the danger in the promotion of the websites and bloggers of the thousands of non-government organisations, is that one day, these tools of soft power could conceivably be used against us.'

'That is my concern exactly, Richard. After all, as the saying goes, those that live by the sword... Anyway, changing track if I may, I want to discuss the real reason that you've been invited to this meeting. We have an unofficial agenda item that I'd like to discuss with you. I appreciate that you'll be shooting from the hip, but I would greatly appreciate your most candid comments. You see, it's time that we made you Brits aware of something of the utmost secrecy - we are planning on having a real go at the Russian Federation.'

The time of reckoning is truly close at hand, thought Director Thomas. 'Something so secret that your president hasn't previously discussed the matter with my Prime Minister?'

'Planning is planning, Richard, but the folks on Capitol Hill have let it be known that they'd like to take advantage of the deteriorating economic conditions created by the economic sanctions and low oil price. We are planning on hitting the Kremlin real hard before the upcoming presidential election. Massive gains have been made in the propaganda war since 2004, despite their wretched international news channel.'

'And that's why you're so sensitive about leaks to the media?'

'Let me put it this way, Richard. If the Russians get wind of what we are up to, we could be looking at a full-scale European land war, and that's the last thing anyone in this room wants.'

I can think of at least three men who might disagree with you, but who I am to correct you, thought Director Thomas, as he scanned the expressions on the faces of those seated about the room. 'What's changed, Ronald? What can you do now that you couldn't back in 2004?'

'I'm not at liberty to provide you with the fine detail, but let's just say that we know, with certainty, that our programme of people power is destabilising the regime. The Russians have been using WikiLeaks against us, but our own reports of offshore tax havens and stories detailing the Kremlin clique's great wealth are gaining traction. Assets are already in place; we are now capable of ensuring that future mass protests will have a real cutting edge to them. If you catch my drift?'

'But the latest RUSI papers indicate that no overt action should be taken against the regime until the current president departs the scene. I don't think that you will find a dissenting voice to that line of reasoning on our side of the pond.'

'That's the beauty of it, Richard. They would never expect us to make a move against them with so many parties concentrating on the Ukrainian and Syrian theatres of war, let alone the problems posed by the situation in North Korea. But what if Russia were to be temporarily barred from the international finance system? Without access to SWIFT we could make a play straight out of the Shock Doctrine 101 and facilitate White Ribbon Democracy demonstrations in every major Russian conurbation. The Kremlin wouldn't know what hit it.'

'And the results of your analysis imply that regime change can be made through people power alone?'

'We could make this work by destroying them from within, by giving pro-democracy candidates our full backing, in addition to hitting them hard with a military option. My view is that we've gone about as far as we can go with our current preferred candidate. To make this work we need somebody new, preferably a woman, somebody seemingly out of nowhere - just like Putin was. Our simulations show that using only four, cruise missile capable, multi-launch B52 bombers, we could bring the Russian high command to its knees.'

Somehow, I've got to downplay the military option, thought Director Thomas, his bright eyes lighting up as played out events in his mind. Now he understood why his American counterparts had disappeared off the radar. Patterson must have had everyone involved in planning this act of mutually assured destruction under lockdown. 'I intend no offence when I say this, Ronald, but won't a play against the Russians completely destabilise the Ukraine? Very careful action would be required to protect the country's nuclear infrastructure. I can't imagine my government sanctioning action that might result in one or more Chernobyls.'

'I take your point, Richard, but we expect resistance to evaporate when the people see that the Kremlin has lost its grip on power. We'd allow the Ukrainian Right Sector groups to mop-up the remnants of the Eastern opposition, but the nuclear power stations will remain out of harm's way. In fact, many Ukrainian nuclear facilities are already under the protection of mercenaries supplied by companies aligned with our democratic aims. Each facility is already armed with stripped-down versions of our high-end missile defence systems. There will be absolutely no chance of a nuclear incident, we have taken all necessary steps to ensure that neither the Russians nor any renegade Right Sector soldiers get anywhere near a single nuclear reactor.'

Changing this man's mind is going to take time, thought Director Thomas. 'Well, if it has anything to do with the Right Sector groups, my advice would be to handle them with the same respect that you'd give to a few kilos of C4. Once that genie is out of the bottle, you'll likely to have a hell of a time trying to put it back.'

Patterson then got up out of his chair to reinforce the request that he was about to make. 'What we want from you, and your government, is a strengthened and sustained social media campaign. We aren't interested in a formal mass media campaign as we expect the Russians to counter everything at the state media level. Can you prepare a draft strategy document for discussion at tomorrow morning's meeting?'

'Of course, strategies for ratcheting up the message a notch or three won't take much time to prepare. But anything I present will be strictly off the record.'

'Don't be worrying about the formalities, Richard. Everything will be explained to your prime minister when the time is right. We all share a common goal, and ultimately, the ends justify the means.'

At the end of the meeting Director Thomas made a beeline for majors Kerry and Weinstock. Events seemed to be moving at such a pace that he wanted to know anything and everything about the fine detail of Patterson's insane plan.

TEN

The walls of the Lieutenant General's office were lined with star charts, photographs of ancient scrolls and cuneiform tablets. The room looked more like the study of an archaeologist than a man who had once commanded a Russian Federation Motor Rifle Brigade, and now commanded a Chechnian Illegal Armed Formation.

Georgy Zhukhov's face was wrinkled, and weather beaten, the product of years of exposure to the elements in many foreign climes. Life for Zhukhov had been hard, but he preferred it that way; it gave him a reason to battle, a reason to maintain his strength and his faculties, which in turn had helped to keep him alive. He was sitting at an ancient oak table hosting a computer screen, keyboard and mouse, a few cuneiform tablets, a notebook, star charts for three individuals, an ancient brown jug, and a copy of a book, written by an anonymous author, entitled the Voynich Manuscript. Zhukhov had drawn star charts from three birth dates; one was his own, one belonged to his long dead son, and the third had been gleamed from the prophecy. All three birth dates were recorded in code hidden within the cuneiform tablets lying in front of him.

Zhukhov was first and foremost a soldier, but slowly, over many years, his skills and thought processes had morphed into those of his enemy. He had taught himself Egyptian hieroglyphs, Assyrian cuneiform, the Alchemists' Green Language, and the arts of astrology and dream interpretation. He had started along the path of ancient knowledge in the hope of understanding the mind of the woman who had come close to killing him in November 1963; his life saved by a homemade nylon and chainmail bulletproof vest. Several of his ribs had been broken but he'd been able to escape after hitting his would-be assassin across the face with a hand-held baton. Zhukhov believed that the same woman masterminded the assassination of his only son, who was killed by a sniper's bullet whilst serving in the ill-fated 40th Army in Afghanistan in 1987.

Zhukhov's foe always seem to hold the best hand, her advantage only increasing as the years took their toll on the aging Russian's physical capabilities. Then a few years ago, Zhukhov's holy order, The GreyFriars, started placing agents inside his foe's evil empire. Many innocents had died over the course of the years, his only son included in their number, but the Lieutenant General had learned from bitter experience that collateral damage had to be accepted if one was to win in war.

The ageing Russian thought he knew things that ordinary men did not know. Everything was written down for all to see but remained hidden from those without understanding. He had read the words of Dante, Roger Bacon, Paracelsus, Tycho Braye, Dr John Dee, Falcanelli and Nostradamus, interpreting their words using the Green Language of the alchemists. He believed that their esoteric works predicted the coming of the End of Days, but he'd also believed that they referred to humankind's last salvation named The Troika - three people who might yet save the world from destruction.

Zhukhov considered himself to be both blessed and cursed. Blessed because he had gained knowledge that might alter the fate of humankind, and cursed because he knew that he might be living at the end of times. There had been many days when he had doubted himself, imagining himself delusional, possibly insane. What kept him going was the knowledge that he had already altered the course of history. He wasn't a great politician or a famous scientist but had killed a President of the United States and lived to tell the tale.

'Come in,' said Zhukhov, his thoughts were interrupted by a knock at the door. A man dressed in monk's attire entered the room, lifting his hood before sitting down at his master's desk. 'Have all arrangements been made?'

'Yes, sir,' replied Pyotr Volkov, the cleverest and most resourceful of Zhukhov's disciples.

'When do we leave?'

'Tomorrow evening. Are you sure it's worth the risk, sir?'

'If we succeed, then I will know that God is on my side. If we fail, I will know that I have been deluding myself and that everything we have done has been in vain.'

'You are certain that she is the one we seek?'

'Her star chart matches the prophecy.'

'But sir, you said that the Troika would be formed by three men. What caused you to change your mind?'

'I'm more certain now than I ever was. The ancient texts don't allude to the sex of the members of the Troika. It was I who assumed that it would comprise three men. Only one other woman has been born in the bloodline of the Enkidu. That woman was Joan of Arc, and she battled in vain against Namdar and the forces of darkness,' said Zhukhov, his attention focused on an ancient brown jug sitting on his desk. 'Yes, it makes perfect sense for a woman to lead us into the final battle.'

'And her father?'

'If we are successful in saving the girl, then all things are possible.'

'Dokukin, Medved and Voronin are in place. Why not leave this in Dokukin's hands?'

'Natasha has many talents, but without my help she has no hope of success. There is no denying that I am old, but none of you are a match for Pirez. She will fear me whilst I'm still able to wield a baton or a knife.'

'What of the witches of Salem? What of America?'

'I don't have an answer for that. I have always been at a loss to understand why Pirez allowed them to abandon the Waxahachie Superconducting SuperCollider.'

'But what if we find ourselves trapped in Britain? What then?'

'God has pointed the way, but we must forge our own path. Deus vult, Pyotr.'

'Deus vult, sir,' replied Volkov.

Zhukhov raised his right hand and Volkov took his leave. When the monk was gone, Zhukhov pondered his charts. He was an old warrior with only the slightest fear of death. But if he were to die, would The Troika die with him? That was a question that filled him with dread.

ELEVEN

Solomon Biratu stared at his Sony tablet with tears in his eyes. He had read the word suicide but couldn't find it in his heart to believe that was how Tatjana had really died. He'd encouraged her to download those files knowing full well what the consequences might be, and now he imagined a chain of events which might have led to her death. How she'd ignored his warning not to load the files onto her own computers and how she'd been systematically tracked down and murdered by fanatical followers of the Church of the Six Salems.

The tall, lean, muscular, mixed-race Ethiopian American had spent two semesters at Kiev's Taras Shevchenko National University studying the mathematical constructs underpinning the five schools of Superstring Theory, believed by many in the Physics community to provide the best hope for the human race to develop the coveted Theory of Everything. Biratu had vastly increased his understanding of the highly mathematical science whilst enjoying a relationship with a captivating Cybernetics undergraduate. Now he'd read that she had taken her own life, choosing to hang herself in the university's halls of residence. He'd spent many a happy hour in her student digs and now tried but now failed to block out the image of Tatjana hanging from a hook that she was said to have affixed to the ceiling. Dying an unnatural death so soon after Mathew5:5's recent postings just didn't seem right. No, she must have paid the ultimate price for his interest in the GreyFriars. He'd filled her mind with talk of esotericism, secret societies, and hidden knowledge, and she'd taken to it like an ill-fated duck to water.

Biratu was a hard-headed scientist but believed in paranormal and occult phenomena, especially ghosts, doing so because he had seen things that he thought were beyond explanation. He'd spent years analysing the mathematical ratios contained within the Great Pyramid of Giza, believing, like many Pyramidologists, that it was a giant stone book, its architecture encoded with arcane knowledge. As a mathematician, he had a sense that the ratios embedded within the ancient structure were a key to a doorway to a new physics that just might open-up humankind's understanding of Dark Energy and Dark Matter. At the very least, he felt that the angle of the Grand Gallery (26 degrees 18 minutes and 9.7 seconds) and the line from the Pyramid's east-west axis, passing directly through the town of Bethlehem, required further study, even if they offered no value to the world of modern science.

Being both handsome and academically brilliant opened many doors for Biratu. And the doors that had initially been closed to him were soon opened after their gatekeepers learned the identity of his adopted mother, Lilith Namdar, the world's richest woman. Tatjana, just like numerous women before her, knew that she had to have him the moment she saw him, Biratu's interest in the occult had only served to make him more alluring to her.

Biratu kept his distance from his peers. He idolised two giants of physics, Albert Einstein and Richard Feynman. Einstein having worked on the periphery of mainstream academia in his early, most formative years, whilst Feynman did little to alter his students' perception of him as a bongo playing frequenter of striptease bars. Biratu imagined himself to be a fusion of the two great geniuses and hoped that one day he would surpass both of them by discovering the Holy Grail that was the Grand Unified Theory of all physical forces. Until that moment came to pass, he was content to spend his time advancing a new theory of gravity.

If Biratu had developed an interest in psychology at an earlier age he might have chosen to study the science of brain function, but his talent for physics had steered him away from other avenues of learning. His conviction that ghosts were real physical phenomena meant that he spent most of his spare time working out ways to record things that go bump in the night, using the highly sophisticated electronic equipment borrowed from university science laboratories. He read anything and everything about magic, cults, and religions. Immersing himself in the opposing but equally weird worlds of particle physics and the paranormal. His interest in the internet chat group, The GreyFriars, originally stemmed from his wanting to try and understand the mind-sets of the people who seemed intent ruining the reputation of the Faithless Freedom Foundation, an NGO created by his adopted mother.

Now he was sitting pondering what a life lived on the fringes was achieving. He was becoming an eternal student, that much was clear. He was thirty years of age and still hadn't completed his PhD. And now it was possible that one of his girlfriends had killed herself because of his obsession with conspiracies and the paranormal. But he couldn't stop himself from believing that Tatjana might have stumbled across the decryption key to Matthew5:5's encrypted files.

Then suddenly it came to him, Tatjana had installed a motion-activated digital video camera in her room. He couldn't guarantee that anyone would be able to see the recordings, as she had encrypted them, but he remembered that the files were stored on the hard drive of her desktop computer. That camera had captured all manner of activity, including a few of their loving making sessions. Solomon hadn't been inclined to see his sexual prowess posted all over the internet, so he'd habitually deleted any and every computer file that he thought might contain their carnal antics. He was the one who persuaded her to encrypt the recordings just in case a jealous lover tried using them in as act of revenge porn. The problem was that only Tatjana had a copy of the decryption key.

It was a long shot, but he wondered whether Tatjana had left the camera running and inadvertently recorded the last moments of her short life.

TWELVE

The esoteric ritual started at midnight, as the dark energy was said to be greatest during the first hour of a new day. The coven members felt the energy coursing through their veins as they watched the Church of the Six Salem's High Priestess use her athame to draw a triangle in the soft earth. After completing the triangle, the High Priestess walked back to where William Meek and the other coven members were standing and drew a large circle around them. Meek didn't care much for it, but he and the other coven members knew that the two-dimensional circle represented a three-dimensional sphere that was meant to keep them safe from any malevolent forces lurking in the Neverworld.

The Church of the Six Salems was very much an American cult, but in the hierarchy of occult covens, William Meek's Pendle came with the kudos of being led by a Witch Queen. Witch Queens were to the CSS cult members what Bishops were to the Christians, in that they were their district's most senior priestesses. Meek had no care who led the masses and certainly wouldn't travel back to his hometown just to watch one in action. He also didn't care much for the formalities of the ceremony, as he was currently standing skyclad trying to stop himself from getting an erection. He'd positioned himself closest to woman with the grapefruit-sized breasts so that he could make a grab for her as soon as the festivities started. He wasn't interested in spells cast by the Priestess; all he was looking for was a bit of hot sex. Standing out under the stars wasn't to his liking, even in summer the cool night air took its toll on his magic wand and crystal balls. Meek thought the women had it easy, as the cold night air only served to make them more alluring, tightening their breasts and hardening their nipples. He was trying not to stare, but he couldn't help himself from sizing up the opposition.

Size wasn't supposed to matter at occult festivals, but he had lost count of the number times the most beautiful woman in a coven had consummated the ceremony with the congregation's most well-endowed man. But tonight, Meek was quietly confident of winning his prize.

Meek had joined the CSS in his early twenties, prior to that he'd been Wiccan, but had soon lost interest in them. Meek found that the Wiccan's were usually up for sex, but he considered them to be glorified tree-huggers, most of them not understanding the true meaning of the words that they so merrily chanted. He never saw himself as a true occultist, his participation in magick not being a means of learning how to conjure spells. No, he thought he could learn that from the internet.

It was through his association with the CSS that Meek got a job at the Faithless Freedom Foundation working as a cyber-security analyst. Before then he'd been very much a black-hatted hacker, destroying computer systems for fun. He soon learned that the CSS and its members were into sex in a big way. The only downside, in his eyes, of the CSS was that he never got to shag a coven leader; the Witch Queens were strictly off limits to ordinary coven members. In fact, in all the time he'd been a member he'd never met anyone who'd slept with one. He'd spent many an hour fantasizing about bedding one but had never come close to realising that dream. He sensed that there was something odd about the CSS High Priestesses, as unlike their counterparts in the Wiccan community they never went skyclad. They thought nothing of going topless but were never seen without a leather miniskirt, stamped with the CSS emblem of the hyena, or their black leather garter belts. What hyenas had to do with the North American towns of Salem was a mystery to Meek, he thought that an emblem of a wolf would be more in keeping with the country's natural predators. He assumed that it was all just some bollocks, dressed-up as esoteric knowledge to keep the higher initiates happy.

His lack of interest in the secret knowledge of the CSS hadn't stopped Meek from advancing up the FFF's greasy pole. No, being a master of the hidden knowledge of computing more than compensated for that. But in the last few years he had learnt that the stated aims of the FFF were at odds with the dark religion he was following. Through his privileged position as a bastion of the FFF's hidden knowledge, he had learnt that the upper echelon of the FFF referred to themselves as The Revelati. It all seemed very strange to Meek, as the CSS members seemed to hark back to an age of worship of pagan gods, whereas, the Witch Queens and their senior leadership, The Revelati, appeared to believe very much in the god of the Christians and seemed to be working to their own, secret, sinister, hidden agenda.

Tonight, Meek forgot all about the conspiratorial thoughts he was harbouring. As a mid-ranking member of the CSS, he'd helped many a nubile young disciple celebrate the climax of an occult ritual, and he lost no time in consummating the mass with the current woman of his desires.

THIRTEEN

Two days had passed since Windsor had seen his MI6 handler and he was getting impatient to know the result of his DNA test. He was starting to wonder what was keeping the man he knew as Michael from getting back to him. With nothing else better to do, Windsor had donned his training gear and made ready to leave the fortress that was his detached three-bedroomed house on the outskirts of East Sussex's County town of Lewes. He had decided that he'd run to Brighton and take a refreshing swim in the sea.

His house and the surrounding gardens didn't look particularly secure, but they were filled with motion sensors and hidden cameras. The front door had three locks built into it, but Windsor only carried keys for two. The third lock served a far more useful function than locking the door as it was fitted with a tiny electronic sensor primed to trigger a silent alarm should the lock be tampered with in any way. The dead bolts set; he started running a well-worn route taking him five miles over the hills of the South Downs. On arrival at the famous pebbled beach, he pulled off his T-shirt and ran straight into the sea and started swimming along the sea front, not straying further than twenty metres from the beach. The current normally ran west to east and he was headed against it for the first quarter mile. Even a man like Windsor felt the cold, but today the sea was a balmy sixteen degrees.

After his swim Windsor found himself a café where he ordered a late breakfast consisting of a mug of tea and two rounds of toast, honey spread on one and Marmite on the other. He hated carrying his special phone as he was certain that Michael and his MI6 colleagues used it to keep track of his movements. But it was a necessary evil, and after logging into the encrypted message service he found the message he'd been waiting for, which read:

We need to talk. 3.00pm, RV # 2?

About bloody time thought Windsor, as he tried to remember the names and the faces of all the women that he'd ever slept with. Having no family or close friends had added to his sense of impregnability. The knowledge of having no one to rely on him had allowed him to take the sort of risks that men in their teens took without thinking.

He checked his watch before keying-in his reply:

Good for me. C U later.

He decided to take a stroll around the old town before heading back home and hadn't gone far when he started noticing mothers and fathers wheeling their children about in pushchairs. He started to wonder how old his own daughter was and what she might look like, regretting that the only thing he really knew about her was that she had been arrested by the police.

Windsor returned to the seafront to perform a little light stretching before running the five miles back home. He was feeling a little sad as he reflected on the relationships that he'd had over the years. There were several women that he'd had short-term relationships with, but none of them were the type that would have allowed a baby to restrict their freedom. Then there were the holiday romances, there had been quite a number of those, and he remembered a few women that he wouldn't have minded giving birth to his children. There was the Aussie girl named Megan he'd hung out with in Bali, an Italian named Allegra he'd met in Rimini, and an English girl named Helen he'd met on the Greek island of Corfu.

He'd almost forgotten about an eccentric amateur magician who said her name was Cassandra, who'd taught him the dark arts of deception. He'd hooked up with her when Michael had insisted that he spend months learning magic tricks, something that Michael had said all field agents worth their salt were proficient in. He had felt confident that Casandra hadn't been a spook as he'd met her at the International Magic Bookshop on London's Clerkenwell Road. He remembered her being a wiz at cards, coins, and close-proximity magic. He'd learnt far more from her than the MI6 trainers that Michael had put him in touch with. Whilst Cassandra had used her sleight-of-hand skills for performance art, Windsor had modified them to improve his proficiency in close-quarter assassination techniques.

Fuck it, of all the women, I bet it was her, thought Windsor. Yes, Cassandra was dippy enough to have had his child without telling him and live the life of a single mum.

༄༄༄༄

Osmond had just posted her first blog on her website in over a week. She didn't know why she had a fear of gene editing technologies such as CRISPR, but she did and felt obliged to act on her fears. She found it hard to argue against the Regenisist narrative that highly targeted gene editing was more natural than evolution, especially in view of such highly impressive feats such as the removal of HIV from human cells and the production of white mushrooms that didn't turn brown. Scientists' dreams of bringing back extinct species like the Woolly Mammoth and the creation of mythological beasts such as Unicorns only made her think of films like King Kong and Jurassic Park. But it was the thought of the creation of Mirror Humans (people immune to all natural pathogens) and chatter about wiping the human evolutionary slate clean that really bothered her. Osmond liked to think that nobody in their right mind would consider doing such things, but history had shown that people had an innate tendency to doing things just for the hell of them.

Osmond had recently been blogging about the dangers posed by CRISPR technologies in human clinical trials. The evolutionary path of humankind was being altered and the public at large either didn't know or didn't care a fig about it. At least they weren't whilst the prospect of designer babies was dangled in front of their eyes.

She didn't like bowing down to the Thought Police, but she was being consciously more selective in the words she had chosen to use in her blog. But until the government started publishing lists of banned words, she couldn't find it within herself to let statements like "It's what nature would have produced." go unchallenged, even if there was a distinct possibility of her being arrested again.

಄ ಄ ಄ ಄

Ian Moore had paid £16.50 for admittance to the *Queer British Art 1861–1967* in London's Tate Britain, one of London's pre-eminent art galleries situated on the north bank of the river Thames, almost directly opposite his Vauxhall Cross headquarters. Moore knew next to nothing about queer art, but he liked to hold clandestine meetings in the building he referred to as the Spider's Web.

Moore thought The Tate made for a good, out in the open, venue. It might not be secure, but people tended to keep to themselves, and it was pretty obvious to those skilled in the art of subterfuge if other people were paying them unwarranted attention. Few foreign agents or terrorists would want to risk compromising themselves by tailing someone through the building's spacious galleries, less than half a mile from the offices of MI5 and MI6. He finally caught sight of Windsor walking nonchalantly through the exhibition in his almost customary uniform of baseball cap and sunglasses. The two acknowledged each other's presence and walked through the galleries together until they chanced upon an empty exhibition hall.

'What is it that you want to tell me, Michael?' asked Windsor.

'The test confirmed what we suspected. You have a daughter.'

'What's her name? Where does she live? And what does she do for a living?'

'Her name is Sanda Osmond, she's thirty years old, lives in London and is currently unemployed.'

'You said she had been arrested.'

'Yes, she's an eco-activist, she has her own website –'

'She's a what?' interrupted Windsor.

'An eco-activist, a tree-hugger. You know, one of them types who's always trying to save the world.'

'What was she arrested for?'

'She was arrested under the Prevention of Terrorism Act, but it's not half as bad as it sounds. She was accused of inciting others to violence. A group of activists' intent on destroying GM crops trials were wearing badges with the logo of her website. A security guard was stabbed, but none of the activists mentioned her name when questioned by the police. It seems that the chaps in the Met were just clutching at straws.'

'So, she didn't do anything wrong then?'

'As far as I can tell, she's as clean as the proverbial whistle.'

'Do you know anything else about her? I mean is she married, has she had any children?'

'She's never been married, and don't worry, Harry, as far as we know you haven't become a granddad. But there is something unusual about her, she knows a lot about computers. She used to be a hacker, nothing sinister, but she did enough to get picked-up by GCHQ's radar.'

'And she's stopped all that now?'

'I had GCHQ go to work on her. They described her status as dormant. That means they haven't recorded her as being involved in any form of cyber-criminal activity in years.'

'The name Osmond means nothing to me.'

'There's no reason why it should do, Harry. Osmond is her stepfather's surname. Her mother is a Helen –'

'Dean,' said Windsor, without missing a beat. Yes, he remembered his daughter's mother. 'Do you know if she is still married?'

Moore scratched the back of his head. He didn't like wasting time on insignificant details. 'Look, everything you need to know about Osmond is on this, Harry,' said Moore as he placed a pen drive into Windsor's left hand.

'I'm sure that it is, but I'd like to know a few details right now, if that's not too much to ask, Skip?'

'Very well if we must. Helen Dean gave birth to your daughter in 1987. She married a man named Benjamin Osmond in 1991. Mother and daughter took the father's family name, and the couple went on to have two more children together, a boy and a girl, named William and Emma. Sanda is likely aware that her siblings are her half brother and sister, but we don't have any definitive proof of that. She hasn't done too badly for herself, graduating with a degree in Sports Science from Roehampton University before going on to work as a personal trainer. Things took a turn for the worse after she joined Greenpeace in 2011. She got herself mixed-up with the New Age movement and went downhill after seemingly becoming obsessed with some bullshit end of the world prophecy in 2012. Now this isn't included on the disk, but to save you time tracking her down, she lives just up the road from here, in Pimlico. The good news is that she's alive and well and currently under our protection.'

'Protection? Protection from whom?'

'You've killed a lot of people, Harry. We think that the national crime databases might have been compromised, so there's a slight possibility that someone out there might attempt to harm her, just to get at you.'

'But you aren't aware of an existential threat?'

'No, Harry, we are just being thorough.'

'Round the clock protection's expensive.'

'Look, we've only just pulled your details from the databases. GCHQ have been tasked with listening for chatter relating to you or your daughter. If they don't pick anything up over the next few weeks, the protection will end, and we will forget that she ever existed.'

'But what if the girl's mixed-up with bad company? With you monitoring her movements twenty-four seven, there's every chance she'll end up getting rearrested.'

'No offence, Harry, but if she's a wrong 'un, what can you or I do about it?'

Windsor smiled. 'Okay, Skip, I'll leave your people to it. After all, this woman Osmond doesn't mean anything to me.'

Moore wasn't sure what to make of Windsor's last comment. He knew that the man was a cold-blooded killer whose only loyalty was for the welfare of his country. So, it was just possible that the man didn't care a fig about his illegitimate daughter. 'Now, Harry, please understand that for operational reasons I'd prefer you not to contact her, no matter how tempting it might be to take a stroll along the river to see her. Currently, you are hidden in plain sight, and it's in everyone's best interests if we keep things that way.'

'Like I said, I'll leave you people to it. Is there anything else I need to know?'

'No, we're done.'

Windsor stood up and walked out of the exhibition hall without giving any of the paintings as much as a second glance.

Moore allowed himself another five minutes before making the ten-minute journey back across the river. He might have told Windsor to keep away from his daughter, but he was very much hoping that the man was going to ignore his request.

Windsor made his way to the gallery's Rex Whistler Restaurant and sat down at a table in an isolated corner of the dining area. After eating lunch, he booted-up his laptop and keyed the words Sanda Osmond + Personal Trainer + London into the web browser's search engine. He opened Sanda Osmond's defunct personal training website and was pleased to see images of an athletic looking young woman he had been told was his daughter. He thought that the girl had her mother's looks and his athleticism. Another link directed him to a website named MutantRainbow.net. He scanned it for a few minutes before satisfying himself that it was unlikely to harbour content warranting his daughter's arrest.

Windsor was pleased when he found a link directing him to the results page of a UK Triathlon held in 2013. It appeared that she had come, what Windsor perceived as being a very respectable, third place in the females' aged 25–29 category. He analysed his daughter's split times with a glint in his eye: 1.5k swim completed in under 22 minutes, 42k cycle in 1 hour 19 minutes and 10k run in 37 minutes. He didn't know much about cycling, but what was very evident to the ex-Special Boat Squadron marine was that his daughter's swimming was up there with his own, and that wasn't something to be sniffed at.

Windsor looked about the restaurant. Most patrons looked to be in the company of friends, but a few tables were occupied by what he thought might be fathers out with their daughters. He couldn't imagine frequenting an art gallery with Sanda, but he thought he would have liked to have helped teach her how to swim. His mind drifted back to the 1980's. He remembered them as violent times, what with the IRA attempting to murder Mrs. Thatcher and senior members of her Cabinet with a one-hundred-pound bomb on 12th October 1984. Five people died in the Grand Hotel, Brighton, including the Conservative MP Sir Anthony Berry, thirty-four others were injured. After that, the gloves came off and the Armed Forces reverted back to the tactics used in the early 1970s, when Operation Demetrius was in full swing. Windsor had seen action in the Falklands in 1982 and although some of the battles were savage, he never came as close to losing his life as he'd done in the counties of Armagh, Tyrone, and Fermanagh. It was then that he first came into close contact with the spooks of MI6 and was properly introduced to the dark arts of kidnap and murder.

He had taken shore leave in May of 1986, and spent a week hiking alone across the volcanic island of Santorini before taking a ferry to Corfu. Helen Dean had told him how she hadn't met anyone like him before. He wasn't the tallest of men, standing 5 feet 11 inches, and had more body hair than she'd have preferred, but his rugged looks, lean muscular fifteen stone physique, great sense of humour and razor-sharp mind more than made up for any shortcomings he might have had. He remembered her being amazed by his ability to speak to other holidaymakers in fluent French, German and Russian.

Windsor remembered flying home to England and spending a week with his foster parents before returning to barracks in Plymouth. If he was honest with himself, he hadn't given Helen Dean a second thought after returning to active service.

FOURTEEN

Namdar was standing on a balcony watching the sun rise over the Seyhan River. The town of Adana might not be a billionaire's paradise, but it was in easy reach of the war-torn countries that she called home. Adana was twenty miles inland from the Mediterranean Sea, in south-central Anatolia, one hundred miles north-west of Aleppo and two hundred miles due north of the Tel Megiddo, better known by its Greek name, Armageddon.

After a few minutes she left the balcony, returning into a huge room containing glass cabinets displaying ancient scrolls, and walls covered with star charts. Ignoring several antique mahogany chairs, she sat herself down, cross-legged, on a rug and poured herself a cup of coffee. She was trying to limit her caffeine intake, but today she needed something to help her focus. Caffeine might boost Namdar's concentration, but drinking it had a substantial downside; the more coffee she drank the less she dreamt, and dreams were her stock in trade.

Namdar had been taught how to interpret dreams by Magi priests, and it was a skill that had served her well throughout her very long life. Recently she'd been dreaming about planetary conjunctions of Mercury, Venus, and Mars; Mercury, Venus, and Jupiter; Jupiter, Saturn, and Venus. *Triplets, always triplets,* she had said to herself many times over recent weeks. Then there were the daydreams, her recollections of days long past. How she'd first been drawn to the banks of Lake Geneva before being chased out of the Holy Roman Empire – the modern Germany - by Pope Innocent VIII's attack dogs, Kramer and Sprenger. *Yes, the old Pope must have had the gift. He'd seen the signs and lost no time in forging a hammer with which to beat her*, she thought to herself.

Namdar now imaged herself in Bavaria, back in the

year sixteen hundred, remembering one of the great witch trials. Was it her fault that illiterate peasants like the Pappenheimers had discovered some of her dark secrets? She remembered Paulus Pappenheimer, his wife Anna, and their children. Namdar wasn't certain whether it was Paulus or his wife, but one of them had witnessed her sharing the secret words of darkness at a gathering of the local Bavarian elite. Illiterate the Pappenheimers might have been, but you didn't need know how to read and write to utter words of power. Yes, Paulus Pappenheimer the cesspit cleaner, had been up at the manor house cleaning out the cesspit that day and must have snuck back, under the cover of darkness, to view the ceremony. Of course, the elites were never going to share their sources of power and arranged for Councillor Wangereck von Romin to have Paulus broken on the strappado. But that was only the start, yes, the Pappenheimers had to be made an example of, and they were executed with maximum prejudice. Namdar remembered their bodies being broken on the wheel, the glowing tongs and the cutting off of bodily parts, before finally being burned alive. Namdar had insisted that some mercy be shown to their youngest boy, who was at least strangled before his immolation. Her thoughts started drifting to Scotland and the Stuart king, James VI, when there was a knock at the door.

'Come,' she said waiting for her personal assistant, Fyodor Maknov, a well-dressed man in his mid-thirties, to make his entrance. 'What is it, Fyodor?' she asked as he entered the room.

'I'm sorry to trouble you, madam, but I've received a report that might interest you.'

'Who submitted it?'

'Director Thomas of –'

'And what does the director have to say?' interrupted Namdar.

'The Americans are planning a colour revolution. A

white one.'

'I wonder what makes them think that Russia will be taken so easily. Is there anything else?'

'Yes, mistress, the director reported that the Black Knight has a daughter.'

'What!' exclaimed Namdar whilst vigorously scratching the back of her head.'

'I don't understand, madam. I can appreciate that this might affect his operational capability, but surely his best days are behind him.'

'How old is she?'

'She's thirty years old.'

'And she lives in America?'

'No madam, she lives in London.'

'But the director submitted his report following his meetings at Fort Mead?'

'Yes, madam.'

'So, he was very likely aware of the existence of the Black Knight's daughter before making his trip to North America.'

'Yes, madam…' said Maknov momentarily lost for words. He could not understand how Namdar could know about Director Thomas's meeting with the NSA. As Namdar's eyes and ears, he assumed that he knew all that his mistress knew. Now it dawned upon him that there must be a lot more to the middle-aged hitman than he had been led to believe. 'My impression is that the director wasn't sure that you would even be interested in knowing such a thing.'

'Is there anything else?'

'No, mistress,' said Maknov sensing an opportunity to delve a little deeper into the background of Harry Windsor. 'Madam, I don't wish to appear impertinent, but is something troubling you?'

'Why do you ask?'

'It is obvious that you haven't been sleeping well.'

'You are very perceptive Fyodor. I expect nothing less from you. Yes, there is something troubling me. Is it not darkest before the dawn? A new age is almost upon us, yet I sense the fates are conspiring against us.'

'But the Black Knight's daughter is an unemployed nobody. How can either of them affect your plans?'

'Our best assassin is an unusual man, is he not?'

'Well, he does seem to be almost infallible. It's a small wonder that he's still alive.'

'So, it might stand to reason that the fruit of his loins might also be special in some way?'

'Yes, but this woman Sanda Osmond she's –'

'The girl's name is Sanda Osmond? Are you absolutely certain of this?'

'Yes, of course, madam.'

'This nobody, might her birth date be 23rd February 1987?'

'Yes, madam, but how could you know that?'

'I been sensing that something was not quite right with the world but had no inkling of the source.'

'How so, madam? Almost everything is in place. Isn't the proposed action of the Americans the final piece of the jigsaw?'

'It is prophesized that others are capable of understanding the ancient texts.'

'You think Dobrynya has the gift?'

'I used to think not, but now... now that we are so close... I'm not so sure.'

'But he is an old man. We receive regular reports on his movements. He hasn't left his mountain base in over two years.'

'He once gave me a memento to remember him by,' said Namdar rubbing her jaw with her left hand. 'I have never underestimated him since. The Book of Veles and the prophecies of Nostradamus might have misled the Hitler's and Khrushchev's of this world, but it was not their destiny to understand such secrets.'

'But Zhukhov is a Russian. I thought that only you, and the descendants of Magog, have the gift?'

'Wouldn't it be prudent to assume that Zhukhov knows much of what I know?'

'Even so, mistress, what can an old man do from a remote mountain monastery?'

'Our computer systems!' exclaimed Namdar, as a thought suddenly crossed her mind.

'Yes, madam?'

'We've suffered many intrusions of late... I want everyone responsible for system security re-vetted as a matter of priority.'

'Yes, madam.'

'Also, cancel all my appointments for the next seven days, with the exception of the visit to TBV Industries and the meeting with the CERN scientists.'

'Yes, madam.'

'And I want to know everything there is to know about this *nobody*, Sanda Osmond. Oh, I almost forgot, Fyodor.'

'Yes, madam?'

'Place a call to Solomon, I wish to speak with my adopted son.'

Fyodor Andreevich Maknov left his mistress to her own devices. He instructed the diary secretary to start clearing down Namdar's diary whilst he initiated urgent inquiries into an unemployed nobody living on social housing in the city of London.

༄༄༄༄

Biratu had watched in disbelief as the coffin was lowered gently into a freshly dug grave in Kiev's Baikove Cemetery. He had contacted Tatjana's parents, Yevheniy and Katerina, soon after reading their daughter's Facebook post and they had invited him to the funeral, apologising profusely for neglecting to send him a formal invitation. He sensed that they were pleased that he had gone to the trouble and expense of flying across the Atlantic Ocean to attend the ceremony, but now he felt bad exploiting their feelings in order to gain access to their daughter's personal effects.

Biratu found himself alone in Tatjana's bedroom, looking at two unopened suitcases, a printer, a laptop, a tablet computer, a desktop computer, and some other items that had been retrieved from her college dormitory. He had told Yevheniy that he wanted to make copies of digital photographs stored on Tatjana's computers as a memory of their time together. Yevheniy had taken Biratu upstairs to Tatjana's bedroom and told him that he was welcome to make copies of anything he wanted, before warning him that nobody had been able to access his daughter's computers because they were password protected. But Biratu was in luck, Tatjana had given him her password when they were dating, and she hadn't bothered changing it. So, he logged straight into the desktop PC and started searching for any files which Tatjana might have downloaded from Matthew5:5's Dark Web sites. He was very surprised that the search came up empty.

Someone's wiped the computer clean, man, he thought to himself.

He knew that there was only one sure way of knowing what had happened to Tatjana, so he initiated a search for all files created on the date of her death. He felt his heart pounding when eleven files were listed on the screen in front of him. Then he took a deep breath and tried opening a file created around lunchtime on 27th July, named DR030315.

'Shit!' he shouted, suddenly remembering that all the digital video files were encrypted. He took a portable hard drive from inside his jacket pocket and a few minutes later had made copies of all the files covering the last few days of Tatjana's life. He was about to return downstairs to the other mourners when the printer caught his eye.

It's a long shot, but what the hell.

He switched on the printer and found one unprinted document sitting in the print queue. He tried reprinting it out, but nothing happened. Then he noticed that the printer was out of paper. He looked about the room and found a half-used ream of A4 paper. He quickly shoved twenty, or so, sheets into the printer and watched as it beeped a few times before printing out a single sheet of paper. He, unlike Tatjana, instantly recognized the four-line paragraph, written in Middle French of the sixteenth Century.

Most French people wouldn't have known what the paragraph alluded to. But Biratu wasn't most people and knew it for what it was, one of Nostradamus's Quatrains. Quatrain IX.44 to be precise, which read:

> *Migrés, migrés de Genefue trestous,*
> *Saturne d'or en fer se changera,*
> *Le contre RAYPOZ exterminera tous,*
> *Auant l'aruent le Ciel signes fera.*

Biratu couldn't remember its interpretation using the Alchemists' Green Language, so instead made a rough and ready English translation which he scrawled beneath the paragraph, reading:

> Flee, flee, Geneva every last one of you,
> Saturn will be converted from gold to iron,
> RAYPOZ will exterminate all opposition,
> Before his advent, the coming the sky will show signs.

Would anybody really be willing to murder people for this? He thought to himself.

With nothing else left to do, Biratu took a photograph of the Quatrain before folding up the sheet of paper and placing it in his inside jacket pocket.

Biratu gave Yevheniy the password to his daughter's computers before leaving. He'd considered telling him about the CCTV recordings but thought better of it. No, the day of his daughter's funeral wasn't the time to make him aware that her suicide, if that is what it was, had likely been recorded for anyone with the relevant decryption key to see.

Biratu thanked Yevheniy and Katerina for allowing him to pay his last respects and left them to their grief. Shortly after climbing into the back of a taxi, he switched on his mobile to find that he had five missed calls and a text message. The text message was from Fyodor Maknov, personal assistant to his adopted mother, Lilith Namdar.

FIFTEEN

It was close to three in the morning and Windsor was lying on his bed staring into the dark of night. He kept repeating the MI6 man's words over and over in his mind, "You've killed a lot of people Harry". Windsor had come to the conclusion that Michael was right, his daughter could be a target for an act of retribution. And that had caused him to spend the last few hours thinking of ways to ensure that Sanda Osmond would be kept out of harm's way.

Windsor was confident that the security services would keep his daughter safe the next few weeks but was worried about what would happen after they lost interest in her. He trusted his handler, Michael, but he had no other contacts within the SIS. In view of all the imponderables, he decided that the best course of action would be for Sanda Osmond to create a new life for herself. Something that would require her to be made aware of her situation, lots of money, and fundamental changes to how she led her life.

Money was something that Windsor had in abundance. He had properties on several continents, many of which he used as safe houses. He had his Armed Forces pension, but the bulk of his wealth came from his SIS commissions. He had been remunerated handsomely over the years for removing flies from the British Empire's ointment. However, his net worth has grown at an exponential rate in recent years due to a completely unexpected source - digital currencies. Michael had insisted on paying him ever greater proportions of his commissions in bitcoins. Telling Windsor that the payments were untraceable and would keep him hidden from the radars of unfriendly foreign governments, terrorist organisations, and Her Majesty's Inland Revenue. Windsor had taken a great risk in agreeing to be paid in electronic tokens, but over the last few years bitcoin's value had risen a hundred-fold. He'd recently cashed in half his coins fearing that the currency was in a super bubble, but that still left him with millions of pounds worth of the encrypted blockchain that he could, at the touch of a button, gift to his newly discovered daughter.

It wasn't the thought of money that was interfering with Windsor's sleep. No, he had plenty enough money to keep the girl safe. What was troubling him was that she would need to become invisible, effectively hiding in plain sight. And then there was the need for her to learn, and master, close-quarter-combat skills. He thought that he could teach his daughter how to hide and fight. The problem was, as he saw it, would she let him? Yes, would she really be willing to cut ties with her family, and start a new life in hiding, on the say so of a man purporting to be her absent father?

Michael won't help me protect her, he hasn't any incentive to, thought Windsor. *The enemy of your enemy is your friend. But who's the enemy, Harry?*

Windsor got out of bed, found a pen and paper, and wrote:

Identify threat, seek allie(s)

That done, he got back into bed and was asleep within seconds of his head hitting his pillow.

SIXTEEN

Windsor wasn't the only one having trouble sleeping. Professor Hilary Washington had been at her desk since six in the morning. It had felt to her like she'd been sitting there for days, as time for her seemed to be running in slow motion. She had hardly slept a wink because today was her day of reckoning. Soon they would try to awaken the first of the synthetic humanoids, and then and only then would the professor know whether she had become the world's greatest living synthetic biologist.

Washington was a forty something single whose inspiration for life came from her work and the millennium spanning TV show Sex and the City. She was tall, slim, possessed high cheek bones, and knew that many men were in awe of her. Every year, for the last ten years, she had made a new year's resolution to find herself a man, settle down, and start a family, but the months passed quickly, and the dream of a family life was fast disappearing with them. The professor was a driven woman, her passion in life being the creation of synthetic humans. Her goal, to create a new model army of genetically cloned soldiers for the United States' military.

A few years ago, she had been forced into taking a sabbatical to work on a top-secret project at an unlicensed Ukrainian company called ThorBaldrVáli Industries, known to many simply by its abbreviation, TBV Industries. TBV was the world leading company in MRT - mitochondrial replacement therapies - understood in simple terms as techniques for the conception of three person babies. The board of TBV had promised the American military unlimited access to its research databases on the condition that Professor Washington be allowed to work on its most secretive project for a period of not less than three years. TBV wanted Washington for three reasons: firstly, she was the world leading expert in her field; secondly, they knew that she secretly worshipped at the Church of the Six Salems; and thirdly, she brought with her materials stolen from the military cloning program, namely some very special DNA.

Professor Washington had been at the vanguard of an ongoing war waged amongst the Pentagon's internal budget holders, the outcome of which would decide the fate of Americas' future fighting forces for the rest of the twenty-first century. There were four main camps: in the first were the generals who wanted to stick to conventional warfare, accepting the inherent financial overheads that came with training and maintaining thousands of combat ready troops; those in the second camp occupied the opposite end of the spectrum, favouring the replacement of manpower with unmanned armed aerial vehicles and other unmanned mobile ground-based munitions, such as driverless tanks, their dream - the creation of a terrifying army of machines that no human force could hope to withstand; the third, favoured the creation of a robotic army, cyborgs of the Terminator movies which to all intents and purposes were simply an advance on human soldiers; the fourth and final group, the professor's group, believed that normal human beings had no place in modern warfare and were afraid of transferring too much power to machines. This last group envisaged soldiers with enhanced strength, speed, and agility; individuals that could be decommissioned at will. Members of this camp were inspired by the movie Blade Runner and dreamt of an army of genetically engineered replicants, a clone army of soldiers with pre-set lifespans, requiring none of the long-term medical and pension costs of regular people.

The professor had worked for the American military on a super-secret project, tasked with creating an army of superhuman clones, although calling it a project was a bit of a misnomer in that she had already been working on it for over fifteen years and there was no hint of an end date. Her team's terms of reference were simple: produce, on production scale, adult male and female fighting units possessing predetermined lifespans, enhanced senses, lightning-fast reflexes, massive strength, great speed and endurance, photographic memories, with thought processes matching the speed of their reflexes. In essence, she had been tasked with creating perfect specimens of humanity, bred under factory conditions, for the sole purpose of waging war.

During the first decade Washington's team had made incredible progress, using DNA rumoured to have been extracted from the bones of ancient giants. Her own view was that the crème de la crème of special DNA at her disposal had been extracted from an extra-terrestrial lifeform, whose body might have been retrieved from an alien crash-landing site such as Roswell, New Mexico back in 1947. But she had it on good authority that it had been extracted from the tomb of Gilgamesh, a mythical Man-God, found in Iraq following the Third Gulf War. The professor's team used to joke that the ancient DNA was the only weapon of mass destruction found in Iraq. But given the choice between two seemingly impossible scenarios, she erred on the side of the extra-terrestrials. Whatever the DNA's provenance it possessed one remarkable quality in that it exhibited all the signs of being created through a process of mitochondrial replacement therapy, meaning that its donor had been the product of a three being conception. The professor was educated in the arts and knew that the mythical Man-God, Gilgamesh, was supposed to be two thirds god and one third human, which allowed the possibility of his having had three parents.

The currency that Washington traded in was facts, and the fact was that the DNA, whatever its origin, had allowed her to create super-sized human beings. Admittedly, some of her earliest specimens were frightening caricatures, their cancer ridden bodies standing at over ten feet with horrific deformities. But the generals seemed ecstatic that the clones were even able to support themselves for only a few hours after being disconnected from their life support machines. Washington had found, through a mixture of trial, error, and luck, that smaller specimens had better bone density and fewer tumours. But two years ago, she hit a proverbial brick wall, the holy grail of creating defect free cloned specimens seemingly beyond her grasp.

It was then that she met with Fyodor Maknov and was made aware of the work of TBV Industries. The generals' first response to the news that greater advances in cloning technology were being made outside of the USA was to have the CIA steal the technology being developed by the secretive Ukrainian enterprise. But eventually it was agreed that more could be gained from sending the professor on a sabbatical, her mission to become fully conversant with the company's proprietary technology and develop the skills to exploit it. What the generals did not know was that the professor did not go empty-handed, she took samples of the ancient Iraqi DNA with her. And the professor could not believe her luck when the scientists at TBV performed a quid pro quo and provided her with their own very special DNA, DNA that didn't come from any synthetic lifeform conceived in an MRT laboratory. No, the donor of the TBV DNA was a human being, who if she was still alive, might actually be immortal. Washington couldn't use the TBV DNA to create super-soldiers, but it offered her something far more valuable, the ability to create highly regenerative stem cells, which she used to lower the incubation periods of her adult clones down from decades to single years.

Washington was again taking huge scientific strides. New CRISPR gene editing techniques allowed her to use myostatin knockouts to produce clones with massively muscular bodies. Her current crop took less than twelve months to grow from stem cells into fully mature adult specimens, standing seven feet tall and weighing-in at 250 pounds. However, there were three major problems with such fast-growing clones: firstly, their brain development was minimal; secondly, their motor skills were poor; and thirdly, all the specimens looked middle-aged, she couldn't produce any that looked under fifty. The final problem was more a question of aesthetics than functionality, but the professor had finally fixed it by suppressing the bcat-1 gene, which is known to promote aging, and synthesizing an XYZ chromosome giving each clone a combination of male and female body parts. In short, Washington had created a species of Transhumans.

There were other long-standing problems which had nothing to do with growth rates, such as language development. The cloned units possessed innate language skills but had no natural language, and although immensely strong they had poor balance and coordination, due in no small part to their having spent the first year of their lives in fluid filled incubators. But those were problems for others to solve, Professor Washington had already accomplished more than enough, ethics and morality aside, to qualify for a Nobel Prize.

Finally, it was time, and the professor went to her laboratory to wake up her most perfect clone, one of the products of experiment F.66 or GoG as some of her colleagues preferred to call it, after the Genome of Gilgamesh. She flooded the transhuman organism's brain with alpha waves and breathed a sigh of relief after the clone responded by generating a full spectrum of brain activity. The professor took another deep breath and gave the order to turn off all life support systems.

An hour later the clone's vital signs were perfect, it was fully able to support itself, its heart pumping fully oxygenated blood to its brain and body. The clone had for a few minutes been awake and even smiled at the scientists standing around it. Then, for reasons unknown to the professor, it had closed its eyes and gone into a very deep sleep. Professor Washington wasn't sure what to make of it all, she had achieved so much but thought that she might have failed at the final hurdle. Her sabbatical was coming to an end, and she would soon be working back with the US Military.

The same could not be said for TBV's chief executive officer, Maksym Nevry, who understood exactly what had transpired in his laboratory. Nevry knew that the transhuman clone was perfect in every way, and had placed itself in a self-induced coma, the GoG being a synthetic body without a soul. All that remained for Nevry to do was to arrange transport of the clone, and exact replicas, to the World's pyramids. He expected to soon be rewarded for his efforts, by being crowned one of the new Kings of the Earth.

SEVENTEEN

William Meek rarely travelled to the US as he could do much of his work on the FFF's American computer network through the intranet from England, but he knew a Witch Queen when he saw one. He had caught a glimpse of the woman's leather garter belt as she entered the mansion house. It looked to have at least twenty buckles stamped into it, telling him that this particular Witch Queen was the High Priestess of at least twenty covens in the state of Maryland. Meek had never seen a Witch Queen at a Church of the Six Salems party before and wondered what she was doing there. He'd heard rumours that some of the FFF elite were going to attend the party and wondered if the Witch Queen had been invited to discuss arrangements for festivities being planned to celebrate the forthcoming solar eclipse.

It was an important year for the CSS, with six towns named Salem predicted to fall within the shadow of 21st August eclipse. In a break with CSS tradition, plans had been made for a High Priestesses from each of the six towns to be made Witch Queens at an initiation ceremony led by the Grand Mistress, Lilith Namdar. As Meek understood it, each of the new Witch Queens would perform a Great Rite as the sun's shadow passed over their respective towns. The location of the festival was a closely guarded secret, with many initiates assuming that it would take place in the first of North America's Salems, the coastal city in Essex County, Massachusetts, famed for the 1692 Witch trials.

Meek was not a member of the CSS elite, but what he lacked in wealth, power, and influence, he more than made up for with his intellect. He knew a fair bit about magick spells but more importantly he knew much more about the dark arts of computing than he did the secrets of the left-hand-path. Meek had drunk several glasses of champagne but was feeling far from relaxed. Usually, he'd have set about the masked women surrounding him like a rutting stag, but tonight he wasn't in the mood for sexual intercourse. Being obliged to attend a sex party not having the same appeal to him as attending out of his own free will. Like many people leading double lives, Meek lived on his wits, and he was at his wit's end, because William Meek was the CSS's enemy within, he was the GreyFriars' blogger Matthew5:5.

A month earlier Meek had hacked into the computer servers he was being paid handsomely to protect and hit the jackpot, as he'd accessed the highly encrypted files reserved for the eyes of the FFF's inner sanctum. He felt sure that the files contained the FFF's true raison d'être, but he had been afraid to open them. Resulting in his uploading them onto the Dark Web for others to take the risk for him.

Many a GreyFriars's follower had died a suspicious death after downloading materials he'd uploaded onto the Dark Web, but this time things were different. All hell had broken loose following his latest indiscretion, and teams of assassins were circling the globe murdering anyone thought to have accessed the files. He now found himself in the difficult position of being sent to America to help CSS agents, working at Fort Mead, find the person or person's responsible for compromising the FFF's systems.

Meek was effectively helping hunt himself down and was worried that he might be given more than enough rope with which to hang himself. He'd spent the last few weeks trying to keep one step ahead of his colleagues in the FFF's Data Security team, who'd uncovered faint traces of his footsteps through the Dark Web. Ordinarily he would have been confident of losing them in the internet's labyrinth of routers and servers, but this time his actions had been accidentally recorded by members of the NSA. They had been scanning offshore bank accounts hidden amongst the world's tax havens searching for links to the Russian President and had inadvertently captured thousands of millions of data packets that had nothing to do with the transfer of foreign exchange. Eventually, agents loyal to the CSS working for the NSA had recognised the traffic for what it was, a cyber-attack on their most holy of holies. Fortunately for Meek his trail ended at the router he'd used in the British Virgin Islands and not back to the router in England that he'd used to launch his cyber-attack from. The CSS's NSA agents, having hit a dead-end, wanted the FFF's most eminent cyber-security analyst to explain to them why and how the hackers had managed to bypass the honey pot traps he'd been responsible for embedding into the FFF's computer network infrastructure.

Meek looked around him, the orgy reaching its climax, wondering how many others knew what he knew, and if they knew whether they even cared. Over the years he'd stolen secret documents that made clear who was behind the revival of witchcraft in the western world. It seemed that Lilith Namdar was the last in a long line of secret female benefactors, who'd used the advertising industry and women's rights movements as a cover for returning the western world to its pagan roots.

Suddenly Meek's thoughts of fear and loathing deserted him. He realized that he had more pressing matters to attend to, not least of which were the firm, rounded, buttocks of a young redhead who'd just started rubbing them against his groin.

EIGHTEEN

Whilst Meek was in the ballroom succumbing to the charms of his masked female friend, more sinister goings-on were taking place in the basement. The Maryland Witch Queen had gone down there to perform a sacred Rite at the behest of the Grand Mistress, Lilith Namdar.

Biratu had recorded many so-called mystics at work over the years and had proved, with the aid of some very sophisticated electronic equipment, most of them to be frauds. He had only ever recorded a few events that he couldn't explain away as mere tricks or illusions in his quest to find a portal to the paranormal parallel world. Biratu found himself in the basement with the Maryland Witch Queen because Namdar had told him that she had heard of an American witch said to be able to conjure all manner of unexplained entities at her Black Masses, and who for the wager of one hundred thousand dollars was willing to allow sceptics the chance to try and prove that she was a fraud. Biratu usually insisted on paying his own way, but he hadn't argued when his adopted mother said that Fyodor would take care of any financial impediments for him. He had produced dozens of mathematical models demonstrating how the fabric of space-time might be underpinned by psychic energy, but to date he had no empirical data to support his hypothesis. Being an ardent follower of the GreyFriars meant that alarm bells started sounding the moment Namdar had mentioned the Church of the Six Salems. Apart from the blogger Matthew5:5 casting aspersions against her, Biratu had never discovered any link between his adopted mother, her favourite NGO or the infamous cult of the CSS.

Biratu felt awkward working in the nude, but the feeling was soon normalized with seven other naked people sharing the room with him. The Witch Queen was the only one wearing clothes, a leather miniskirt, and a garter belt, and she was now busy drawing nine pentagrams into the soft earth of the basement floor with her athame – a black handled dagger. Whilst the Witch Queen was preparing her magick circle Biratu spent his time making final checks of his sensors and computers. He'd been told that during the ceremony the room would be illuminated solely by candles made from human fat. He thought that the use of candles might be a ploy to limit his ability to record the event, but he wasn't worried by the prospect of soot and lack of light as his cameras worked in ultraviolet and infrared.

Biratu then joined the seven naked coven members, comprising four women and three men, in a circle before two of their number, a man and women, broke off to join the Witch Queen. The couple placed large candles in the centre of each of the pentagrams, before lighting them whilst the Witch Queen drew a triangle into the earth.

The repugnant smell of the candles made Biratu want to gag, but the others seemed used to the foul odour. He thought that the Witch Queen looked hot in her garter belt and miniskirt, but the feeling of nausea was doing a good job quelling his sexual urges. He watched as the Witch Queen placed the tip of her athame into two bowls, one containing salt the other water, before moving them into a pentacle drawn in the middle of the altar. She placed the dagger on the altar whilst pouring the salt into the bowl of water. She picked up the athame and started moving deosil fashion, clockwise, marking-out an incomplete circle in the soft earth. Then she then beckoned Biratu to join her, kissing him as he entered the circle before spinning him around one revolution, again in deosil fashion. Biratu followed the Witch Queen's lead and beckoned a female coven member to join the two of them in the incomplete circle before kissing her and spinning her once around. This continued until all of them were within the bounds of the circle, after which the Witch Queen draw her athame through the earth, closing the circle around them. Three coven members then took turns walking deosil around the inside edge of the circle, carrying the consecrated water, incense, and an altar candle. There was a pause, before all the coven members raised ceremonial daggers whilst watching the Witch Queen draw the outline of a pentagram in the air in front of her.

The ceremony now reached the point that Biratu wished could have been performed in private. With the Witch Queen giving him the sign that it was time for him to give her a fivefold witches' kiss. Biratu duly complied by kissing her feet, her knees, her navel, and her breasts, before finally kissing her full on the mouth. There was no disguising the fact that despite his obvious embarrassment and the foul smell of the candles, he had become sexually aroused by the experience. With all the coven members now staring at his erect penis.

The things that I do for science, thought Solomon slowly shaking his head.

The Witch Queen had told Biratu at least a dozen times before the start of the mass that, no matter what happened, he must not under any circumstances leave the circle drawn into the earth. She has explained to him that the circle served as an impregnable three-dimensional sphere that elementals (spirits, familiars, and demons) could not penetrate. Her plan was to summon an elemental into the confines of the triangle, where it couldn't cause anyone physical harm, whilst allowing it to communicate with the coven members through psychic projection.

Biratu believed in the existence of elementals. He thought they were ever-present in the three-dimensional world inhabited by humans but remained invisible because their astral world existed in additional dimensions of space-time. He thought that ghosts and other entities sometimes emerged from the ether in much in the same way as the seven colours of the rainbow emerged out of translucent sunlight.

The Witch Queen rang a handbell and Biratu joined the others in dancing and chanting. This was the moment that held most interest for him, as the simple ringing of a bell symbolized the start of a sacred Rite and was used to call the Universe to attention. An act supposedly having the ability to stop the flow of time for the very briefest of moments. And this was the moment, in the convoluted proceedings, when Biratu expected to earn a cool hundred thousand dollars. He had planned to disprove the Witch Queen's extraordinary claim using five, synchronised to the picosecond, electronic clocks. He'd brought two clocks down into the basement with him, left one in his car, left a fourth in his apartment, and locked the fifth in a cupboard housed in the physics laboratory of a university campus. He hadn't been sure what he would witness during the Black Mass but was confident of two things; firstly, that he would record any discrepancy in the flow of time lasting more than a trillionth of a second; and secondly, that the Witch Queen didn't have a cat's chance in hell of making it happen. He was just beginning to lose interest in the ceremony when something unexpected happened, as an image began to materialise within the confines of the triangle.

Biratu had witnessed many hoaxes over the years and thought that the blurred image looked to be nothing more than a man-made hologram. Up until this point in the ceremony the coven members had been happily chanting, with smiles on their faces. Suddenly the atmosphere in the room changed as everyone, including the Witch Queen, looked a little frightened. The chanting petered out as the coven members huddled together at the centre of the circle. Biratu ignored them and remained standing just inside the perimeter but felt the hairs on the back of his neck rise as he watched the image of a Baphomet - a horned man with breasts, and the face and legs of a goat – formed before his eyes. It was the most lifelike hologram he'd ever seen and if he hadn't known better, he'd have believed that the image had taken solid form. A cold chill enveloped his whole body when he realised that he recognised the image. It was something straight out of his boyhood nightmares.

How could they know? he thought to himself.

The entity, still standing within the confines of the hand-drawn triangle, tried to take a step toward the circle but seemingly bounced off an invisible wall. Biratu's curiosity then got the better of him. He was about to take a step out of the protective circle when the Witch Queen pulled him back by his left arm, which was no easy task considering that he weighed over ninety kilos. Then, for what seemed to be an age, but probably lasted no more than a few seconds, the hologram, elemental or whatever the hell it was, started snarling and roaring as it tried to free itself from the confines of the triangle, bouncing off its invisible walls dozens of times a second. Then, as suddenly as it had appeared, it was gone.

The Witch Queen went through the motions of formally ending the Rite, but Biratu sensed that the coven members were truly afraid to leave what they obviously perceived to be the safety of the circle. The Witch Queen stepped out first and turned on the electric lights before rubbing the triangle out of existence in her bare feet. Only when the triangle was gone, did the coven members dare move from where they had been standing.

'Does that always happen, man?' asked Biratu.

'No… no, I've never seen the Baphomet before. We are all truly blessed,' said the Witch Queen.

The other coven members thanked the Witch Queen for the conducting the mass and hastily left the basement, looking eager to return to the upper floors of the house. Biratu wasn't sure what to make of it all. He walked over to his equipment and was elated to see that it had recorded several terabytes of data. Whatever the entity had been, a man-made fake or genuine elemental from the aether, it had disturbed the room's energy field, providing him with a data set for his mathematical models. He was keen to check the time logs but knew that would have to wait until he returned the recording kit to the university's physics laboratory.

'Do you have a shovel?' asked Biratu.

'What?'

'A shovel, I want to dig the floor up. I mean, all this is too good to be true, man. There's got to be some electronic wizardry buried in the earth,' said Biratu as he passed an EMF recorder over the earth floor. *Strange, but I'm not getting a reading, but something's got to be buried down there.*

'What are you trying to measure with that machine?' asked the Witch Queen.

'This is an electromagnetic field reader. It should have picked-up the residual energy from whatever you used to create the hologram.'

'It hasn't detected anything, has it?'

'That doesn't mean that there isn't anything to detect. This is a portable, the equipment connected to my computers is much more sensitive.'

'Will a spade do? I have one on the altar?'

Biratu scooped-up a handful of soft earth, it was moist and loose between his fingers. 'Thanks, it's not ideal but should do the job.'

'Trust me, you won't find anything,' said the Witch Queen as she continued to stare at the ground. 'Who are you? I was told that you are just a physicist, but the Elemental, it recognised you... I saw the look in its eyes.'

Biratu laughed. 'Come on babe, you're good, but none of this is real and I'll prove it soon enough.'

The Witch Queen walked slowly toward the open door and closed it, before locking it with a brass key. She then walked back over to where Biratu was digging before licking both her index fingers and running them over her nipples.

'Look, you're hot but can't we do this another time?' he asked, suddenly remembering that he was still stark naked. 'I'm going to dig-up whatever's been buried down there, then I'm going back to my lab to analyse the data on my recorders.'

'Kiss my feet. Do it now!' barked the Witch Queen.

Biratu smiled but carried on digging.

'I order you to touch yourself!' she barked again.

'Don't forget who arranged for me to be here, babe. You've put a good show on for me, but I don't remember seeing anything in the small print about me having to give myself a hand job.'

'Very well, do as you please. I was told that you are here because you are a sceptic. Is that true?' asked Witch Queen, regaining her composure.

'I sure am, babe. What of it?'

'If I'm the charlatan that you say I am, then you shouldn't mind giving me something to remember you by. What do you say, can I take something from you?'

'What do you mean, babe? Are you saying that you want something instead of one hundred thousand dollars?'

'You are obviously a very special person. I would like a keepsake to remember you by.'

Biratu stopped digging and looked up with a blank expression on his face.

'What? Are you still after some of my sperm, babe?'

'No, just a lock of your hair will suffice. We collect samples from all our coven members.'

'Okay, babe. I think you deserve a lock of my hair as a reward for the show you put on for me. You can have it on one condition. That you get me a shovel and stay out of my way until I've finished digging up the floor.'

'I promise on all that is holy,' said the Witch Queen as she walked over to the altar and picked-up a pair of scissors.

'Just to clarify, we are talking about the hair on my head, aren't we, babe?'

The Witch Queen smiled. 'Yes, the hair from your head will do just fine. Not everything we do is connect to sex.'

'You could have fooled me. Okay, take a little of what you fancy, then get me a shovel.'

Ten minutes later a fully clothed Biratu, minus a lock of hair, was digging into the soft earth with a shovel purloined from the groundsman's shed. He dug down several feet into the soft earth before satisfying himself that nothing was hidden there. He spent another ten minutes searching the rest of the room for holographic equipment but found none. All of this was done under the watchful eye of the Witch Queen.

'I don't know how you did it, but I've recorded all that I needed to. The thing with my hair was a nice touch, but none of this esoteric bullshit will work with me.'

'In that case, I bid you goodnight... my Lord of Physics.'

༺༺༺༺

Meek had ventured outside the mansion house to have a smoke. He was standing around the back of the building, where the staff had parked their cheap cars, when his attention was caught by a tall muscular mixed-race man loading what looked to be very expensive electronic equipment into the back of a car. Even though everyone wore face masks inside the house. He was sure that the man stood in front of him had not attended the orgy, and yet Meek found something strangely familiar about him.

'Hi, sorry to trouble you, but would you like a hand with any of that?' asked a half-cut Meek.

'What? No, I'm fine, man, but thank you for offering,' said Biratu, suddenly noticing the short, dumpy, drunk looking man. 'These bags contain delicate electronic equipment, so I'm going to handle them one piece at a time.' Just like Meek, Biratu didn't recognise the man standing in front of him in the moon light, but he sensed that he knew him from somewhere.

'If you don't mind my asking, what were you doing with kit like that in a place like this?'

Biratu laughed. 'Well I'm afraid that's a little complicated –'

'If I didn't know any better, I'd guess that you came here to measure disturbances in electromagnetic energy fields, interrupted Meek.

'That's exactly what I've been doing,' said Biratu, thinking that the drunken man must have been responsible for setting-up the hologram in the basement. 'You worked all that out from the labels on these boxes?'

'I'm interested in tech stuff. I work in computing. Social media, cryptography, that sort of stuff. Please accept my apologies for my obvious state of inebriation, but I'd be very interested in knowing more about what it is that you do?'

'You're an Englishman?'

'Yes, I live in England, I'm over here on business.'

'Unfortunately, I can't tell you what I've been doing here tonight. I signed a non-disclosure agreement. But if you still feel the same way tomorrow morning, why not give me a call as I'd be happy to provide you with an overview of what I do. However, I'm into my quid pro quo, man.'

'What?'

'You said you work in computing?'

'Yes, social media and cryptography.'

'Here's the deal. I'll tell you about what I do if you can explain the world of encryption technology to me,' said Biratu as he watched Meek's eyes light-up.

'It's a deal,' said Meek, turning his head left and right for any eavesdroppers. 'My name's William. Could we meet for a coffee or something one evening this week? I'm returning to the UK on Saturday.'

'My name's Solomon,' said Biratu, shaking Meek's hand. 'In that case, how about we meet tomorrow for lunch?'

'Yes, that will be great. But please bear in mind that I still might be a little hung over.'

The two men exchanged mobile phone numbers before Meek returned to the mansion house, leaving Biratu to finish loading up his car.

NINETEEN

Biratu arrived at the coffee house just before one p.m. and was pleased to see William Meek waiting outside for him. There was no particular reason for it, but he'd taken an immediate liking to the man. The two men entered the cafe and a few minutes later they were sat down with coffee and cake, ready to discuss the intricacies of their chosen fields of interest.

'So, if I've got this right, you're a particle physicist with an interest in occult phenomena,' said Meek.

'My day job is in particle physics, but I investigate paranormal activity as a hobby. And if truth be told, I'm hoping to find something that proves that there is more to life than what we experience with our five senses. I'm really interested in ghostly apparitions and their like.'

'I know that you can't give me any specifics about what you were doing last night, but I'm guessing that you were searching the old mansion house for poltergeists and other unworldly phenomena.'

'Something like that, man. Let's just say that I'm interested in recording the electronic signatures of what might be called entities that flitter in and out of our three-dimensional world.'

'What do you mean by our three-dimensional world?'

'In mathematical terms, there might be an infinite number of dimensions occupying the space that we're sat in right now. It's just that we can't see or feel them.'

Meek looked slowly around the café. 'So, you're saying that right here, right now, in this café, there are ghostly phenomena inhabiting the same space as us?'

'I don't know about living beings, but that's exactly what I'm saying.'

'Do you have any proof of that?'

'Unfortunately, not, but from time to time I see stuff

that is kind of there but not there. If that makes any sense?'

'Not really,' said Meek. 'How about telling me a little about yourself? Where you grew up, that kind of stuff.'

'I don't see how that's relevant to what I believe in, but okay, I will do, as I can't see how it can hurt any' said Biratu, speaking around a mouthful of blueberry muffin. 'I wasn't born in America, I moved here in my teenage years. I was born in a small village in the Arsi district of Ethiopia's Rift Valley, south of our capital city, Addis Ababa. My life changed when representatives of one of the hundreds of western NGO's came to our village promoting a nationwide mathematics competition for children under the age of ten. I was only eight at the time and had little formal education, but I ended-up winning the grand final and 50,000 Ethiopian Birr for my family. That was about two hundred dollars back them, it might not sound like much, but it was a huge sum of money to us,' said Biratu pausing to take another bite out of his muffin.

'What's any of that gotten to do with entities in other dimensions?' asked Meek.

'I used to have lots of strange dreams and sometimes I'd see things that I knew couldn't be real. I haven't ruled out that I'm just prone to seeing hallucinations, but they seem real to me so I'm kind of devoting my life to proving they really exist.'

'Sounds fair enough to me. So, how'd you go from winning an African mathematics competition to ending up here?'

'Just before my ninth birthday my entire family died in a house fire. I was found outside of the building wrapped in a blanket. One of my uncles took me in, but after a few weeks he gave me up to representatives of the NGO who ran the competition. They'd heard about my plight and offered to take care of me. They took me to Addis Ababa and paid for my education at a prestigious church school. One thing led to another, and now I'm studying for a PhD in elementary particle physics.'

'I hope that you don't take this the wrong way, but aren't you a little old to be studying for a PhD?'

'No worries, man. I went kind of rogue for a few years. Travelling the world, that sort of stuff.'

'This NGO, what was it called?'

'You probably haven't heard of it, it's the Faithless Freedom Foundation.'

Meek's face broke into a big smile.

'You know it, man?'

'This might sound a little weird to a man who believes in the paranormal, but I work for them.'

'What were you doing up at the house last night?' asked Biratu, now more certain than ever that Meek must have had something to do with the hologram he'd seen.

'I was there for the party.'

'You had nothing to do with what I was doing down in the basement?'

'I don't know if you noticed, Solomon, but there were well over a hundred people there. I don't think that any of us knew that you were down the basement searching for ghosts.'

'Okay, so what's your background, William?'

'I was born and still live in England. I grew up in a little known village called Barley, in a local government district called –'

'Pendle,' interrupted Biratu.

'I had a feeling that you might have heard of the place.'

'Heard of it! I've been there, man. It's the starting point of the Pendle Hill walk.'

'So, you know all about the witch trials of 1612?'

'Yes, they aren't very different to our Salem witch trials of 1692.'

'Anyway. My upbringing was pretty boring. Like you, I'm shit-hot at maths. I've always been a bit of a rebel and used to be a computer hacker. I was sort of bribed into changing from poacher to gamekeeper. I get paid good money to protect the FFF's computer systems from people just like I used to be, and you can't work in cyber-security these days without knowing loads about encryption technologies. That's about it, really.'

'No wife and children?'

'Nope.'

'Me neither.'

'What can you tell me about the world of encryption?' asked Biratu, who was hoping against hope that he'd found someone who could help him open the encrypted digital video files he'd copied from Tatjana's computer.

'I'm sure that we've got plenty of time for me to bore you with what I know about encryption. This stuff about other worlds interests me.'

'Like I said, man, I can't tell you what I was doing up at the house last night because I've signed my non-disclosure agreement. But I'll tell you a little more about what I believe, William. The Bible says that there are two types of being, those made from clay, people like us, and those made from fire, angels, demons, and things that go bump in the night. My theory is that the angels and their ilk are made from Dark Matter and coexist in a six-dimensional world filled with Dark Energy, but that's just my theory,' said Biratu before taking another bite out of his muffin.

'So, you're saying that you believe that this missing matter that you physicists' like to talk about, is hiding, in plain sight, in hidden dimensions?'

'I'm working on a new theory of gravity, which I'm hoping will prove that gravity crosses the boundaries of the two worlds.'

'Sounds complicated. Okay, how about you ask me what it is you want to know about encryption? I'm assuming that you've got some very important documents that you want protected.'

'Actually, I'm hoping that you might be able to help

me decrypt a digital video recording.'

And there I was, beginning to think that you might be interested in decrypting some much sought after files uploaded onto the Dark Web by my alter ego Matthew5:5, thought Meek, before asking 'What standard was the recording encoded in?'

'256-bit AES.'

'Then you already know that what you're asking me is impossible, man.'

'I thought as much, but since you're an expert I thought it was worth asking the question.'

'As I'm an ex-hacker it was a question well worth asking. What are we talking about, a recording from a fixed position camera, like a security camera?'

'Yes.'

'Well, my friend, where there's a will, there's usually a way. A brute force attack aimed at discovering the encryption key is impossible, but assuming that on average at least 95% of the recording is a fixed image there are things that we can do. Are we talking about kit purchased in the USA?'

'No, it's Ukrainian,' said Biratu wincing.

'That's actually a good thing, Solomon. I've been doing quite a bit of work in Russia, so I guess we are talking about a SECAM recording.'

'So, you know more than a little about optics and holography?'

'I work in cyber-security. I'm sorry, but I can't see what that has got to do with optics and holography.'

'I'm sorry, William. I keep forgetting that regular people aren't obsessed with light and energy the way I am.'

'What I'm trying to ascertain is how the image files were constructed. You know, the number of frames a second, the number of lines on a screen, that sort of thing.'

'It sounds like you might actually be able to help me.'

'Running a decryption app worth its salt is going to require access to a decent sized GPU node cluster.'

Biratu laughed. 'I've got access to a forty-four node, NVIDIA Tesla C2050 GPU with 3 gigabytes of memory, sitting on top of a 64-bit Linux cluster platform. Will your app run on that?'

'Forty-four nodes should just about do it,' joked Meek. 'I can't risk sending you something over the Web, but I could let you have an app on a write-protected disk two days from now.'

'That fits my schedule.'

'It'll be menu driven and should be almost as simple as plug and play. But just so you know. If it doesn't work, you'll have to visit me in the UK if you want another one.'

A short while later the two men left the café. Meek had purposely not asked if his newfound friend had any connection to the FFF's founder, Lilith Namdar, but had an intuition that he had. He did not believe that Biratu really wanted an app to decrypt a video file, as he had an inkling that his new friend just might be the kind of person who read the posts of the GreyFriars's blogger, Matthew5:5.

TWENTY

Faced with the prospect of an afternoon in front of the television, Osmond decided to go for a run. She walked out of her council estate and onto the embankment of the River Thames, where she stopped to do some stretching. She was about to set her stopwatch when she was suddenly overtaken by a feeling of nausea. She leant on the embankment wall, looking out across the river at the old Battersea Power Station, in the hope that the feeling would pass. Then, as suddenly as the feeling had overtaken her, it was gone. So, she set her stopwatch and started running.

Osmond was well aware that running along the riverside pavements wasn't supposed to be good for her joints, but she had been doing it was years without any ill effects and soon settled into her stride. She intended to run the three and half miles at six minutes per mile pace and wasn't expecting to be overtaken by any other runners. So, she was more than a little surprised when a heavy-set man with silver-white hair edged in front of her on the steps leading up to Albert Bridge, forcing her to play catch-up as they ran over the bridge towards Battersea Park. She wasn't happy at being overtaken by a stocky old man but assumed that the old fella would soon run out of steam. It actually took her a full four minutes before retaking the lead and she could still hear the man's footsteps as they both crossed Chelsea Bridge. Osmond had a half mile left to run, and the old fella was matching her stride for stride. Ordinarily, Osmond would have considered a man running so close behind her to be some sort of pervert, but not this man, he was obviously a serious runner who'd set his mind on trying to beat her. So, she wasn't at all surprised when he stopped about thirty metres further along the road from where she had stopped, and she watched him for a few seconds with interest as he tried to recover his breath.

She finally turned her attention away from him when she started her warm-down stretches and didn't notice him approaching her.

'That was some... some run, it's not often... that anybody outpaces me,' said the middle-aged man still trying to catch his breath.

'I only did the one lap, I started and ended here. It's about three and a half miles,' replied Osmond.

'I know, I... I started, right behind you. I'm staying at Dolphin House. I like to get out and run when my schedule allows.'

'I hope you don't mind me saying this, but you run really well for a man of your... build.'

'For a second there, I thought you were going to say, for a man of my age. I used to be a lot faster, but the years take their toll on all of us.'

'I'll count myself lucky if I'm running anywhere near as well as you are ten years from now.'

'I'm Harry by the way,' said the man, holding out his right hand.

'I'm Sanda, nice to meet you, Harry. Did you say that you're staying at Dolphin House?'

'That's right, I sometimes stay there when I'm in London on business. You see a lot of interesting people about the place.'

'I know that quite a few Members of Parliament are supposed to have apartments there. I've lived around here for years, I used to swim there when I was at school.'

'You not working today, Sanda?'

Osmond smiled. 'No, I'm sort of between jobs at the moment.'

'I don't know why, but I thought that you might be a personal trainer.'

Osmond smiled again. 'Actually, I used to be one, but I haven't done that for a few years now.'

'You should give it another go. You're obviously

committed to keeping yourself fit and people are willing to pay good money to somebody who can encourage them to do the same.'

'Like I said, I gave all that up a long time ago.'

'I hope that you don't take this the wrong way, but I don't really like running out on my own. I'm likely to be in London for a few more weeks and I'd really appreciate it if you'd go for a run with me. I'll understand if you say no, but it's just that we seem so evenly matched. What do you say?'

Osmond laughed. 'I actually prefer running on my own, but yes I'd be happy to go for a run with you.'

'That's great. Look here's my number,' said Harry Windsor giving Osmond a bogus business card. 'Give me a call when you are planning on running again. I've got a few gaps in my schedule. If I'm lucky, I'll get a second chance to beat you.'

'I'll give you a call, Harry,' said Osmond as she placed the card in the zip pocket of her shorts. 'Have a good one.'

'You too, Sanda.'

Osmond waited for a break in traffic before running across the road and walking the rest of her way back to her flat. When she got there, she took a proper look at the man's business card, it read:

Henry Windsor
Exaurare Consulting Limited

Osmond performed a quick internet search and found links to a company website saying that stated that Henry Windsor was an Aerospace and Defence Technologies consultant working out of Lewes, in East Sussex. Half-assured that Windsor wasn't a stalker, she forgot about him and jumped into the shower.

Biratu had spent over fourteen hours in the Physics Department of the American University analysing the energy readings he'd recorded at the Witch Queen's sacred Rite in the basement of the mansion house. He wasn't remotely tired as adrenalin had been surging through his veins from the moment his atomic clocks proved that for the briefest of moments, time had actually stopped at the moment the Witch Queen had rung her hand bell. Whether he could convince anyone in the scientific world that it had happened was a different matter, but problems like that could wait for another day.

Time seemed to be playing games with him as he waited to see if his Superstring based gravity equations concurred with his results. At any moment he would know whether a semi-naked woman had opened the gateway to a hidden world using nothing more than a black-handled dagger, a hand bell, and a few foul-smelling candles.

'Awesome!' shouted Biratu. There was no disputing it, the energy disturbances he'd recorded in the basement of a mansion house in Maryland correlated exactly with hypothesised particle strings of the subatomic world. If his equations were right, eight evaporating black holes suspended in a massive electromagnetic field could be used to create a wormhole between the three-dimensional world inhabited by human beings, and the six-dimensional world inhabited by entities such as the Baphomet.

Knowing he was right was one thing, proving it was quite another. But unlike the pioneering scientists of bygone days who might have to wait decades before they could test their theoretical theories, Biratu knew of one place on earth where his mathematical theory could be tested immediately. In the engineering reality, that was the Large Hadron Collider.

Biratu knew that if he could just find a way of convincing CERN's administrators to run an experiment that deliberately created eight micro black holes, he'd likely find himself standing on the intellectual shoulders of Einstein.

Biratu, suddenly exhausted by his mental exertions, lay down on the lab's Lino floor. Whilst he lay there, he remembered that there was something of greater importance than fame, prestige, and fortune. He had to find a way of decrypting the recordings made by Tatjana Umansky's hidden dormitory camera. Yes, until he had proved what had happened to her, academic acclaim would have to wait.

TWENTY-ONE

Richard Thomas was feeling nervous and confused. As he could not understand what was so important that it had caused Namdar to breach protocol and insist on meeting him on the CCTV ridden streets of London. Wanting to get out of sight of any cameras, he hastily climbed into the back of Namdar's Rolls Royce Ghost when it stopped beside him in the little side street.

'Good morning, Richard. I hope you haven't been waiting long,' said Namdar.

'Good morning, mistress. No, I've only been here a few minutes,' said the MI6 director, lying.

'Have you any idea why I am here?'

'I can only think that you would like to hear a firsthand account of my meeting at Fort Meade.'

'Am I to infer from your response that you have left something of interest out of your report?'

'No, mistress, my report included all salient points. In that case, what else can I help you with?'

'As you know, I've always paid a keen interest in Harry Windsor, the man known to many of our disciples as the Dark Knight.'

'Which is why I made reference to his fathering a child in my report.'

'But you delayed notification until after you had travelled to America, why is that?'

Thomas could feel his face beginning to flush with embarrassment. 'With respect, mistress, the woman is an out of work eco-blogger. I didn't want to waste your time with such trivia.'

'Wouldn't it have been wiser to allow me to be the judge of the importance of such a matter?'

'But I only delayed informing you by a few days. I had other priorities, not least of which is the location of the encrypted files stolen from the central servers.'

'I want you to understand that I am not pleased by the delay, but I accept, that from your perspective, news of Windsor's daughter would seem insignificant in comparison. However, my feeling is that an attempt will be made on Sanda Osmond's life. Under no circumstances should anyone intent on harming her be allowed to escape.'

'Who might make such an attempt, mistress?'

'Windsor assassinated a Soviet Union colonel in 1987. That man's father is still alive and, in my opinion, will seek revenge for the death of his only son.'

'By Soviet colonel, I take it that you mean the son of one Lieutenant General, Georgy Zhukhov?'

'I'm impressed, Richard. Apart from Fyodor, I didn't think any other of my disciples would be aware of such an important detail.'

'How is possible for Windsor to have killed Zhukhov's son? He wasn't working for us in 1987.

'He just happened to be in the right place at the right time.'

'So Zhukhov thinks that we were responsible for his son's death, because of something Windsor did during his time in the Armed Forces?'

'Let us say that it is a contributing factor.'

'But Zhukhov is an old man, a shadow of his –'

'Disciples within the FSB report that he is physically fit and in complete possession of his faculties.'

'Why would Zhukhov involve himself in such an undertaking, when his people could kidnap and transport her to most any destination of his choosing?'

'Please work on the premise that Zhukhov will soon arrive in London, if he is not already here.'

'That explains why Manning has placed the woman under surveillance.'

'I had the surveillance team put in place as a buffer. Any assault on Osmond will have to go through them first.'

'But, mistress, why use our disciples to perform such a task? Sacrificing unbelievers in one thing, but our own people!'

'Isn't their safety assured, now that you know what we are dealing with?'

'Yes, mistress,' responded Thomas, lying.

Namdar's expression indicated to Thomas that she knew that he was lying but wasn't concerned about it. 'Tell me, what is it that you learned from Mr. Patterson?' she asked, much to his relief.

ɷɷɷɷ

Captain Natasha Dokukin had instructed her two faithful lieutenants, Milan Medved and Andrei Voronin, to watch the girl between six in the morning and ten at night, doubting that anyone would approach her outside of daylight hours. Whilst her Lieutenants had been watching the girl, Dokukin had been busy sorting out logistical matters - safe houses, firearms, and vehicles, in readiness for Grand Master Zhukhov's arrival in the country.

Dokukin's life had been made easier than she had expected because her contact at the Russian Embassy had delivered everything exactly as requested. Osmond's biological father contacting her had complicated matters. Dokukin knew Windsor to be an extremely dangerous man and hoped that she didn't have to deal with him until reinforcements arrived.

TWENTY-TWO

The head of cyber-security at the Faithless Freedom Foundation's offices in the United Kingdom, Julian Snowden, was starting to crack under the pressure. He should have been immune to the repercussions of a data breach in the foundation's U.S. headquarters. Yet, for reasons unknown, his right-hand man's trip to North America had resulted in the searchlight moving across the pond. Nothing had been said, but he sensed that he, and his team, had become the focus of the FFF's internal investigations. Today, Snowden and his number two, William Meek, had been summoned to a meeting with Edward Manning, the FFF's Vice President of Public Relations. Manning's job title sounded innocuous, but it was common knowledge what he did for a living. Manning was the FFF's defacto Witchfinder General, a man charged with hunting down disciples who'd strayed from the path of light.

Manning was responsible for maintaining the FFF's charitable image, a task he performed using any means necessary. He was an imposing figure, standing six feet four inches in height and weighing-in at an athletic two hundred and fifteen pounds. Most of his acquaintances were afraid of him and people who knew him well were petrified of him - something he often used to his advantage. He was a health fanatic, obsessive about keeping himself in shape and was very particular about what he ate and drank. He took an immediate dislike to anyone not looking in the optimum of physical condition, something that was never going to bode well for a junk food eating, short, dumpy man, with personal hygiene issues, like William Meek. The two men had met several times before, and it was obvious that Manning detested Meek, but as Meek was the FFF's resident computer genius, he had no other choice other to put up with the smelly, dumpy little man. Today Snowden sensed all that was about to change.

'Meek did excellent work stateside, Julian. His contributions were most welcome. In fact, his insights, combined with some sterling work performed by the boys and girls at the NSA, have helped us track down the data breach to... to right here in the UK,' said Manning, who had deliberately paused to heighten the effect of his words.

'I'm glad that William was able to help. You've got more than your fair share of problems over there,' said Snowden.

'Our disciples didn't have a clue where the latest breach was launched from, but we got lucky, the NSA inadvertently recorded the cyber-attack but lost the trail in the British Virgin Islands. Now, with William's help, the guys stateside followed the trail right here, to the good old Blighty.'

'Since we are having this conversation, I'll take it that you haven't narrowed the search down to any particular router?' asked Snowden.

'We came pretty close. Which is why you two gentlemen are here with me this morning,' said Manning, clearly scanning Meek's, and Snowden's expressions.

Up until that very moment, Manning had assumed that Meek was the traitor he sought, but now that he was face-to-face with the two UK data security leads, he sensed that Snowden was the man with something to hide. 'I've got an itch that I keep scratching. The folk's stateside just don't understand how the hacker managed to steer clear of our honeypot traps. I'm no cyber-wizard but I left William's briefing thinking that the only guys in the world outside of the U.S. capable of such an attack were you two fellas, or possibly somebody working for you. Don't worry, I'm absolutely certain that you and your staff are clean, Julian, but I have to rule out the possibility that we're not dealing with an inside job. So, all UK cyber-security staff will be required to attend a series of vetting interviews. We aren't seeing anyone in any particular order, but I thought that we might as well start at the top. So, you two boys are up first. I'll be conducting the interviews myself and I'll be starting with you, William. I want you back here in thirty minutes, if that's okay with you?'

'Yes, thirty minutes will give me plenty enough time to reschedule my day but aren't there any forms to fill in?' asked Meek.

'I won't be wasting time with any of that psychobabble nonsense, William. I'll be using plain old question and answer sessions, just like we did back in the good ol' days,' replied a smiling Manning. 'Okay, William, get yourself out of here.'

Meek tried to play it ice-cool, taking a sip of cola before gathering up his things and leaving Snowden's office.

'William is a good man,' said Snowden when Meek was gone.

'He's a wiseass son of a bitch,' said Manning.

'I know that he can be a little disrespectful at times, but that's to be expected. After all he's still a hacker at heart.'

'The man goddamned stinks,' said Manning, finishing his rant. 'Anyway, enough of that, I want you to run an audit scan of Meek's IT account before I meet with him.'

TWENTY-THREE

Many hours had passed before Biratu was able to run Meek's decryption program on his multi-server array, without it crashing the system. The configuration issues, finally, over, Biratu hoped that he could finally get to work on decrypting the jpeg files. He took a deep breath and hit the Enter key before sitting transfixed by the slowly spinning icon which told him nothing more than that the program was finally doing something.

Biratu knew that months might pass before he got a result, but he just couldn't pull himself away from his computer. Then, much faster than he could have dreamed possible, the spinning icon was replaced by a message asking if he would like to view or save the decrypted file. He saved the file in several locations, including his pen drive, before trying to open the decrypted video file.

The file opened first time of asking, and there, displayed on the screen in front of him, was a recording of Tatjana's room on the day that she died. Standing right in the middle of her room was a masked man whose movements must have set-off the camera's motion sensor. Biratu paused the recording after watching the man affix a hook into the ceiling, close to a lightshade.

What to do Solomon? asked the voice inside his head.

He took a few deep breaths and restarted the recording, watching as the man hid in the ensuite bathroom, then after another thirty seconds the recording ended. The second file was decrypted as quickly as the first. This recording allowed Biratu to watch Tatjana enter her room and make herself a cup of tea before sitting down at her computer. He couldn't see what she was looking at on her computer screen, but she was writing in a notebook.

Could she have decrypted the files? asked the voice in his head.

Biratu paused the recording after watching the masked man creep out of the bathroom. Tears were streaming down his face as he looked at the image of the man standing behind Tatjana with a cord held in his gloved hands. Finally, he restarted the recording and watched as the man wrapped a cord around Tatjana's throat and pulled her backwards out of her chair. He couldn't believe how very matter of fact it all looked and was glad that the camera didn't include a microphone. He was sickened by the recording, but his predominant feelings were of anger and the desire for revenge.

ಜಜಜಜ

Windsor was surprised to see the incoming call from Sanda Osmond's mobile. He had been planning another *chance* meeting with her but hadn't managed to think of any believable scenarios that would allow him to make first contact. He couldn't think why his biological daughter would bother arranging a running session with a middle-aged man she'd met running along the river embankment, but he was very happy to take the call.

'Hi, Harry speaking,' said Windsor.

'Hi Harry, this is Sanda Osmond.

'Oh, hi Sanda, how are you?'

'I'm fine, Harry. You said that you'd be up for a run, so I was wondering if you're free sometime tomorrow morning?'

'I'll just check my calendar, but I don't think that I've gotten anything scheduled for tomorrow morning. Yes, great, I'm free. What time were you thinking of heading out?'

'How does nine o'clock sound?'

'Perfect. Where should I meet you?'

'I don't know if you remember the Boris Bike rack over in the -'

'Yes, I know where that is.'

'I'll see you there then.'

'That's perfect. Oh, I nearly forgot. How far are you intending on running. I thought that we might run the same route as last time if that's okay with you.'

'Sounds good to me. I'll see you tomorrow morning.'

'Bye,' said Windsor before disconnecting the call.

Osmond wasn't sure exactly why she'd rung Windsor. She wasn't sure if it was the personal trainer in her, but she was genuinely interested in learning how the middle-aged man had managed to keep himself so fit.

TWENTY-FOUR

Biratu had been thinking long and hard about whether he should return to Kiev and show Tatjana's parents the recording of their daughter's murder. As unpalatable as it might be for them, they would at least know that she hadn't taken her own life. But a thought was still troubling him. Would the killer ever be brought to justice? He thought that the answer to that question was no. Tatjana's murder was not the random act of a lunatic, the man who killed her was professional and he had at least one accomplice. There was no escaping it, Tatjana had been killed by the hand of an assassin most likely working for the Church of the Six Salems. Letting Tatjana's parents have the recording might only serve to upset them. What was needed was the help of somebody with power and influence, and despite a very obvious conflict of interest, Biratu decided to request help from his adopted mother, Lilith Namdar.

Namdar was a notoriously difficult woman to arrange a meeting with, and a lot of people were willing to spend a lot of money just to be in the same room as her. Yet for all the demands on her time, the billionaire philanthropist always found a window to see Solomon Biratu, the orphaned boy from Ethiopia. And, as strange as it seemed to Biratu, his adopted mother called him first. Namdar requesting that he travel to London to meet her. Her assistant going on to book him a first-class plane ticket and a room at the Shangri La Hotel in Europe's tallest building, the Shard.

'It is good to see you my son' said Namdar rising from the carpeted floor with all her usual vigour.

'It is good to see you, mother. You look well,' said Solomon in measured tones which in no way matched the brash Americanisms he liked to use in casual conversation.

'Would you like to join me in a cup of coffee?'

'Yes mother, I'd love to.'

'You look tired, Solomon. Why don't you extend your stay and have yourself a proper holiday?'

'I'm fine mother. I'm a little jet-lagged, that is all.'

'Very well, as you wish. Now tell me, Solomon, what you have been up to?' said Namdar as she served each of them a small cup of freshly brewed coffee.

Biratu scanned her face for any visible signs of aging, and as usual found none. To Biratu's eyes, his adopted mother hadn't aged as much as a day in all the years he had known her. He also thought that Namdar moved with the fluidity of a woman of much younger years. And nothing ever got past her, she had a mind like a steel trap. He had spent many hours thinking about what he was going to tell her but still wasn't sure how to begin. In the end, he decided to start by telling her about the world of high-energy physics and his potential discovery of a gateway to a parallel world.

'My flight was most comfortable, mother, but you shouldn't have paid for my ticket, I have enough money these days to pay my own way.'

'Solomon, I've tried not to spoil you and have left you to your own financial devices, but you should allow me the privilege of removing unnecessary financial burdens from your shoulders. I trust that your research grant doesn't allow the cost of first-class air travel or even a single night's stay under the roof of this architectural masterpiece.'

Biratu smiled as he remembered trying to turn right as he stepped onto the plane and, ever so discreetly, being ushered to his left into the first-class cabin. 'It is good to see you mother, we should meet more often. I must apologise for only contacting you when I need something.'

'Don't be silly my boy. Wasn't it I who contacted you? But I sense that there is something troubling you, my son. What is it?'

'I don't want anything from you mother, well not

anything in the material sense.'

Namdar placed a slightly wrinkled hand on Solomon's shoulder. 'You make an old woman very happy. Nothing would please me more than to assist you with a personal dilemma. Now, tell me what is troubling you?'

'The Black Mass that you suggested I attend, it led to the most amazing outcome.'

'I had been informed that there might be something of interest for you there, but that was only rumour.'

'As unbelievable as this is going to sound, I witnessed and more importantly recorded events that I think may have led to my making one of the greatest discoveries in science.'

'I hope that you are not getting ahead of yourself Solomon, after all there are many charlatans out there. But please tell me more.'

'I am as certain as I can be that I witnessed the summoning of an entity from another dimension into our world. Initially I was skeptical, thinking it to be nothing more than a hologram, some trick of the light, but my readings tell me different. I have no means of knowing whether any symmetries were broken -'

'Solomon, please try to remember that I'm a businesswoman, not a scientist,' interrupted Namdar. 'You say you witnessed an entity materialise within the room that the ritual was held in?'

'Yes, mother.'

'And what makes you so sure that this entity crossed over what you call, a dimensional boundary?'

'The entity disrupted electromagnetic fields in a very specific way, its signature matching theoretical constructs in the field equations I'm using in my quest for a new theory of gravity. I think that I have discovered a mathematical construct linking the three-dimensional space that we live in with the nine-dimensional space hypothesised by String Theory.'

'If I understand you correctly, you are saying that you have discovered a means of creating a gateway to a parallel world?'

'Exactly!'

'And you discovered all of this by attending a single esoteric gathering?'

'Yes, mother.'

'I'm sorry, Solomon. I don't profess to understand what you are telling me, but I would have expected you to have been pleased by your discovery.'

'I'm a thirty-year-old man with no standing in the scientific community. I mean, I haven't even completed my doctorate yet. No self-respecting scientist is going to take me seriously.'

'But hasn't it been your ambition to emulate your hero, Albert Einstein? Who was he when he first submitted his theories? You, like him, might change our understanding of the world in which we live, hopefully earning yourself a Nobel Prize in the process.'

'That is my hope, mother.'

'Don't let this be a burden upon your young shoulders my son. I am only a humble businesswoman, but I have many contacts in the scientific community. I am sure that I can arrange for your theory to be given a fair hearing.'

'But what if I am wrong? Think about what that might do to your reputation?'

'I pay people very good money to protect my reputation, my son. Did not Einstein explain the intricacies of energy and matter with the simplest of equations?'

Biratu burst out laughing. 'Unfortunately, my equations are far from simple, mother. I have no E equals MC squared.'

'Tell me, Solomon, are you planning on proving your theory by inviting members of the scientific community to watch esoteric services being held in the basements of mansion houses?'

'That's one of my problems. I can't mention the paranormal. To do so would be tantamount to committing an act of intellectual suicide.'

'Are you saying that you can prove your theory using equipment in a scientific laboratory?'

'No laboratory in the world has equipment capable of creating a single black hole, and I need to create eight of them, simultaneously.'

'Now I understand your discomfort, my son. I'm no expert but talk of black holes sounds a little frightening. I can't imagine there is a laboratory in the world that would encourage you to create one.'

'Actually, mother, I am not stuck. There is one place on earth where my mathematical constructs could immediately be turned into a physical reality for all to see.'

'Are you talking of about nuclear reactor?'

'No, we already have lots of those on the planet. No, I am talking of about the world's greatest machine, the Large Hadron Collider.'

'Ah, the particle accelerator housed in Switzerland.'

'You've heard of it, mother?'

'Who hasn't? Even I know that the machine was built to prove the existence of something you scientists call The Higgs Boson, which the news media prefer to call the God Particle. If I am not mistaken, the particle's existence was proven in 2012.'

'You never manage to surprise me, mother. You are a true polymath.'

'Do you believe in fate, Solomon?'

'Well yes, I suppose that I do. Why do you ask?'

'Do you know what I am doing here in London?'

'No, mother. You said on the telephone that you wished to meet with me because we hadn't seen each other for such a long time.'

'In between attending business meetings, I am here in London to be wined and dined by two of CERN's most senior scientists. The administrators at CERN wish to thank me for funding the Emerging Nations' Mathematics Competition, the very same prize that you won as a child. The scientists are going to provide me with an overview of future research projects that CERN hopes to fund through private donations. I have no wish to become a cash cow, milked to fill shortfalls in grants allocated by the central governments of the developed world, but I sense that I can use the opportunity to further your research.'

'But mother, if I hand the details of my theory over to these people, what is to stop them from claiming it as their own?'

'Ah, finally we move into an area in which I have some expertise. I have a small army of legal people working for me. It will be a simple matter to have them draw up a non-disclosure agreement to be signed by the CERN scientists in advance of our meeting.'

'Thank you, mother. Your plan sounds like an excellent way of promoting my theory. Tell me, why is it that you were so keen to speak with me or did you truly want some family time together?'

'What do you think, Solomon? You know that I hate communications devices. I wanted to have a proper conversation with you. That is all.'

'I'm afraid that something else is troubling me, mother. Something far more important than my work.'

'Are you ill, Solomon?'

'No, I'm in the best of health.'

'Then what is it?'

Tears filled Biratu's eyes, and he took several deep breaths before he was able to say the words. 'A good friend of mine has been murdered.'

'What?'

'A good friend of mine has been murdered, but everyone thinks that she committed suicide.'

'You're not in any trouble are you, Solomon?'

'No, mother, I am fine.'

'But you speak of murder.'

'Please let me explain. The matter is complicated, and indirectly involves you.'

'I don't understand, are you accusing me of being involved in murder?'

'No, of course not, mother.'

'Then what is it?'

'You fund many NGOs.'

'Yes, what of it?'

'Your favourite, the one you devote the most time -'

'The Faithless Freedom Foundation, an organisation dedicated to the freedom of all individuals, no matter what their faith, race or gender,' interrupted Namdar.

'You must be aware of views of the anti-capitalist groups, which say that your NGO is just a tool of Western soft power that helped catalyse the revolutions of Eastern Europe and the -'

'Of course, I am. But even if that were true, does it make me a murderer?'

'No mother, of course not. Please let me finish what I am trying to tell you.'

'Very well, I will try not to interrupt again.'

'I had a Ukrainian girlfriend; she was a student at the Taras Shevchenko National University in the Ukrainian capital city of Kiev. She was also a follower of an internet group calling themselves the GreyFriars. A group devoted to thwarting the actions of a secretive witchcraft cult, The Church of the Six Salems.'

'The very same esoteric group whose sacred Rite I sent to you watch?'

'Yes, it is mother, but there's more to than that. This group, the GreyFriars, they say that there are links between the cult and your NGO.' Biratu scanned his adopted mother's expression for any sign of recognition of what he was telling her, but her demeanour didn't change. 'A hacker calling himself, Matthew5:5, well known to users of the Dark Web, says that encrypted files recently hacked from the computers at the FFF's headquarters, link the NGO to the Six Salems. My girlfriend was in possession of a few of these encrypted files when she was murdered.'

Namdar looked, unblinking, at her adopted son for a good while before speaking. 'Solomon, I don't wish to hurt your feelings, but the story you have told me sounds fanciful at best. It is clear to me that you are under a great deal of stress, and it is normal for stress to warp one's objectivity. I will not dismiss what you have told me, but you must appreciate that prolonged exposure to -'

'But I have proof that Tatjana was murdered, mother!' exclaimed Biratu.

'Tatjana?'

'Tatjana Umansky. I have a recording of her murder.'

Namdar placed a kindly hand on Biratu's shoulder. 'My son, there are people that for one reason or another try to exploit our grief for their own ends. You know far better than I that in this digital age images can be doctored to show any abomination.'

'But the recording is mine, mother.'

For the first time Namdar's expression changed, only the faintest of grimaces was perceptible. But Biratu saw it and Namdar was aware that he'd noticed it. 'This recording, do you have it with you?' she asked as nonchalantly as she was able.

'Yes, mother, I have a copy with me.'

'Have you brought it to the attention of the police?'

'No, nobody has seen it except me.'

'Then why not take it to the police before bringing it to me? Do you honestly think that I had something to do with this young lady's death?'

'No, mother. It's just that I don't think that the police will take me seriously. I want the perpetrators brought to justice and I believe that your involvement will provide the best chance of justice being served.'

'Tatjana's parents, have they given you their blessing for you to approach me?'

'No, mother, they know nothing about it. I didn't want to upset them unnecessarily.'

'As always, you have done the right thing, my son. I don't know if you are aware of the international police force, Interpol?'

'Yes, mother, I have heard of them. You think that they might be able to help?'

'They operate in many areas. In recent times my NGOs have had dealings with them regarding the sorry business of people smuggling.'

'You think they have the jurisdiction to investigate the suspicious death of a Ukrainian university student in the city of Kiev?'

'Article three of their constitution forbids them from investigating religious crimes, but you believe this young woman was murdered by a secret society?'

'Yes, mother,'

'So, yes, I see no reason why they wouldn't be interested.'

'Would my name be mentioned, mother?'

'I don't envisage them needing to know who passed the recording onto me. You said that the young woman, Tatjana, is a Ukrainian national?'

'Yes, mother.'

'If I remember correctly, the Interpol National Central Bureau for the Ukraine is part of the Ukrainian national police force. Give me a copy of the recording and I will have Fyodor make the necessary arrangements. I promise that your name will be kept out of this.'

Ten minutes later the two of them were sat on a rug watching the recording with tear-filled eyes; Biratu's pain stemmed from the evil that had been done, Namdar's from the evil yet to be done.

TWENTY-FIVE

Osmond jogged out of her estate onto Grosvenor Road at ten minutes to nine to see Harry Windsor already out waiting for her. He was leaning against a tree trunk stretching his gastrocnemius and soleus muscles.

'Hi Harry, you're keen, aren't you?' asked Osmond after crossing the main road.

'I'm fine Sanda. I'm just looking forward to our run. Do you need to warm up before we get started?'

'No, I'm all good to go.'

'Is it alright if I take another minute to finish-off my stretches? I'm afraid that these days I seem to spend as much time stretching as running,' said Windsor.

'Stretch away, Harry, I'm not in any hurry. And besides we're early yet,' replied Sanda, deciding to fill in the time performing a few stretches of her own.

Windsor used the time to search for Michael's security service minders, as he thought that one of them had followed Sanda out onto the embankment. The well-built man in his mid-thirties, wearing a grey T-shirt, jeans and what looked like a pair of combat boots, stood out like a sore thumb to him. Windsor spent a few seconds studying the man stopped on the opposite side of the road pretending to read from the screen of his mobile phone. A few joggers were on the pavements, but nobody else caught Windsor's eye. 'I'm sorry about that, I'm all ready to go now,' said Windsor, satisfied that he'd seen all there was to see.

Osmond let Windsor set the pace, and he went too fast to allow them to chat along the way. The little conversation they indulged in revolved around asking each other if they were comfortable with the pace. Osmond couldn't believe how such a powerfully built man was able to run middle distance so quickly, but she wasn't surprised to see him struggling for breath at the end of the run.

'Bloody hell Harry, you sure run fast for such a big guy,' she said.

Harry laughed between gasps of air. 'I'm not bad... not bad... for a... for an old man. Even if... I say so myself.'

'You must have been some athlete in your youth.'

'I'm ex-army.'

'I came across a couple of really fit fifty-year-olds when I was working as a personal trainer. They were either good at running or weights, but I never came across anyone who could do both.'

'There's plenty of us out there. I guess that fellas like me don't use personal trainers that often. You might want to give the personal training another go. According to what I read in the newspapers; underemployed people are supposed to be stuck in front of plasma screens eating pizza all day. You definitely don't match that stereotype.'

'It can be like that sometimes, but I keep myself busy. I'm a blogger. I spend a lot of my time researching stuff, then I write or talk about it on the net.'

'What do you blog about?'

'Gene therapies, genetically modified foods and the like.'

'So, you're into saving the planet?'

'Who isn't?'

'And does blogging give you enough money to pays the bills?'

'There's money to be made from it, but I don't do it for that.'

'I don't know the first thing about blogging, but I can't believe that it takes up too much of the day.'

'You'd be surprised. It can take hours of reading time. But I have to admit that I've been thinking about getting back into the world of properly paid work. My savings are right down, and I might have to start borrowing money soon.'

'If you blog like you run, I'm sure that you could find a way of making money out of it. I hate being beaten at anything, and I could tell that you could have left me if you'd have wanted to.'

'Maybe, but we weren't racing each other.'

'If you're up for it, I'd like to do this again sometime. I'm going to be in London for another couple of weeks before my contract finishes.'

'Okay, Harry. It makes a change running with someone who pushes me to the limit. I don't get to run with many people who can do that anymore.'

'Me neither. I've got to get off now. Please send me a text when you fancy another run.'

'I will do, Harry. Have a good one.'

Windsor started jogging slowly in the direction of Dolphin Square but stopped, after he'd gone about fifty yards, pretending to do up his shoelace. He was looking out for his daughter's shadow, the man in the grey T-shirt. Windsor saw him waiting for her just inside the council estate. He was just about to return to where he had parked his car when he noticed a woman in her late twenties wearing a blue T-shirt crossing over the main road. *She doesn't look right*, he thought to himself. He hadn't noticed her earlier and guessed that she'd been watching him and Osmond from the shadows. He had no reason to think it, but something told him that this woman and the man in the grey T-shirt weren't part of the same team. *Could somebody have found her so quickly?* That was a question to which Windsor required an urgent answer.

Osmond walked slowly back to her flat, oblivious of what was going on around her. She was tired but pleased with the run. The old fella had really pushed her. She wasn't happy about getting slagged-off about being unemployed, but she sensed that Harry's heart was in the right place.

ଘଘଘଘ

Biratu and Namdar were seated in a Michelin-starred London restaurant with two senior CERN nuclear physicists, Professor Liana Malashenko, a Ukrainian national, and Dr Carman Abrahams, an American. Biratu was well acquainted with Professor Malashenko's research into five quark atoms but knew nothing about the American. Much to the embarrassment of the CERN scientists, it was obvious to Biratu that neither of them had ever heard of him or the subject of his PhD thesis.

'Carman, if I've understood you correctly, you specialise in transforming theoretical mathematical constructs into computer models that ultimately can be tested by physical experiment in one of the Collider's many detectors,' said Namdar, having waited until after the desserts had been ordered before making her pitch.

'Yes, Lilith, that is correct. Our computer models give the administrators a degree of certainty that the high energy collisions will bear fruit in the detectors,' replied Dr Abrahams.

'Solomon tells me that his research has led to some very interesting developments in what he calls Gauge and String Theories. He believes that your Collider could be used to create something he calls a wormhole between our world and one of possibly unlimited, extra-dimensional, parallel worlds.'

'That's very interesting, Lilith, but even if it were theoretically possible to create such a gateway, the Collider wouldn't be the place to do it. Its function is to collide particles at massive speed and record the exotic particles created by the collisions.'

'But that's the point,' said an excited Biratu. 'Not only does the Collider have the energy to create the wormhole, but there should be an asymmetric build-up of Gravitons on either side of the gateway, allowing us to measure gravitational leakage between the parallel worlds.'

'So, you're an advocate of the Many Worlds Theory, Solomon?' asked Dr Abrahams.

'Not in the classical sense. I think that there might only be as few as two parallel worlds.'

'And you believe that recording of the emergence and or disappearance of Gravitons in the Collider's detectors will be enough to proof your theory?' asked Dr Abrahams.

'Exactly!' replied Biratu.

'That's very interesting, Solomon,' said Dr Abrahams giving Solomon a forced smile before turning to face Namdar. 'Well, Lilith, I'd be very happy to help Solomon in any way that I can, but unfortunately our research projects are approved several years in advance of –'

'Actually Carman, ad hoc projects are approved all the time. I am very confident that the board would look favourably on testing Solomon's hypothesis, if one of your models demonstrated that it was feasible to do so,' interrupted Professor Malashenko, who had been watching as Namdar's expression hardening. The professor being worried that millions of dollars of funding might be lost by not indulging the billionaire businesswoman's aspirations for her adopted son.

'I won't pretend to understand the amount of work involved in building one of Carman's computer models, Liana, but it would so please Solomon if he could take his research to the next level.'

'Actually, as luck would have it, Carman is between projects at the moment. I see no reason why she couldn't immediately start working with Solomon to build a basic simulation program. Isn't that right, Carman?'

'What? Yes, I'd be delighted to,' replied Dr Abrahams, giving the professor a look that hinted that she might have to reschedule her summer holiday.

Namdar allowed herself a smile. 'In that case, I'm very

pleased to inform you both that I've decided to double the funding I currently make to your auspicious organisation. My personal assistant, Fyodor Maknov, will oversee the transaction details.'

Biratu spent the next ten minutes acquainting Dr Abrahams with the finer details of his theory. The doctor, under the watchful eye of her professor, converting Biratu's theoretical constructs into collision energies, luminosities, and inverse femtobarns. To Biratu's surprise, Dr Abrahams seemed to have an innate understanding of his experiment and the physical requirements needed to test it. Within a few short minutes she suggested, with some confidence, that his experiment could be tested using quark-gluon plasma created from the residue of heavy-ion collisions within the ALICE detector, in an experiment running not longer than two minutes.

TWENTY-SIX

Windsor had positioned himself on the roof of a tower block overlooking Osmond's first floor flat. He had purposely not chosen the rooftop providing the best view as he'd guessed, correctly, that it was already in use by what he hoped was Michael's security service's team. He'd been totally unprepared for the sight of a second surveillance team and had still had Moore's words ringing in his ears, "You've killed a lot of people Harry". He couldn't believe how unprofessional he'd been and vowed not to let himself get caught unawares again.

From his vantage point he could see at least one person on the roof of the building that provided the best view of Sanda's apartment. Whoever was up there had a better view of him than he had of them, so he was careful to keep himself concealed from view and only used his binoculars under cloud cover, limiting the possibility of reflected sunlight giving his position away.

Where's the other team, Harry? asked the voice in his head.

The hours had passed slowly, but Windsor was an expert in the art of watching and waiting, having been trained by the SBS to sit cross-legged in a small box for hours at a time. Then he noticed movement coming from his daughter's flat, the lights went out and a few seconds later Sanda Osmond was on the move. She was heading in the direction of the local shops with a long-life shopping bag in her hand. He was just about to leave his vantage point and make his way to ground level when he saw a heavyset man climb out of a car parked at the end of Osmond's block. He hoped the chance had come to locate the operating base of the second surveillance team.

Osmond had disappeared from view with Michael's grey T-shirted shadow following close behind her. It was then that the woman who had been wearing the blue T-shirt finally broke cover. Windsor decided to stay put on his rooftop vantage point as he had some serious thinking to do.

His original plan had been to try and get to know his daughter through her passion for sports, but the sight of a second surveillance team changed everything. The little voice inside his head was telling him that he should have listened to Michael and kept well away. Well, it was too late for that now, he'd contacted her, vastly increasing the chances of her being snatched or murdered. He decided that there was only one thing for it, he'd go hell for leather and tell her everything. The decision made; it was now just the case of choosing the right moment to do so.

༒ ༒ ༒ ༒

Namdar was sat alone drinking mint tea, eating dates, and wondering what had caused her to change over the years. It was true that after hundreds of years, life had become boring, but she had learnt so many things and could so very easily have been a force for good. But the longer she had lived, the longer the Accuser had had to work on her, gnawing away at her day and night until she had cracked. It was her interest in magic that did it for her, making it so easy to cross over to the dark side. She sensed that the god of the Christians had no time for oracles and soothsayers, even though he had provided the warning that saved her, and her husband, from the flood. Once she had been a priestess, but now she was nothing more than a liar and a murderer. She had done some abominable things over the centuries, but her disciples had done worse, far worse. She had drawn the line at eating babies, but not so the Pappenheimers and others like them.

Recently she had felt the Dark Lord stirring in his pit, sensing that his day of resurrection was close at hand.

Originally he'd come to her in dreams, teaching her the power of sacred words and symbols. Through him she learnt the power of light and how a super collider could be used to mirror the rainbow, corrupting humankind's covenant with God. Billions would die, but was that so bad? After all, she had been wishing for death for centuries. No, death wasn't to be feared, it is what might come after it that one should fear - the eternal wailing and the gnashing of teeth.

She smiled as she looked into the flames of the fire-holder. The Russian had hurt her physically all those years ago, but the closest Namdar could remember coming to defeat was at the hands of the Maid of Orléans. Now, at this vital time, another female descendant of Enkidu looked set to do battle with her. The Maid of Orléans had gotten lucky, she had been no stranger to the dark arts and had stolen an item of Namdar's power from her, her Bellarmine or Witch Bottle. Now, in the present day, Namdar thought it possible that fate might allow the Russian to take the girl under his wing. So she intended to ensure that the woman was powerless to battle against her.

Namdar stared, smiling, at the flames of the fire-holder, remembering the last agonies of the Maid of Orléans. *Your fate awaits you, Sanda Osmond, O great protector of humankind.*

TWENTY-SEVEN

Osmond returned to her flat with a full bag of food shopping in hand. The stocky man in the grey top had followed her all the way, and following him was the woman of the second surveillance team. Windsor watched as the stocky man climbed back into the parked car and the woman sat herself down on a bench in a children's playground providing good views of Osmond's apartment. Windsor, having decided to throw caution to the wind, called Sanda's mobile.

Osmond saw Windsor's name on the display and had thought about letting his call go to voicemail before she picked it up. 'Hi Harry, how are you?' she asked.

'Hi Sanda, I'm good thanks. I got to thinking after our run yesterday that I might be able to help you out on the job front. I know that you said that you're pretty much committed to your blogging, but I've got a proposal that I think you might be interested in. A contact of mine in the City mentioned that she is looking for a personal trainer to work with some of her wealthiest clients, it would be a part-time zero-hours contract arrangement, but the money sounds excellent. I'm just over in Lupus Street, so I was wondering if I could let you know the details over a cup of tea. What do you think?'

'Well, it's all a bit sudden Harry... but if you're over the road, then fine, come on over and we can discuss it.'

'I was hoping that you'd be at home, what's your address?'

Five minutes later Windsor walked slowly over to his daughter's tower block. He took the opportunity to take a closer look at the car the heavyset man was sat in and wasn't surprised to see another man sitting in the front seat next to him. He rang Osmond's doorbell and used the time she took to open the door to observe the woman sitting on the bench in the children's playground. He was trying to get a fix on where the rest of her team were based, but nothing in the woman's body language gave their observation post away.

'Hi, Harry. Come on in,' said Osmond.

'Thanks for seeing me, Sanda, I'm sure that you won't regret it,' said Windsor sensing that she wasn't keen on letting him in.

A few minutes later the two of them were seated in her front room sharing tea and cookies.

'Sanda, what I'm about to tell you is going to sound very weird, but I can't see any other way around it,' said Windsor taking a deep breath. 'I didn't just happen to bump into you when you were out running. I planned to meet you that way.'

'What!' exclaimed Osmond, thinking that she might have inadvertently let a weirdo into her flat. She was a powerfully built woman, but she knew that she was no match for a man of Windsor's physicality, and started to look about the room for anything that she might be able to use as a weapon if things turned nasty.

'Look, just hear me out and I'll explain it all to you.'

'Well, ah, well, ah... okay, fire away, Harry.'

'I think that you know that your father, Benjamin, isn't your biological father. He met and married your mother after you were born. Well, I knew your mother before they met, and –'

'No fucking offence, Harry, but are you trying to tell me that you're my biological father?'

'Er, yes.'

'This is all a bit much for me to take in. Even if what you're saying is true, couldn't you have thought of a better way of telling me?'

'I didn't want to include your mother in any of this.'

'Couldn't you have emailed me or something?'

'I'm afraid that there wasn't time.'

'What? Why not?'

'There are reasons why I didn't want to include your family in this. I mentioned when out running that I used to be in the Armed Forces. Well that part was true, I was a member of the Special Boat Squadron, they are like –'

'I've heard of them. They are like the SAS.'

'That's right. Well, when you're in the Special Forces you see a lot of active service. Look, what I'm trying to say is that I've killed people for Queen and Country, a lot of -'

'What's so complicated about that? Soldiers kill people all the time.'

'Please let me finish.'

'Okay.'

'I chose never to get married or start a family because I wanted to be absolutely certain that there would never be any risk of someone harming my family in revenge for something I might have done in the line of duty.'

'Don't tell me Special Forces soldiers don't have families. I might not know about how armies work, but soldiers are just regular people.'

'Alright, there's no time for me to get into the details. Can you just please try and accept that what I'm telling you is the truth?'

'What you're trying to tell me is that you got my mum pregnant and left her to bring me up all on her own!'

'No, that's not it at all. I barely knew your mother. We had a holiday romance and returned back to our normal lives. At least, I did. She obviously became pregnant with you, and up until a week ago I didn't even know that you existed.'

'How can you know all that if you haven't been in contact with my mum?'

'When you were arrested, the police collected a sample of your DNA.'

'What?'

'The police took a sample of your DNA. Your DNA was matched to my DNA, and without getting into the finer details, the people that I work for made me aware of your existence.'

'I don't know what to think or say, Harry. What you're saying sounds too complicated to be made up. But why tell me this right now? I mean, couldn't you have waited until we went out on another run or something like that. You said that there wasn't time, what did you mean by that?'

'I don't want to worry you, but there are people following you.' For the first time, Windsor had said something that Osmond knew to be true. Up until that moment she'd been tempted to throw Harry, or whatever his real name was, out of her flat. But the mention of people following her struck a chord. 'You've seen them, haven't you?' continued Windsor.

'Yes, I've seen them, but I thought they were police.'

'There are two teams out there. I know that one of them belongs to the Security Services.'

'And the other?'

'I don't know who they are, but I have to assume that they don't have your best interests at heart.'

'Okay, suppose what you've told me is true. What am I supposed to do about it?'

'I'd like to get you out of here and take you to a place of safety.'

'Hold on. You really expect me to believe you, when you say that you're my biological father and want to drive me off to a place of safety?'

'No offence, Sanda, but I'm in your home. If I wanted to harm you, don't you think that I'd have done so by now? Alright, I might have a way of proving this to you.'

'How? Are you going to call my mother?'

Osmond looked on in horror as Harry unbuttoned his jacket and pulled out a large handgun.

'This is a real gun, it's a Glock 22, standard issue to UK police firearms units. If I wanted to harm you, I could simply shoot you dead. Take a look at it. Don't worry, the safety's on,' said Windsor handing her the gun.

Osmond took the gun. It was heavy, weighing over two pounds. It looked professional and expensive. It certainly wasn't the type of weapon that the average lunatic would be carrying around with him, not in England at least. She was trying to weigh up her options. She was tempted to call her mum and confront her with what Harry had told her but thought better of it. But she couldn't bring herself to leave the safety of her home on the say so of a man she didn't know or trust.

'Look, Sanda, you could simply call the police, but my feeling is that might only compromise your safety. How about I escort you to the MI6 building at Vauxhall Cross? We'd be there in minutes. What do you say?'

'The MI6 building?' asked a confused Osmond.

'Yes, it's the home of the UK's Secret Intelligence Service. It's covered in green glass. You might have seen it in a James Bond movie.'

'Fuck it. Let's do it,' said Sanda giving Windsor his gun back.

'Alright, but I need to make a call first,' said Windsor retrieving a mobile phone from his backpack. 'Hi, Michael, this is Harry Windsor. I'm putting you on loudspeaker. Listen, I need a favour from you.'

'Who else is with you, Harry?'

'Sanda Osmond. We are in her apartment.'

'I see. What is it that I can help you with, Harry?'

'My daughter, I think that her safety has been compromised. I want to take her to Vauxhall Cross.'

'What are you talking about, Harry? You know my people are outside, guarding her apartment.'

'There's another team out there with them. I don't know who they are or what they want. I just want the girl out of here.'

'Listen, Harry. Stay put and I'll send in another team to pick you up. Sanda will be perfectly safe in the meantime.'

'Another team! Wouldn't it be quicker to have the existing team bring us in?'

'You said that my people have been compromised. It will be better to leave them in situ and have a specialist extraction team pick you up.'

'But that's going to take time to arrange!'

'Just stay put, Harry, and I'll have them pick you up in a jiffy. Sanda, how are you?'

'I'm fine, but very confused.'

'I don't know what Harry has told you, but don't worry about a thing. My people will bring you in. I can't guarantee that things will become any less complicated, but I promise that you, and your family, will be safe.'

'Thank you, Michael.'

'Harry, the code word is Excalibur. Have you got that?'

'Excalibur. I copy that.

'I'm going to hang up now as I've got a few phone calls to make. Remember, don't let anyone in unless they give you the code word. Goodbye.'

'Sanda, I need you to lock the front door and leave the key in the mortice lock. I don't like it, but I suppose we'd better do as he says,' said Windsor.

'Have you got a backpack?' asked Windsor after Sanda had locked the door.

'Yes. Why?'

'Fill it up with any possessions that are important to you. You know, money, photos, that kind of stuff. Take the photos out of their frames if you can, you don't want anything too bulky.'

'You don't think that I'll be coming back here?'

'To tell the truth, I've got no idea. Better safe than

sorry, eh?'

After Sanda had locked the front door and gathered her things, the two of them sat down in silence whilst they waited for Michael's extraction team to arrive.

Half an hour passed, and there still wasn't any sign of the cavalry. Windsor took a look through a window providing a view of the children's playground, and wasn't surprised that the lady had gone. He looked out of all the other windows but didn't see any sign of Michael's extraction team. Finally, he double-checked the window providing a view of roof being used by the original surveillance team.

'I don't like it,' said Windsor. He was still looking up at the rooftop when he saw several bursts of light. 'That's not right.'

'What isn't, Harry?' asked Osmond.

'We can't wait any longer, we need to get out of here right now,' said Windsor ignoring the question.

'But Michael said to wait.'

'Michael's not here, I am, and I say that we've waited long enough. Come on, grab your bag we're getting out of here.'

'Okay, dad, the ball is in your court,' said Osmond, her tone filled with sarcasm.

Windsor winced on hearing his daughter call him dad.

Osmond didn't know why, but she trusted Windsor. So, she picked up her backpack, unlocked the front door, and the two of them made their way downstairs.

Windsor left his lightweight jacket unbuttoned, allowing his easy reach of the Glock housed in a shoulder holster under his left arm.

'Where are we going?' asked Osmond when they reached the pavement.

'I parked my car in the next block, it's a white BMW convertible. Stay two steps behind me and everything will be just fine. Tell me if you see anyone you don't recognise, male or female.'

'What happens if someone gets in our way?'

'Don't worry about a thing. I might have to break the speed limit once we're in the car, but apart from that there shouldn't be any problems.'

Two men suddenly appeared at the end of Osmond's block.'

'Just in case you were wondering, Harry, I don't recognise either of those men,' said Osmond, her voice rising to soprano.

'I had a feeling you were going to tell me that. Alright, we'll go around the other way, out onto the main road.'

The two of them turned around and saw a little old lady with a walking stick coming their way, coming fast behind her were two men, and the woman who'd been sitting on the bench.

'I don't know those -'

'Don't worry about them, we will be fine,' said Windsor placing his right hand over Glock hidden beneath his jacket. He carefully sidestepped the old lady as he braced himself for the confrontation that lay ahead. Windsor was oblivious to the old woman's sudden change of direction and didn't see her raise her metal walking stick, but he did feel the electricity when it started pulsing through the back of his neck.

Osmond stopped in her tracks as Windsor collapsed onto the pavement beside her. She could only watch in horror as bullets started flying out of the front of the old woman's walking stick. She looked-up to see blood and bone spattering off of the two men and the woman before all three of them hit the pavement. It was only as they lay dead on the pavement that she noticed the guns in their hands. She turned around and saw two men lying on the pavement at the other end of the block. Two other men were standing over them discharging handguns into them. Osmond was stood frozen to the spot as the men with guns jumped into a car, accelerated down the road, and skidded to a halt next to her. Sanda turned to see the old woman's outstretched hand in front of her.

'Come with me if you want to live' said the old woman, her voice sounding like an Eastern European woman of much younger years. The old woman grabbed her arm and pulled her to the back car. 'Come with me if you want to live' she repeated as she opened the boot and pointed, indicating that Osmond should get in.

Osmond looked around at the dead bodies strewn across the pavement. She very much wanted to live, so without hesitation she climbed into the boot as instructed.

TWENTY-EIGHT

Director Thomas was sat ashen faced as he listened to Ian Moore's description of Sanda Osmond's kidnap. In truth things could have been a lot worse. Several CSS disciples might have been shot to death, but Harry Windsor had been found alive, lying unconscious next to three of the bodies. And somehow, against all odds, the bodies had been removed from the scene before the arrival of the police and without anyone managing to record the event on a mobile phone. In fact, all that the emergency services personnel found when they arrived on site was a lot of blood, fragments of bone and a number of bullet casings. The evidence pointed to a number of people being very badly injured, but there was nothing to prove that anyone had actually been murdered. To all intents and purposes, it looked like the London council estate had been the site of another, very bloody, drugs related postcode gang dispute.

'Where is Windsor now?' asked the director.

'He said that he intended to return to his home in Lewes,' replied Moore.

'And you think he believed you when you told him that a media blackout had been imposed because the incident was being treated as an issue of national security?'

'Yes, sir. He had no reason not to.'

Director Thomas turned to his deputy director. 'Liz, who selected the disciples making up the surveillance team, you or Ian?' He was careful not to look Elizabeth Middleton full in the eye. He might be in Namdar's top tier, The Revelati, but he was under no illusions of what a priestess was capable of. Middleton was a coven leader; she might not yet have graduated to Witch Queen status, but she knew how to harm people wielding the ancient words of power.

'Ian did,' she replied. 'It made more sense for him to

do so as he works out in the field.'

'And who was responsible for the arranging the clean-up operation?'

'I was,' said Middleton.

'Very well, we will draw a line under Osmond's capture. They didn't leave her dead at the scene so we must assume that they wanted her alive. That leaves the question of how we are going to get her back?'

'My guess is that they have moved her to a safe house. Ultimately, this might well play into our hands,' said Moore.

'How so?' asked the director.

'I've got no evidence for it, but I think that Zhukhov is here in Britain. The Mistress will likely forgive our debacle should we capture or kill him before he has a chance to escape.'

Director Thomas knew that Moore was right. Their lives depended on capturing the Russian. 'Assuming that you're right, Ian, how do we go about finding him?'

'The Black Knight will find him for us, he has a sense for these things.'

'And how do you propose that I articulate this strategy to the Grand Mistress?'

'There is nothing else that we can do, sir. Either they make a mistake, we get lucky, or we rely on Windsor finding them for us. If I were a betting man, my money would be on the latter of the three.'

'Unfortunately, there's a lot more than money at stake here, Ian,' said the director giving his fellow disciples a wry smile.

৩৩৩৩

Windsor was still kicking himself for being so easily duped. It was bad enough his making a grab for his daughter without having an exit strategy, but missing the woman disguised as a senior citizen was a complete amateur's mistake. He didn't believe that he deserved to wake up on the pavement, he felt that he should have been killed along with the members of Michael's surveillance team. The only upside was that Sanda had been snatched rather than murdered. He wasn't one to rely on luck, but he knew he needed some now. He took a deep breath and activated the transponder, twenty seconds later he exhaled with a smile on his face. He had a signal.

Either they haven't discovered the transmitter I planted in her backpack, or they want me to find her, said the voice in his head.

ଘଘଘଘ

Namdar, flanked discreetly by her bodyguards, met Biratu at the Kingston-upon-Thames's ancient market.

'How well do you know Kingston, Solomon?' she asked.

'Not that well. I stopped here when walking along the Thames path a few years ago,' replied Biratu.

'Kingston has a lot of history, Solomon. There has been a market at this site for over eight hundred years. And until seventeen-fifty, Kington boasted the only other bridge over the Thames other than London Bridge. Back when the first bridge was built, King Egbert of Wessex, grandfather of Alfred the Great, held his Great Council here. Of course, back then it was a small town, quite separate from the great city that is London. The Great Council was attended by the King, his noblemen, Archbishop Ceolnoth of Canterbury and twenty-four of his bishops. It made a compact of mutual support and co-operation between church and state. An interesting model, no doubt copied by others. But that is not what I wanted to show you.'

'Are we going to visit a church?'

'No, Solomon, Kingston contains a treasure far greater than any church.'

A few minutes later the two of them were standing on the outskirts of the grounds of the town hall.

'Is this what you wanted to show me, mother?'

'No, not the council building. What I want you to see is just over there,' said Namdar, pointing at a lump of rock enclosed behind a circular metal fence.

Namdar's eyes seemed to mist over as the two of them approached the rock.

'What is it, mother?'

'This, my son is the Sarsen Coronation Stone, used to crown seven Anglo-Saxon kings. Some say that it has a twin, that it is one of two stones removed from Stonehenge over a thousand years ago. Others, that this stone might once have had an anvil affixed to it, to hold the sword used by the magician Merlin to prove that Arthur was the true heir to the throne of England. Now that would be a thing, would it not? But alas, that's likely to be a story told to keep the tourists happy,' continued Namdar, her face breaking into a mischievous grin. 'Even so, what is beyond dispute is that seven ancient kings thought the stone important enough to be seated upon it when their crowns were placed upon their heads.'

'Why would such an important relic of history be lying out here, unprotected from the elements, with few who know or care of its existence?'

'I don't know, Solomon. It is one of life's mysteries, but fortunately it has weathered well. I come here once a year, just to look at it and imagine the events that have surrounded it for millennia. To try and get a sense, a feeling, of the ancient kings who felt compelled to gain legitimacy from a lump of rock. But most of all, I like to think about the fabled magician, Merlin, imagining the look on his face as Arthur freed the sword from the stone.'

'Why do you care for ancient fables, mother?'

'I suppose that I just like the old stories, I feel that

they give life a sense of wonder. Something that has been lost to many in our modern times. Come, let us take a walk along the river.'

TWENTY-NINE

Osmond was taken to a shower room where she was told to clean herself up by a male guard. Twenty minutes later the same man escorted her along a corridor and told her to wait outside a room whilst he knocked at the door.

'Enter' called out a woman, whose voice Osmond recognised as that of the old lady who'd pole-axed Harry Windsor before shooting three people to death. The guard escorted her into a large office where she saw an old man seated behind a desk and a woman, who looked to be in her late twenties or early thirties, sat to the side, on a sofa.

'Please sit yourself down, Sanda,' said the old man, his voice containing traces of what Osmond thought might be a Russian accent.

Osmond sat down opposite the old man whilst scanning the room, its walls plastered with strange charts and ancient writing. On the desk in front of the old man was a book that included the name Nostradamus in its title.

'The first thing that I want you to know is that we wish you no harm, Sanda. My name is Georgy Zhukhov, I was once a Lieutenant General in the Russian army. You have already met Natasha, albeit in a different guise. I assume that you have many questions, and you will be allowed to ask them as time allows. However, first I must tell you a story. Would you like a drink, tea, or coffee before I begin?'

'May I have a cup of coffee, Mr. Zhukhov?'

'Would you like milk and sugar?'

'Milk and two sugars. I don't normally take sugar, but under the circumstances I think I need some.'

Natasha served the coffee whilst Zhukhov started telling his tale.

'In the nineteen-sixties I was an officer in the Soviet Union's Main Intelligence Administration, called in my language, the Glavnoye Razvedyvatelnoye Upravlenie, better known as the GRU. Just like today, we had many problems with the foreign policy of America. Things were worse then, than they are now, but at least we no longer have the threat of nuclear war hanging over us like the Sword of Damocles. I spent most of the decade stationed in Cuba and played no small part in General Castro's repelling the Bay of Pigs invasion in April of sixty-one. I also oversaw the siting and construction of the ICBM missile silos that led to the Cuban Missile Crisis in October of sixty-two. The Soviet General Staffs were very keen in those days not to lose their foothold in the Caribbean, and officers, just like myself, were tasked with gathering intelligence on the possibility of American sponsored invasions of Cuba. It was then that I became acquainted with a woman calling herself Qarinah Pirez. Pirez had extraordinary powers of persuasion and managed to convince me that a second Cuban invasion was being planned for December of sixty-three. The proposed invasion, supposedly authorised by the Kennedys, was to receive full American air support. Such an assault was assessed as being unstoppable with the military capability at ours and Castro's disposal. But Pirez did much more than simply provide us with intelligence of the forthcoming invasion, she suggested a means of averting it. Proposing that we assist in the assassination of the then American president, a certain Jack Kennedy.'

'With all due respect to you, Mr. Zhukhov. Even if what you say is true, what has any of this got to do with me?'

'My intention is to provide you with some background information concerning the woman that you, I and your biological father, must do battle with.'

'What?'

'Please let me finish my story, Sanda,' said Zhukhov raising his right hand. 'It was Pirez who chose Dallas, arranged for me to be positioned on the grassy knoll, and set Oswald up as the patsy. This woman was a master strategist, able to plan years in advance. If my research is correct, she approached Oswald as early as 1958, when he was a US Marine private, responsible for protecting U-2 spy planes at the Atsugi airbase in Japan. Whatever else Pirez might have done, the rest they say is history. Tell me, Sanda, do you believe my story?'

'Before I answer that, I have a question of my own.'

'What is it?'

'What did this woman, Qarinah Pirez. What did she expect to gain from President Kennedy's death?'

'Back then, I assumed she wanted what most other people wanted – money. But over the years I began to understand that Kennedy's death should have ended America's plans to be the first nation to put a man on the moon.'

'And how would that have helped her?'

'Have you studied Economics?'

'I know a little.'

'Good. This is all about finite resources and Opportunity Costs. You see, Pirez wanted the money Kennedy allocated to his moon project spent elsewhere.'

'So, your country, Russia, assassinated President Kennedy because it wanted the United States to spend the moon project budget money on something else?'

'No, we did it to stop a second invasion of the Bay of Pigs.'

'Okay, this is all so weird that I'm even willing to accept that you might have killed President Kennedy.'

'Good. Then we can continue, said Zhukhov glancing at his star charts. 'You asked what this has got to do with you. As unfathomable as it may seem, rather a lot.'

'But I wasn't even born in 1963.'

'I'm afraid that if you have any doubts about the veracity of my first story, the next one is far less believable.

There now lives a woman, Lilith Namdar is her name, a name you might recognise as belonging to one of the world's wealthiest individuals. This woman is a well-known philanthropist and is a patron of many good causes. It is less widely known that she is the founder, and leader, of a non-governmental organisation called the Faithless Freedom Foundation. So far, so good. But what is much less well known is that the FFF is the public face of a secretive esoteric cult going by the name of the Church of the Six Salems, whose goal is the replacement of the World's established religions by the worship of witchcraft. It is even less well known that Namdar intends to use the cult to help bring about the End of Days, as described in the Book of Revelation. How do I know this you might ask? Because my disciples and I have been battling against the CSS for decades. Now Sanda, tell me, do you believe that story?'

'I still don't see what any of that has got to do with me,' said Osmond, looking at Zhukhov as if she thought him a little mad.

Zhukhov paused, and took a deep breath. 'Qarinah Pirez and Lilith Namdar are one and the same person. Her tactics have changed over the decades, but her ambition remains the same, to initiate the tribulation, Humankind's last seven years on earth. And you, my girl, might be able to stop her.'

'What? Me? Why? How?'

'Yes you, but you will not work alone. Prophecy states that you will work with two others.'

'Prophecy? What prophecy?'

'There are many prophecies, but the one with the greatest meaning is contained within this book,' said Zhukhov pointing at the book lying on the table in front of him. 'All is hidden in one of Nostradamus's quatrains, the one numbered IX.44. I have marked the pages showing the original Middle-French and its translation into modern

English.'

There was a page marker inserted in the book, Osmond opened the book and read the quatrain and its meaning:

> Migrés, migrés de Genefue trestous,
> Saturne d'or en fer se changera,
> Le contre RAYPOZ exterminera tous,
> Auant l'aruent le Ciel signes fera.

> Leave, leave Geneva every last one of you,
> Saturn will be converted from gold to iron,
> RAYPOZ will exterminate all who oppose him,
> Before the coming Heavens will make a sign.

'I'm sorry Mr. Zhukhov, I haven't a clue what any of that means. That, in itself, must make it clear to you that I can't be the woman you're looking for.'

'But weren't you born on 23rd February 1987?'

'Yes, but so were lots of other people.'

'And are they direct descendants of Enkidu?'

'Who?'

'He doesn't know it yet, but your biological father and I are brothers. You and I share the same bloodline.'

'Brothers? But you are so much –'

'Older? Yes, I am. Your father and I were born to different mothers, twenty years apart. You felt something when you entered the room, did you not?'

'Yes, I did, but I assumed it was just fear.'

'Now think back, you experienced the same feeling when you first met Harry Windsor. Didn't you?'

'Now that I think about it, yes, maybe I did. I don't want to show you any disrespect Mr. Zhukhov, but the things you are saying about me just can't be true.'

'My only son died on the day that you were born, killed by a sniper's bullet in Afghanistan. The man who took the fateful shot was part of an eight-man team of Special Forces soldiers smuggled into the country to eliminate high worth targets in the Soviet Army. That man was Harry Windsor. Something that I have waited thirty long years to discover.

'You think that Harry Windsor is my father, your brother, and that he murdered your son?'

'I don't think anything. I know all three to be true.'

'Is this all about revenge?'

'Qarinah Pirez would have liked events to have unfolded that way, but I have seen through her deception. I cannot lie. I would very much like to take my revenge for the death of my son, but for the good of the World, I cannot.'

'But if this woman Pirez wanted me dead, why am I still alive?'

'For several reasons, but the most important of which is that she knew that I would break cover to contact you. Her expectation being that I would kill you. Your life for the life of my only son,' said Zhukov whilst opening a drawer and pulling out a file. 'I have placed myself in great danger by coming to England, so I'd be grateful if you could read the contents of this folder. We will talk again later. In the meantime, you are at liberty to roam freely about the building, but please don't try to leave. You will be well catered for; we have a kitchen and a cook.'

Osmond browsed through the file. There were photos of strange charts, scrolls and stone tablets.

'I know that there is much to absorb. Please give some thought to the words I have spoken whilst reading the documents. Hopefully, things will start to make sense to you as the days go on.'

Natasha got up off the sofa and opened the office door, Osmond took it as her cue to leave.

THIRTY

Julie Barrett stepped out of her work office building into bright sunshine, the Forensic Administrative Assistant loved the light and warmth of the summer months. She'd almost taken early retirement the year before as the nights lengthened in advance of another gloomy British winter, but then changed her mind when she'd calculated the harsh reality of what her pension would force her to live on. Her husband of thirty-seven years had had a gambling problem and had never paid into his firm's generous company pension scheme or taken out life insurance, so when died in an accident Julie found herself facing an uncertain future. But she hadn't been dealt a completely bad hand, as her job had unexpectedly provided a means for her paying off the mortgage on her semi-detached two-bedroomed house. She wasn't rich, by any stretch of the imagination, but recently fate had been on her side, and she now had a nest egg to fall back upon. If winter ever got too cold and bleak for her, she now had sufficient resources to take early retirement.

Her rail journey home had been uneventful, with her passing the time as she usually did, reading a novel on the train. Then, a few minutes after leaving the train station, something unusual happened. A burgundy-coloured Rolls Royce Ghost pulled-up alongside of her and a woman called out of a window asking if she would like a lift. Julie hesitated, but she had never been inside a Rolls Royce before, so couldn't resist the chance of taking a seat inside of one as the chauffeur held open the passenger door for her.

'My name is Lilith Namdar, it is a pleasure to make your acquaintance…'

'My name's Julie.'

'It is a pleasure to make your acquaintance, Julie.'

'Nice meeting you, Lilith.'

'Where are you heading, Julie?'

'I'm just on my way home from work, I live in Victoria Drive.

'Excellent, Oleksiy will drive you home.'

'I hope that you don't take this the wrong way, Lilith, but why would you go out of your way to offer me a lift home?'

'You are direct and to the point, I like that in a person, Julie. With your permission I'd like us to take a longer route to your home as I have a business proposition to put to you. If you have no interest in what I have to say, I'll instruct Oleksiy to drop you at your doorstep and that will be the end of the matter. What do you say?'

'Sitting in here sure beats sitting in front of the telly with a cuppa.'

'You see Julie our meeting is no accident. I have been told that you process DNA test results for the Metropolitan Police Service. Is that correct?'

Namdar looked at Julie through her bright, friendly eyes, watching to see where Julie's eyes moved prior to answering the question.

'Why would a woman like you care for the work that I do?'

'But is it true? Do you process DNA test results for the Metropolitan Police Service?'

'Yes, I do, but I'm guessing that you already knew that.'

Eyes to the left, good. So, it is truth to the left and lies and misinformation to the right with you my dear, thought Namdar.

'Some people, me included, think that a DNA profile opens a window into the very soul of a person. People are willing to pay substantial amounts of money to know the inner secrets of their peers, business partners and lovers. Please tell me, Julie, how many bedrooms does your home have?'

'What? Why?'

'I'm interested in gaining an understanding of your financial circumstances. I repeat. How many bedrooms does your home have?'

'Two bedrooms, I live in a semi-detached house with a small back garden.'

Eyes up and to the left, recalling the picture in your mind. Good, you speak the truth, my dear.

'Can you hear the trains from where you live?'

'I hear them well enough.'

Eyes to the side and to the left, searching for a remembered sound. I am reading you like one of the books you like to read on the train, my dear.

'And the sofa in your living room, is it fabric or leather?'

'What? Look what is it that you are after, Lilith?'

'I will get onto that soon enough. Your sofa, is it fabric or leather?'

'Oh, alright then if you insist, it's fabric. I've never liked leather; I find it too cold in the winter.'

Down and to the left, remembering the feeling of the seat. Quite excellent.

'So, yours is a simple life, you don't have extravagant tastes.'

'I live within my means. I spend what I can afford to.'

'Ah, there we have it. Now, do me a favour, Julie. Please picture your dream home in your mind. What sort of house would you like to live in? Don't concern yourself with such trivialities as money.'

'Look, I think that I know what this is all about now. Am I in any trouble?'

'No trouble at all, my dear. Now please tell me, what sort of house would you like to retire in?'

'If you insist on going through this whole rigmarole. I'd like a nice little bungalow in a village close to the sea, with a decently sized garden. That would suit me just fine.

Up and to the right, creating a picture in your mind.

'Excellent, you have provided me with everything I need to proceed.'

'Proceed with what?' said Julie giving Namdar a puzzled and slightly worried look.

'Someone paid you a paltry sum to provide them with the name of a man whose DNA was recently removed from the national database. I am willing to pay you half a million pounds if you are willing to give me the test results of fifty people currently residing on that database. What says you to that?'

'But all the records are monitored by an electronic auditing system. Someone will find out what I've done. It's one thing providing the name of a man included on the database, it's quite another accessing and copying files.'

'Very well, make it one million pounds then. Five hundred thousand up front, with instalments of fifty thousand to be paid for each batch of ten records that you provide me with. This is a once in a lifetime offer, and I want an immediate answer. Will you, do it?'

Namdar could see that Julie was already imagining spending the money. Julie's eyes were darting right and moving up and down to the right.

'But I'll get caught, I'll lose my job, they might even –'

'What, prosecute a fifty-seven-year-old lady? Surely not. And besides, would they really risk making the public aware that their priceless DNA is being sold to the highest bidder?'

'Okay, I'll do it.'

'I do have one proviso before we cement our deal.'

'What's that?'

'I need to know that I can trust you to keep your mouth shut, come what may.'

'How can I possibly convince you of that?'

'There is an element of trust in every business transaction. It is all well and good inserting penalty clauses into contracts, but some people are greedy and let the money blind them to their obligations. Before we discuss anything else, I would like the name of the person who paid you for divulging the name of the man whose DNA matched that of Sanda Osmond.'

'Hold on, are you trying to trick me?'

'What do you mean, Julie?'

'Well, if I tell you that so easily. Who's to say that I won't do the same if someone asks me about you?'

'Excellent, Julie. That is the perfect answer. For you to even think of asking me that question, inspires me in confidence in you. In fact, you are just the type of person with whom I like to do business. However, give me the answer and I'll place twenty thousand pounds into your handbag. After all, it's not like you'd by breaking any promise that you made to them?'

'How so?'

'I assume that the person in question never gave you their name and I'd imagine that they might have taken some trouble to disguise their appearance. Am I right?'

'He did his best to disguise his appearance, I'll grant you that,' said Julie as she thought back to her meetings with the man in the hat who wore sunglasses in the middle of December. Her eyes darting left, both up and to the side as she scanned her memories.

'Why don't you just tell me how it all began?'

'It all started back in the summer of 2006. It was a nice sunny day, so I ate my lunch in the square. I've had money troubles as far back as I can remember, and this man tells me that he's willing to pay me good money if I was willing to stick one of them pen drives into my work computer. I'd never seen one before, they were new back then. He told me that it contained the DNA profiles of eight men and that he'd give me ten grand if I'd insert the drive into my computer's USB socket. He said that I'd receive another hundred thousand if I ever got a match for one of them on the criminal database. To tell the truth I didn't have the first clue what he was talking about, but I took the money and did what he asked. I was worried sick about it for couple of months, but over time I forgot all about it. My husband was still alive then, God rest his soul. But we burnt through the money quickly enough, what with his gambling and all.'

'Julie, I am but a simple woman. You say that a man paid you ten thousand pounds to load a computer program onto your office computer system?'

'Yes, that's right.'

'And you had to do nothing more?'

'Actually, I had to load the drive into my computer each time they changed it. That's right, I've reloaded the drive several times over the years,' said Julie, looking up and to the left.

'But then, a few weeks ago something unusual happened, you received a message informing you that a profile matched one of those given to you eleven years ago. I'm assuming that you were given a telephone number to call in such an eventuality. Did the same man pay you for the information?'

'Yes, it was the same man. He was older, but it was him hiding behind a pair of sunglasses. He approached me in the square, just like the first time.

'Do you recall the day and time of your last meeting?'

'Yes, it was on Wednesday between twelve and one. All of our meetings were during my lunch breaks.

Eyes to the top left. Excellent.

'You have an excellent memory, Julie. I'm sure that it has served you well over the years, but I'm afraid you have no more use for it,' said Namdar as she jabbed a needle into Julie's hand.

'Ouch! What have you done to me?' said Barrett just before she slipped into unconsciousness.

Later that night, Namdar lay in bed mulling over the events of her day. Top of her list was her conversation with the now deceased, former Metropolitan Police Forensic Administrative Assistant. She was certain that everything Julie Barrett had told her was true, and that meant that the Russian General had gone to extreme lengths to avenge the death of his son. What she couldn't understand was how Zhukhov had had the foresight to collect all traces of DNA left in the final firing positions by the eight British Special Forces soldiers smuggled into Afghanistan to assassinate his son, Ivan.

For all her intelligence, Namdar could not understand the logic behind Zhukhov's planting of the DNA profiles onto the Metropolitan Police's crime database. She had been sleeping badly for weeks, but tonight she sensed that she would sleep easily on the expectation that Zhukhov's contact at the Russian Embassy would soon be in the hands of her interrogators.

But Namdar wasn't granted a peaceful night's sleep, instead she experienced a succession of nightmares. Her mind had been filled with images of nuclear weapons and the faces of British traitors who'd gifted nuclear secrets to the dictatorships of the East. Images of Hiroshima, Nagasaki, and Semipalatinsk, formed a montage with the faces of Maclean, Burgess, Philby, and numerous others who she'd lured along the left-hand-path as they drank copious quantities of alcohol at Frisco's nightclub.

When Namdar finally awoke drenched in sweat, she was imagining Zhukhov collecting skin cells from the Dragunov SVD semi-automatic sniper rifle used by Harry Windsor to murder his son. She lifted the duvet to let freshened air get to her wet body and wondered if she had missed something. Something seemingly insignificant, a Rubicon, a proverbial butterfly flapping its wings that would ever so slowly bring a mighty storm to her door.

THIRTY-ONE

The file Zhukhov handed to Osmond was filled with references to the Holy Bible, prophecies of Nostradamus, events leading up to a global apocalypse, satanic rituals enabling the release of the Antichrist into the world, total eclipses, murders of Russian journalists, and machines called particle accelerators. Everything she read led her to believe that she was being held captive by a manipulative, possibly insane, cult leader.

If Zhukhov was correct, she and two others were going to save the world from a destructive event starting on 21st August. And just like all good cult leaders, Zhukhov wasn't certain what the cataclysmic event was, and even if they were able to stop it, and there would be no way of knowing whether they had been successful in saving the world for another seven years.

Osmond concluded that Zhukhov was most likely a fantasist or a fraud, but if agreeing with him was going to keep her alive, she was intent on playing along with most anything that he, and his disciples, asked her to do.

૩૩૩૩

Dimitri Obolensky's official role was that of a special adviser to the Russian Ambassador on the vagaries of the UK petrochemical industry; unofficially, he was one of many spies working for the Russian Embassy in London. During his lunch break he had bumped into an old friend, and the two of them had arranged to meet later in the evening to catch up on old times, over a vodka or three. His friend had suggested they meet at a Russian bar in Hackney. The bar was out of Obolensky's way, but he thought it might make a welcome change from the approved haunts frequented by embassy staff.

Obolensky travelled by tube from Queensway to Bank station, where he booked a taxi to take him the rest of the way to the bar. He was a little surprised when a Mercedes with blacked out passenger windows pulled-up alongside of him and more surprised when he was approached by an attractive South African lady just as he'd opened the rear passenger door. The last thing he remembered was a stinging sensation on the right-hand-side of his neck before he awoke to find himself in what appeared to be an abattoir, hanging by a meat hook impelled deep into his anus. His mind was groggy, but he was painfully aware that his body was trembling with cold, even though his brow was dripping with sweat. He looked down to see a puddle of blood on the stone floor that he assumed had formed from the blood that was slowly seeping from his bottom and dripping down his legs. All embassy staff had been warned, months before, to be extra vigilant on nights out as the war of words between East and West was forever being ramped-up since the invasion of Crimea. Obolensky thought the situation he found himself in was reminiscent of the old Cold War.

We cannot have reached the stage where our spy agencies have taken to impaling each other's agents on meat hooks. No, this has to be something different, said the voice in his head.

Obolensky's worst case scenario was that he'd been kidnapped by members of ISIS. If they had him, he surmised that it would only be a matter of time before he was placed in front of a video camera and murdered. He surmised that if the worst came to pass, having his head cut-off slowly with a combat knife was preferable to being burnt alive in a wire cage.

'Do you know why you are here my friend?' asked a heavily accented male South African voice from behind him.

'It does not matter why I am here. Proper channels should have been used before things were allowed to go this far,' said Obolensky, trying to sound calm and authoritative in spite of the pain pulsing through his body. 'You must understand that the repercussions will be most severe.'

'For you, my friend, there are no proper channels. You have been a naughty boy and we have brought you here to give you a good spanking.'

'This must be some kind of mistake. I am an analyst at the embassy, I advise the Russian Ambassador on matters relating to the petro-chemical industry.'

'Are you trying to tell me that you don't know an FSB General, named Zhukhov?'

Obolensky's head dropped, years of experience told him that he was a dead man, and that the remainder of his life would be filled by pain and suffering. He wondered how many hours he might survive impelled on the meat hook and what methods his interrogators would use to make him talk. The most that he could hope for was a quick death.

The South African moved swiftly, wrapping muscular arms around Obolensky's body, pulling it down hard onto the hook. Obolensky's bloodcurdling scream was met with laughter.

'It hurts a lot more when you're awake, eh my friend. You didn't squeal like a pig when I put you up there,' said the interrogator as he loosened his grip. 'I'm told that you are a smart man Mr. Obolensky. And if you are half as smart as they say you are, you will already know that there is no going home for you. The best that I can do for you is make it quick. You met my wife earlier; she doesn't like this side of the business and would prefer you not to suffer any more than is absolutely necessary. So why don't you do us both a favour and tell me what I need to know? Can you do that for me?' asked the interrogator, looking directly into Obolensky's eyes as he spoke. 'Come on, my friend, what says you, will you play ball?'

'What more can I tell you that you don't already know?'

'Then you tie my hands my friend. My wife will be most upset, but what can I do? I am afraid that things will get very nasty very quickly,' said the interrogator before picking-up a two-inch long needle from a table and positioning it under the fingernail of the middle finger of Obolensky's left hand. 'Last chance, my friend,' said the interrogator just before ramming the needle under the nail, all the way down to the cuticle.

Obolensky immediately forgot about the pain in his backside. For him, a living hell had just begun.

༄ ༄ ༄ ༄

Windsor was seated in a grey Range Rover, parked in a sports ground about a quarter of a mile from the business park, where the transponder said his daughter's kidnappers had taken her to. He was watching the live feed from the cameras of a state-of-the art drone he was operating from controls built into the steering wheel. He was planning on breaking into the warehouse complex and rescuing Sanda, something he thought he could do more effectively on his own. He was an expert in counter-surveillance measures and had taken every precaution to ensure that none of Michael's people had followed him, including changing the number plates on his car.

Apart from reassuring himself that he hadn't been followed, the drone footage allowed him to view all the CCTV cameras surrounding the warehouse complex listed as the premises of Gusinsky Import/Export. Getting close to the building undetected was going to be difficult, but he had worked out a route taking him through a wooded area. He'd also found a blind spot in the camera coverage that would allow him access to the roof of the building. He had been trying to work out how he was going to get through the very solid looking steel door that accessed the flat roof when it was opened by a man smoking a cigarette.

You should have read the warnings on the packet, Skip. Smoking kills, said the voice in Windsor's head.

THIRTY-TWO

Gaining access to the roof had been easier than Windsor had expected. He'd climbed up a drainpipe hidden from view of the numerous CCTV cameras. Now he was seated, considering his options, awaiting the return of the rooftop smoker. The use of lethal force was his simplest option, but he was giving serious thought to sparing as many of the kidnappers' lives as possible. He was certain that the woman disguised as the senior citizen had chosen not to kill him, and circumstances allowing, he hoped to return the favour. But he couldn't understand why she had spared his life when she had been happy to take the others. If on the other hand he discovered that Sanda had been murdered or tortured, he planned on killing everyone in the building without mercy.

When the rooftop door finally opened, Windsor was pleased to see the lone smoker step out into the night on his own. He pressed the prongs of a taser into the back of the man's neck, placed tape over his mouth, and bound his hands and legs together with plasticuffs. The smoker regained consciousness to see Windsor standing over him holding a large combat knife.

'In a moment I'm going to remove the tape from your mouth, when I do you are going to tell me where I can find the young woman you kidnapped. If you attempt to call out or if I don't believe what you tell me, I will cut your throat. Are we clear?'

The man nodded his head.

Windsor placed the knife against the right-hand side of the man's neck with his right hand, removing the tape with his left hand. 'Okay, where is she?' he asked.

'Room on ground floor. Room number five. I speak truth,' said the man in a heavy Russian accent.

Russians, I should have known, said the voice in Windsor's head. 'How many levels are there between here and the ground floor?'

'Two.'

'How many people in your team?'

'Six people, two sleeping.'

'Where are they?'

'Two sleep in rooms on first level. Others, ground floor.'

'Is the woman alone?'

'Yes, she alone. We no harm her.'

'You speak truth, you live. Understand?'

The man nodded.

Windsor placed a fresh piece of tape over the man's mouth before entering the building. A few minutes later he was standing in the ground floor corridor outside of room number five. He tried the door. It was unlocked, so he opened it and stepped inside.

ຎຎຎຎ

A few things struck Biratu as odd about Dr Abrahams and her computer simulation program. Firstly, he couldn't understand how quickly she'd modified the program to incorporate his experiment, it was almost as if the simulator had been designed with his experiment in mind; secondly, the American seemed to have absolutely no interest in adding her name to his scientific endeavour. He could only conclude that Namdar must have paid CERN and Abrahams a huge sum of money for their goodwill. Only five days had passed, and they were ready to feed the data recorded at the black mass into the simulator program.

'This is the moment of truth, Solomon. We will know whether we can run your experiment in the Collider within the next few minutes. I'd have liked to have been able to create a visual representation of the gateway, but as I explained earlier, coding the graphics could have taken

THE KEY TO THE PIT

weeks and would have added nothing to the outcome. The optimum score is six hundred, but anything between five and seven hundred and we will be cooking with gas.'

'It's as simple as that?'

'From my perspective, yes, but Professor Malashenko will have to jump through a few hoops to get the experiment approved by the Board. However, we are getting ahead of ourselves, as everything depends on passing the simulator test first. I have to run three slightly different programs to be sure of eliminating any false positives.'

The two scientists then sat in silence looking at Dr Abrahams' monitor. Finally, the screen burst into life, white typeface on a green background.

'Green screen, we are in business!' exclaimed the doctor. 'Now we just need to know the fault tolerance. Remember, anything between five and seven hundred and we are in business. As the saying goes - as above, so below.'

Biratu recognised the quote as belonging to Hermes Trismegistus and thought it a strange thing for a particle physicist to say, but he quickly forgot about it when he saw the final reading, his experiment had scored six hundred and sixty-six points.

൮ ൮ ൮ ൮

Osmond was lying on a bed when the door opened. She assumed that one of the Russians had come to check on her and nearly didn't recognise Windsor standing in the doorway with the index finger of his left hand raised to his lips. She was just climbing off the bed when a wall-mounted monitor burst into life.

'I have been expecting you, Mr. Windsor,' said a voice that Osmond knew to be Zhukhov's. 'Please remain calm as you and your daughter will not be harmed.'

Windsor looked left and right along the corridor; it was empty.

'Both the room and the corridor are wired with explosives, if I intended to kill you, you would already be dead. Please check under the bed if you don't believe me.'

Windsor lay on the floor and bit into his lower lip when he saw the plastic explosive.

'You have no other choice other than to trust me, Mr. Windsor. You and Sanda will not be harmed, I only wish to speak with you. I promise that your liberty will be returned to you after our conversation. What do say, Mr. Windsor? Are you willing to talk to me?'

Windsor said nothing as looked up at the monitor, weighing up his options.

'We were aware of the tracking device long before we brought Sanda here. I am taking a great risk in meeting you this way. The sooner we speak the better it will be for all of us. Please say something, Harry.'

Windsor turned to Osmond. 'Has anyone harmed you, Sanda?'

'Nobody's laid a finger on me. I'm absolutely fine.'

Windsor turned to face the monitor. 'Who are you and what do you want from me?'

'My name is Georgy Zhukhov, formerly Lieutenant General, Zhukhov of the Russian army, and I would like to meet my half-brother.'

'What?'

'You and I are long lost brothers, Harry. Soldiers who have served our nation states with distinction, but now we have one final mission, that we must complete together.'

THIRTY-THREE

Namdar was pleased that her instructions had been obeyed and that the Russian was still alive when she arrived at the warehouse.

Obolensky had told his South African interrogator a great many things, but what Namdar wanted to judge with her own eyes was how much of it was true. The Russian managed to raise a wry smile when he saw her, recognizing her instantly, realising that someone with authority had come to question him and that the hours of pain and suffering might soon end.

'Dimitri, how has it come to this? If you had only given honest answers to the questions, put to you,' said Namdar shaking her head from side to side.

Obolensky hung silently from the meat hook, but his silence spoke volumes.

'Please understand that you are in the hands of people expert in human physiology. They have the capability to keep you alive for many days. You only serve to prolong your agony by trying to deceive us. What do you say, will you play ball?'

Obolensky remained silent but was biting hard into the gum shield that had been inserted into his mouth, steeling himself for the terrors to come. But Namdar was prepared for such an eventuality. Following a wave of her left hand, the South African interrogator held a tablet computer in front of the tortured man's eyes.

'Zhukhov chose well. You were no doubt selected because you are an unattached orphan, a man who, at face value, is beholden to no one. However, Dimitri, you might be interested in the contents of the live video feed being displayed on the computer screen. That is the St Petersburg home of Mitrofan Bondarev, is it not? The kindly man who did so much to help when you were growing up in the orphanage. Now either you answer all my questions honestly or you see the refrigerated lorry, the one with the logo of a local meat processing company? Inside are seating arrangements similar to your own. I am afraid that Mr. Bondarev, and his wife, may soon have their favourite armchairs replaced by something far less comfortable. So, I ask you one last time, Dimitri, will you answer my questions truthfully?'

The expression on Obolensky's face answered Namdar's question, but she waited patiently for him to verbalise his response.

'There... there is no need... for you to harm Mr. Bondarev or... or his family,' said the Russian, struggling to form his words.

Namdar nodded and the South African removed the gum shield from Obolensky's bloodstained mouth.

'Death is coming for me, there is no need for them to suffer. I promise to tell you the truth.'

'I wish that I could have you freed from the hook, but to do so with the crude tools at our disposal would be a most painful experience. The best that I can do for you is to have you lowered to the floor.' Namdar waved her left hand again and the South African started working a pulley, slowly lowering Obolensky until his feet were in contact with blood-soaked concrete.

Obolensky's legs were cold and numb, but he was able to stand on them, greatly reducing his suffering.

'Please start by telling me exactly what was on the pen drive that you persuaded the old lady to load onto her work computer?'

Obolensky smiled a sad smile, as he imagined the fate that must have befallen the Metropolitan Police administrator. 'The drive contained DNA profiles of eight men thought to be British soldiers. I was told was that what Zhukhov was interested in was discovering the identity of the man who murdered his son in Afghanistan.

Staff at the embassy viewed it as a vanity project, but the old general has many friends. Nobody thought that anything would ever come of it,' said Obolensky before going into a spasm. 'Please, may I have something to ease the pain?'

'You will receive nothing until you have answered all of my questions. I am afraid that we cannot give you anything that might inadvertently cloud your precious memories, but you may have a little water,' said Namdar before nodding in the direction of the South African who then carefully poured a few mouthfuls of water into Obolensky's mouth.

'Thank you,' said Obolensky. 'Who would have believed that there would ever be a match? The last time I met the woman at the forensic science laboratory she told me that she was thinking of retiring, so I didn't even know whether she was still employed at the facility.'

'And when did you first approach the lady?'

'First contact was made way back, probably in the summer of the year 2006.'

Namdar noted the movement of Obolensky's eyes, which moved up and to the right as he spoke. 'But you have missed out an important part of the story. Who obtained the soldiers' records from their Ministry of Defence?'

'What do you mean? What records?' said Obolensky looking confused.

'Come on Dimitri, do you take me for a fool? Have you forgotten what is at staked for Bondarev and his family?'

'No, I have not forgotten. You must believe me, I don't know what arrangements exist between the GRU, FSB and staff at the British MOD. I am just a mid-ranking official; I work in industrial espionage. I know nothing of any value about military matters here or in the Motherland. Please, you must believe, I am telling you the truth,' said a pleading Obolensky.

'I believe you Dimitri,' said Namdar looking at the movement of Obolensky's eyes. 'And you must believe me when I promise you that no harm will come to Bondarev if you continue to tell me the truth. Now, if I might summarise? You gave Mrs. Barrett the pen drive in 2006 and last met with her a few weeks ago, presumably following Zhukhov being informed of a match against the DNA database?'

'Yes, that is correct. I paid the woman for the names of the people flagged-up by the system. I have never met or ever had any direct contact with Zhukhov.'

'Who at the embassy is his contact?'

'And if I give you that person's name, won't he or she suffer the same fate as me?'

'That person will die, but the Bondarevs will live.'

'Very well, before I give you his name, I want you to understand something. You are an extremely rich and powerful woman. You kill me and nobody will much care. However, you kill a senior official at our embassy and the repercussions will be most severe. My country is willing go to war over such indiscretions.'

'Thank you for the warning, Dimitri, I shall bear it in mind. Now, can you please give me the name of Zhukhov's contact?'

'His name is Captain Alexander Kornienko, he is –'

'The Defence and Naval Attaché. Yes, he would be the logical choice. Then it only serves for me to thank you for your cooperation, Dimitri.'

Namdar gave the tired looking South African the signal he had been waiting for and he fired two small calibre rounds into the back of Obolensky's head. The 21-millimetre bullets destroying much of Obolensky's brain as they bounced around the inside of his skull. One round would have sufficed, but the South African was nothing if not meticulous in the performance of his work. The job over, he could return to his wife and get himself some much-needed sleep. The disposal of Obolensky's body was the concern of others.

🕮 🕮 🕮 🕮

Biratu was bouncing between elation and depression. Elation because Dr Abrahams's had confirmed the feasibility of creating a stable gateway between the parallel worlds within the confines of the CERN collider, and depression because no progress had been made in finding Tatjana's murderer. With the simulator program out of the way, he couldn't think about anything other than the masked man in the recording. He didn't like to pressure his adopted mother, but he decided to give her a call.

'Hello, Solomon, how can I help you?' asked the ever-present Fyodor Andreevich Maknov.

'Is it possible to speak to my mother, Fyodor?'

'Unfortunately, not. Ms. Namdar is in meetings all day today, but I will inform her that you called. Is there anything that I might help you with?'

'Actually Fyodor, I was ringing to ask Lilith if there had been any developments regarding the recording, I gave her.'

'You have called at an opportune moment, Solomon. I have just this very moment received an update from a Ukrainian official working for Interpol. I wasn't intending on contacting you with the news without first discussing the matter with your mother, but I suppose it couldn't hurt to give you the details.'

'Please tell me what you know, Fyodor.'

'Very well, Solomon. The authorities in Kiev have several suspects in custody, but their legal representatives have challenged the provenance of the recording. I wouldn't normally be so bold, but would you consider flying to the Ukraine to provide the authorities there with a formal statement? I have received assurances from people at the highest level that your anonymity will be guaranteed until the matter is sent for trial.'

'Do you think a statement from me is really necessary, Fyodor? I mean, the recording couldn't possibly be used to positively identify the man who murdered Tatjana.'

'All I know is that a request wouldn't have been made to Ms. Namdar unless they thought it absolutely necessary in facilitating matters. That said, we don't need to arrange anything just yet, I'll discuss the matter with your mother and –'

'I'm sorry to interrupt you, Fyodor, but there is no need to wait. I'm happy to provide them with a statement if they think that it will help convict Tatjana's murderer.'

'Excellent, sir. Leave the arrangements to me. I'll email your itinerary in due course.'

Biratu suddenly remembered the debt owed to William Meek for providing him with the decryption program and sent him a text which read:

> Hi William,
>
> Just to let you know that your program worked great, man. I'm living it up, at the London Ritz.
>
> Solomon

Biratu had been wary of involving his adopted mother in Tatjana's murder, but now he felt glad that he had done so. He just hoped that the officers of Interpol hadn't found any connection between Tatjana's death and Lilith Namdar's favourite NGO.

THIRTY-FOUR

Meek sensed that the finger of suspicion had moved from himself to his boss, Snowden. Only a fool would have failed to notice that Snowden was just a salaried employee of the FFF, whereas Meek was a fully paid-up member of the CSS. Snowden was a married man who, to Meek's knowledge, only attended the satanic rituals he was obliged to and none of the mansion house orgies. Meek, on the other hand, attended the orgies with abandon and was known to complain when not invited to some of the more exclusive mansion house events.

Meek was sitting in Manning's office when the FFF enforcer took an urgent call.

'This is Solomon Biratu we are talking about? You're absolutely certain of this?' asked Manning into the speaker with a look of incomprehension on his face. 'I'm sorry, Fyodor, but I must insist that you send me something in writing. No, I'm sorry, sir, I won't involve my folks in this unless I get something in writing from you. I understand what you are saying, but either I hear the words directly from the mouth of our Mistress or you put it down in black and white for me.'

Meek had never seen Manning display emotions other than anger, pleasure, and boredom, but now he saw a new emotion on the man's face - fear.

'Is there anything wrong, Edward?' asked Meek, pretending to look concerned.

'You still here, Meek?' said Manning, suddenly remembering Meek was in the room with him. 'Get yourself out of here, I'm busy.'

Meek got up and left with the name Solomon Biratu ringing in his ears.

Is this a trap? They must know that I've met him. But what if they don't? Manning could have had a confession beaten out of me if he wanted. No, they don't know that I know him, said the voice in Meek's head. *Solomon's got to be in serious trouble, but how the hell can I help him?*

'What did he want from you?' asked a nervous looking Snowden when Meek returned to his desk.

'Nothing, I was in there for less than a minute when he took a call. He kicked me out straight after that.'

'Oh, okay,' said Snowden. 'He called you in for nothing?'

'You know him, boss, it's probably all part of his mind games,' said Meek as he waited for the highly secure email to arrive in Manning's inbox.

'Anything wrong, William?' asked Snowden.

'What? No, I'm just double checking that the secure servers are operating correctly. I don't want to give Manning another stick to beat us with.'

'Good thinking, William. I'm off to a meeting. Oh, make sure that I'm the first to know if you discover any anomalies on any of the servers.'

'Will do, boss,' said Meek who was sat staring at the screen of his computer. He'd heard the rumours telling of how Manning's people were travelling the world, murdering anybody suspected of downloading the files that he, in the guise of Matthew5:5, had stolen from the FFF computers and uploaded into the Darkweb. And now he sensed that his new friend, Solomon Biratu, was about to become another casualty in his private war against Lilith Namdar. He took a deep breath and logged into the account of his boss, Julian Snowden, located Fyodor Maknov's email and copied it to a temporary folder. He took another deep breath before opening and reading the contents, which read:

THE KEY TO THE PIT

Dear Edward,

Further to our conversation I am writing to confirm, against protocol, that Solomon Biratu is to be moved to a secure location, pending further instruction by an appropriate authority.

SB is currently resident, Ritz Htl, London.

Yours,
Fyodor Maknov

Meek copied the email to a pen drive and logged out of his manager's account. He then took a laptop computer from a cupboard, walked into the computer room, and plugged the machine into a secret network port. He signed into the Darkweb under his pseudonym, Matthew5:5, and posted the following message into multiple forums:

An urgent message for a man of GREAT WISDOM,
You are in more danger than you can ever know :
Rats UnderNeath, from, Railings In The london Zoo.
Hope to meet you on TOR one day, where is heart.

A few minutes later Meek had returned the laptop to the cupboard and sat pondering the consequences of his actions.

THIRTY-FIVE

Zhukhov hated reading from computer screens and asked for the message to be printed out onto a sheet of paper. He was looking at what purported to be an urgent message from the blogger Matthew5:5, written in the form of a quatrain.

'What do you think, General?' asked Dokukin.

'I know no more than you do, Natasha. Our Trojan horse is trying to send somebody a warning. I think the important questions that need answering are: who is the intended recipient? And what is he, she, being warned about?'

'My immediate thought was that the message was meant for you, sir.'

'I'm flattered, Natasha, but no, I don't think our messenger is trying to warn us. Please ask Sanda and Harry to come here, I would like to hear their thoughts on the matter.'

'But, General, what can they know?'

'I think that it will be interesting to find out, don't you?'

A few minutes later Osmond and Windsor were sitting at Zhukhov's desk, each with a pen and pad laid out in front of them.

'For reasons that have yet to be determined, someone embedded deep within the Faithless Freedom Foundation has aligned themselves with our cause. This person, we think likely to be a man, has been posting defamatory information about the FFF on the internet for the last few years. A few weeks ago he uploaded dozens of encrypted files onto the Darkweb, stating that he'd hacked them from the FFF's headquarters' computer servers requesting that his/our followers should try and decrypt them. Bearing in mind that a number of people thought to have downloaded the files are now dead, I would be grateful if the two of you could give me your thoughts on meaning of a message, he posted less than an hour ago,' said Zhukhov, turning to face the wall mounted plasma screen. Please try not to overthink things, I'm interested in knowing what, if anything, pops into your minds.'

'Is there any significance in the message being written in the form of a quatrain?' asked Osmond.

'Who knows? It is possible that the format was chosen just to help catch the intended recipient's attention,' replied Zhukhov.

Osmond and Windsor sat in silence for a minute, after which time Windsor's pad remained empty, whereas Osmond's contained the words:

> An urgent message for (King) Solomon.
> You are in more danger than you can ever know.
> Run from the Ritz (London).
> Hope to meet you on a tor/hill, close to home.

'Your pad is empty, Harry,' said Zhukhov.

'And why wouldn't it be, we don't know the code used to encrypt the message.'

'Yet Sanda and I reached the same conclusion, said Zhukhov, turning his pad over for all to see. 'Tell us, Sanda, why did you write what you did?'

'I know the theory behind coding and decoding messages but have never used any manual techniques. So, I tried to interpret the quatrain using nothing more than common sense,' she replied.

'Go on, Sanda, tell us more,' said Zhukhov.

'The message seems to have been written by somebody in a hurry, with a specific individual in mind. Somebody the sender might know socially. The sender also knows that the recipient is interested in the prophecies of Nostradamus, which is why a quatrain has been used. I think capital letters have been used as a crude attempt to direct the recipient to the most important parts of the message.'

'So why not simply telephone or text the recipient?' asked Windsor.

Osmond looked to Zhukhov, but he stared back at her, indicating that she should answer Windsor's question. 'Because the sender knows that the recipient's phones and computers are being bugged' replied Osmond.

'If all this is true. What, if anything, should we do about it? asked Zhukhov.

'If you think that the recipient is valuable to your cause, you could send somebody over to the Ritz hotel to check on them, said Windsor. 'I could go with them if you like.'

'We have our Troika, Harry. I think it would be prudent for us to stick together until our moment in destiny reveals itself to us,' said Zhukhov.

'Then we should all go,' said Osmond.

'I don't think that would be wise, Sanda. Our foe has huge resources at her disposal. If we were discovered in central London, escaping the city would be impossible.'

'But are we any safer staying here?' said Windsor. 'I found you easy enough. It will only be a matter of time before they do. And isn't London the only place in the country providing you with a guaranteed place of refuge?' asked Windsor.

Zhukhov broke into a smile. 'And what makes you think that we will be made welcome at the Russian Embassy, Harry?'

'You got into the country under the radar of our border security. You have vehicles, high quality weapons, sophisticated communications equipment and at least one safe house. That tells me all I need to know.'

'You surmise correctly, Harry. We have friends at the Embassy, but it is not a given that we will be safe there.

The CSS has disciples embedded within all the world's security services.'

'You said that we have until August 21st to save the world from catastrophe. I can't see how we are going to achieve that hiding here.'

Zhukhov sat in silence, his head bowed, and his fingertips pressed together. Finally, he lifted his head and looked up at Windsor. 'Do we have your word of honour that you willing to help us, Harry?'

'I've already told you. I might not understand what's going on, but it's clear to me that whatever it is, it involves Sanda. I'll help you for as long as that helps her. I can't say more than that,' replied Windsor.

'I need to let you know something, Harry.'

'And what's that?'

Lilith Namdar has an adopted son; his name is Solomon Biratu. He is a mixed-raced man originating from Ethiopia but has spent most of his adult life living in the United States of America.'

'You think that this message was meant for him?'

'I don't know, Harry, but we will find out soon enough. It's time for us to go mobile.'

॥॥॥॥

Meek watched as two of Manning's people arrived at Snowden's desk. They weren't the usual cerebral looking types one encountered in vetting interviews. No, Meek thought these men looked like battle-hardened soldiers.

'Mr. Manning wants to speak with you,' said one of the men to Snowden.

'Can you let him know that I'm just in the middle of something? I'll be with him in about five minutes.'

'He's not in his office. We have instructions to escort you to him.'

'But, I've just got –'

'Whatever it is that you are doing can wait.'

'Have you any idea how long this is going to take? Edward knows that I was planning on leaving early today, it's my daughter's birthday.'

'I wouldn't worry about that, Mr. Manning's not very far away.'

Meek grimaced as he watched the heavies escort Snowden out of the building. *After they've finished with him, they'll come back here for me,* said the voice in his head.

Meek shut down his computers, collected his belongings, and went for a piss, before walking to the car park and starting on a long drive, north.

THIRTY-SIX

Biratu had been watching the recording of Tatjana's murder for what seemed like hours when he received the following text from an unknown number:

> They say the meek will inherit the earth.
> Let's hope that it doesn't come to that.

'What's this crap?' Biratu asked himself whilst typing "the meek shall inherit the earth" into his browser. He shook his head, laughing when he saw the results, which read:

Matthew 5:5 is the fifth verse of the fifth chapter of the Gospel of Matthew in the New Testament. It is the third verse of the Sermon on the Mount, and also third of what are known as the Beatitudes.

'It can't be, man,' said Biratu as he accessed the Darkweb through the TOR browser and found a new message from the blogger Matthew5:5 waiting to read:

> An urgent message for a man of GREAT WISDOM,

King Solomon was a man of great wisdom. This message has got to be meant for me, said the voice in his head.

Biratu found himself a pad and a pen and wrote out what he recognised as being a quatrain. The second, third and fourth lines read:

You are in more danger than you can ever know :
Rats UnderNeath, from, Railings In The london Zoo.

Hope to meet you on a tor/hill, close to home.

Biratu thought that the second line was self-explanatory. "You are in danger". The third line seemed more challenging. "Rats UnderNeath, from, Railings In The london Zoo."

Capitals in the first line caught your eye and could mean the message is for a man named Solomon, so what is the point of the capitals in the third line?

Biratu wrote out the capitals individually:

R U N R I T Z

What the hell does that mean, man? He asked himself. Then he noticed the crest of the writing pad he was using, and the words written underneath it:

The Ritz London

No way, man. That can't be right, said the voice in his head as he split the capitalised letters into two separate words and filled the gap with the words "from the", changing the words to:

RUN from the RITZ

Shit. Does William want me to run from the Ritz?

Biratu rewrote the quatrain on his pad, which now read:

> An urgent message for Solomon,
> You are in more danger than you can ever know :
> Run from the Ritz in London.

Hope to meet you on TOR one day, home is where the heart is.

'What to do?' Biratu asked himself. Then he reread the anonymous text message:

They say the meek will inherit the earth. Let's hope that it doesn't come to that.

He looked again at the last line of the quatrain "Hope to meet you on TOR one day, home is where the heart is". 'Does he want to communicate with me through the Darknet?'

What does he want? To communicate with me on The Onion Router or meet him on a TOR, like Glastonbury Tor, or does he want to meet me somewhere else?

Biratu was having trouble believing that William Meek was the conspiratorial blogger, Matthew5:5. But somehow it all made perfect sense. After all, what were the chances of meeting an expert in computer encryption at the mansion house just after he'd attended a Satanic Rite conducted by a Witch belonging to the Church of the Six Salems? Everything seemed to point to Meek, and the blogger, being the same man.

Tatjana was murdered because of the blogger's last post. Are you trying to redeem yourself by saving me?

Whilst Biratu was still trying to make sense of it all, Fyodor Maknov's email with his travel itinerary arrived in his inbox. It said that a car would collect Biratu at eight the next morning, taking him to the airport in plenty of time for a lunchtime flight to Kiev.

Biratu telephoned the airline pretending to have a query about the booking. He was greatly saddened at being told by the customer services agent that the flight and his booking reference number didn't exist.

'Home is where the heart is, man,' said Biratu to himself as he started to pack-up his belongings.

THIRTY-SEVEN

Namdar's Rolls Royce Ghost arrived at the main entrance of the Ritz less than ten minutes after Biratu walked out carrying a large suitcase and a backpack.

'I don't think that this is a good idea, mistress,' said Maknov just before the chauffeur opened the rear passenger door for her.

'I want to see Solomon for one last time. It is most unfortunate that things have had to end this way. I've always felt obliged to look after him after having his family burnt to death.'

'But mistress, we don't even know if he's here. His mobile is switched-off and there's no answer from the phone in his room.'

'Go and see if he is in his room, I will wait in the lobby for you.

Five minutes later Namdar watched a nervous looking Maknov questioning a hotel doorman. He finally approached her with his head bowed, not wanting to look her in the eye.

'Where is Solomon?' asked Namdar without giving Maknov a chance to speak.

'He's gone, mistress. The doorman saw him leave with his suitcase about twenty minutes ago.'

'Has Solomon checked-out of the hotel?'

'No, madam, but his room is empty. We must assume that he isn't planning on returning. The doorman said that Solomon was heading in the direction of the underground station.'

'Something must have happened for Solomon to lose trust in me' said Namdar. 'What exactly did you say to him on the telephone?'

'Nothing, mistress. A-all I t-told him is w-what you t-told me to say. Nothing more,' said a stammering Maknov.

Namdar sat in silence staring hard at Maknov.

'All I told him was that Interpol in the Ukraine wanted a statement from him confirming how he came to be possession of the recording. I can only go on how he sounded, but there was nothing in the tone of his voice to indicate that he didn't believe me.'

'Very well, Fyodor, I believe you. Then somebody else has alerted him to the danger he was in,' said Namdar rising from her chair. 'I want to speak with Manning as soon as we are back in the car.'

Namdar and Maknov sat in silence during the five minutes that passed before Manning finally answered the phone.

'What kept you, Edward?' asked Namdar.

'I apologise for keeping you waiting, mistress. I was just in the middle of a particularly challenging security vetting interview,' said Manning, his forearms smeared with Snowden's blood. 'Is Fyodor not with you?'

'Yes, Fyodor is here, but I would like to ask you a few questions before I pass him onto you.'

'I see,' said Manning, trying but failing to swallow some saliva. 'What is it that I can help you with?'

'I was led to believe that Solomon's welfare was now in your hands, yet none of your people are in evidence at the hotel.'

'You are at the hotel?'

'Yes, I am here, but Solomon isn't. Both he and his belongings are missing.'

'I didn't think it necessary to send anyone there, mistress. Fyodor led me to believe that my people were to pick him up tomorrow morning.'

'So, what, if anything, did you have in place today?'

'Only the measures we always take.'

'Meaning?'

'I've been monitoring his communications equipment from over in the States. Is there a problem?'

'Yes, there is a problem. Solomon has left the hotel in a hurry, and nobody knows why or where he has gone to. I want you to send your recordings to Fyodor immediately.'

'Yes, mistress. I'll see to it right away.'

ಬಬಬಬ

Dokukin had reached the Ritz with minutes to spare and spotted Biratu just before he left the hotel and walked to Green Park station, where he caught an underground train to King's Cross Railway station. She was within earshot of him as he ordered a single ticket to a town she had never heard of, called Skipton, and now found herself in the same rail carriage as she pretended to read a newspaper.

'General, the captain has sent a message stating that that Solomon Biratu is on a train heading north to a small town named Skipton. He must change trains along the way, in the city of Leeds.'

Zhukhov was sitting in the back of an SUV with Osmond and Windsor. All of them called up maps of showing Skipton on their tablet computers.

'Do any of you think that you know where he is going?' asked Zhukhov.

'Looks like he's planning on losing himself in one of the national parks. That would be a good way of becoming anonymous,' said Windsor.

'And what do you think, Sanda?'

'I think that the person who sent him the warning had a particular meeting place in mind,' said Osmond as she typed "Skipton + Local Attractions" into her browser. The results left her none the wiser, but her expression changed after keying in the words "Skipton + Witchcraft".

'What is it, Sanda?' asked Zhukhov.'

'I think I know where he's going,' she said with a broad grin on her face.

THE KEY TO THE PIT

༄༄༄༄

Maknov was seated ashen faced in the back of the Rolls Royce. Only he, Namdar and Manning knew of her decision to have her adopted son killed, and yet somehow the CSS's nemesis, the blogger Matthew5:5, had learnt of their plan and warned Solomon to go on the run. Maknov knew that only he or Manning could have leaked the information. And even he could not bring himself to believe that Manning would do such a thing.

'Tell me what's troubling you, Fyodor,' asked Namdar in gentle tones.

'There is no explaining how the blogger could have known our plans.'

'Isn't it obvious? Manning must be a traitor, must he not?'

'No, mistress, I can't believe that.'

'Then that only leaves you, Fyodor.'

'I know, mistress. But I promise you that it was not me. You must know that I would never betray you.'

'Unfortunately, there is only one way that anybody can be sure of such things, Fyodor. You know what that is as well as I.'

Maknov felt his heart pounding in his chest. He looked momentarily toward the passenger door, it was unlocked. His inner voice was screaming at him to run, but he remained sat in his seat, awaiting his mistress's judgement.

'Don't be afraid, Fyodor, it hasn't come to that. I trust you implicitly. There must be a rational explanation for what has happened. I sense that the answer is well within our grasp.'

'What do you mean, mistress?'

'The warning was written in haste. Somebody has either eavesdropped on your telephone conversation with Edward or intercepted your email to him. Get me a list of the full names of all Information and Communications staff working at the Cheltenham office.'

'But mistress, what will a list of names tell you?'

'Just do as I ask, Fyodor.'

Five minutes later Namdar had her answer.

'I don't know how I could have been so stupid,' she said.

'You, stupid? Impossible, mistress.'

'Our troublesome blogger, he goes by the name Matthew5:5, does he not?'

'Yes, mistress, but –'

'How well do you know your Bible, Fyodor?'

'I make it my business to know it very well. Why do you ask?'

'And what does Matthew tell us in chapter five, verse five?'

'That the meek shall inherit the –'

Maknov looked again at the list of employees' names, his eyes stopping at the name of an employee responsible for the implementation of cyber-security.

THIRTY-EIGHT

The tearoom was closed when Biratu arrived in the village of Barley. He'd been tempted to check into a bed and breakfast so that he could ditch his suitcase but had thought better of it. It was a pain having to lug his belongings, but he decided to keep them with him as started walking along Barley Lane in the direction of Pendle Hill. He was well on his way to the summit when his attention was caught by a light coming from a barn. He stopped to look at the building and saw what looked like someone signaling to him from inside the building with a flashlight.

Biratu hoped that William Meek was in the barn waiting for him, as he left his rucksack and suitcase by the side of the path and started to walk at pace towards it. He was about forty metres from it when William Meek came running out of the front door brandishing a large knife, followed a few seconds later by two men and a woman.

'Run, Solomon! Run, Solomon!' Meek was shouting at the top of his voice.

Biratu froze to the spot and watched as one of the men grabbed Meek by the shoulder, only for the dumpy little man to spin around and plunge the knife into his assailant's stomach. Biratu watched in horror as the man fell to the ground, only for the second of the two men and the woman to grab hold of Meek's arms. Meek possessed far greater strength and agility than his build had suggested and easily knocked the second man to the ground and was only taken down when the woman grabbed hold of his windpipe.

Biratu was thinking about running over to assist his new friend when two more men appeared from around the back of the building. He watched as the man Meek had stabbed got to his feet and didn't seem to have a spot of blood on him. The woman continued to hold Meek down as all four men started walking towards him.

'Don't worry, Solomon. You and your friend are safe with us,' said the lead man who Biratu thought looked to be in his seventies. 'You have nothing to be afraid of.'

Biratu assumed that he was about to be beaten to death but watched as the woman allowed Meek to get to his feet.

'Are you alright, William?' Biratu called out.

'I'm fine, Solomon. They didn't hurt me.'

'And our man's fine too, just in case you were wondering young man,' said the lead man. I insist on the wearing of body armour. It can be a bit of an inconvenience, but one never knows when one might need it. Eh Roman?'

'The stab proof vest did its job, General,' said Roman Utkin, the youngest of Zhukhov's disciples.

'Excellent, then it would be wise for us to return to the relative safety of our vehicles. I will not force you to join us, gentlemen, but I am of the opinion that it would be in your best interests to do so,' said Zhukhov.

'Do we have any choice?' asked Meek.

'We have a common enemy. It is my opinion that without our assistance that it will only be a matter of time before they find you. We didn't come here to coerce you into doing anything against your will. The choice is yours to make, gentlemen.'

Ten minutes later Biratu and Meek were in a three car convey heading west towards the M6 motorway, sitting in the back of a Mercedes V-Class MPV in the company of Zhukhov, Osmond and Windsor.

'I think introductions are in order. It is a pleasure to meet you, Solomon. I am Georgy Zhukhov and it is my privilege to lead a little-known religious order called the GreyFriars. This is Sanda and Harry, and in the front of the vehicle are Natasha and Pyotr.'

'If you people are the GreyFriars you must know what happened to Tatjana.' said Biratu, not knowing what else to say.

'We find ourselves in a very complicated situation, Solomon. I know that your friend here, for reasons unknown, has been helping our cause in the guise of the blogger Matthew5:5. As for you, I know everything and nothing about you. It was Sanda who guessed that you would both meet on Pendle Hill.'

'Meek sat in silence, still unsure as to whether he and Solomon had fallen into the hands of Manning's people.

'Why have you got it in for my adopted mother? She hasn't –'

'All in good time, Solomon,' interrupted Zhukhov. 'First I would like to know the true identity of your friend, if he will tell us his name.'

'Can you prove who you say you are?' asked Meek.

'No. But Lilith Namdar's people aren't known for their subtlety. I can't imagine that they would waste their time playing this little game with you.'

'Okay, I can live with that' said Meek, still not knowing what to believe. He was surprised he was still alive and was hoping to keep things that way. 'My name is William Meek and I grew up in the little village next to Pendle Hill.'

'And how is it that you discovered the link between the Church of the Six Salems and the Faithless Freedom Foundation?'

'I work for the FFF in IT security. I'm an expert in encryption technologies.'

'And the FFF has allowed a man with no interest in the occult to guard its most secret treasures?'

'No, they aren't that naïve. I'm also a card-carrying member of the CSS.'

'And what is your connection to Solomon?'

'Not much I'm afraid. I only met him a few weeks ago at a CSS party in -'

'No, that's not quite right, William. We met after your party. I was at the house on other business,' interrupted Biratu.

'And what business might that have been, Solomon?'

'I'm a particle physicist. I had been invited to the house to observe a satanic rite held in the basement.'

'And the lady, Tatjana, that you mentioned. Who is she?'

Biratu's head dropped and his eyes moistened. 'She was my girlfriend. She's been murdered.'

Zhukov had originally intended to return to the relative safety of the offices of Gusinsky Import/Export but now decided, on nothing more than his gut feeling, to head north towards the Lake District national park. Zhukhov, Osmond, Windsor, Biratu and Meek spent the best part of the two-hour drive telling each other their life stories.

THIRTY-NINE

Windsor hadn't slept well. He was in a virtual no man's land; he'd somehow cut himself off from his MI6 handler and aligned himself with an apocalypse obsessed cult leader who claimed to be his half-brother. He'd spent most of the last week doing something that he rarely did, he'd been acting on instinct. His life in the armed services had revolved around planning, and Benjamin Franklin's maxim "If you fail to plan, you are planning to fail!" had served him well over the years. Now he'd finally thought of a plan, he was keen to get on and implement it.

'Georgy, I've been thinking. I need to spend some quality time with my daughter.'

'But, Harry, I've already explained to you. We need to stay together. It is the only way.'

'Maybe so. But it seems to me that whatever plan you were working to has gone out of the window now that Solomon and William have arrived on the scene.'

'Time is short, Harry. I sense it.'

But Natasha has told me that you were once absolutely certain that the apocalypse was coming in September 2015, with the last of those blood moons. Now you're absolutely certain that it's going to start with an eclipse of the sun, and Natasha says that you've also mentioned another date in September.'

'I will reiterate what I have already told you, Harry. None of you are prisoners, I might not like it but you are all free to leave. But if we start going our separate ways who is to say that we will ever be reunited?'

'Apocalypse or no, I want to spend a week with my daughter. If I understand all this correctly, you're of the opinion that the world isn't going to end in a bang, it's going to be another seven years before it's all over. On the assumption that you are right, Sanda is going to need to learn certain skills to help secure her future. I can teach my daughter how to hide and how to survive.'

'And what of the two of us, my brother?'

'There'll be time enough for us to get to know each other along the way.'

'And once you're gone, how do you propose that we communicate with each other?'

'I've seen your shortwave radios and one-time pads. Don't tell me that you haven't got access to a number station?'

'You see a lot, Harry,' said Zhukhov bowing his head and pressing his fingertips together, as if in prayer. 'Very well, take your week. But we won't be returning to London, we have another safe house close to the port Harwich. I'll give you a one-time pad, use it to listen out for messages.'

FORTY

Zhukhov had instructed Volkov to drive Windsor and Osmond to the town of Kendal where they hired their own car for the drive up to the Scottish university town of Stirling. They were now sitting outside a café which provided stunning views of Stirling Castle.

'What are we doing here?' asked Osmond.

'I'm a native of the south, Lewes in East Sussex is my hometown, but I love to come here when I feel the need to get away from things,' said Windsor, as he looked northwest toward the lower Scottish Highlands and the peaks of Ben Vorlich and Ben Ledi.

'Are you telling me that you've brought me here so that I can chill out for a few days?'

'I'm not sure what I've brought you here for. I need a few days to try and get my head around what's going on.'

'I've got something that I need to do, Harry, and you're not going to like it.'

'And what's that, Sanda?'

'I want to telephone my parents; I need to let them know that I'm safe. I can't believe that they haven't tried contacting me after Natasha murdered those people on my estate. They're most probably worried sick about me.'

'But we can't afford to give your location away. If Georgy's right about what's happening, we need to stay off the entire communications network.'

'And say they report me as a missing person, what then?'

'How about you do something old school?'

'What?'

'How about writing them a letter?'

'They will think that that's an odd thing for me to do and it'll take days to get to them.'

'Won't they recognise your handwriting when they see

it?'

'Of course, they will.'

'I can't even imagine how all this must seem to you, but a letter's the only way.'

'But won't the postmark give our location away?'

'I'll post it from somewhere else. How about telling them that you're on an impromptu tour of Britain's' national parks. That sounds like the sort of thing an unemployed eco-blogger might do.'

'Okay, Harry, I'll buy some stationery. But I want my letter posted today.'

'No worries, I'll get that done for you.'

'So, you're a bit of a mountain man, Harry?'

'Actually, no. I love the water and the sea,' Windsor said in between taking sips from a mug of freshly brewed tea. 'I think that's the reason why I joined the Navy.'

Osmond took a sip of cappuccino, it tasted good. In fact, it was far better than she could remember drinking in the London franchises. Then a frown shot across her face. 'I'll ask you again, Harry, apart from Scotland being one of your favourite holiday destinations. What are we doing here?'

'They say, Skip, that Stirling is the gateway to the Highlands. It's rough country from here on in. Places, where our foes, assuming that they actually exist, will lose their technological advantages over us. There are many good reasons for coming here.'

Osmond took sip of coffee as she looked out towards the hills. 'How did you meet my mother?'

'I'm afraid that it's all very simple and complicated at the same –'

'Look, don't beat about the bush. I'm a big girl, so whatever it is, I'll just take it on the chin. So just get on with it.'

'I had shore leave in the summer of 1986 and decided to spend it in the Greek islands. I went hiking, alone, across Santorini in the first week before making my way to Corfu. I met a group of women sunning themselves on a beach, one of them was your mother. Anyway, one thing led to another and we spent the best part of a week together before going our separate ways. I returned to my life in the SBS and as far as I knew she returned to hers as an office worker in London. We hadn't agreed to keep in contact and I've never seen or spoken to her since.'

'And how is it that we've ended-up in this mess?' she asked, keeping her gaze fixed on the hills.

Windsor looked about them, checking that no one else would overhear what he was about to say. 'Well, if Georgy is to be believed, not only are you my daughter, but he's my long-lost brother and I'm responsible for shooting dead his only son,' he said before bursting out laughing.

'But you believe him. Don't you, Harry?'

'All I know is that I was smuggled into to Afghanistan in 1987 with seven blokes from the SAS, we split up into two teams of four. All of us were dead shots but one of the SAS guys and me were the sniper specialists. We took out a number of high-profile Soviet targets, but I was the one that pulled the trigger on a young Russian colonel that Georgy says was his son.'

'So how did he find us?'

Windsor smiled as he remembered taking the shot with the unfamiliar Dragunov sniper's rifle. 'After killing the colonel, we did as we always did and cleaned-out our FFP, I mean the forward firing point. It's standard procedure not to leave anything behind that might identify us as being British Army, but we didn't reckon on the march of technology.'

'What do you mean?'

'These days, we bag up our ablutions.'

'That sounds nice, not.'

'Anyway, it appears that some bright spark had the bright idea of bagging-up anything that might have contained our DNA. I think that Georgy's original plan was to try and use the DNA samples to help him avenge the death of his son. Somewhere along the way he's managed to convince himself that he's part of some special warrior bloodline tasked with saving the world.'

'But you believed, Georgy, when he said that this woman, Lilith Namdar, is immortal and that you, me and him are special?'

'It makes no sense that we can't be killed by regular people, but will still die of old age.'

'But you believe him, don't you?'

'I don't know what to believe anymore,' said Windsor raising his hands in an act of submission. 'But I remember something I thought was a bit weird at the time. His son, we were sent to kill him because the Mujahidin were afraid of him. They'd supposedly tried to assassinate him many times without success and a rumour was spreading throughout Afghanistan that he might be protected by God. Now, Holy Warriors aren't too effective when they get it into their heads that they might be fighting against one of God's chosen ones, so we were sent in to stop that myth gaining traction.'

'And you killed this man with a single shot?'

'That was the weird bit. I can feel the sensation even now. It was like there was a connection between us. I was certain that we'd made direct eye contact with each other even though I was looking at him through a rifle scope from nearly a mile away.'

'And that's why you haven't been in contact with the authorities?'

'I guess so. Like I said, I need some time to think this through,' said Windsor before finishing the rest of the mug of tea. 'I take it that your mother didn't tell you anything about me?'

Osmond smiled as she scanned her biological father's face, noticing the similarities with her own facial features.

'No, mum never said anything about you. Not once, not ever.'

Windsor felt a little disappointed on hearing that, but in a way, he was relieved that the lady he knew as Helen Dean had chosen to do things that way.

'As far as I'm concerned, my dad's a man named Benjamin Osmond and nothing will ever change that.'

'That's fair enough, Skip.'

'Have you ever had a normal job, Harry? You know, something that hasn't involved killing people?'

'Look, it's just how life turned out for me. I was a marine in Her Majesty's Navy, and now... now I'm an assassin. Yes, I kill people for money, but I've been doing it for the good of the country.'

Osmond shook her head in disbelief. 'I'm sorry, but in my book that doesn't make you any better than the bastards who killed Solomon's girlfriend. I'll bet that –'

'Now hold on for a minute,' cut in Windsor. 'Can you let me tell you a bit more about myself before you make your mind up about what I might or might not be?'

Osmond bit into her lower lip and stared at the man that she wished wasn't her biological father. 'Alright, what else if there to know?'

'Okay, I kill people, but they're not just any people. As far as I've been led to believe, I work as a contractor to Her Majesty's government. In many ways what I do now is no different to what I did during my days in the Royal Navy. I assassinate people perceived to be a threat to our country but are beyond reproach, due to the complexities on international law.' Windsor looked his daughter directly in the eye. 'You've got to understand that there are a lot of very bad people in the world and that people like me help keep people like you safe from them. No offence, but Solomon's girlfriend is most probably dead because somebody in the intelligence community hasn't done their job properly.' He could see the disappointment in Sanda's eyes. But if she was disappointed in him, that was the fault of her mother. 'The only good that can come from any of this, is that I should be able to keep you out of harms –'

'What does that mean? What can you do?' snapped Osmond.

'If Georgy is telling the truth and people are trying to kill you, then you can't do much better than have me as your bodyguard. Also, if this lady, Lilith Namdar, really is behind all of this, then all this should end with her. I'm an assassin, one of the best. If I kill her, you can go back to leading a normal life.'

'And what if Georgy's setting you up? What if he's trying to trick you into killing her?'

'I'm impressed, Sanda, that's one of the things that's been bugging me about all of this.'

'No offence Harry, but you and Georgy see the world through the eyes of soldiers,' said Osmond looking back toward the rolling hills. She couldn't believe that this was how the world worked. The man sitting opposite her might be an assassin, but she felt sure that most things in the modern western world weren't settled through the barrel of a gun.

'You're right Sanda, I'm no diplomat. I was a soldier, trained to kill. I've seen many things that could never be justified in a civilised society.' Windsor threw a few pieces of marmalade covered toast in the direction of a hungry looking pigeon that had been hovering around their table. 'Okay, this is my version of history. I'm not saying that it's the right version, but it fits well with the life that I've led.' Windsor paused for a few seconds. 'You're a young woman but must know about the cold war, right?'

'Yes,' said Osmond breaking into a smile. 'But I'm not that young.'

'So, you know that the West were indirectly at war with the old Soviet Union. That is, up until December 1991, when the Soviets ran out of money and their world collapsed around them.'

'Yes, I'm aware of that.'

'There are people in authority who would like you to think that after the collapse of the Berlin Wall that we and the Russians suddenly became the best of friends. But things aren't like that and haven't been for centuries. Have you heard of the Great Game?'

Osmond started laughing. 'I'll take it that it doesn't have anything to do with football and the World Cup?'

'No, but in a way even football is included in it. The Great Game is the name given to struggle, between the old British and Russian empires, for the control of India. It was coined by a British Intelligence Officer, a bloke named Arthur Connolly way back in the early 1800s. Anyway, India's grown too big and powerful to be controlled by the likes of us or the Russians, but that hasn't stopped us from playing a modified version of the game, with some new players thrown into the mix. These days it's us, the Saudis and the Americans against the Russians, Iranians, and Venezuelans. The game has always been played out in the manmade hell hole that is Afghanistan. We invaded the country three times between 1839 and 1919, and in recent times the Russians invaded in 1979 and with encouragement from men like me, they left in 1989. Britain went back in with the Americans in 2001, and as you might know, we are still there in one capacity or another. At the end of the day, the power that subdues the Afghans will one day be able to take Iran. That said, these days the Iranians aren't powerless to stop foreign powers from taking them over, so they get to play the game as well but have little choice other than to side with the Russians to keep us and the Americans at bay. No doubt they'll come knocking on our door one day, should the Russians get too close to them for comfort. What I'm trying to say is, if you view world events as they relate to the United Kingdom through the lens of the Great Game, then many senseless government decisions suddenly become very understandable.'

'You're telling me, that all you have to do is find and kill this woman Namdar and everyone can get back on with their lives?' said Osmond looking at the greying middle-aged man sat in front of her. Harry was very fit and strong for his age but at the end of the day he was just one man and she couldn't visualise how he could fix the mess they found themselves in.

'Yes, that would seem the best way to sort this mess out.'

'And in the meantime, I have to hide from everyone including my own family?'

'Look, Skip, I can appreciate that you don't want to put your family through the agony of not knowing what has happened to you, but there's no other way. If you –'

'If I contact them, I'll put myself in danger! How do you know that will happen?'

Windsor held up his hands not knowing what to say.

FORTY-ONE

Edward Manning's heart was racing. He was sitting in a car with three of his most trusted men, a few minutes' drive from a warehouse where he had been told to meet the Grand Mistress, Lilith Namdar. He knew better than most that bad things happened to people in disused warehouses and today he had a feeling that some of those bad things just might happen to himself. His nerves weren't helped when he and his men were met at the entrance of the warehouse by two men he had never met before.

'Greetings, Mr. Manning. We have been expecting you,' said the shorter of the two men with an outstretched right hand.

'Who do you guys work for?' asked Manning whilst shaking hands.

'We work directly to the Grand Mistress, Edward. Why do you ask?'

'Oh, I thought you might be working in the British Security Services, that's all.'

'I'm afraid that his is a private meeting, Mr. Manning. Your friends will have to wait for you in the car.'

'It's been a long drive; can't they at least use the toilet?'

'They look like big boys to me. They can go find a tree to take a piss on.'

Manning nodded and his men returned to the car whilst the second and larger of the two men frisked him. 'I'll look after that for you, Mr. Manning. No weapons allowed inside. Lilith Namdar's orders,' said the man after his massive hand pulled a pistol from the ulster concealed under Manning's lightweight jacket.

Manning was escorted to a large room containing a meeting table, chairs and a meat hook hanging above a blood-stained concrete floor. For the first time in his life Manning started to feel some empathy for the people he'd tortured over the years.

'Sit yourself down, Mr. Manning, the Grand Mistress will be will you shortly,' said the man who'd greeted him at the front door.

Manning sat down at the table, his heart racing as his he looked over at the South African standing guard at the door. He quickly rose from his chair when Lilith Namdar entered the room accompanied by two men he recognised as Fyodor Maknov and Richard Thomas. Manning's nerves finally settled on the sight of the South African minder leaving the room.

'Good morning, Edward,' said Namdar. 'Please sit yourself back down.'

'Good morning, Mistress,' replied Manning whilst nodding a greeting at Maknov and Director Thomas.

'My apologies for holding this meeting in these less than salubrious surroundings, but needs must, gentlemen,' said Namdar. 'It would appear that fates are conspiring against us. Edward, you and Richard are going to have to start working closer than you have ever done before.'

'With respect, Mistress, I'm coming under heavy pressure to explain my intervention in Sanda Osmond's disappearance,' said Director Thomas.

'I am sure that you will find a way to justify your actions, Richard. Yours will continue to be a surveillance role. Edward's people will be responsible for any unsavoury activity. Isn't that right, Edward?'

'Yes, of course, Mistress,' said Manning.

Maknov passed three manila folders around the table. 'Memorise the contents of your folders gentlemen as you won't be allowed take them with you at the end of the meeting,' said Maknov. 'We believe that Zhukhov and his most competent GreyFriars's disciples are here in the UK. The Black Knight has fallen short of expectations and has vanished into thin air. We also believe Solomon Biratu and William Meek to be on the run together. Solomon's trail stopped at Pendle Hill and Meek vanished shortly after the internet warning issued by the blogger Matthew5:5. This meeting has been convened to discuss what, if anything, should be done to rectify these matters.'

'I've arranged for the Ukrainian authorities to raise an Interpol Blue Notice against Solomon Biratu. He is now the sole person of interest in what is now being treated as the suspicious death of Tatjana Umansky,' said Director Thomas.

'Excellent, Richard. And what about you, Edward, what have you been up to?' asked Namdar.

'I don't wish to make excuses, but I've just spent the last month covering the globe fixing Meek's latest security breach.'

'Damage caused by a man that you have twice vetted, Edward,' said Maknov.

Manning said nothing in response to Maknov's diatribe, his throat was dry and he was finding it hard to swallow, let alone speak.

'All that is in the past, Fyodor, we must take back control of the future. Now is not the time for divisions and infighting,' said Namdar, to tone of her voice making it clear that she wasn't interested in the blame game being played out in front of her. 'Fortunately, we have a lead of sorts. Intelligence gathered by our South African friends points to Zhukhov having allies at the Russian Embassy, the most important of which is the Embassy's Defence and Naval Attaché, Captain Alexander Kornienko. Fyodor has placed Kornienko under surveillance. I would like you two to take up the reins and put something more substantive in place. Do you think that you can manage that between yourselves, gentlemen?'

'Yes, of course, Mistress,' said Director Thomas. 'But the Russian Defence –'

'No buts, Richard. Not now that we are so close to achieving our goal.'

'Yes, Mistress.'

'Remember, Zhukhov is the key. Eliminate him and our opponents will dissipate into the ether.'

ಠಠಠಠ

Osmond had spent hours thinking about her family, which seemed strange to her as she had fallen out of touch with them in recent months. She'd found fewer reasons to visit the family home now that her younger siblings were away studying at university. Her brother, Billy, was studying Economics and Politics at the University of Kent in Canterbury and her sister, Emma, was studying Economics and French at Nottingham University. Osmond hadn't undertaken formal study since finishing her Sports Science degree back in 2008 but she liked reading. She didn't have much time for novels and tended to spend her time reading articles relating to climate change, genetically modified foods and gene editing.

So far, she had managed to remain calm in spite of the storm blowing around her, but she couldn't understand why Harry was so adamant that Russia was Britain's great enemy. She didn't know a lot of history, but she thought everyone knew that the Russians were Britain's allies in two world wars, fought against the Germans. She knew far less about the Crimean war, but she'd heard of Florence Nightingale and the Charge of the Light Brigade. All she really thought she knew about Russian people, apart from their being good chess players, was that they were supposed to be hard drinking, sports drugs cheats, with a shed load of aging nuclear weapons at their disposal. As far as she was concerned, Harry's talk of communism and the cold war was the concern of old men. She was too young to have any recollection of the Berlin Wall coming down in 1989 and only had the faintest of memories about the collapse of the Soviet Union in 1991.

Windsor was under stress, he might not care much for caffeine but he was feeling lost without access to the technical gadgets provided to him by people, like his MI6 handler, Ian Moore. But what was he to do? Zhukhov had tried to convince him that one of the world's richest women was the leader of a witchcraft cult intent on bringing about the end of the world, and that he and his recently discovered daughter were amongst the few people on planet earth able to stop her. He wouldn't have given Zhukhov the time of day if it hadn't been for the fact that the British media had run stories describing the murder of at least six people on a Central London estate as a pitched battle by rival drugs gangs. He'd been sorely tempted to put the battery back into his secure SIS mobile so that he could try and speak to Moore. The only thing that had stopped him was the thought it might compromise Sanda's safety. He'd spent years looking after number one, but now he had a ball and chain attached to his ankle, in the shape of his daughter, and it was starting to make him feel like a caged animal. It had been the stories told by Biratu and Meek that had finally stirred him into action. But he was faced with a dilemma, sensing that if he pushed Sanda too hard, she would push back, refusing to do anything he might advise her to do. His other problem was that he'd tied himself to Zhukhov and only had six days before he and Sanda had to travel to the port town of Harwich. He desperately wanted to broach the subject of teaching Sanda what he considered basic life skills, but didn't have a clue on where to start.

FORTY-TWO

Windsor had reserved himself and Sanda a table for two at the five-star hotel he'd booked them into. He'd waited until after through their starters before broaching the subject that had been troubling him for the last few days. He was chewing slowly on a succulent slice of pan-seared breast of partridge whilst scanning the faces of the other diners and was pleased to see that they were all deeply engrossed in their own private conversations.

Okay, go for it, Harry, said the voice in his head. 'Have you given any thought as to how you are going to live after this is over?' he asked after taking a deep breath.

'Yes, I have but you aren't going to like what I've decided to do,' said Osmond, with a look that told him that he was going to have great difficulty in changing her mind.

'What do you mean by that?'

'We both know that my life has changed forever. Even if this woman, Namdar, is removed from the frame, there's always going to be the chance that someone will want to avenge some grievance or other –'

'What are you telling me, Skip? Are you saying that you just want to go back to your old life and hope for the best?'

'No, that's not what I'm saying, in fact that's the opposite of what I was saying,' said Osmond before bursting out laughing.

'What's so funny, Skip?' asked Windsor as he scratched the back of his head.

'You are.'

'How so?'

'Has anyone ever told you that you refer to anyone who's pissing you off as Skip?'

Windsor's brow furrowed and he bit into his lower lip before his face finally broke into a smile. 'No, nobody has ever told me that, Sanda. But now that you mention it, I think that you might be onto something. But what's that got to do with all this?'

'Absolutely nothing, it's just an observation. However, in answer to your original question. Yes, I know exactly what I want to do in the immediate future... I want to become more like you.'

Windsor gave his daughter a blank look. 'And what's that supposed to mean?'

Osmond paused and looked around at the other diners and then back across the dining table to Windsor. 'The way I see it, only someone like you would stand a realistic chance of surviving an attack by people like these Russians. Not that you fared too well when Natasha tasered you.'

Windsor raised his right hand as if about to break into a tirade, but gently lowered it again.

'I'm just ribbing you, Harry, you need to lighten-up a little. Physically, there isn't too much difference between us. You might be stronger than me, but I'd wager that I'm fitter and faster than you –'

'Now hold on for a minute –'

'No, you hold on, just hear me out. You're not the man you used to be. You might not like to hear that, but the sands of time take their toll on everybody. And yet you've managed to convince yourself that the only thing between my living and dying is your ability to protect me.'

Windsor picked up his glass of wine and sat back in his chair, mulling over what Sanda was saying to him.

'For starters, you can teach me how to shoot a gun,' continued Osmond. 'No doubt you're an expert in unarmed combat but believe it or not I actually know a little bit about fighting. I did a little judo as a child and more recently I've been into boxerobics. So, I know how to throw a punch and control a fall. It's not like I'm a total novice on the physical combat front. As for things like home security and checking vehicles for bombs and the like. I'll bet that there are some standard techniques that you can show me.'

Windsor laughed. 'And how long do you think that it will take to get you up to speed with all of that? You know, before I could leave you to your own devices?'

'I learn fast. So, I reckon that I'd be pretty handy after about three or four months.'

'Okay, I'll concede that a hell of a lot can be achieved in three months, especially as you're minded to stay the course,' said Windsor as he cut himself another piece of partridge. 'But we've only got five days before we're supposed to rejoin the Russians.'

'I bet that there's a lot that I could learn even in such a short space of time.'

'And how long do you think it takes to create somebody like me?'

Osmond gave Windsor the once over. 'Well, you've most probably been trained in all sort of stuff that wouldn't be relevant to me –'

'But all the training I did was devised specifically to create men like me, little whirlwinds of destruction. Remove any part of that training and you lose some of the man,' interrupted Windsor.

'Alright, I'd guess two years, tops.'

'I did three years in the marines and it was a full two years before I was the finished item in the SBS. I kid you not, it takes four to five years of hard graft to become someone like me.'

Osmond swallowed a mouthful of baked goat's cheese tart. 'Are you telling me that it can't be done?'

'No, there's a lot that you can learn, but there are many things you can only learn through experience gained from being out in the field,' said Windsor before taking another sip of red wine. 'And then there's the little matter of whether you've actually got what it takes to take another person's life. They make it look easy on the television and in films but trust me, some people can't do it even when their life depends upon it.'

'Hold on a moment, who said anything about taking lives?' said Osmond.

'But you said that you wanted to be like me.'

'Up to a point.'

'Sorry to trouble you but is everything to your satisfaction?' asked the waiter in a faint French accent.

'Yes, Skip, everything is fine. The food is excellent,' said a Windsor smiling.

The two of them burst out laughing, as it dawned upon Windsor that he'd just called the waiter, Skip.

'Are you sure, sir?'

Oui, tout est complètement à notre satisfaction. La perdrix est l'un des meilleurs que je ai jamais goûté,' said Windsor in his best French accent.

'Merci monsieur, je vais passer vos compliments sur le chef,' replied the waiter before topping up their wine glasses and moving off to attend to another table.

Windsor then looked across to Osmond.

'Have you got the time, Sanda?'

'Yes, it's…,' Sanda gave her wrist a puzzled look. 'Actually no, I think that I must have forgotten to put my watch on.'

Windsor smiled. 'Are you sure, I could have sworn that you were wearing it when we met in the bar.'

Osmond gave Windsor a suspicious look. 'What, you've got my watch!'

Windsor placed his right hand under the table and raised it again holding Osmond's violet coloured Garmin Forerunner 10 GPS Running watch.

'I've got a couple of questions for you. How many tables, not including this one, are there in the restaurant? How many are taken? Oh, and just to make things a little more difficult, how many fire exits, including the main entrance to the restaurant, are there?'

'Okay, I'd guess there are eleven tables in here of which seven are taken. As for the fire exits, I guess that there's two of them,' said Osmond just about resisting the urge to look about the restaurant.

'That's quite good going, but there are fourteen tables in here, nine of which are occupied and there are three fire exits, said Windsor closing his eyes. 'If you take a look around the room, there are two people on the adjacent table and two more on the one closest to that one. The table after that is vacant, the table next to that one has four people sitting at it and the next one is vacant. The one after that has two people sitting at it, the next one has three people sat at it, the one after that is vacant and the next is occupied by a man in a blue jacket who looks to waiting on someone to join him. The next one is vacant, the one after that is occupied by two people, the one after that has three people, the next one two people and finally the last one is vacant. Am I right?' said Windsor with a look of satisfaction on his face.

Osmond was surprised and impressed by Windsor's impromptu demonstration of his skills of observation and memory. 'That's pretty good but there aren't four people seated at the table over there, there's only three of...' she replied, seeing that Windsor had made a mistake. But as she was speaking the words, she noticed the half-drunk glass of wine in front of the empty chair.

'That lady sat there has just nipped off to the restroom.'

'Okay, I'll give you that one. So, you've got a blinding memory, can speak fluent French and have the ability to remove a watch from a woman's wrist without her noticing. But what of it?' asked Osmond whilst refastening her wristwatch.

'I'm also fluent in Russian and Farsi, and as for being able to remove your watch, sleight of hand is one of the most useful skills that I possess and I didn't learn it in the armed forces.'

'Now what are you trying to tell me?'

'That before someone like you can dream of becoming someone like me, you need to become proficient in all manner of skills. Some of which, no disrespect intended, you're now too old to master.'

'Neither of us are as young as we might like to be, but like I said, I learn fast.'

Windsor finished off his partridge and took a large sip of wine. 'All right, I won't dispute that you have the mental and physical capabilities, and you certainly have the incentive to put the effort in and stay the course. But if you insist on going down this road, you'll lose something.'

'And what might that be?'

'Your humanity! I don't consider myself to be a monster, but… but I'm far from what you might call a compassionate man. There's no way around it, in becoming more like me you'll lose much of what makes you the woman you are.' Windsor placed his wine glass on the table and looked Osmond straight in the eye. 'By the time I'm finished with you, you will have changed. You'll be much harder with people. Do you really want that?'

'And if I don't, I might suffer a violent death.'

'Alright, we need time to give this some proper thought,' said Windsor doing his best to disguise the pleasure he felt in Sanda having made such a choice by her own volition. 'For starters, I'll show you how to shoot a gun and you'll have to demonstrate that you have what it takes to take a life.'

'I already told you, Harry, I'm not interested in killing anyone. There's got to be a limit in what we can reasonably cover in five days.'

Windsor smiled. 'There's a lot that can be learnt in that time. Don't look so worried, Sanda. I'm not going to have you rubbing out tourists or anything like that. No, we will start nice and easy, a deer should just about do it.'

'What, you want me to kill a deer?'

'Yes, and I believe that you are in luck.'

'And why's that?'

'We're in the middle of hunting season. My preference would be a Red Stag, but a Fallow Buck should be enough to test whether you've inherited your biological father's killing genes.'

'Why a deer?'

'Because they are big animals. Trust me, there's a significant difference between the killing a game bird and a deer. And there's a huge difference between taking the life of a deer and that of a person. Oh, and whilst we're about it, there's something else that would be good for you to start on with.'

'And what's that?' asked Osmond.

'I'm competent in several languages. You could do a lot worse than start learning to speak and read the language of our newfound Russian friends. You've got some cash. Take yourself into Stirling tomorrow, it's a university town so they'll have loads of language programs for you to choose from. I wouldn't bother with any written materials for now, that will just confuse you. Oh, and another thing, there's another book on your kindle that you might want to get to grips with, it's by a fella named Buzan, he specialises in memory enhancement techniques. He's written a load of them.'

'Is that it? You don't want me to read a copy of War and Peace whilst I'm about it?'

'Hold it there, Skip,' said Windsor, his temper flaring. 'We're in a shitty situation. All I'm trying to do is mitigate the risk, so that you can go back to living as near normal life as possible.'

'I know where you are coming from,' said Osmond raising her hands up in front of herself. 'I'm trying my best, but you've got to understand that I've got a lot on my mind. I'm not finding it easy to concentrate at the moment.'

'Okay, I'm sorry. But as the saying goes, every journey starts with a first step. Oh, I've just remembered something else.'

'What, you want me to buy a top hat and a white rabbit?'

Windsor gave Osmond a hard stare.

'Chill out, Harry. I was just ribbing you. I meant for that sleight-of-hand thing you mentioned.'

'Oh that,' said Windsor breaking into a smile. He was glad that Osmond had tried to lighten the mood. 'Don't worry about that, we won't be calling in Derren Brown just yet. What I was going to say is that as I won't be with you all the time, you need to take steps to minimise your risk of running into trouble. Get yourself a sunhat and a pair of sunglasses, try not to drink too much, be careful who you get talking to, and if you sense that you are in real danger make your way to a police station.'

Just then the waiter arrived with their main courses. The steak was a little rare for Windsor's liking, but he took some pleasure from winding Sanda up as the blood red juices oozed from the cuts, he made in it with his steak knife. He gave Osmond a wink before turning his gaze to a painting of a stag hanging on the wall on the far side of the restaurant.

FORTY-THREE

Meek and Biratu found themselves on a campsite, without access to the internet, with a group of Russians professing to be the GreyFriars. The only one who didn't seem to mind being without life's electronic staples was Zhukhov, who was glad that the two westerners would have little to do other than talk. He was hoping to learn why the fates had brought them together so close to the North American eclipse. But first he wanted to convince them that they were dealing with a person who had been alive for at least a thousand years.

'As I've already alluded to gentlemen, I first met Namdar when she was going by the name of Qarinah Pirez. It was in the guise of Pirez that she managed to persuade my government to assassinate Kennedy by leaking the President's plan to provide US air support for a second invasion of Cuba in December of 1963. I only became suspicious of Pirez's motives after breaking into one of her apartments and stumbling across a notebook containing coded notes. Photographs of the pages are included in your folders,' said Zhukhov.

'I have to admit that to my untrained eye the handwriting and the doodles in Pirez's notebook match the hand that wrote the Voynich Manuscript,' said Meek.

'A document dating back to the fifteenth century,' said Zhukhov.

'Assuming that I accept that she authored the document, why did she bother to write it in the first place?' asked Biratu. 'I mean it's just a mishmash of sketches of plants, women in bathtubs and indecipherable charts?'.

'Have to you ever read C. S. Lewis's The Magician's Nephew?'

'The prequel to the Chronicles of Narnia. What of it?' asked Meek.

'The "wood between the worlds" is a pertinent construct is it not? It's a gateway to a multiverse accessed through pools of water. What if Lilith Namdar was acquainted with Vivienne, the mythical Lady of the Lake of Arthurian legend? A woman presumably capable of moving between dimensions via a body of water. Might she not doodle on the possibility of doing the same thing?'

'You really believe that Lilith was alive six hundred years ago and, at that time, believed that parallel worlds were accessible by submerging oneself in bodies of water?' asked Biratu.

'Yes, I do,' replied Zhukhov. 'But I think that she altered her beliefs after Einstein published his Theories of Relativity. In 1935, the concept of an Einstein-Rosen bridge was established, a gravitational tunnel or wormhole created by pulling apart two entangled black holes, forming theoretical shortcuts through the universe. It wouldn't have taken a great leap of her imagination to see the possibilities of using such a bridge to open a connection to the hidden dimensions of space-time.'

'Just so I can be sure that I haven't misunderstood any of this, man. What you're proposing is that my adopted mother wrote the Voynich Manuscript and has spent the last six hundred years changing her identity whilst travelling across the continents of planet earth?' asked Biratu.

'That is the conclusion I reached back in 1963 and I've not read or seen anything since that has caused me to change my mind. Also included in your folders are photographs of other documents that I found to be in Pirez's possession. They were written in modern code and relate to what can only be described as particle accelerators. Of course, I couldn't immediately understand them, but she made the most amateur of mistakes in leaving her code book in the same room as the rest of her belongings. Even with the code book, it took me a number of weeks to understand what her notes alluded to. It was only on the day that we killed Kennedy that it all started making sense to me,' said Zhukhov as he remembered that fateful day. 'She thought that his moon project would die with him. She seemed obsessed with the building of particle accelerators and was worried that their development and construction was being curtailed by what she viewed as Kennedy's presidential legacy project. That thought made me very nervous, as I sensed that Pirez would want to tie up any loose ends connecting her to the deed.'

'The writing in the notepad does look very much like Lilith's,' said Biratu.

'The plan was for me to meet-up with Namdar, with the two of us driving over the border into Mexico. She told me that she intended to lie low in the Middle East, whereas arrangements had been made for me to return home to the Motherland,' continued Zhukhov.

'That's when she tried to kill you?' asked Meek.

'Yes, she shot me several times in the chest, but I was wearing a prototype bulletproof vest, a garment in the early stages of its development. The first of its kind. I kept it for luck, it's in a wardrobe in our monastery.'

'But this is the bit I still don't get,' said Meek. 'You said that Pirez, Namdar or whatever name she chooses to go by, is immortal. So how come you were able to injure her?'

'I didn't know about such things back then. She had a gun but I managed to lay my hands on a club. I hit her in the face with it and made a run for it. I was certain that I'd broken her jaw. I heard the bone break under the impact.'

'No disrespect intended, Georgy, but if Namdar has been alive for thousands of years, shouldn't she be covered in scars and have all sorts of physical afflictions?' asked Meek.

'All that is explained in the ancient texts. Harry, Sanda and I are descended from an ancient bloodline dating back to a mythical man beast, named Enkidu, who lived in what is now modern-day Iraq. I have DNA evidence to support my claim. The texts state that this man, Enkidu, and all of his descendants are able to inflict pain and physically damage demigods and other immortals living amongst us. Obviously, he, and we, don't have the power to kill such beings, else they wouldn't be immortal. I remember the expression on Pirez's face like it was yesterday. She looked more shocked by my having hurt her, than by the injury itself.'

'And that's why you, Sanda, and Harry, are special?' asked Biratu.

'Yes, exactly, Solomon.'

'So where, if anywhere, do William and I fit into all this?'

'I don't know, but our stumbling upon you both at this juncture makes me think that you are both integral to the prophecy. In fact, there is something that I want to find out as a matter of urgency.'

'What's that?' asked Meek.

'All will be revealed in good time, William, but for now I would be grateful if each of you will provide me with a sample of your DNA.'

'I won't ask why you want them, but how are you going to test them?' asked Biratu.

'I am not without friends, Solomon. I have a contact at the Russian Embassy in London who should be able to help us.'

'I don't personally subscribe to fate and luck,' said Meek. 'But it does seem strange how we've all ended up together. Not that I like quoting Donald Rumsfeld, but I think that we need to draw up a grid to record what we think we know, and what we know we don't know.'

'What do you mean, William?' asked Zhukhov.

'We need to list our known knowns - the things that we know we know, the known unknowns - the things we know we don't know, and that should leave us with the unknown unknowns - things we don't know we don't know.'

'How will that help us, William,' asked Zhukhov.

'I don't know why, but I sense that we are missing something. I've worked for the FFF for years and the link to the CSS is there for all to see. But the CSS has a grading system that works something like the one used by the Freemasons. They have a series of ranks or degrees, awarded to members on the attainment of ever higher levels of esoteric knowledge. But in the CSS, some initiates, important people, are promoted up through the ranks with great rapidity. Way faster than anybody could ever hope to learn via the intricacies of Namdar's dark religion. The top tier inhabits in a special club. They attend exclusive masses, with rooms set aside for them at the larger parties. Most initiates don't get past the third degree. I'm on level five and I'm not in the same league as the top tier disciples. I've sometimes thought that Namdar might be running two separate cults, but I've never discovered anything proving that. And then there is Solomon. Why would Namdar invest so much time and effort in you? You were clearly very important to her plans. The question is why?'

'I've already told you. She took me under her wing after my foster family died in a fire,' replied Biratu.

'That was after you won a prestigious mathematics competition run by her favourite NGO?' asked Zhukhov.

'Yes, but I was only a young boy. How could she know what I might or might not go on to achieve in life?'

'Tell me again, Solomon, what exactly is it that you do?' asked Zhukhov.

'I'm trying to find the Grand Unified Theory. A theory describing all physical properties within the Universe.'

'Would you describe yourself as being just like the other scientists trying to discover the same thing?' asked Zhukhov.

'No, I don't think that I'm like the others. As a matter of –'

'What's that you have there, Georgy?' interrupted Meek when he noticed the general holding a small brown jug.

'What? Oh this, it's a –'

'I know what it is, Georgy. It's a Bellarmine jug. And it looks like a very old one,' said Meek.

'I was told that this object once belonged to Joan of Arc,' said Zhukhov.

'And where did she get it?' asked Meek. 'I know that she died in the fifteenth century, but that bottle looks way older than that.'

'You know your antiques, William,' said Zhukhov.

'I don't know about that, but I know a witches' bottle when I see one. I'm from Pendle, English witch country. Do you keep it for luck?'

'It is rumoured to have once belonged to Namdar.'

'Is there anything inside of it?'

'A few locks of hair.'

'Are you aware that if it contains Namdar's hair, the bottle can be used against her?'

Zhukhov smiled. 'I have tried to use it many times over the years, but to no good effect. I was hoping that Sanda might have more success. I intend to give her the jug when she and Harry return back to us.'

'How about letting me have a crack at it, Georgy?' asked Meek.

'Wish away, William, but be very careful with it. In the interim we have work to do, so if you don't mind, your DNA samples please, Gentlemen?' asked Zhukhov.

Biratu had been about to tell Zhukhov about his experiment at the collider but the moment was lost in the sands of time.

FORTY-FOUR

Osmond couldn't see him but she assumed that Windsor must be following her, she was certain that Harry wouldn't let her wander the streets unprotected. But she was wrong, Windsor didn't have any choice other than to leave her to her own devices as he had her training programme to organise. Not that Osmond minded being left on her own, as it gave her time to read her book on Psychic Self-Defense, in between perusing Russian language DVDs and self-help books purporting to show how to master one's memory. She'd also purchased a book entitled *Sleights of Mind*, which described what seemed to her to be the exciting discipline of neuromagic. Osmond knew that she wasn't going to become a conjurer any time soon but was interested in understanding how the human mind was deceived by magic tricks, just like the one employed by Windsor when he'd surreptitiously removed her wristwatch.

༜༜༜༜

Whilst Osmond was milling about in the streets of Stirling, Windsor was busy visiting a few old contacts from his days in the Armed Forces. He'd just arranged for himself and Sanda to visit a shooting range and was now sitting in the lobby of a large house on a private estate owned by an old colleague of his from his SBS days.

'It's good to see you, Harry,' said General Spalding shaking Windsor firmly by the hand.

'And you, sir. Thank you for agreeing to see me at such short notice.'

'Don't be ridiculous, my man. It's a pleasure to see you my dear fellow. You've kept yourself in excellent shape I see. You bloody nearly took my hand off with that grip of yours.'

'Oh, I'm sorry, sir. I didn't mean –'

'Think nothing of it, my man. If I had more people like you about the place, I wouldn't be letting myself go to pot. Come with me, we can't have you sitting in the lobby,' said the General leading Windsor to an opulent room on the first floor.

'Drink, Harry?'

'I'll have a Scotch, General.'

'Excellent. Now that we're a bit more comfortable, you can tell me what's brought you here to see me after all these years?'

'I'll get straight to the point, sir, I'd like a favour from you.'

'You can have anything you want. Just tell me what I can do for you.'

'I'm up here on holiday with my daughter and I'd like to take her out hunting.'

'Your *daughter*, Harry, I see,' said General Spalding raising an eyebrow.

'What? Oh yes, my daughter. I'd like to take her out stalking, outside of a gamekeeper's prying eyes.'

'I know exactly what you mean, my man,' said the general giving Harry a knowing look. 'Anything that you and your *daughter* get up to is nobody's business but your own. I'm sure that the young filly couldn't be in better hands. When were you thinking of bringing her here?'

'The day after tomorrow.'

'That's a pity, I'd like to have hosted a dinner party in your honour, but I'm going away on business. Will you be around next week?'

'I'm afraid not, General.'

'Some other time then, Harry. But make sure that you bloody come back soon. It's been too long, my man.'

'Don't worry, sir, I'll be back before you know it.'

'Excellent. Leave everything to me, Harry. You and your lady friend will be well catered for. Please ask for

Clive when you arrive in reception. He'll kit you out and explain the lay of the land. I'll have him direct you to an area of the estate that I keep for personal use. Nobody will disturb you if you know what I mean!'

'Thank you very much, sir.'

'You see much of the old platoon, Harry?'

'No, sir.'

'That's a pity. You're all such good, fine men. But then you were always a bit of a lone wolf. Most of the Scots lads still live around these parts you know. You might want to knock on a few more doors before leaving.'

'Yes, sir.'

'I'm sorry about this, Harry. I'm entertaining today, so I'll have to be off. Please feel free to make yourself at home.'

'You're very kind, sir, but I'd better be off myself.

ഇഇഇഇ

Namdar was sitting all alone in a candlelit room remembering how she started on her quest to free herself from the bondage of life. She remembered fleeing the Holy Roman Empire for Scotland and travelling from there to England. It seemed that witchcraft and the hunting of witches followed her everywhere she set up home. She'd escaped the potential tortures of Nider's Formicarius, Sprenger's Malleus Maleficarum, and Bodin's De La Demonomanie, only to be exposed to the strictures of King James VI's Demonologie. It wasn't until she settled in Pendle that there was any repeat of the Bavarian experience, the ill-fated Pappenheimers being substituted for Demdike and Chattox. She might have stayed longer in England if it hadn't been for that self-styled Witchfinder General, Matthew Hopkins. Yes, he'd followed her trail, forcing her to flee across the ocean to the settlements of the Presbyterians of New England. It had been centuries since anyone had pursued her with the fanaticism of Hopkins, and she often wondered if he and Zhukhov shared the same bloodline.

'Oh, why couldn't I have killed him when I had the chance?' she said to herself as she looked into the flames of the fire-holder.

FORTY-FIVE

Getting Osmond access to the gun club had been even easier than the Deer Hunting Estate, as Windsor had been a member for many years and was on very good terms with the owner. The club contained three ranges in all, a 25-metre range with firing points used for handgun practice, a 50-metre range used predominantly for the shooting of air rifles and a 75-metre range used for the firing of live rounds from real rifles. Windsor had made reservations for four sessions. Two for today and two in a few days' time.

'I'm sorry, Sanda, but we are going to have to do this the hard way,' said Windsor as he removed the headphones covering her ears.

'What? Why? Do you want me to go deaf or something?' she asked.

'It's very easy to lose concentration when the adrenaline kicks-in amidst the smoke and noise. Practising this way will increase your ability to focus should you ever find yourself in a real firefight. I'm afraid that if you find yourself needing to fire a gun, the chances are that you will be up against someone discharging their own weapon at you. Muffling the sound of these things is all well and good if you're intending to take the odd pot shot at a deer, but it's a completely different ball game in a combat situation.'

'Very well, I can see your point, Harry,' said Osmond as she took aim on the twenty-five-meter range with a SIG Sauer P226 pistol. It was a large weapon, capable of holding fifteen cartridges and weighing-in at just over two pounds. She fired off two rounds, both shots missing the target.

'That was very well-done Sanda. You might not have hit the target but your body posture was good, your aim steady and most importantly you hardly flinched when the pistol discharged. You're definitely not afraid of loud bangs.'

Osmond gave Windsor a big smile. She had been expecting him to have concentrated on the numerous errors she was sure she was making and was surprised that Harry was proving to be a good teacher.

'Fire off another two sets of two. Focus on the dead centre of the target. You want to visualise the bullets passing right through the target and embedding themselves in the sandbags behind it.'

Osmond discharged another four rounds and was pleasantly surprised to see all of them hit the target. Windsor had spent ages the night before talking about grouping. So, she was very pleased that most of her shots were very close together.

'Are you sure that you've never fired a gun before? Not even an air pistol?' asked Windsor.

'Apart from on the X-box, this is the first time I've even held a gun.'

'I'm not one to give praise where it isn't due. So, you can take it from me that you are off to a very good start. Maybe these computer games serve some useful function after all,' said Windsor looking genuinely pleased with the progress his daughter was making. 'Okay, change the magazine and empty the entire next clip into the target.'

Osmond fired round after round, hitting the target every time.

'Okay, repeat that with the remaining four magazines and then we'll move over to the rifle range,' said Windsor.

Osmond loaded the next magazine into the pistol. This time she imagined the target to be a real person and tried her best to aim for the heart. Windsor noticed that the bullets were landing higher and to the left of the target.

'What are you doing? I thought I told you to concentrate on just hitting dead centre?'

Osmond pulled out the empty magazine and loaded the next one into the weapon. 'I was just aiming for the heart. I want to practice making a clean kill.'

Windsor looked Osmond up and down. 'And what if the person you're shooting at is wearing body armour?' asked Windsor. 'If you're adamant about making a clean kill, you'll need to make a head shot, but we're a long way off you doing that. Just concentrate on hitting the centre of the torso for now. Remember, two shots at a time, grouping the entry wounds.'

Osmond emptied the remaining rounds into the target, again not missing with a single shot. When she was finished, the two of them walked over to a seventy-five-meter firing range.

'There are different methods that can be used to shoot a rifle, and the preferred method is not the one I favour, said Windsor as he removed a C8 SFW assault rifle from its carrycase and pointed it at the target. 'Conventional wisdom states that you should pull the trigger when you have fully exhaled the air from your lungs, whereas I prefer to pull the trigger when I have taken a deep breath. The trick is to pull the trigger at the end of a breathing cycle, but I find the downside of taking a shot when you've breathed out is that you have to wait a full breath cycle before taking your next shot.' Windsor entered a crouched position and aimed the rifle at the target, took a deep breath and fired. He breathed out and in again, set himself and took the second shot. Osmond looked at the target through a pair of the binoculars; both bullets had hit the centre of the target and looked to be less than an inch apart.

'That looks like pretty accurate shooting to me,' she said.

'True, but how do you take say three or four shots in quick succession? Let me demonstrate,' said Windsor, setting himself and taking another deep breath before firing four rounds at the target. 'Right, now it's your turn,' he said handing Sanda the rifle.

Osmond took hold of the assault rifle, entered a

crouched position, steadied herself, looked through the weapon's iron sights, took a deep breath and gently squeezed on the trigger. The weapon discharged and she tried to ignore the recoil into her shoulder as she focused her mind on the next trigger pull. From the look on Windsor's face, Osmond assumed that she'd scored a bull, but when she looked at the target through the binoculars, she saw nothing that indicated that she'd even hit the target.

'You missed the target. But don't let that put you off, most of what you did was very good. There are twenty-four rounds left in the clip, fire them off as you like. When you have finished, I'll change the target cover so that you can start over from scratch.'

Osmond noticed that she started hitting the target after about her fifth shot, even managing to group the last three shots together. She waited for Windsor to change the target cover before reloading the rifle.

'Okay, this time I want you to fire off two rounds at a time, same as you did with the SIG,' said Windsor as he raised the binoculars to his eyes.

Osmond emptied the magazine and didn't miss with a single shot.

'Okay, you've got four more clips. Fire them off in your own time and we'll be done for this morning.'

A few minutes later Osmond's first live-fire shooting lesson was over. Leaving father and daughter looking pretty pleased with themselves.

༺༺༺༺

Captain Natasha Dokukin knew that by travelling back to London she was placing herself and her men, Milan Medved and Andrei Voronin, in grave danger. But the general had been adamant Meek's and Biratu's DNA samples needed analysing and there was only one person in the UK able to arrange that for them. Neither she nor

Zhukhov even knew if the Defence and Naval Attaché, Captain Alexander Kornienko, would be at the Russian Embassy in London to meet her. She'd tried calling Kornienko several times on his secure mobile without success. So, she was greatly relieved when they arrived at the embassy and were told that not only was Kornienko in the building, but he would cut short the meeting he was in to see her.

'Is Zhukhov safe?' asked Kornienko immediately Dokukin, Medved, and Voronin were shown into his office.

'Yes. But we have all gone mobile,' replied Dokukin.

'Why, has the safe house been compromised?'

'Things have become complicated. We discovered two more links in the chain.'

'Then why the personal visit?'

'With respect, sir, you've been ignoring our calls.'

'Obolensky is missing, presumed dead. I had to assume that he'd been taken in an effort to get to the General.'

'Do you think Obolensky talked?'

'Everyone talks. But he couldn't have given you away as he didn't know the whereabouts of the safe house.'

'You think they will come for you next?'

'I haven't left the grounds of the Embassy in days now.'

'Please explain, sir?'

'In 2008 the General convinced the powers that be that the European Super Collider had to be stopped at all costs. I must hand it to the man, he led that operation without loss of life. But what was the end result of his actions? A temporary halt in experiments of a year, only to be followed by improved security arrangements. We have learned from bitter experience that only a suicide squad will be able to take down the facility for good.' Dokukin, Medved and Voronin looked at each other with expressions of alarm on their faces. 'Am I to take it that the General has not made any of this clear to you?'

'We know next to nothing about the 2008 assault, other than it was a success,' said Dokukin.

'Am I correct in assuming that the General will not be leading any future assault on the complex?'

'Very probably, sir. But you used the words bitter experience. What did you mean by that?'

'We went through the same scenario in 2015. The General convinced all relevant parties that we had until the last of the four blood moons to disrupt the Collider. We think that your predecessor and his team were purposely allowed entry into the twenty-seven-kilometre service tunnel so that their bodies could be obliterated by the combined effects of super magnetism and radiation. Media reports stated the charred remains of a furry creature were found close to a gnawed-through power cable. That was one way of describing events. But all that matters is that the mission failed and, strangely, the world did not end. Now the whole cycle begins again.'

'But, sir, I have read copies of the ancient texts and am in agreement with the General that Tribulation will likely start this year.'

'And which date do you subscribe to, the date of the eclipse or the date of the astrological alignment?' Dokukin did not respond to the question. 'Are this year's events so very different, Captain?' Again, Kornienko's question was met by silence. 'You must try to appreciate my situation. Your activities haven't gone unnoticed in Moscow. The British Foreign Office are using their back channels to try and ascertain whether rogue elements of the SVR are operating in their capital city. I have placed my head on the block by formally notifying the President's Office that the British are trying to blame your nefarious activities on an ISIS cell operating out of the Motherland. So, I hope you will appreciate my reasons for asking why it proved necessary to shoot, what I hope were Namdar's people, to death on a London council housing estate?'

'I am as certain as I can be that Namdar's people had the woman Osmond under surveillance. We anticipated her biological father contacting her, but everything changed when he arrived at her home with the intention of moving her to a place of safety. Namdar's people moved in on him, forcing us to intervene.'

'How many of them were killed?'

'Two people were killed on a rooftop overlooking Osmond's apartment and five were killed at ground level. We incurred no casualties.'

'And you are absolutely certain that they were Namdar's people and not members of the British Security Services?'

'No, I am not. But the fact that we were able to escape so easily from central London speaks volumes in itself, does it not?'

'I thought as much, but it helps to know the facts. I was hoping that the British might have snatched Obolensky with the intention of using him as a bargaining chip, but that seems less likely with each hour that passes.'

'I am sorry, sir, Obolensky was a good man.'

Thank you. But we must get on with this murky business. So please tell me why you are here?'

'The General wants two DNA samples analysed as a matter of urgency.'

'The additional links the in chain. I see. It can be arranged, but you must remain at the embassy until we have the results. I will smuggle you and you men out the building when the time is right.'

'We don't have much time.'

'It will take as long as it takes, but you should receive the results back tomorrow morning.'

'Thank you, sir.'

'Just so that you know, I have been made aware of a strange development.'

'Meaning?'

'The Ukrainian authorities have raised an Interpol Blue Notice for a man named Solomon Biratu. Lilith Namdar's adopted son. Am I to infer from the expression on your face that you know of his whereabouts?'

'You are very perceptive, sir.'

'You trust this man to betray his krysha?'

'He believes that Namdar had his girlfriend murdered.'

'The lady referred to in the Blue Notice? Could this not be all part of an elaborate ploy?'

'As I said, sir, time is short. We are chancing everything on his being honest with us.'

'And why after all these years of planning are you all in England? What assets do we have in Switzerland, Germany, Japan or America? My feeling is that Namdar has tricked you all into coming here. The sea port is your only exit and should anything happen to me you will be stranded here.'

'Then I wish you good health and a long life, sir.'

'Unfortunately, one must hope for the best but always plan for the worst. We live in interesting times, Captain. Make yourselves comfortable, you are to remain in my office until I get the test results back to you. Please make full use of the on-suite bathroom facilities.'

'Yes, sir.'

FORTY-SIX

Windsor and Osmond left the hotel at five in the morning for their day's deer stalking on General Spalding's estate, in the heart of the Spey Valley. Spalding had said that Windsor and Osmond would be left to their own devices as long as they steered clear of the hunting lodge and other accommodation facilities. The estate was described as an area of outstanding natural beauty, providing a mix of rugged hills and dense forest. Osmond thought that all the beauty in the world wasn't going to make up for the fact that she was going there to murder a deer.

'Sanda, I've got to check-in with the gamekeeper, present him with my DSC2 certification, that sort of thing. Whilst I'm doing that can you get the backpacks out the boot?' asked Windsor.

Osmond was waiting next to the Land Cruiser with two Vorn rifle backpacks at her side when she heard the sound of a horse's hooves. 'What's that, Harry?' she asked.

'It's a Garron pony,' said Windsor as he approached the vehicle with a white pony in tow.

'What, you want me to shoot that as well?'

Windsor burst out laughing. 'No, game reserve rules. We can't leave carcasses out to rot on the hills. You're a strapping lass, but you'd never be able to haul a dead stag back here.'

'Are we guaranteed to see any deer today?'

'It's normal to go a day or two without seeing one. So no, you might not have to shoot one, but don't get your hopes up.

'How close will I need to be to take a shot?'

'The open sights on our rifles are set to 65, 150 and 250 yards, but I'd prefer you to use the scope and try taking one out from about three hundred metres.'

'Just don't accuse me of missing on purpose. I mean,

the firing range was only seventy-five metres long.'

'Don't sweat it, Sanda. I wouldn't have brought you here, if I thought you weren't capable of making a clean kill.'

'What?'

'No pressure, but any animal's welfare will be better served by your taking it out with a single shot.'

ಉಉಉಉ

Dokukin, Medved, and Voronin had spent an uncomfortable night in Kornienko's office and were feeling restless when he returned waving a business card in his hand.

'I apologise for the delay, but I have the results,' said Kornienko handing Dokukin the business card. 'The results are in the microdot embedded in the dot above the lower-case letter, i.

'Do the results mean anything to you?' asked Dokukin.

'This is all very strange. If the test results are to be believed, one of the men is Zhukhov's son and the other is a close relation.'

'What?'

'My sentiments exactly, Captain.'

'How can that be?'

'I was hoping that you could tell me that. You might be better placed directing that question to the General. Can you tell me who these men are?'

'No, not at this late stage. The less you know about them the better. Do you know who the other man's father is?'

'That man's name is Shahram Abbasi. He was an Iranian nuclear scientist.'

'What do you mean by *was* a nuclear scientist?'

'We think he was assassinated in Paris about a month ago.'

'Surely you must know if he was murdered or not?'

'Unfortunately, I don't. The man's life seems to have ended in a similar fashion to that of the traitor, Edwin Carter. But without access to the results of any biopsies, urine, or faecal samples, we will never know how he really died'.

'Do you think he was he murdered to tarnish the image of the Motherland?'

'I don't think so. Who could accuse us of going to such lengths to kill our allies?'

'Polonium is a very difficult substance to gain access to. Is it possible that the same batch of poison was used to commit both murders?'

'An interesting question, captain. I asked one of our nuclear scientists the same question and received the following by way of a response. As you might already know, Polonium-210 is colourless, tasteless, and only fifty nanograms is sufficient to kill a full-grown man or woman. However, Polonium, like all radioactive elements, is unstable and has a half-life of one hundred and thirty-eight days, meaning that it decreases in potency as time passes. You'd need to quadruple the dose from the original batch for every year that passes to achieve the same lethal effect. Agent Carter was eliminated in 2006, so if the same source material was used to murder Abbasi, the assassin would have had to have been originally supplied with at least one hundred and fifty milligrams of the stuff. So, in answer to your question, yes, it is quite feasible that the same batch of poison was used to commit both murders.'

'In which the first lethal dose would be the size of a microdot whereas the second lethal dose might cover the dot above a lower-case letter, i.'

'A most prescient choice of analogies, captain.'

'I'm sorry to spring this upon you, sir, but the General had one other request to make from you.'

'What is it?'

Dokukin unfolded a piece of paper before passing it to Kornienko. 'He wants those digits included in the daily number station transmissions for at least the next two weeks, starting from this evening.'

Kornienko took a long look at the five-digit numeral code. 'I don't suppose you know what the message is?'

'The General didn't tell me what it means.'

'He has others in the field?'

'I don't know.'

'Very well, consider it done,' said Kornienko before bursting out laughing.

'What's so funny, sir?'

'I was just thinking that this is so old school. Micro dots, and coded radio messages transmitted over short-wave radio. Who would have believed it possible in this day and age?'

'The General has little trust for the digital communications network.'

'Let me know when you are ready to leave. I have arranged for a road traffic accident to be staged in front of the main gate. You will be smuggled out amidst the chaos. Two dark blue Land Rover Defenders will be parked-up outside the embassy, get into the one to the left of the building, the decoys will get into the other one. The driver will take you anywhere that you want to go. After that you are on your own.'

'Thank you, sir,' said Dokukin, Medved and Voronin in unison.

۩ ۩ ۩ ۩

Windsor and Osmond had leading the pony slowly over the rolling hills for a little over three hours when they stopped for a break.

'I don't suppose you brought a flask of coffee with you did you, Harry?' asked Osmond after she watched Windsor fill a plastic mug with hot tea.

'No, I'm afraid that it's tea or water.'

'In that case I'll have tea then. But I'm going to get a blinding headache if I don't have a proper coffee soon.'

'You'll be fine, Sanda.'

'No offence, but what's the big deal about coffee? Millions of people drink the stuff every day.'

'It's probably just an old school service thing, but soldiers like me have been taught that computers and coffee are for Americans,' said Windsor filling a second plastic mug with tea. 'We Brits thrive on talent and tea.'

Osmond laughed. 'What, you've got it in for the Americans as well as the Russians?'

'No, it's nothing like that,' said Windsor smiling. 'Maybe I'm just jealous of them. I used to think that the Americans' got everything a bit too easy,' said Windsor before swallowing a mouthful of hot tea. 'To my mind there are a good number of U.S. soldiers that would fall to pieces if you removed their GPS trackers and deprived them of coffee and burgers for a day. Fortunately for them there aren't many nations with the firepower to deprive them of their home comforts.'

'You stole the sachets of instant coffee from my room last night, didn't you?'

Windsor burst out laughing. 'What makes you say that?'

'Sometimes I think that you're from a different planet, Harry,' said Osmond vigorously scratching the back of her head. 'Yes, I've got a fucking headache and whose bloody fault is that?'

'So, it's point proven then.'

'All right, so regular people don't function too well without a morning coffee, but are you telling me that it's not the same for you and all your tea drinking buddies?'

'Believe it or not, no it's not. Look, you said that you wanted to be more like me. Well, people like me don't cling to props, we function under our own steam,' said Windsor pulling a can of cola from his backpack. 'I'm told that this stuff works wonders for caffeine withdrawal symptoms.'

Whilst Osmond gulped down her cola, Windsor scanned the horizon with a pair of high-powered binoculars. Then he moistened the index finger of his right hand by placing it into his mouth before waving it above his head.

'We're in luck; there's a group of three female roe deer about three quarters of a mile away. We're upwind of them, so there's a good chance that we'll get close enough for you to take a shot at them.'

'How do you know that they are female dear? Is it because they haven't got antlers?'

'Yes, it's easy to tell them apart at this of the year, but it isn't always the case. Males and females both have white fur on their hindquarters, it's called a caudal patch. It is heart shaped on the females and shaped like an oval on the males. Take a look through these,' said Windsor passing Osmond the binoculars. 'Can you see the heart shapes?'

Osmond zeroed-in on the three deer, they looked to her to be in the prime of their short lives. 'Okay, let's do it,' she said passing the binoculars back to him.

It took about ninety minutes for them to cover nine hundred metres. Windsor insisted on crawling much of the way, so as not to risk spooking the deer, which were happily eating grass on a ridge. Then Windsor gave the signal that they were finally in a good spot for Osmond to take her shot. She watched as he placed his rucksack on the ground, lay in a prone position and rested the barrel of his rifle on top of the pack. She replicated his stance and about a minute later found herself agonising over whether or not she should shoot one of the deer. Everything was as she had visualised it would be. The deer were about three hundred metres away but she should see them clearly enough through the scope. She thought that hitting the target would be easy, but making a clean kill, to minimise her target's distress and suffering, was likely to be a much harder proposition.

Windsor had shown her on a diagram where the animal's heart and lungs were. A shot a little above and back from the animal's front leg would be perfect. She slid the safety off and nestled her cheek onto the comb, took a deep breath and gently squeezed the trigger. She felt the recoil and hoped her aim had held true.

'Sorry, I missed, Harry,' said Osmond as she watched all three deer bolt as the report rang out over the hills.

'Not so fast, Sanda,' said Windsor, just as one of the deer hit the deck as the other two made good their escape over a bank.

'Grab your kit and get yourself moving!' barked Windsor who was already on his feet pulling the pony along behind him.

A few minutes later Windsor and Osmond were face-to-face with the badly wounded animal.

'You need to put it out of its misery,' said Windsor undoing his jacket and pulling out a P226 pistol. 'Use this, a single shot to the head will do it.'

Fuck it, thought Osmond. Her hands were shaking and she couldn't think straight. When she saw the animal fall to the ground, she hoped that it was dead. Now she was up close watching it struggling to regain its feet in a pool of blood. She'd only winged the deer, hitting it high, above its front leg, missing the vital organs. There wasn't a lot of blood but she felt like vomiting. But she didn't hesitate and quickly removed the pistol's safety and fired two shots into the top of the animal's head.

'Good job, Sanda,' said Windsor. 'Now we that have to load our friend here onto the back of pony and we can get on our way. Luckily you didn't hit it in the guts, else the carcass would have been ruined.'

Osmond faffed about trying to pick the deer up without getting any blood on herself.

'One day, Sanda, if you're very unlucky, you might come face-to-face with somebody intent on harming you. In such a situation you'll need four things to survive. Luck, hand-to-hand combat skills, iron determination, and willingness to do horrible things without hesitation. So, try not to let a little blood and brain get in the way of your loading our friend onto the back of the pony.'

'Did you choose a white pony on purpose, Harry?' asked Osmond before finally grabbing hold of the carcass with both hands and hauling it up onto the pony's back.

'Actually, no. But you're right, the white ones sure show off the blood. Here, clean yourself up,' said Windsor passing Osmond a canister of water and a micro towel. 'We'll take this little fella back to the lodge; they'll skin him before placing him in the game larder. After that, we can head back to the hotel for a well-earned dinner.'

The two of them didn't speak much on their trek back to the lodge or on the long drive back to the hotel. Osmond spent much of the journey picturing the badly wounded animal and wondering what sort of person could make a career out of shooting fellow human beings to death.

FORTY-SEVEN

Osmond's mood had been low since she'd shot and killed the deer but Windsor hoped to re-energise her with the next stage of his training plan. She found him seated in his hotel room in front of a wooden table covered by books, packets of playing cards, and large metal coins.

'What are the magic props for?' she asked as she sat herself down at the table.

'As I hope that I've made clear, your future welfare will depend on more than knowing how to shoot a gun and speaking a few foreign languages?'

Osmond picked up one of the coins and manoeuvred it clumsily through the fingers of her right hand. 'I'm guessing that this is what the coins are for?'

'Yes, they help improve manual dexterity. They also play a role in hand-eye coordination, as do the playing cards,' said Windsor getting up from the table and picking-up a rectangular wooden tray from a sideboard. He placed the tray on the table in front of Osmond, together with a notepad and a pen before setting the stopwatch function on his wristwatch to zero. 'I'll give you fifteen seconds. Look at the stones in this tray. I want you to memorise how many there are, their exact positions, and their colours. Starting from, now!'

Osmond looked at the brightly coloured stones sitting on a layer of sand, she counted sixteen of them. She was still trying to memorise their colours and locations when Windsor shouted "STOP" and covered the tray with a sheet of black card. She spent the next minute drawing the outline of the tray, the position of the stones on the pad and was halfway through labelling stones with their colours when Windsor interrupted her.

'How are you getting on?'

'Give me another twenty seconds and I'll have it all

done, Skip.'

'Oi! That's my bloody line. Alright, I'll give you another fifteen seconds to finish labelling them up.' When Osmond was finished Windsor removed the card covering the tray and they both checked the locations and colours of the stones against her drawing. His eyebrows narrowed slightly and he sat up a little straighter in his chair. Sanda had drawn the outline of sixteen stones. Their sizes and positions were almost a facsimile copy of the real thing, and she'd managed to get half the colours right.

Osmond was feeling very pleased with herself but sensed that Windsor wasn't happy with her efforts. 'What's the matter, Harry? Don't tell me you were expecting me to get all of the colours right?'

'No, far from it. That's the best first-time effort that I've ever seen. I suppose it might just be beginner's luck, so how about you give it another go?' Windsor then moved the tray over to the sideboard and started removing the stones, being careful to wipe the residue of sand from them as he did so. Then he placed them into a black velvet bag, half-filled with other coloured stones, before giving the bag a good shake. He then grabbed a few handfuls of stones from the bag and positioned them on the tray. He covered the tray up with the sheet of card and placed it back on the table in front of his daughter. 'Right, you know the drill. You've got fifteen seconds from, now!'

Osmond was surprised that she could hold the image of the tray in her mind's eye. This time Windsor waited until she had completed her sketch before removing the card cover.

'Fucking hell,' was all Windsor he could think to say.

Osmond's sketch and the positions of the stones in the tray were nigh-on identical, and she only got two of the stones' colours wrong.

'Okay, once might be down to luck, but twice implies a degree of talent and skill,' said Windsor picking up a book.

'Cop a load of this,' he said handing Sanda a copy of Rudyard Kipling's novel *Kim*. 'You might want to give this a read. It's a fictional story, but is accredited with bringing the Great Game into mainstream consciousness.'

Osmond looked sceptically at the book whose name she remembered from childhood. 'I haven't read it, but if I remember correctly, it's just a story describing the adventures of a boy and an old priest as they travel through India. How's that connected to the Great Game and the concepts behind your training programme?'

'Part of the story describes how the young boy, Kim, trains to become a British Spy,' said Windsor as he flicked through the pages of the book. 'Look, this is where Kim is introduced to the *Jewel Game*, the exercise you've just performed.'

'All right, I suppose that this jewel game, as you call it, might help improve my memory, but what of it?'

'Remember when we were at dinner and I told you how many people were sitting at each table in the restaurant. Did you think that was natural talent or a learned skill?'

'Well, I suppose I thought it might be a bit of both, but I still don't see how perfecting such a skill benefits me.'

'It's all about situational awareness. The most basic example I can think of is taking note of where the fire exits are in a building. Imagine automatically committing the location of each and every fire exit into your memory. It might sound a bit dull, but in an emergency, you will move without thinking toward an exit whilst others are running around like headless chickens. Take my word for it, a few seconds saved here and there can make all the difference between life and death.'

FORTY-EIGHT

Zhukhov had ordered Pyotr Volkov to guard the safe house in the team's absence. Volkov had spent the time monitoring CCTV cameras and shredding documents brought over from Chechnya. Zhukhov hadn't liked leaving Volkov to fend for himself but knew that the man was ideally suited to the task. Dokukin might have been Zhukhov's captain but Volkov was smarter and better able to think on his feet.

Now that they were back, Zhukhov wanted one task completed before all others. He wanted Meek to transpose their ever-expanding grid of known unknowns onto the large whiteboard affixed to the wall in the room he was using as an office. The question he most wanted an answer for was, who were the Troika? He'd purposely left it off the grid when they were travelling, but had a feeling that Dokukin, Medved, and Voronin would soon arrive with the answer.

֍ ֍ ֍ ֍

Namdar's private jet landed at Kish International Airport on the sun-drenched island off the South-West coast of Iran. She would have preferred to have held the last meeting of the Grand Council in Iraq, the land between the rivers, but the ongoing war against ISIS didn't allow for it. Unlike the luxurious suites booked for the members of the Council of TwentyFour, Namdar's chauffeur drove her to a dilapidated building in the town's old quarter. Maknov and her bodyguards hated the place, but the ancient building reminded Namdar of some of the best days of her long life. The facilities were basic but contained a fire temple and other minimalist comforts of what she considered to be a real home from home.

In a few hours' time, she would distribute final orders to the twenty-four men she'd personally selected to rule the earth under the supreme command of the Dark Lord. They were clever but ruthless men, men she was certain would plunge the world into war and chaos. Men who when the time came, could be relied upon to start wars, collapse the financial system, create food shortages, disrupt power grids, poison water supplies and unleash global pandemics. The coming apocalypse wouldn't be unleashed by the Devil, God or the Angels, but by humankind against itself.

ഇ ഇ ഇ ഇ

Zhukhov read the report embedded in the microdot and smiled. He didn't understand much of the technical jargon, but finally, after all these years he had his answer. He'd already guessed that either Solomon or William was his son, but now he had something tangible to prove it. Then after a few seconds his face transformed into a mask of sadness at the thought of what must come to pass.

'It is a lot to take in, I know, General,' said Dokukin.

Zhukhov said nothing as he removed the business card from the microscope, rose to his feet and turned to face the whiteboard. She watched him as he wrote a question "Who are the Troika?" in the space headed Known Unknowns. Then he turned and answered his captain. 'Yes, Natasha, a long time ago I lost what I thought was my only son. Today I've discovered that I had not one but two sons. I am an old man and thought that I'd experienced all of life's twists and turns. But how wrong I was. There are so many things that we don't know or understand.'

'When will you tell them?'

'Soon, but first I'd like to know when they will start transmitting the message from the number station?'

'Captain Kornienko said he expected to do so from

this evening.'

'Excellent. Let me know when it is done. The Iranian scientist, my half-brother, do you know anything about him?'

'No, General.'

'Oh, Natasha, I almost forgot to ask. Did Kornienko have anything else to report?'

'No, sir. Nothing.'

Zhukhov stared hard at the business card before shaking his head and placing it into his breast pocket.

ಌಌಌಌ

Windsor was knocking at Osmond's hotel room door, half an hour after they had said their goodnights, with a portable radio in his hand.

'What is it, Harry? Has something happened?'

'There's been a change of plan. Georgy wants us to return to the warehouse.'

'How do you know?'

'The message will be repeated in a few minutes time. That should leave just enough time for you to get yourself acquainted with the one-time code.'

'The what?'

'The one-time code. Georgy told me to listen out for messages sent over the airwaves.'

'Has he got a radio transmitter?'

'It would seem so. Basically, he wants us to return to home base, pronto.'

'Why?'

'Who knows? Maybe he wants to brief us on the next phase of his mad plan.'

'You're still not convinced that any of this is real are you, Harry?'

'Until I learn any different, I have to continue to assume that I'm an assassin working for Her Majesty's government.'

'But all of this is so far-fetched, it must be real.'

'It's a pity. I would have liked an extra day with you.'

'What for?'

'You know, a bit of plain old father and daughter time.'

'You're turning soft, Harry.'

'Well, there's that and two other skills that I want you to get to grips with.'

'What are they?'

'Hand-to-hand combat and surveillance countermeasures.'

'Why haven't we started them before now?'

'The ability to disable an aggressor with your bare hands is one of the most useful skills that anyone can possess. But learning to fight is a brutal, unpleasant business, and you might get injured in the process. As for surveillance countermeasures, to my mind they are a mixture of situational awareness and common sense. I thought it best to get you up to speed on memory enhancement techniques first.'

'I'm sure that you won't be able to teach me anything that can't wait until we return to the warehouse.'

'Who knows how much time you will have to learn anything when we get back there? I want us to go on an early morning run followed by an introductory CSC session. We'll check out after we've had a late breakfast.

'CSC?'

'Close quarters combat. Don't get into a sweat about it, we won't get into any of the real physical stuff,' said Windsor as he turned the radio on. 'We've got about a minute before they repeat the broadcast. I hope you know your Russian digits from zero through to 9.'

Osmond listened as a female voice with a Russian accent spoke a few nondescript words before reading out streams of five-digit numbers, repeating each set of numbers twice. Osmond hadn't had much time to look at the one-time code, but she understood the meaning of the message clear enough. 'It's such a simple code, Harry. Namdar's people are bound to be able to decipher it.'

'Simple it might be but decipher it they won't. Without their one-time codes, messages like this are almost indecipherable.'

'Apart from the GreyFriars, who's using them, Harry?'

'You'd be surprised, all the main powers of the world use them. People like me and Zhukhov have been using them for decades.'

'So how come I've never heard of them?'

'Why would you? Who goes to the trouble of scanning the world's short wave radio frequencies unless they have to? Look, it's getting late and we are going to have to be up extra early. I'll knock for you at five forty-five.'

FORTY-NINE

Osmond thought she'd woken from a dream about an eclipse of the sun, only to find her bed surrounded by women she assumed to be witches, one of which was just a head floating over her bed. Then, after a few seconds, they vanished into the semi-darkness. She couldn't sleep after such a disconcerting awakening and spent her time trying to remember the exact content of her dream. She remembered seeing a woman, she thought to be a witch, with the number 666 tattooed into her forehead. Then there was an eclipse of the sun, a giant burning pyre of wood, and towns named Salem. But there was something else, something she could only half remember, but whatever it was had seemed important. Then, as the dream faded from her mind, all she could think of was the number 666 and a town whose name she couldn't remember.

It started with a C. I know that it did. Said the voice inside her head.

She was still trying to remember the name of the town when Windsor knocked gently on her hotel room door. All thoughts of her dream were forgotten when she and Windsor set off on their run. A quarter of an hour passed when Windsor had them that a break in a semi-secluded field.

'Okay, Sanda, tell me, what do you know about unarmed combat?' asked Windsor.

'I might actually know more than you think. I already told you that I did some judo when I was a kid.'

'How long did you stick at it for?'

'Long enough to reach fifth Mon.'

'A two tag Yellow belt?'

'That's right, Harry.'

'Then you should know all about throwing, falling and trying to maintain your balance whilst knocking your opponent off theirs.'

'It was a long time ago, but I'd like to think that I can control a fall.'

'And have you ever been in a *real* fight?'

'Not since I was at school. I was about twelve. I remember there being a lot of hair pulling.'

'Did you win?'

'What do you think?' asked Osmond with a cheeky grin on her face.

'The judo should come in handy, but you will have to learn to dispense with any niceties you might have learnt as a child. You're going to have to learn to inflict real pain and trauma.'

'And how are you going to teach me that?'

'I can't. I can show you a few moves and techniques, but you'll only really learn the horrible stuff by doing it. First things first, attack is the best form of defence. Never let anyone take the first shot at you.'

'So, if I understand you correctly. You're saying at the first sign of trouble, I should punch somebody in the face?'

'No, definitely not. Never punch anyone if you can help it, it damages the hands. You need to get to the stage where you're automatically hitting with open hands - using your palms like fists, jabbing your fingers into somebody's eyes or taking head shots with your forearms.'

'That's great, Harry. I'm looking forward to that, not.'

'Your preferred method of attack should be a palm strike to the jaw, what we in the Armed Services call a chin jab. It's a pretty handy manoeuvre for a woman because it's easy for you to swing your open hand up and under the chin, just like this,' said Harry slowly jabbing Osmond under the chin with the palm of his right hand. 'You can give me a couple of shots after I put my gumshield in. Go on, give me a couple of shots.'

Osmond stood left foot first whilst she swung her open hand up and under Windsor's chin.

'You're a natural,' said Windsor as he removed the gumshield. 'Okay, the next one is the eye jab. It's very simple, all you have to do is jab your outstretched hand into your attacker's eye, just like this. Okay, your turn.'

Osmond did as she was told, flashing her leading hand out at great speed.

'You're very fast, my girl,' said Windsor, looking impressed by his daughter's athletic prowess. 'Now we've got the basics of attack out of the way, you need to learn defence. I don't know what they taught you in the dojo but in the Forces, we use the tactical Y.'

'The what?'

'The tactical Y, it's easy. You're at the bottom of a capital letter Y, your attacker is in the apex of the Y. Your job is to move out of your opponent's way, along the upper arms of the Y, attacking from the side and back.'

'What's the point of that? Surely, I'd better off just keeping my distance?'

'But what if your attacker has a weapon, such as a knife or a gun?'

'I suppose I could just try running away.'

'Not that I had too much time for the SAS, but one of their founding fathers, Jock Lewes, had a maxim that I believe in.'

'And what's that?'

'When you start running, you stop thinking.'

'I suppose that makes sense.'

'I don't want to encourage you to place yourself in danger, but if I suddenly pulled a gun on you, the best thing you could do is to move up along one of the arms of our imaginary Y and attack me from the side or back.'

'How am I supposed to jab someone in the chin or poke their eye from the side or back of them?'

'You'll have to improvise.'

Osmond and Windsor spent the next hour practicing

fighting before jogging back the hotel. Osmond was glad for the time that she'd been able to spend with her biological father, but now that they were going to leave the hotel she started to think of home and her real family.

༄༄༄༄

Namdar was sitting cross-legged on a mat in a candlelit Fire Temple, daydreaming about her long life and the changes that had taken place over the millennia. First, there had been the Flood, an event like no other. Another three hundred and fifty years passed before her husband died, and she started to believe that she might actually be immortal. Until then she'd assumed that, when the time came, they would both depart the physical world together. Eventually, she was forced to leave her homeland in order that she would be forgotten about in the mists of time. She travelled far and wide and was set upon by vagabonds and thieves several times before she realised that none could harm her. She acquired great knowledge over the centuries and eventually migrated to the land of Egypt where surviving members of the Nephilim had set up home. Egyptian society treated women well, even foreign woman, and over the generations and many changes of identity, she was finally welcomed into the echelons of the Egyptian elites to help fill the void left by the departure of the Nephilim from the earth. But Egyptian society began to crumble and she decided to migrate back east, finally setting-up home in the land called Persia, where she converted to the religion of fire.

As for the lives of ordinary human beings, they'd hardly changed for thousands of years. She'd lived through the worst of times, the great plagues, like the Black Death. But in modern times, nothing could match the scale of pain and suffering caused by the Spanish Flu and two Great Wars. The thought that she was about to unleash the war to end all wars troubled her, but in reality, she thought to herself, what chance did humanity really stand? Families sought to gain material advantage over other families; religions over other religions; cities over other cities; countries over other countries and races over other races? She had personally selected twenty-four men who placed their selfish aspirations above the rest of humanity. Seven and half billion people were about to suffer slow horrible deaths, whilst twenty-four of their number would rule as kings; at least until the end of the Tribulation.

Pain and suffering would be inflicted onto billions so that she could free herself from the bondage of life, such was her pact with the Dark Lord. Yet as the second hand of the clock of humanity was about to strike midnight, she was worried that Zhukhov, that fly in the ointment, was still alive and recruiting powerful forces against her.

'Oh, why couldn't I have killed him when I had the chance?' she asked herself. Her thoughts were broken by a knock on the door.

'Come in,' she called out through the darkness.

'I have good news, mistress,' said Maknov as he entered the room.

'What is it Fyodor?'

'Manning thinks he's located Zhukhov's hiding place.'

'A disciple based inside the Russian Embassy alerted Director Thomas to some unusual activity. Kornienko cancelled half his meetings yesterday in response to the arrival of three unexpected visitors. He tried to smuggle them out of the embassy this morning but Manning's people tracked them to a business park in north-east London.'

'And what makes Manning so sure that Kornienko's guests are connected with Zhukhov? His recent record has been less than good.'

'Kornienko requested urgent testing of two DNA samples. He –'

'What incentive did Zhukhov have for taking such a risk?' interrupted Namdar.

'Because the results of the test say that he has fathered a second child, he has another son.'

'Then question we must ask ourselves is. Is it a coincidence that Zhukhov sent Kornienko two DNA samples so soon after Solomon and Meek so recently vanished off the face of the earth?'

'Exactly, mistress. Manning wants your permission to storm the building.'

'What type of building is it?'

'It's a warehouse complex, leased to a Russian company, based on the outskirts of London.'

'But Solomon disappeared in the north of England. Is Manning certain that Zhukhov is in the building?'

'No mistress, but –'

'But nothing. Tell Manning to stand down. If he has Zhukhov cornered we will be able to deal with him at our leisure. Instruct Manning to keep the building under surveillance. I want definitive proof that Zhukhov is there whilst I think of how best to deal with him.'

'Yes, mistress. Is there anything else?'

'Is everything ready for the gathering?'

'Yes, the last of the Grand Council members touched down three hours ago.'

Have my plane readied, we will travel to London tonight.'

'But, mistress, you can't, the Grand Council? You will miss the dinner. Your leaving early might be misinterpreted,' said Maknov.

'The Council members have had good lives have they not, Fyodor?'

'Yes, mistress.'

'And they have been promised that they will soon rule the world as great kings, will they not?'

'Yes, mistress.'

'Then it is reasonable to assume that they will view my early departure as an enhancement of their positions. With me gone, they will start to deal directly with the Dark Lord.'

'Yes, mistress.'

'Then make ready the plane and return back for me in one hour, Fyodor.'

Maknov bowed his head before vacating the temple, leaving Namdar to return to her daydreams.

༄༄༄༄

Zhukhov requested that Meek and Biratu join him in his office. On the middle of his desk was the portable microscope, a bottle and three glasses.

'It's not quite Tsarskaya Gold, but it hits the spot,' said Zhukhov as he poured each of them a glass of ABSOLUT Elyx single estate vodka. 'In Rus, we say that drinking is enjoyment, and we cannot live without it. To our good health, gentlemen.'

'To good health,' replied Biratu and Meek.

'I sense that you have something important to tell us, Georgy,' said Biratu.

'Where to start? Oh, where to start, gentlemen?' said Zhukhov.

'What's the microscope for, Georgy?' asked Meek.

'On the microscope is a business card from our benefactor at the Russian Embassy. Hidden in the dot above the lowercase letter, i, is a microdot which includes, amongst other things, your DNA results. It might be easier if I tell you what it says, but feel free to read the results at your leisure,' said Zhukhov pouring himself another glass of vodka. He waved the bottle in the direction of Meek and Biratu but each declined the invitation. 'It seems that we are all related. It seems that you two gentlemen are Sanda's cousins and William's father was another of my brothers. Whereas, your father, Solomon, is very much –'

'You're my father! No fucking way, man!' shouted Biratu.

'I am afraid that it's true, the test results have not been tampered with in any way.'

'No disrespect intended, pa, but I don't know if you noticed, but you're a Russian dude and I'm a mixed-race man who was born in the heart of Africa.'

'What can I tell you? I travelled a lot in the services of the Motherland. I first served in Ethiopia in 1977, during the Ogaden War. I was very much involved in the successful beating back of the Somalian army.'

'But I wasn't born until eighty-seven.'

'Once we enter a country my nation never really leaves.'

'It's all well you two playing happy families, but what do you know about my father?' asked Meek.

'Unfortunately, he is now deceased, he passed away earlier this year. By all accounts he was a very clever man. His name was Shahram Abbasi, he was an Iranian professor of nuclear science.'

'How did he die?'

'Officially of natural causes, but there is evidence of foul play, he might have been poisoned whilst on a business trip to Paris.'

'Now hold on a moment there. You said this man is your brother, yes?'

'Yes.'

'According to your prophecy, mere mortals can't kill us and you're saying that he didn't die of old age. So, one of his relations must have killed him, making you and… Windsor… the most likely suspects. Are you telling me that Windsor murdered my father?'

Zhukhov poured each of them another glass of vodka. 'Please remember that Lilith Namdar could be responsible for the man's death.'

'But Windsor's an assassin, he makes his living by

murdering people. What's to stop him trying to murder the lot of us when he gets back here?' asked Meek.

'Please remain calm, William. Harry and I are not monsters. We are nothing more than patriots who served our countries to the best of our abilities. By all accounts Professor Abbasi went to Paris with the intention of assisting Syrian nuclear scientists in the building of a nuclear device, something that the Secret Services of many countries are likely to have taken a great dislike to.'

'This is crazy, Georgy. Is Windsor working for the Church of the Six Salems or not?' asked Meek.

Zhukhov had his hands palms up in a sign of resignation when Dokukin entered the room.

'Sorry to disturb you, general, but you said to inform you the moment Sanda and Harry arrived.'

༄༄༄༄

Although part of Iran, the island of Kish was easily accessible to people from the West and there was none of the iron adherence to Islamic law found on the mainland of the country. Kish was a flat but beautiful island surrounded by sandy beaches and coral reefs, but that's not why the billionaire owners of the twenty-four private jets had landed there. They were there for the final meeting of the Grand Council, Namdar's Council of the TwentyFour, before the start of the Rapture and their seven-year rule as kings of the earth.

Much of Kariz underground city was open to the public but hidden from view were a series of chambers that no tourist ever saw. The Grand Chamber was a massive subterranean room of strange beauty. The room was filled with throne-like chairs placed in the pattern of a semi-circle around a large, beautifully decorated, throne of royal proportions. Separating the lesser thrones from the central throne were four stone columns and the chamber was lit by an eerie blue-white light emanating from plasma balls built into its walls and domed ceiling.

To the sound of trumpets, two massive wooden doors were opened and twenty-four robed men led by Maksym Nevry, the CEO of TBV Industries, entered the chamber taking their seats on the lesser thrones. A few minutes later the trumpets sounded again and the twenty-four men rose as Lilith Namdar strode into the chamber, taking her seat on the central throne. Namdar looked about the room at the men she had selected to do her bidding. She had made them all rich beyond their wildest imaginations. She had trained each of them in the art of Semiotics, the study of signs, sigils and the secret power of the occult. She and these men had prepared the way for the Lord of the Light. In addition to building the scientific tools of humankind's destruction, they had spent billions promoting self-interest, the sexualization of children, sexual perversions, gender dysphoria, tattoos, and witchcraft, to a global audience.

'Welcome gentlemen, today I greet you as citizens of the World, but the next time that you meet, a power far greater than I will seat each you on the Stone of Destiny, crowning you Kings of the Earth,' said Namdar in a voice that filled the great chamber.

The twenty-four men bowed their heads before chanting as one, 'He that was, now is not, but will be again! He that was, now is not, but will be again! He that was, now is not, but will be again!'

'We owe great thanks to Maksym Nevry for creating the body that will house the Lord of the Light in human form,' continued Namdar.

'He that was, now is not, but will be again! He that was, now is not, but will be again! He that was, now is not, but will be again!' the twenty-four men continued to chant.

'He, in the form of what might be called, "They", will allocate your kingdoms to you and give you directives on how to rule.'

'He that was, now is not, but will be again! He that was, now is not, but will be again! He that was, now is not, but will be again!' came the response.

'But now the time has come for each of you to receive his mark,' said Namdar as the huge doors opened and two hooded men carrying a high-powered laser entered the chamber to the fanfare of trumpets.

All was silent as each man received his mark, a miniature laser-branded tattoo, burnt into his forehead. Then, to great applause, the hooded men left the chamber.

'My time on the Grand Throne is over,' said Namdar rising from her seat. I am sorry but I cannot stay for Humankind's last supper, gentlemen. There are tasks to be attended to, that only I can complete.'

Namdar strode out of the Great Chamber for what she hoped would be the last time of her life, leaving the twenty-four men to a night of feasting, drunkenness, and sexual debauchery.

Twenty minutes after Namdar departed the ancient underground complex, thirteen explosive charges were detonated above the heads of the men who had been expecting to be the last Kings of the Earth. Seconds later, the Council of the TwentyFour and the Grand Chamber, were no more.

FIFTY

Zhukhov now knew that Windsor had murdered one of his sons and their brother. He'd spent a largely sleepless night wondering if he too had been manipulated by Namdar into murdering some of their relatives. It was with those thoughts filling his mind that he'd asked Windsor to join him in his office.

'We didn't really get to talk last night, Harry. How did you and Sanda get on in Scotland?'

'Much better than I was expecting we would. I was hoping to persuade her to start learning skills better suited to our world when, right out of the blue, she suggested doing so herself.'

'And how did she get on?'

'She took to it like a duck to water. She's a natural. She can now shoot rifles and handguns and has started learning a few essential unarmed combat techniques. She's cobra fast, strong, smart, and keen to learn. What more could we ask for?'

'And how about you, Harry? Have you come down on our side or are you still making your mind up?'

'I haven't tried contacting my MI6 handler, if that's what you're asking? So as insane as all this seems to me, I don't see how I've got any other choice other than to keep playing along with all this.'

'I suppose it all comes down to trust, Harry. I have to trust that you're not an assassin loyal to Lilith Namdar's' Church of the Six Salems, and you have to trust that I'm not some insane cult leader.'

'Are you saying that you don't trust me, Georgy?'

'I wanted say that, but my contact at the Russian Embassy believes that you have a penchant for poisoning people with Polonium-210.'

'Even if that were true, what business of is that of

yours?'

'Because last night I learnt that William's father was a man named Shahram Abbasi.

'Do you have indisputable proof of that?' asked Windsor shaking his head in disbelief.

'I have DNA evidence, but no way of proving that the tests results weren't rigged. All I know is that Abbasi was our brother and he didn't die from natural causes. Did you kill him, Harry?'

'I'm not confirming or denying anything.'

'William became most upset at the news. He's unsettled by your presence here.'

'He'll get over it.'

'On the whiteboard behind me is an area headed, known unknowns. Inside is a question. It reads, who are the Troika? I know now that it isn't you, me, and our brother Shahram. So, the most likely answer to the question is that the Troika are Sanda, Solomon, and William. Unfortunately, there can be only one unpalatable outcome if that is true.'

'And what's that, Georgy?'

'That soon, both you and I shall be dead.'

'Well, I guess that's just the way the cookie crumbles, Skip.'

'I've drawn-up a list of priority actions required to put an end to this saga.'

'And what might they be?'

'Firstly, the elimination of Lilith Namdar.'

'Something you say no mortal can do.'

'Secondly, the elimination of her Grand Council. Something I thought only a powerful nation state had the power to do.'

'What do you mean by that?'

'The GreyFriars and the Church of the Six Salems are but two of many secret societies. At least one of the others wields as much power as the CSS.'

'And who might they be?'

'The Illuminati. I had for years assumed that I'd evaded Namdar's security apparatus solely through God's protection, but recently I've been led to believe that an earthly power has been busy at work, keeping her assassins from my door.'

'Meaning?'

'That the Illuminati are also in an age-old battle against her, the CSS, and her almost mythical group of men, called the Council of the TwentyFour. I have intelligence indicating that the Illuminati are planning on removing Namdar's council from face of the earth.'

'And thirdly?'

'Thirdly, the elimination of some, preferably all, of Namdar's Witch Queens.'

'But you said that there are at least fifty of them, spread over every North American state?'

'I know, Harry. But it can't be for nothing that Namdar named her witchcraft cult, the Church of the Six Salems, can it?'

'Is there anything else?'

'Yes. I am certain that Namdar intends to utilise one of the World's particle accelerators to create a gateway to Satan's pit. I have assumed that the largest of them, the Large Hadron Collider, will be used for this task, but I'm still searching for a sign, a prophetic warning, to point the way.'

'Then it is cards on the table time, Georgy.'

'What do you wish to confess, brother?'

'I've been waiting patiently for you to ask me to do something that could be used to discredit my country's security services. Helping destroy the world's most famous machine wasn't on my list, but it certainly meets the criteria.'

'But I don't need your help with that, Harry. Believe it or not - I have Solomon, William and Sanda in mind for that task.'

'So that can only mean that want me to assassinate Namdar's Witch Queens?'

'Is that something you think you could do without discrediting the reputation of your beloved United Kingdom?'

'I've never killed anyone not deemed to be a threat to national security, and I'm not planning on starting now. However, such talk is an irrelevance.'

'Why might that be?'

'Because if I'm not mistaken, we're sat here in the UK whilst Namdar's witches reside in America.'

'I know my request doesn't make any sense in the here and now, but please give it due consideration. Somehow, I sense that future events will make it very clear to you that their elimination is essential to humankind's survival.'

'And what of this business about the so-called Illuminati getting involved in this? How's that supposed to work?'

'Embedded in the lowercase letter, i, of this business card is a microdot. Amongst other things, it contains details of the Iluminati's plan to eliminate Namdar's Grand Council. Please take the business card and the microscope and guard them with your life.'

'You'll be planning on making me an executor of your legal estate, next.'

Zhukhov laughed. 'In our line of business, we must hope for the best but plan for the worst. Oh, I almost forgot. There's one last thing, Harry.'

'What's that?'

'Sanda. I don't wish to sound sexist, but she is a woman.'

'I kind of noticed that, Georgy.'

'We battle against witches, Namdar the chief of them.'

'So?'

'Sanda might have a psychic connection to them.

There are powers at work that remain hidden from me. That's all there is to say, Harry,' said Zhukhov before giving Windsor a hug.

'What's that in aid of, Georgy?'

'I just want you to know that I harbour no bad feelings about what happened to my son. We are all but pawns in a cosmic chess game. Can you please ask Natasha to come and see me?'

Windsor collected up the business card and the portable microscope, leaving a sombre looking Zhukhov to his planning and scheming.

۞ ۞ ۞ ۞

Six black Range Rover Sport SUVs were parked at a North Circular road service station when Namdar arrived there in her Rolls Royce.

'Has my journey been worth the effort?' she asked Manning as he took a seat next to her.

'There has been no sign of Zhukhov, but Windsor and his daughter arrived there yesterday evening. We've detected a lot of movement in the facility, there are at least ten people in there.'

'Then I was right to come here. But taking them down with the Black Knight in their midst will be no easy task.'

'With respect, mistress. He's only one man and his best years are clearly behind him.

'You have the nets and their rocket launchers?'

'Yes, but –'

'Good, instruct your people not to waste bullets on Windsor, his daughter, Solomon, or the man named Meek. They are to be taken down in the weighted nets. Make sure to leave Zhukhov to me.'

'But –'

'But nothing, Edward. Just for once, please do exactly

as I command you to.'

'Yes, mistress.'

'And, Edward, I trust that you and Director Thomas have arranged for us to proceed unmolested?'

'All has been arranged, Mistress.'

Unknown to the Metropolitan Police or staff at the Highway's Agency, the eye-catching convoy of seven cars was making its way at high speed to the business park housing the premises of Gusinsky Import/Export. All public CCTV cameras for miles around had been switched-off following instructions emanating from the upper echelons of Vauxhall Cross.

FIFTY-ONE

The first thing that Manning's men did upon their arrival at the business park car park was to cut the tyres of all vehicles parked outside the offices of Gusinsky Import/Export. Then, when everyone was in position, three holes were blown into the walls of the warehouse complex and armed men started piling into the building. The Russians had been quick to react but four of them were shot to death in seconds. Everyone else took up defensive positions in the largest room of the complex.

'Sanda, grab a weapon!' Windsor shouted to his daughter, but she ignored him and left the AK-74 assault rifle on the floor beside her.

'Even if you don't intend to use it, pick it up whilst you still have the chance!' Windsor shouted again. This time Osmond grabbed the rifle.

Manning's men ignored the orders they'd been given and left the rocket propelled net launchers behind before storming the main room, concentrating their fire on the man they were most afraid of, Harry Windsor, better known to them as the Black Knight. Inexplicably, none of their bullets hit the target.

Zhukhov used the moment to seize the initiative, and Windsor watched in amazement as Zhukhov got up from where he'd been sheltering and started walking directly at their assailants, firing off round after round from an AK-47. Windsor wasn't sure what compelled him to do it, but he too jumped to his feet and joined Zhukhov in the counterattack. Ten seconds later five of Manning's men lay dead whilst the others ran for cover.

Windsor led the way along the corridor leading to an exit with Zhukhov guarding their flank. Once out in the car park the Russians ignored their own damaged vehicles and ran towards Namdar's Rolls Royce and Manning's SUVs.

Namdar's chauffeur jumped out of the car and managed to fire off a few rounds from his handgun before being shot in the face by Dokukin. Whilst Maknov, who had no wish to become a martyr, lay curled up in a ball hoping that no one would notice him in the back of the car.

All the SUVs had been left unlocked with their keys in the ignition. This enabled Dokukin and Medved to jump into the driver's seats of two of the vehicles whilst Voronin and Volkov shot out the types of the others. Biratu and Meek clambered into the same car as Medved and Voronin whilst Windsor and Zhukhov unloaded the last of their bullets in cover fire. Then, just as they were running out of ammunition, they heard the booms of the rocket launchers. Windsor dived to the ground out of instinct and watched a weighted net fly harmlessly over his head, but Osmond and Zhukhov weren't so lucky. Windsor managed to untangle his daughter from the net that had knocked her to the ground just before Namdar took aim at them with a hand-held pistol from just inside of the main door of the building. 'Shoot her, Sanda!' he shouted.

'I'm sorry, I can't do it, Harry!' she shouted back at him.

Zhukhov had only just managed to get back onto his feet when the first of Namdar's bullets smashed into his shins. He screamed out in agony and collapsed back onto the tarmac.

Windsor grabbed the AK-74 from his daughter and peppered the doorway with bullets. He then turned to face Zhukhov but sensed that there was no saving the old war horse, so he forced Osmond into the back of the car.

'Natasha, Ostav' menya! Ostav' menya!' shouted Zhukhov.

Dokukin revved the engine violently but waited until Windsor had closed the door before accelerating out of the car park, turning south onto the North Circular road. All the while screaming obscenities into her throat mic.

Windsor didn't like the words he heard but found himself in agreement with most of what she said. His daughter had let them down, and another of his brothers was going to die a slow horrible death.

'You know where you are going?' he asked.

'We have vehicles in a garage a short distance from here. We must lose this car, they are bound to be tracking it,' said Dokukin.

'What's the plan after that?'

'We swap vehicles and make our way to the seaport.'

'But I left the bag containing the microscope and the microdots. They'll learn everything, the mission's sunk without -.'

'I have the bag. I picked it up when I realised that you and your daughter had forgotten it. Fortunately, some of us are professionals.'

'Steady on there, Natasha. Sanda's just a civilian. I might have left the bag behind, but if it hadn't been for me none of us would have gotten out of there alive.'

Dokukin ignored Windsor and recommenced swearing into her throat mic.

൝൝൝൝

When Zhukhov regained consciousness, he found himself tied to a chair with a cannula inserted into his left forearm. In front of him Namdar stood holding a baseball bat.

'The best you can hope for, General, is that I allow you to receive pain relieving morphine through the cannula. Maybe you would like a little now?' she asked him.

Zhukhov ignored her and focused his attention on the bat.

'You and I have a score to settle,' said Namdar rubbing her jaw. 'I will return the favour, after you have told me what I want to know,' she said before swinging the bat down onto Zhukhov's left knee. Whilst he was screaming out in agony, Namdar calmly took aim and smashed the bat onto his right knee. 'Maybe now you would like a little morphine? Yes? No? Tell me what you know!'

Apart from screaming out in pain, Zhukhov didn't utter a word.

Namdar nodded at Manning, who walked over carrying a pair of gardening secateurs.

'One last chance before this starts to get messy, Georgy. Come on, talk to me. Tell me what you know?'

Zhukhov closed his eyes tight shut as he tried to prepare himself for what was coming next. He felt his right hand being was forced open and the secateurs positioned over his little finger. He started screaming again as his little finger bounced off of the concrete floor. He kept his eyes shut whilst the next finger was cut off by teeth of the secateurs. He opened his eyes just in time to see a grinning Manning cutting off his middle finger.

Manning, assisted by one of his henchmen, made ready to cut off Zhukhov's index finger when Namdar raised her left hand. 'How about a little morphine, Georgy? What do you say?' she asked.

Zhukhov tried to ignore her and clamped his eyes tight shut again. Manning smiled as another of Zhukhov's fingers hit the bloodstained concrete floor. Manning was positioning the secateurs around Zhukhov's thumb when Zhukhov opened his bloodshot, tear-filled, eyes. 'Please make him stop!' he pleaded.

'And you will start talking, Georgy?'

'Yes, anything. Just make him stop.'

Namdar nodded and Manning backed away with a look of disappointment in his eyes.

'That's better, isn't it?' said Namdar after pressing the button on the morphine dispenser. 'Now tell me, what do you know of my plans?'

Zhukhov waited a few seconds to enable the morphine to work its way through his bloodstream. It was only a few drops, but it immediately eased most of his pain. 'None of this makes any difference, you've already been defeated.'

'What do you mean by that, Georgy?'

'It is obvious that nobody has dared tell you about Kish,' said Zhukhov turning to face an embarrassed looking Manning.

'What do you know of Kish?'

'Enough to know that your Grand Council is no more,' said Zhukhov forcing a smile. The expression on Manning's face told Namdar all she needed to know. 'What else haven't they told you? Yes, I am about to die a horrible death, but I've achieved what I set out to do. Knowing that I've been a step ahead of you ever since Dallas is what is making this bearable for me.'

'You delude yourself, General.'

'Do I? Then how is it that Meek managed to embed himself in the heart of your organisation without being caught? Could he really have done that without my help?'

'You lie!' barked Namdar.

'And the girl, Sanda Osmond, she grows stronger as you grow weaker.'

'Impossible, she knows nothing of magick and the old ways.'

'Your Witch Queens are being drawn to her when surfing the outer plains. She has awoken on several occasions to find them attacking her in her sleep, but they don't have the power to penetrate her aura. And because of that, they fear her. But I guess that you remain, like so many other things, ignorant of this too.'

'None of this makes any difference. None of you is a match for me.'

'Individually we are not, but you are no match for the Troika. Sanda, Solomon, and William share the same bloodline, and are prophesised to defeat you,' said Zhukhov before started to laugh uncontrollably.

'What's so funny?'

'You are. You think that you are invincible, but you are not. 'I took something of yours when I broke into your apartment all those years ago.'

'You took nothing from the room. You were too stupid to even remove my code book.'

'I took something that I knew you wouldn't notice. I removed a few strands of hair from a pillow, in addition to the numerous photographs I took of your other materials.'

'You're a fucking liar,' said Namdar suddenly losing all composure.

'The girl has your hair safely enclosed in your Bellarmine jug. Only time will tell what use she puts it to,' said Zhukhov before mouthing a kiss.

Namdar smashed Zhukhov about the face and head several times with the baseball bat before Manning was able to stop her.

'Mistress, please stop, there is much more that he can tell us.'

'Wrong again!' shouted Zhukhov just before the cyanide hidden in a capsule in his now broken tooth was absorbed into this bloodstream.

Namdar and Manning could only watch as Zhukhov died in front of them, his hideous grin forming into a death mask.

'He tricked you into killing him,' said Manning forgetting himself.

'Bring Fyodor to me at once, I need to speak to him before anything else goes wrong.'

Manning nodded for his henchman to get Maknov, but his order was met by a shake of the man's head.

FIFTY-TWO

It was late into the night when Medved and Volkov drove their respective MPVs into the grounds of a farmhouse just over a mile from the town of Harwich. Dokukin noticed that the kettle in the kitchen still felt warm to her touch, indicating that the farmer (a deep cover Russian spy, known as an Illegal), his family and his dogs had not long vacated the premises. The farmer grew lavender and was glad that the crop had recently been harvested and sent to auction, else he'd never have been able to explain to his wife why they were taking a very impromptu holiday. There were no livestock other than a few noisy geese, which Dokukin thought would make for a reliable organic burglar alarm.

Dokukin surveyed the premises with Medved, Volkov and Windsor before walking into a relatively empty barn. 'This is where we will interrogate him,' she said. 'Get a chair from the kitchen and tie him to it.' Medved, a bear of a man, went to collect Maknov from the boot of one of the MPVs whilst Volkov went back the farmhouse to collect a chair.

'Has he told you who he is?' asked Windsor.

'No, but we will find out soon enough. Milan discovered him cowering the back of the Rolls Royce and had the good sense to throw him into the boot of his car.'

Maknov was pale with fear when they brought him into the barn. He had soiled his expensive clothes and stunk of urine and excrement. He hadn't recognised any of the Russians but stopped in his tracks at the sight of the man he knew to be the Black Knight, Harry Windsor.

'This man knows what a murdering bastard you are, eh Harry?' said a smiling Dokukin. 'You should be afraid of all of us, as we're all murdering bastards, my friend. You're lucky that Pyotr couldn't find a metal chair as I'd have fried you on it, like an egg. Now take off your stinking clothes, we need to clean you up before we get started.'

Maknov remained silent whilst removing his clothes and scanning the faces of those around him. Medved and Volkov took turns throwing buckets of water over him, before Medved finally tied him to the chair.

'You answer my questions honestly and you will not suffer any pain. That is the arrangement. Do you understand?'

Maknov nodded that he understood.

'Now tell me, who are you?'

'My name's Arron, Arron Kravets, I'm Lilith Namdar's butler.'

'You dress very well for a butler, Arron. Your mistress pays well, no?'

'All of the staff dress well. The mistress insists upon it.'

'And it is usual for her to take her butler with her to a gunfight?'

'Everything just happened so quickly. The chauffeur drove us to a service station. We were there for only a few minutes before joining a convoy of cars to the warehouse. Look at me, I'm not a soldier. I was instructed to wait in the car. Please believe me, I am telling you the truth.'

'Shall I check his identity on the internet?' asked Medved.

'No, the name might be a code word,' said Dokukin. 'We can't afford to give our location away.'

'Why don't I blow one of his knee caps off,' said Windsor, removing his SIG Sauer P226 pistol from his shoulder holster.

'That won't be necessary, Harry,' said Dokukin. 'Get him on his feet,' she ordered Medved and Volkov.

Whilst Medved and Volkov untied Maknov, Dokukin threw a rope over one of the crossbeams supporting the barn roof. Medved held Maknov as Volkov tied his hands above his head. Then Medved pulled the rope tight, forcing

Maknov to stand on his tiptoes.

'Milan, go to the farmhouse and prepare dinner. Put some music on. Make sure to play it loud, very loud.'

'Yes, captain,' said the giant Russian before marching out of the barn.

'I'm going to give you one last chance. Tell me who you really are or things are going to end very badly for you,' said Dokukin.

'I already told you. My name's…' said Maknov before he started screaming.

'You have a low threshold for pain, Mr. Kravets,' said Dokukin as she removed the thumb of her right hand from a point between Maknov's right shoulder blade and his neck. 'It might interest you to know that the Chinese had documented four hundred and nine acupoints, also known as vital points, by the year 1815. An acupoint is a soft point on the body that can by pressed to soothe pain or as I have just demonstrated, can be used to inflict extreme pain by pressing a point called the Empty Basin. The area in your shoulder is one of seventy-four tactical points, pain causing regions, but I also know the location of ninety-six paralyzing points and thirty-two lethal points.'

Dokukin took a step toward Maknov and he instinctively responded by trying to kick out at her, but failed to do so because a kneeling Volkov was holding his legs together.

'Hold him steady, Pyotr,' said Dokukin as she launched a finger strike to the front of Maknov's neck. He responded by letting out a blood curdling scream, his body jolting as if hit by an electric cattle prod in response to the feelings of pain and paralysis flowing between his neck and shoulder. 'That point is called the Energy Abode - it's recognised as a paralysing point. Now what happens if I hit you here?' said Dokukin as she punched Maknov in an area just below his belly button.

Maknov couldn't breathe and clamped his teeth

together so hard that he thought they might break.

'Just in case you were wondering, that was one of the lethal points. It's called the Passage of Origin,' said Dokukin before letting loose a frenzy of jabs and punches all over Maknov's body. She only stopped hitting when he lost consciousness.

'Was that really necessary?' asked Windsor.

'It's payment in kind for Georgy.'

'And what if he is only a humble butler, what then?'

'I'm hungry, Pyotr. How about we have ourselves a snack before dinner?' said Dokukin, ignoring Windsor, and walking back to the farmhouse.

Windsor didn't like what he was witnessing but he knew he'd done worse in the name of Queen and Country.

FIFTY-THREE

Namdar was beginning to believe that the fates might be working against her. She'd inadvertently killed Zhukhov, Maknov had been snatched from her car, and Director Thomas's communications blackout had backfired, allowing the GreyFriars to make their escape without leaving a trace. Edward Manning was beginning to think that he might have been wise to have made his escape with them.

'Edward, why do you believe that they couldn't have travelled further than five miles? asked Namdar.

'Richard Thomas's people had all CCTV coverage in a five-mile radius from the warehouse switched-off.'

'And it was Director Thomas who advised you to disable the tracking devices in your vehicles?'

'He told me that it was the only way of keeping below GCHQ's radar.'

'I value the words of a dying man, Edward.'

'What do you mean, mistress?' asked Manning, instinctively reaching for his Beretta Px4 Storm handgun.

'With Zhukhov gone your priority is the Bellarmine, I want it found. Without Zhukhov to lead them, the others are just paper tigers.'

'But, mistress, what about Maknov?'

'Fyodor's loss is most unfortunate, but his misfortune is telling is it not, Edward?'

'I don't understand what you're getting at.'

'It is clear to me now, that a few weeks ago, Fyodor, started filtering out bad news. The most recent example being his decision not to inform me of the events in Kish. Such derelictions to duty deserve serious punishment do they not?'

'Yes, of course they do,' replied Manning, his heart racing as he wasn't at all sure where Namdar was going with her line of questioning.

'Well said, Edward. I trust that you will continue to serve me better than Director Thomas has?'

'With respect, mistress, how was Richard to know that Windsor and the others would use my vehicles to make their escape?'

'Are you telling me that you wish to take responsibility for the debacle, Edward?'

'No, but –'

'Please give me your pistol, Edward,' interrupted Namdar.'

Manning started to feel a tingling sensation in his hands and wrists and thought that he might be on the verge of a panic attack, but he did as he was instructed and passed Namdar his gun.

'Was it you, Edward, who informed representatives of the illustrious brethren, the Illuminati, when and where the last meeting of the Council of TwentyFour would be held?' asked Namdar, releasing the pistol's safety catch.

'No, of course not.'

'Somebody close to me has been liaising with the Russians.'

'I can assure you, mistress, that it was not me.'

'I thought that Fyodor might be responsible for such treachery,' said Namdar replacing the safety and giving Manning back his gun. 'I didn't know until just now that Director Thomas was our traitor. The demise of the Grand Council is most unfortunate, but prophecy only states that twenty-four men will be crowned Kings of the Earth. It is my privilege to choose the men whose names will be recorded in the *Book of Kings*. Your name, Edward Manning, will be the first entry made in the great book.

'What does that mean, mistress?' asked Manning.

'It means, Edward, that soon the fate of billions will be in your hands. You can't see it, but the Dark Lord's aura has already started to engulf you. It will get stronger by the day. The feelings of superiority you currently feel over your fellow man, will soon increase one-hundred-fold.'

ருருருரு

When Dokukin, Windsor, Medved and Voronin returned to the barn they found an unconscious Maknov, dangling by his wrists. But all that changed when Medved cracked a smelling salts capsule under Maknov's nostrils.

'Tell me, Mr. Kravets, are you going to persist with this charade?' asked Dokukin as Medved and Voronin took a firm hold of him.

'Please stop, I promise that I will tell you everything that I know.'

'Then start by telling me who you really are.'

'My name is Fyodor Maknov, I am... was, Lilith Namdar's Private Secretary.'

'Then you must know a great many of her secrets, Mr. Maknov.'

'I have served Lilith Namdar faithfully over many years with the secret hope that she would reward me by making me one of the Kings of the Earth. But all that I was going to receive for my loyalty, were the crumbs from her table. I have no wish to die. Let me live and you will know all Namdar's' secrets.'

'I could tell you that we won't harm you, but why would you trust what I say?'

'Do I have any other choice?'

'And if I let you live, what is to stop you running straight to your mistress?'

'Over the last few months, she has become paranoid, punishments are being meted out to all those suspected of disloyalty. She knows that you have me, how do you think she will instruct them to debrief me?'

'You must already have concluded that I and my fellow Russians are disciples of order of the GreyFriars, and as such cannot lie on oath. I swear to you, on all that is

Holy, that neither I nor my men will harm you.'

'Thank you.'

'However, I cannot speak for Mr. Windsor or the others, but I have no reason to assume that he or anyone else will disrespect my wishes. Understand that you will be placed under house arrest until this is over,' said Dokukin before focusing her attention on Medved and Voronin. 'Take him to the farmhouse, let him bathe and find him some clean clothes. Fyodor will be joining us for dinner.'

FIFTY-FOUR

Maknov nodded a greeting at Solomon Biratu when Voronin escorted him into the farmhouse kitchen. 'Fyodor, what are you doing here?' Biratu asked, not believing his eyes.

'It doesn't matter why or how I am here, Solomon. Believe it of not, it is great to see that you are alive and well.'

'That's enough of the small talk, Solomon,' said Dokukin. 'Fyodor has important information to tell us.'

Maknov looked around the room before sitting down. Seated at a large wooden dining table were Dokukin, Windsor, Medved, Volkov, Osmond, Biratu and Meek. Dokukin was at the head of the table with Volkov sat next to her with a pen and paper laid out in front of him. Although Dokukin was clearly in charge of proceedings, Maknov found himself drawn to the British woman he knew to be Sanda Osmond.

'Have we met before?' asked Osmond wondering why Maknov was staring at her.

'No, but it is my pleasure to make your acquaintance, Sanda,' said Maknov. 'In fact, it's my pleasure to meet all of you.'

'Please remember that you are our prisoner, Mr. Maknov,' said Dokukin which prompted Maknov to raise his hands in an act of submission.

'I know that there are only nine days until the solar eclipse, but you must understand that Namdar trusts nobody. Everyone who serves her, does so on a need-to-know basis.'

'Please start, by telling us what her travel arrangements are for the next two weeks.'

'On Saturday she will take an overnight flight to St. Louis Lambert International Airport. From there she will be driven to the town of Carbondale in the state of -'

'Carbondale, I know that name,' interrupted Osmond.

Maknov looked at Dokukin. 'Do you mind if I ask Sanda a few questions?'

'I don't see why not, but keep them brief and to the point,' said Dokukin.

'Thank you,' said Maknov turning to face Osmond. 'How do you know the name of that town?'

'This is going to sound ridiculous, it came to me in a dream,' said Osmond.

'Did a specific person speak the town's name?' asked Maknov.

'I can't think of any better way of describing them than as a group of witches.'

'Can you remember anything else about the *dream* that you had?'

'I remember a strange symbol comprising three letters. That's right, the name Carbondale and the strange symbol.'

'Can you draw it for us?' asked Maknov.

Volkov passed Osmond the pen and paper, on which she wrote: ٦ ٦ ٦

'You might not know it, Sanda, but that symbol is the number 666. It is the sign of the Beast,' said Maknov.

'That's all very interesting Mr. Maknov, but I would like to know the purpose of Namdar's visit?' asked Dokukin.

'She will be presiding over an eight-day festival of magic being held in the woods at a point marking the intersection of the two solar eclipses.'

'Two eclipses?'

'Yes, the first one, taking place on Monday 21st and the second one on the 8th April 2024.'

'Do you think that is wise?' Windsor asked as Dokukin placed a tablet computer on the table.

'The manager of this farm is an agent of the SVR. All digital communications made from here are sent over a

Russian equivalent of TOR. Namdar's people at GCHQ won't easily discover our internet searches. It should take them days to get a fix on our location,' said Dokukin before typing Carbondale, Illinois into the search engine.

'That's very interesting,' said Dokukin before passing the tablet computer around the table. Everyone's eyes were immediately drawn to the town's zip codes. There were three of them: 62901, 62902 and 62903. 'So Namdar is travelling to Carbondale, a town at the centre of two solar eclipses, separated by almost seven years, the prophesised length of the Tribulation. Tell me, Mr. Maknov, is that just a coincidence?'

'No, it's no coincidence. Namdar is going there to create six new Witch Queens.'

'How is that possible?' asked Meek. 'According to CSS orthodoxy, no North American state can have more than one Witch Queen.'

'Six coven leaders will be promoted to Witch Queens, one for each of the six towns of Salem falling within the shadow of the first total eclipse. Each one is to perform a sacred Rite as the spirit of the Dark Lord replaces the light from the sun as the moon blocks it from view,' replied Maknov.

'Is she travelling anywhere else?' asked Dokukin.

'No, Carbondale is her last stop.'

'Georgy asked me to assassinate the Salem witches on the day he was taken,' said Windsor. 'He said that it was imperative that were eliminated before the eclipse.'

'What else do we need to know, Mr. Maknov?' asked Dokukin.

'The giant particle accelerator, the Large Hadron Collider. She is planning on using it to create a cosmic gateway. The scientists who built and run the great machine are ignorant of its supernatural capabilities, but Namdar has a number of disciples working there.'

'Meaning what?' asked Biratu.

'The machine is situated on an ancient cosmic ley line connecting Stonehenge to the Great Pyramid of Giza. A few weeks ago, Namdar and I witnessed rivers of cosmic energy, created within the collider, pulsing between the two ancient monuments. The Great Pyramid is connected by ley lines to every other ancient pyramid in the World.'

'And why is that of importance to Namdar?' asked Dokukin.

'It is part of her pact with the Dark Lord.'

'The Dark Lord?'

'The Devil. She believes that the Devil, and his demons, will be released into the World via electromagnetic gateways embedded within the ancient pyramids.'

'You said that you've already witnessed the connecting-up of the pyramids. What role can a solar eclipse play in all of this?' asked Dokukin.

Maknov shrugged his shoulders, which sent waves of pain cascading through his body. 'I'm afraid that I don't know,' he finally answered as the pain gradually subsided.

'But you say she will be in Carbondale on August 21st?'

'I'm responsible for organising her travel arrangements. It would be most unusual for her to travel anywhere without my knowledge. The five points of the pentagram are: the sacred Rite to be held by the Salem Witch Queens, the writing of twenty-four names into the Book of Kings, the two solar eclipses and the running of Solomon's experiment in the Large Hadron Collider.'

'Solomon's what!' shouted Dokukin. As all eyes focused on Lilith Namdar's adopted son. 'Is this true, Solomon? Do you have an experiment scheduled to run on the Collider?'

'Actually, I do. I don't know why I didn't mention it. I didn't think that it was important.'

'So Namdar has arranged for an experiment of yours to run in the Collider, with the sole purpose of creating a gateway to this six-dimensional paranormal world you told me about, and you didn't think it was important!' said a disbelieving Meek.

It was Biratu's turn to shrug his shoulders.

'Namdar believes that the conjunction of Solomon's gateway, the geomagnetic disturbance created by the eclipse, and the sacred Rites are the conditions necessary to free the Lord of the Light from his pit.'

'Did you get all that, Pyotr?' asked Dokukin, as Volkov finished labelling his drawing of a pentagram on a sheet of A3-sized paper.

'I have recorded everything, captain,' replied Volkov.

'With the greatest of respect, you have not recorded everything,' said Maknov.

'What do you mean by this?' asked Dokukin.

'You talk like you are only dealing with Namdar. She is but the tip of the iceberg. Underneath her are the CEOs of massive multinational corporations, political leaders, senior civil servants, and scientists. All have started to turn our world upside down. Drugs, criminality and violence are on the increase. Chaos rules whilst our leaders call white, black, and try to obscure the difference between a woman and a man. All of this will accelerate before your eyes should see succeed in freeing the Dark Lord from his pit.

'I might be new to all of this, but it seems simple to me. Defang the Cobra and we can get back on with our lives,' said Windsor.

'If it was only that easy, O great knight,' said Maknov. 'You must believe me when I tell you that Lilith Namdar would willingly give you all that she owns, if you could painlessly end her life on this earth.'

'I don't care what any of you say. Nobody lives forever,' said Windsor clearly losing patience with the discussion. 'I say, enough of this, already. We know all the elements of Namdar's plan. The question is. What, if anything, are we are going to do about it?'

'No one but God can influence the two solar eclipses,' said Dokukin.

'I have been reliably informed that the Revelati Grand Council has been eliminated,' said Maknov. 'However, whilst Namdar is in possession of the ancient book, she is at liberty to write any names that she chooses inside of it.'

'So, if we can't influence the eclipses or get a hold of the ancient book, that leaves the Salem Witch Queens and Solomon's experiment,' said Volkov.

'I can't believe that I'm saying this, but I can deal with the Salem witches,' said Windsor.

'Don't talk rubbish, Harry. The chances of any of us escaping this little island you call home via air travel, are nigh on impossible,' said Dokukin.

'You forget, Natasha, I'm an international assassin. I have many identities, a number of which I'm certain my MI6 handler doesn't know about. I have many contacts in North America. Trust me, getting out of the country on my own and taking out a gang of broomstick wielding women will be child's play.'

'And what of the Collider? I've been told that it's a death trap, but the General was adamant that the Troika can disable it,' said Dokukin.

'You're seriously suggesting sending Sanda, Solomon and William on a suicide mission?' asked Windsor.

'What else do you suggest, Harry? You're saying that it needs to be you who travels to North America, you can't be in two places at once,' said Dokukin.

'Who says that I need to be. All being well, I'd be back in good time to assist in any attack on the Collider.'

'But the prophecy says that the Troika will, as you say, defang the Cobra,' said Dokukin.

'Now hold on a moment. I'm guessing that all of you are Russian Special Forces, and you're trying to tell me that a mission that's beyond your capabilities can be completed by three civilians?' said Windsor.

'Sanda will be fine, Harry. With Namdar in America, who can hurt her?' said Dokukin.

'I guess that makes you Russians pretty redundant in all of this,' said Windsor.

'Far from it, Harry. A few of us will assist in any assault on the Collider,' said Dokukin. 'Tell me Solomon, you must have one or more collaborators at CERN, who are they?

'Namdar arranged for me to deal with a CERN scientist named Dr. Michaela Abrahams.'

'I know that name,' said Meek. 'She's a member of the CSS.'

'Will she be running your experiment on the Collider?' asked Dokukin.

'No, she created the computer program that will be used to test my gateway. I'm guessing that somebody without any connection any of this will run it.'

'Let me guess, Solomon. Your experiment, is it scheduled to run for less than two minutes?' asked Meek.

'How could you know that?' asked Biratu.

'In which case, I'd wager a million dollars that it's going to be sitting on the computerised job queue to run just as the shadow of the eclipse passes over the last of the six towns of Salem,' said Meek.

'So, technicalities aside, someone needs to deal with Abrahams. So, you see, Harry, us Russians are not as redundant as you might like to think we are,' said Dokukin. 'However, I have grave reservations about sending Sanda, Solomon and William on a mission to disable the Collider. No disrespect intended, but they clearly don't have the skills, and Sanda certainly doesn't have the stomach to take a life, no matter what the consequences of her inaction.'

Osmond looked over at Maknov. 'Please tell me, Fyodor. This lady, Lilith Namdar, you likely know her better than Solomon or anyone else does. Is it really possible that she has been alive for thousands of years?

And is she really capable of bringing about the end of humankind?'

Maknov didn't answer. The expression on his face answered Osmond's questions for her.

FIFTY-FIVE

Namdar's convoy took two hours to travel the ninety-four miles from St. Louis Lambert International Airport to the town of Carbondale, Illinois. Manning had asked her to cancel the festival as he was certain that Maknov would be forced into disclosing her travel itinerary. But the 2017 Festival of Magick had been years in the making. All fifty Witch Queens were to bear witness to the formal christening of their church, the Church of the Six Salems. The festival would see six Salem witches elevated to the highest rank of their order, becoming Witch Queens, answerable to nobody other than their pagan Gods. Namdar's presence was essential, as she was required to cast each of the great circles for the six Rites of Passage.

The CSS disciples had been told that a great day of reckoning was at hand, the events of 1692 avenged as the shadow of the great eclipse passed over each of the six towns of Salem, drawing down the Sun and Moon, and opening the Gateway of Light. In truth, none of Namdar's disciples completely understood what was meant by that, but all of them wanted to bear witness to the formal baptism of their sacred church. And tonight, the woods surrounding Salem Road, Makanda, the epicentre of the 2017 and 2024 North-American solar eclipses, would be filled by followers of the most secretive of the pagan religions.

Unbeknown to Namdar's minders, Windsor was already in the woods, watching and waiting, with a Heckler–Koch HK G28 sniper rifle fitted with a suppressor and an otoelectronic night vision adapter. He'd flown into Arkansas International Airport using one of a small number of passports that he'd kept secret from the man he knew only as Michael. Windsor had estimated that he had about a one in five chance of his biometric data giving his true identity away. He was taking huge risks with his personal safety and was loving it.

Ordinarily, a night-time assault in unfamiliar woodland would have been one of Windsor's worst nightmares, but not on this shout. He'd barely had time to complete any sort of meaningful reconnaissance but had been lucky enough to witness the positioning of a large throne on the main stage, before it had been covered up to protect it from the elements. Windsor was now getting used to the idea that nobody, other than Namdar or one of his own relatives, could kill him, but he knew very well that he wasn't immune from capture, pain, and torture. He remembered how Georgy had had his legs shot out from under him and been taken down by weighted nets. He didn't believe that anybody was truly immortal and hoped to be able to prove it by training his rifle on Namdar after he'd finished with the Salem witches.

ඕඕඕඕ

Whilst Windsor lay hiding in the woods of Makanda, Dokukin and the others had joined a coach party crossing the North Sea on a ferry bound for the Hook of Holland. It was a high-risk strategy, and neither the tour guide nor the coach driver was aware that seven of their passengers had been booked onto their four-day Amsterdam & the Hansa Towns of Old Holland tour by an Illuminati disciple allied to Russia's SVR. But everything had gone to plan and they had long escaped into the ether by the time the tour guide had finally got around to reporting their absence to the Dutch police.

Dokukin had kept her promise to Maknov. He'd been left chained to a wall with a week's worth of provisions and arrangements had been made for his release after the eclipse. Uncomfortable he might be, but he was almost certain to live.

THE KEY TO THE PIT

𒀭𒀭𒀭𒀭

All the Witch Queens were dressed the same and looked to Windsor's eyes to be indistinguishable from one another. They were topless, wearing leather miniskirts, with leather garters wrapped around their right thighs. He had a clear view of Namdar who was sat on her throne, but he couldn't take a shot at her. His primary objective were the Salem witches, it being crucial that he killed as many of them as possible before even thinking of trying to inflict pain and suffering on Namdar.

Windsor zeroed in on Namdar because he wanted to be as sure as he could be that she wasn't wearing a bullet-resistant vest. Then he turned his attention back to the Witch Queens who were now sprinkling each other with what looked to be salt and water. From his vantage point he could hear the ringing of hand-held bells and lots of chanting. Finally, Namdar rose from her seat and six woman were led toward a huge fire-rimed circle. Windsor made ready to take his first shot, but by the time he'd set himself, the group of six had stopped behind the trunk of a large tree. There was nothing for him to do but wait.

Windsor felt strangely uncomfortable at the thought of having to shoot dead a group of unarmed semi-naked women and wished that the Church of the Six Salems were just like all other covens in having female and male leads. He'd have felt much more comfortable shooting six unarmed men to death, but times had changed and he'd had to change with them. Whilst he was waiting, he zoomed in on an emblem embedded on the front of Witch Queens's miniskirts, it bore the image of a hyena.

Then something happened that temporarily made him forgot about the purpose of his mission. All the Witch Queens removed their miniskirts and were standing completely naked apart from their garter belts. That hadn't surprised him because he'd been told that it was normal for witches to attend their festivals skyclad. What he hadn't been expecting was that they were all very clearly, men. Large-breasted men with thoughts of a sexual nature on their minds.

The Salem witches had moved from behind the tree and were now standing out in the open, but Windsor had failed to take a single shot. In the time it took to compose himself, the moment was lost, as the group were surrounded by fifty Witch Queens with hard-ons who had formed a circle around them. It wasn't a pretty sight, but Windsor watched the Witch Queens getting close-up and personal. Fortunately, it wasn't more than five minutes before the last of the Witch Queens shot his load and Namdar gave the signal to them to break from the circle, leaving the six Salem initiates out in the open.

'Start shooting soldier, this might be your last chance,' Windsor said to himself.

Three heads exploded in quick succession, the air turning into an aerosol of blood and bone, but Windsor kept his focus, and three soon became five. He squeezed the trigger twice more and five became six. He swung the rifle eight degrees to the right and was surprised to see Namdar still sitting unprotected on her throne. He'd used nine rounds to make what he was sure were six kills, giving eleven rounds to use on Namdar. He took a deep breath and squeezed the trigger only to see Namdar to vanish from his sights. The next two rounds missed their target, slamming into the velvet covered throne. The destruction of the throne caught Namdar's attention and caused her to spin around to see what had happened, just in time for four rounds to slam into her chest, spinning her around the other way.

You certainly bleed a lot for an immortal, thought Windsor, before unloading the six remaining rounds into the scattering Witch Queens.

Windsor dropped the rifle, switched-on his night-vision googles, pulled out his SIG Sauer P226 pistol and started marching, at speed, in the opposite direction to the mayhem he'd created in the forest clearing. He marched a half a mile through dense woodland before reaching a glade where he'd parked a Taurus 2×2 All-Terrain Motorcycle. He couldn't ride quickly in the dark, but he hoped that he'd soon be much further away than they'd think to look for him with their helicopter mounted thermal imaging cameras.

FIFTY-SIX

Windsor escaped the U.S. by flying out of Nashville International Airport to Munich, Germany, with a stopover at Newark Liberty International Airport, where he'd caught an Airbus A340-600. He was feeling surprisingly refreshed, having managed to sleep for over five hours on the overnight flight. Everything had gone so smoothly, that he wasn't the least bit surprised when he was challenged at Passport Control by two nondescript German customs officials. He was sure that the game was up as they led him to an interview room, a short distance from the customs lobby.

He was trying to control his breathing when a third official entered the room. The third man was dressed in an expensive suit and had an air of authority about him. Windsor watched as the man ordered the two customs officials out of the interview room, leaving the two of them alone together. Windsor had noticed that the man spoke German with a faint English accent and couldn't fail to notice that the lights above the CCTV cameras changed from green to red, indicating that they had been switched-off. His hands were free, and he was considering overpowering the mystery man who had sat down across the desk from him.

'It's my pleasure to meet you Mr. Windsor, I've heard so many good things about you,' said the Englishman breaking into a smile.

'And who might you be,' asked Windsor.

'Richard Thomas, UK Secret Intelligence Service's Director of Cyber Terrorism.'

Windsor's body stiffened. He was now expecting to be told that Michael really did work for MI6 and that he'd been conned into travelling to North America to commit a senseless act of mass murder.

'May I call you, Harry?'

'Call me whatever you like, Mr. Thomas.'

'Please try to relax, Harry. I could easily have had the BND rendition you to a far less favourable location if I had wanted to. All I want is a chat, and then you to go on your way.'

'How did you find me?'

'Michael, has records of all your fake documentation, even the passports you had made up on the side. You were allowed to leave the United Kingdom and return back to Europe on his say so.

'Why would he do that?' asked Windsor.

'Michael's a double agent, he's working for us and for Lilith Namdar. I'm afraid that Ms. Namdar is a very clever lady, she's got hundreds of us running around in circles.

'What is it that you want to know from me, Skip?'

'The Russians have a saying, Harry. You only find free cheese in a mousetrap. Lilith Namdar's free cheese was given to you in the woods, south of a little town named Carbondale. I am trying to find out more about the mousetrap she has enticed you into.'

'So, you know where I've been and what I've done.'

'Most, but not all. I know that a number of women were shot to death, their bodies moved to sites all over the country, which is why there have been no reports in the media about a mass shooting. A total of six missing persons reports has just been filed in six towns named Salem, and a middle-aged woman, whose description matches Namdar's, has been found shot to death in the woods, presumably in the location where her assailant killed her.'

'What has any of that got to do with me?'

'I'm not accusing you of anything, Harry, but you need to know that Lilith Namdar never left the UK, the lady found in the woods was her body double.'

'Why don't you just cut to the chase, Richard?'

'Before I do that I'd like to know if Georgy explained to you where you fit into Namdar's plans?'

'What do you mean?'

'Let me put it this way. Why do you think that Namdar had you surreptitiously placed under MI6's wing?'

'Why don't you dispense with the guessing games, Skip, and just get on with it?'

'Very well, Harry. Namdar accidentally recruited one of your relatives onto her Grand Council. This man was as greedy and power-hungry as are all would-be Council members, but ultimately it wasn't in his nature to help destroy the World. He started leaking the true purpose of Namdar's secret churches and NGOs. In fact, that's how William got started in all of this, but I digress. This man, a Russian, started leaking stories to the Russian news media, but one by one, all of the journalists he contacted were eliminated. Obviously, Namdar needed a cover story for their demise, and linked their deaths to the Russian Regime. This all worked brilliantly for her. You, her chief assassin murdering each of them to order, whilst British Intelligence happily followed the crumbs that conveniently led to Russia's door.'

'I can't confirm or deny anything that you've told me, Richard, but what you've said is very interesting. So here I am in Germany, what do you make of that?'

'I would surmise that they let you out of England so that they could follow you back to where your daughter, Sanda, is hiding out with what's left of Zhukhov's Russian disciples,' said director Thomas opening Windsor's suitcase. Thomas then waved a scanner over Windsor's belongings, finding not one but two tracking devices. 'My guess is that these little beauties were added to your luggage by somebody working in the baggage handling team.'

'With respect, Richard, I don't see what you gain from our conversation. You seem to have all the boxes ticked.'

'I was wondering if you can help me. Have you ever

dealt with anyone purporting to be from MI6, other than the man you know as Michael?'

'Let's just say that that name might be familiar to me, but I don't know any others.'

'I know the identities of most of the CSS/Revelati agents working within the SIS and Security Services and we're following Michael's every move in the hope of uncovering most of the rest of the network.'

'I hope that goes well for you.'

'Did it ever occur to you why they started paying you in bitcoin?'

'Bitcoin? That's this so-called new-fangled currency of the modern world, isn't it?'

'You see, Harry, the very real clamp-down on money laundering meant that Namdar couldn't risk paying you with fiat money, as she was certain that one day the UK authorities would red flag you. Now that wouldn't have been a problem for them if you were a bona fide MI6 contractor, but the truth is, Harry, that you aren't one. You've become, by no fault of your own, Lilith's Namdar's most feared assassin – her people refer to you as the Black Knight.'

'Hold on for a moment. Even I'm aware that somebody has been murdering dozens of Russian defectors and journalists over the years. Those deaths look, from my perspective, to be all part of the ongoing Great Game.'

'What is the Great Game, Harry? Is it a battle between East and West or is it something more sinister? Might it be a millennia-long struggle of good against evil, waged by supra-national secret orders, such as the Revelati, Illuminati, and the GreyFriars?'

'You're telling me that somebody has got themselves a passport straight to Hell because they've been inadvertently batting for the wrong side?'

'You and I both, Harry. But I like to think that we are part of the Bund der Perfektibilisten as they like to say in these parts. I find it interesting that you should be travelling to Ingolstadt in preparation for the final battle.'

'What makes of think that I'm travelling there?'

'Let's just say that I have an innate sense for such things.'

'Are we done, Richard?'

'Yes, apart from a few administrative details.'

'Such as?'

'I've had some documents made up for you that neither Michael nor anyone else in Namdar's organisation will have any record of. My suggestion is that you cross the border at Salzburg using your existing documents and then high tail it to Osternberg, where hopefully you'll get across the border unchallenged using my documents. Time is of the essence. It is common for outgoing vehicles to be stopped for customs and refugee checks. If you give me the details of your vehicle, I will ensure that you are pulled over so that Namdar's people know that you have crossed the border.'

'Okay, I'll be driving a silver Audi A8.'

'Are you are a competent motorcyclist?'

'What? Yes? Why?'

'In the bag are a crash helmet, boots and motorcycle leathers. I'd suggest that you take your backpack but leave the rest of your luggage here.'

There was a knock on the door and a lady in dressed in motorcycle leathers entered the room.

'Bitte warten Sie außerhalb,' said Director Thomas and the woman left the room as instructed.

'Let her ride pillion until you reach your car, which I'm assuming isn't parked in the airport car park. The two of you riding together should help keep them off of your tail. I wish you well in your quest, Great Knight.'

Director Thomas then left the room, leaving Windsor to change into the motorcycle leathers.

FIFTY-SEVEN

Michael, aka Ian Moore, was in the Berlin headquarters of the BND, the German Federal Intelligence Service, when Windsor's border crossing at Salzburg was red flagged. Michael had taken charge of the operation after German Intelligence had lost Windsor as the airport. But he knew Windsor too well to allow himself to relax now.

You're too cautious and too smart to drive straight to Ingolstadt. Aren't you, Harry, thought Moore.

Moore walked over to a quiet corner of the open-plan office and called Manning.

'Have you found him?' asked Manning.

'He's just crossed the border into Austria at Salzburg. He's driving a silver Audi A8, I've just texted you the registration number.'

'Where do you figure he's heading?'

'My guess is that he's being overly cautious, but he's time limited, so has few options available to him. My money's on his crossing back into Germany at Osternberg or Braunau am Inn.'

'Let me assure you, son, you've got more riding on this than your paycheck. Now tell me again. Where to you think he's going?'

Moore walked across the room and spent about thirty seconds looking at a large wall map of Europe. 'Okay, add Suben to the list, he might try driving over the border via the A8 motorway.'

'I don't want him stopped again!' barked Manning into his smartphone. 'He can't be given any reason to believe that we are tracking his movements. All I'm interested in is his leading us to the girl. Have the border guards make a record of every silver Audi that crosses the border at those three locations.'

'But —'

'But nothing, son! Get this done like your life depends on it,' said Manning before disconnecting the call.

ujujujuj

It was an hour-long drive between Salzburg and Osternberg, but Windsor completed the journey in under fifty-five minutes, including a brief stop to change out the motorcycle leathers and change the car's number plates. He had been stopped at the border into Salzburg as the man, claiming to be Director Thomas of the SIS, said he would be. He didn't notice any extra security precautions back at the German border, so he hoped he'd crossed back undetected.

From Osternberg, Windsor took the B299 straight to Ingolstadt. What with getting stopped, at Director Thomas's request, and taking a massive detour, he arrived at the safe house six hours behind schedule.

'It's good to see you, Harry, but what kept you?' asked Dokukin.

'I decided to make a detour in and out of Austria,' said Windsor, prompting the Russians to reach for their weapons. 'Everything is fine, I haven't seen any sign of Namdar's people. Where's Sanda?'

She's next door playing with coloured rocks in a box of sand. I don't know why the General thought she was so important. No offence, Harry, but I think that she is a dead weight to us,' said Dokukin.

'And where are the others?' asked Windsor, choosing to ignore the remark.

'Talking in another room. They are always talking.'

'And Maknov?'

'We left him chained to a wall back at the farmhouse. He will be fine. The farmer has been instructed to return for him on August 22nd.'

'I need to let you know something.'

'The real reason why you were delayed, Harry?' asked Dokukin.

'I got stopped at the airport by a man purporting to be a member of the Illuminati. It would seem that you are not the only people intent on saving the world. You'll have to take my word for it, but the Freemasons appear to be on your side and trying to help us.'

'Who? How? Why?' asked Volker, the man Windsor thought to be the most intelligent of the Russians.

'I was detained at the airport at the request of a man named Richard Thomas. He told me that he is MI6's Director of Counter Terrorism, a role he combines with working for Namdar and the Illuminati.'

'You trust this man, Harry?' asked Dokukin, her hand moving instinctively over her gun.

'If he was working for Namdar, he could have had his people follow me straight here without the need for the performance at the airport. Either he's working to the most subtle of plans or he was telling me the truth. He told me something that I'm sure he wouldn't have done if it was just a set-up.'

'And what was that?' asked Volkov.

'He knew that I'd killed all six Salem witches.'

'Is that it?'

'No.'

'What else did he tell you, Harry?' asked Dokukin.

'For starters, that you happen to have a safehouse here in Ingolstadt!'

'What!' said Dokukin. 'The General's contact at the Embassy assured us safe passage here.'

'The town claims to be the birthplace of the Illuminati,' said Windsor looking irritated. 'But I'm sure that you already knew that!'

'It could just be coincidence,' said Dokukin.

'Director Thomas knew that I was coming here. Something that he could only have known if the General's contact is also a member of the Illuminati.'

'You said there were a few things, Harry. What else is there?' asked Volkov.

'Did any of you know that the Witch Queens, as you call them, are all men?'

'That's rubbish, Harry, I've seen a good few of them up-close-and-personal,' said Meek.

'Well, I've seen them skyclad. Trust me, each and every one of them is a man!'

'That might explain where the Baphomet fits into all this,' said Biratu.

'Everyone please forget all about transsexual Witch Queens for the moment. I just want to know what you did out there, Harry?' said Dokukin.

'In addition to killing the Salem witches, I hit Namdar with at least four rounds to her chest. It was dark, but she had blood all over her. She looked very mortal from where I was lying.'

'Unlikely, but a possibility,' said Dokukin.

'Well, Thomas told me that Lilith Namdar never left the United Kingdom. He said she sent a body double in her place.'

'You think they assumed we would make Maknov talk and would learn her travel itinerary from him?' asked Dokukin.

'That wasn't it. According to this man, Thomas, they allowed me to travel to America just so they could follow me back to you. I can only surmise that the Salem witches are a red herring.'

'But that goes against the prophecy,' said Dokukin.

'I know diddly-squat about your prophecy, but it seems to me that Namdar has been using it against you. Although I'll admit that right up until the point where I miraculously dodged dozens of bullets, I assumed that you and the General were full of shit. Now I consider myself to be a fully paid-up member of the GreyFriars and I'm quite willing to believe that this gentleman, Thomas, and the rest of the Illuminati, think that my daughter might just hold the key that saves the world.'

'It doesn't matter what Sanda knows. All we have to do is stop Solomon's experiment running in the Super Collider. You honestly think she will be of use on such a mission?' asked Dokukin.

'And what use will you, Peter, Andrei and Milan be on such a mission?' asked Windsor.

'I think your trip to America had gone to your head,' said Medved. 'Do you think that they will lay out a red carpet for her visit?'

'What's going to happen is that the Troika will access the Collider service tunnel and delete Solomon's computer program,' said Osmond as she walked into the room.

'And you, William, and Solomon will incapacitate all the guards on your way down there, will you?' asked Dokukin, her tone brimming with sarcasm.

'No, Harry will clear the way for us.'

'And what if something happens to Harry?' said Volkov.

'Pyotr's right, Sanda. We won't get in without their help,' said Windsor.

'They can't all come with us,' said Sanda.

'And why not?' asked Dokukin.

'Remember, somebody's got to take care of Abrahams. She's got all the details of Solomon's equations and likely has the beta programs on her home computers. Every trace of the program needs to be destroyed, otherwise Namdar might find another way of opening the gateways.'

'And how do you know this?' asked Volkov.

'Because I saw it all in a dream,' replied Osmond.

FIFTY-EIGHT

Windsor found his daughter sitting at the kitchen table with a cup of strong white coffee, an old brown jug, a very rudimentary looking wax doll, and a few rusty nails in front of her. She was sat there staring into space and didn't notice that anyone else was in the room with her.

'What is it, Sanda? Are you feeling homesick again?' he asked.

'No, it's not that,' she said looking at the jug.

'What's that?' he asked.

'It's a witches' bottle, Georgy gave it to me. He gave me some old spiel about it being used against Namdar by Joan of Arc.'

'And you believe that?'

'I don't know what to believe anymore. But Georgy said that we can use it to defeat her.'

'And how's it supposed to work?'

'He said that the bottle contains a lock of Namdar's hair. He wanted me to make a wax image of her, push nails through it, then place the nails in the bottle and urinate into it.'

'And have you done that?'

'What? Are you telling me that you suddenly believe in all this witchcraft crap?'

'Aren't you the one trying to convince everyone that you've got to storm the Large Hadron Collider because of stuff you saw in a dream?'

'Yes, I know, it's crazy!'

'Up until a few days ago I didn't think that I was immune to knives and bullets, but now I'm beginning to think otherwise.'

'Georgy told me that I could only make the wax image from a memory. He said that I had to see her with my own eyes for it to work.'

'Well, you've seen her now.'

'And that's why I've made this.' said Osmond pointing at the doll. 'You know, it's weird. Ever since he gave me the bottle, I have had all manner of weird dreams and started experiencing a load of déjà vu - conversations and stuff, just like the one we're having right now.'

'In that case you might want to crack on and run that wax doll through with those rusty nails,' said Windsor before bursting out laughing. 'Hey, do you think that Joan of Arc used it as a hot water bottle?'

'Who knows, Harry? I was trying to push the nails into the wax image before you came in, but the wax is to stiff, bits just keep falling off of it.'

'Have you tried heating up the nails?'

'You reckon that'll work?'

'Like a hot knife through butter, as they say.'

'Alright, I'll give that a go. Then I'll hope that this cup of coffee works its way through me, so that I can finish the job off.'

Windsor winced. 'That's too much information for me, girl. I think I'd better leave you to it.'

۩ ۩ ۩ ۩

Unknown to Windsor, Manning's people had tracked him from Osternberg to the safe house. His fabricated number plate had red-flagged on the APNR system because another vehicle with the same registration had been recorded as being driven some four hundred miles away in the city of Berlin.

Manning was intending on launching his attack when Windsor, and the others, next attempted to leave the building. His men had been thoroughly briefed that they should shoot the Russians and take down all others using weighted nets. But that all changed when a very agitated looking Namdar appeared on the scene.

'Edward, get your people in there immediately,' she commanded.

'But, mistress, it will be so much easier to deal with them out of doors.'

'There is no time left for that. Zhukhov wasn't lying. The girl, Osmond, has my Bellarmine.'

'I appreciate that you are concerned about the jar, but it is just as likely to get damaged in the building as it is out here.'

'You appreciate nothing, Edward. I want the bottle taken off the girl immediately.'

'But we aren't ready yet.'

'I don't care how many of them get away. Just get me my Bellarmine back!'

'Yes, mistress. Leave everything to me. We will storm the building five minutes from now.

༄ ༄ ༄ ༄

Osmond had just finished pushing the last of the heated rusty nails through the wax image when the front door was smashed in. She was alone in the kitchen and the kitchen was the closest occupied room to the front door of the building.

Four huge men stormed into the building wearing googles and full body armour. They came in pairs, the lead man armed with a Taser and a baton, the man behind carrying a large, weighted, net.

Osmond reacted too slowly to escape the kitchen. Her path was quickly blocked by the first of the men, who immediately shot her with the Taser. To his surprise, although Osmond was clearly in pain and disorientated, she didn't pass out and managed to pull the wires out of her stomach with her bare hands. But the time taken to free herself from the Taser allowed the second man to cover her with the net he was carrying.

Dokukin was also confronted by the second pair of giants. She fired several rounds into the first of the two men's bodies but was rendered unconscious by the Taser before she could take a head shot. One of the giants was about to smash her skull in with his baton when Volkov dived onto him. The giant man was too strong for Volkov and sent him flying through the air. He raised his baton for a second time but took two rounds to the face from Windsor's SIG Sauer P226 pistol. This caused second the man with him to turn his back on Windsor, hoping that the body armour would do its job and that he wouldn't end up dead.

Windsor lost no time in shooting the second of the two men in the back of the head, but the bullets ricocheted harmlessly off his Kevlar helmet. The big man knew when he was beaten and started running for the front door, only to find his path was blocked by the two men carrying a struggling Osmond out of the building.

Biratu and Meek weren't sure what to do. They'd opened a trap door that led to the sewers but didn't want to leave the others behind. Meek helped Volkov get to his feet whilst Biratu pulled the wires of the Taser from an unconscious Dokukin.

Windsor was stood motionless, not knowing what to do. He could hear Sanda struggling, but there was no way that he could get past the giant blocking his way in the corridor. He'd unloaded the rest of the magazine into his back of the man without any effect. Then whilst reloading the weapon he settled on a course of action. He put the Sig back into its holster and unsheathed a six-inch military fighting knife, and rammed it into the giant's throat. The huge man fell to the floor, allowing Windsor to clamber over the top of him. There was no hail of bullets this time, instead he found himself confronted by a group of men dressed in full body armour, carrying Tasers, batons, and nets.

Sanda had been dragged about ten metres from the building by the time Windsor got outside. He was feeling confident of getting her back until he caught sight of Namdar out of the corner of his left eye, causing him to think that one or both of them was about to die. He fired a few rounds into the faces of the men who were stood between him and Sanda, killing them instantly, but the two huge men dragging Sanda along had their backs to him and he knew that there was no taking them down.

'Have they got the bottle? I don't see it, where's the bottle?' shouted Namdar.

Windsor knew that it was a long shot but he ran back into the kitchen and found the brown jug lying on the kitchen table. He grabbed it and ran straight back out of the front door. 'I know you want this!' he shouted. 'Tell them to let the girl go and you can have it!'

Namdar was already starting to feel unwell and couldn't think straight. She knew that the Bellarmine was really only dangerous in the girl's hands, but she hadn't had sight of her own witches' bottle since Zhukov stole it from her back in 1963. 'Let her go!' she commanded.

'But, mistress,' said Manning.

'I already told you, Edward, the bottle is the priority.'

'Let the girl go,' said Manning into his throat mic, but the two giants pretended that they hadn't heard him.

'This is Manning speaking. Let the girl go, that's an order,' barked Manning for a second time before the men reluctantly released Osmond from their grasp.

Windsor saw Namdar being handed a machine gun. He forced his Sig into Osmond's hands and started running to his right, waving the brown jug in front of him.

Namdar only had eyes for Windsor and her Bellarmine.

'Sanda, shoot her!' shouted Windsor.

Osmond raised the handgun, aimed directly at Namdar, but couldn't bring herself to pull the trigger.

Namdar used Osmond's hesitation to take cover, whilst keeping her sights trained on Windsor.

'Bloody shoot at her, Sanda, you've…'

Windsor's voice was suddenly drowned out by the reports from Namdar's machine gun. This time the bullets didn't miss him. His body was peppered with holes, the force of the impacts spinning him around before sending him sprawling, motionless, onto the ground.

Osmond froze, as the images of Windsor being shot to death were burned into her brain cells. Then, after a few seconds, that felt like minutes, she recovered her senses and ran back to the relatively safety of the building.

Namdar changed out the magazine and unloaded a second clip into a motionless Windsor for good measure. Then she strode over to Windsor's lifeless body, hesitating for a few seconds, before bending down and removing the unbroken Bellarmine from the death grip of his right hand.

'We must continue the assault, mistress,' said Manning.

Namdar held the Bellarmine in both hands and closed her eyes tight shut. 'Don't bother, Edward, they are already underground, I can sense it. You'll never find them. Get this place cleaned up and ship everybody out. Our work here is done.'

ቦቦቦቦ

Harry Windsor had been a true British patriot. So, in a perverse sort of way, it was fitting that Namdar ordered his body parts buried on Holy ground, in each of the four countries making up the United Kingdom.

Manning had wanted to burn the body, as he had done with Zhukov's, but Namdar wouldn't allow it. So, he had his men cut the arms, legs, and head, away from the torso - instructing that the arms be buried in Northern-Ireland, the legs in Scotland, the torso in Wales, and the man's head in England.

There was no time for mourning her biological father's demise for Osmond. She, Medved, Voronin, Meek, and Biratu had to get themselves to the area above the twenty-seven-kilometre long Large Hadron Collider tunnel, whilst Dokukin and Volkov started the hunt for Dr. Michaela Abrahams.

Dokukin's last words to Osmond were: "You let the General die, and now, because of you, your father is dead. In honour of their memories, I beg you, stop thinking and start acting. You have a date with destiny, for the sake of the World, don't let us down!"

FIFTY-NINE

It was Monday 21st August. The fateful day had arrived, leaving Osmond, Meek, Biratu, Medved, and Voronin, just over five hours, if Lilith Namdar and Georgy Zhukhov were to be believed, in which to save humankind from the start of the seven-year Tribulation - the collapse into chaos before the prophesised the End of Days.

The group of five had made their way to a small town named Meyrin, on the outskirts of Geneva, where Zhukhov believed a stairwell led down into the Collider's service tunnel. It was supposed to be one of a number of stairwells allowing emergency escape from the ATLAS detector. The Russians had spent hours looking at the area on Google Maps but hadn't been able to identify anything resembling a subterranean access point. So, it was decided that the only way that they were going to know whether or not the shaft existed, was to look for it with their own eyes.

The five of them drove around the town until they passed a garish industrial complex that wasn't in keeping with any of the other buildings in the area. They parked about a hundred metres from the complex. Osmond, Meek and Biratu sitting in the car whilst Voronin and Medved went to take a closer look. The Russians lit-up cigarettes about thirty yards from a perimeter fence whilst Osmond scanned the facility through binoculars - it was all CCTV and razor wire.

'There's a sign, I think it says that the complex is supposed to be a recycling plant,' said Osmond.

'I know that the Swiss take their recycling seriously but that place looks like Fort Knox,' said Biratu.

Osmond checked her wristwatch, it had just gone five in the afternoon, leaving them less than three hours and twenty minutes to access the subterranean complex and find and delete Abrahams's computer program. *Where is the time vanishing too?* Asked the voice inside her head.

'What did you say, Sanda?' asked Meek and Biratu simultaneously.

'Oh nothing,' said Osmond, wondering if she really had spoken out loud. 'Let's hope that Milan and Andrei get a better idea of what this place is than us.'

A few minutes later they had their answer.

'We fucked-up Sanda,' said Medved.

'Why? What have you done?'

'Nothing, and that's the problem. We should have brought a drone with us. Without one, we are never going to get a proper look inside there.

'Who's to say that they haven't installed radar to protect against aerial surveillance?' said Meek.

'The way I see it, we have two options. Either we go in, guns blazing, or we can find ourselves a bar, eat, and weigh up our options, said an exhausted looking Medved. 'Who knows, if we are lucky, maybe we find someone who works at the facility inside of one!'

'I can't think straight, I've got a blinding headache, I'm dying for a cappuccino,' said Meek.

'Me too, man. I've been feeling bad all morning,' said Biratu.

'But we're running out of time, Milan,' said Osmond.

'I am very aware of the time. But, unlike Napoleon Bonaparte, who forgot all about his maxim that an army marches on its stomach, contributing to his losing the Patriotic War of 1812, I think we should eat and take stock of our situation,' said Medved.

The five of them took a short walk along the road and entered the first bar that caught their eye.

'I need to sit down, guys. I'm not feeling very well,' said Biratu.

Medved and Voronin refused to order anything that sounded German, so everyone settled on a starter of fritto misto, followed by main courses of mushroom risotto, trout, salad and polenta in a tomato sauce. All washed down with numerous cups of black coffee and bottles of mineral water.

'You Swiss certainly take your recycling seriously,' said Osmond to their waiter.

'What do you mean?' he replied.

'We noticed the facility up the road. It looks better protected than some of our English banks.'

'Oh, that place. No recycling goes on there.'

'But the sign, I'm sure it said they recycle there.

'Take my word for it. It's a government owned facility, they do no recycling there. Your eye was caught by the armed security guards, yes?'

'Oh yes, all very strange,' said Osmond.

What do you think, Milan?' asked Osmond after the waiter had moved on to another table.

'It's in the right location. And who protects rubbish with armed guards and razor wire? I say we go in.' said Medved.

๗๗๗๗

Namdar had paid English Heritage millions of pounds for exclusive access to the Stonehenge, but money meant nothing to her now. She would have willingly handed over billions of pounds to be able to sit at the centre of the ancient stone circle. The fact that she was sat on the Stone of Kings was an added bonus. She'd made up her mind to steal it when she last visited Kingston with Solomon. Hundreds of years had passed since she had last sat on it, but she sensed that it had lost none of its power. She hoped that she was now only hours away from death, but time seemed to be running in slow motion for her.

Manning had assured Namdar that every precaution had been taken at CERN, but she had heard similar assurances from him so many times before. Her only real reassurance had come from knowing that she'd made her own arrangements, with heavily armed mercenaries guarding every emergency exit stairwell, leading up from the twenty-seven-kilometre-long subterranean tunnel.

She was holding her Bellarmine jug close to her chest, but without the hair samples she'd requested, it was useless to her. The Maryland Witch Queen was flying over from America with what she said were samples of Solomon's and Meek's hair, but Namdar wasn't sure that she would arrive before the start of the eclipse.

ଉଉଉଉ

As time slowed for Namdar it sped up for Osmond and the others. It was seven o'clock, Geneva time, leaving them only one hour and twenty-one minutes before the shadow of the Total Eclipse passed over the small town of Carbondale, Illinois.

The group were again stood outside the perimeter fence of the facility they thought housed the stairwell leading up from the ATLAS detector. They had been hoping for a delivery, a shift change, anything that might necessitate the front gate being opened, but nobody went in or out in the whole time that they were out there.

'We can't just sit here, we've got to do something, Milan,' said Osmond.

'I have a plan. We have a huge quantity of explosives in our vehicle. I will crash through the gates at speed and blow the place to pieces, hopefully, taking out most of the guards out in the process,' said Medved.

'But what about civilian casualties? People in the town might be killed or injured,' said Osmond.

'Enough of such talk, Sanda. We lost the General because –'

'And I lost my father,' interrupted Osmond.

'Do you really believe that Milan and I are going to get

into that tunnel without causing a few civilian casualties?' asked Voronin.

Osmond's head dropped. 'Okay, you're right. I know you are. It's just that I've dedicated years of my life to trying to save humankind, I can't believe that the only way to do it is by killing innocent people.'

'And what about my life, Sanda? You aren't concerned that I'll likely blow myself to pieces?' asked Medved.

'Ty sam sobirayesh'sya matratom, Milan?' asked Voronin.

'What did he say?' asked Biratu.

'He wants to know if Milan is intending to become a suicide bomber,' said Osmond.

'Neit, Andrei. We will place an accelerant at window height. Shoot it when I have taken cover,' said Medved.

'What happens after that?' asked Meek.

'We run into to the middle of the facility, all guns' blazing, said Medved. 'I'm hoping that we will find a hut or similar looking building in there. If this place contains a stairwell down to the Collider, it's got to be at the heart of the complex.'

At exactly seven-thirty in the evening, fifty-one minutes before the eclipse was due to pass over Carbondale, Medved smashed through the gates at fifty miles per hour. He hit the brakes hard, but still crashed into one of the compound buildings, causing the vehicle's airbags to explode into life, trapping him in the driver's seat. He was shaken by the impact but managed to cut his way to freedom.

In the time that it took Medved too take cover behind a low wall, dozens of guards started descending on the area, like soldier ants swarming out of a nest. The men had been paid to shoot first and ask questions later and weren't intent on taking any prisoners. They sprayed the car with machine gun fire, inadvertently detonating the explosives the

Russian's had packed into the vehicle. The explosion was massive, instantly killing seven of them.

Medved was safe behind the wall but thought his eardrums had burst, leaving him temporarily deaf in both ears. He had been close enough to the blast to have burst his lungs, but he'd saved himself by having the composure to keep his mouth open, equalizing the air pressure.

Voronin charged into the compound, the others following close behind him. He was firing at anything that moved. He'd told to others to start shooting when he stopped to reload his weapon. He didn't think it would be enough to guarantee victory, but providing the three foreigners did as he asked, they had a chance of success.

Sanda was facing her worst nightmare. Two guards appeared from behind a wall whilst Voronin was changing the magazine on his machine gun. She aimed her weapon which was set to fully automatic mode but couldn't bring herself to pull the trigger.

Voronin looked-up to see two men pointing their guns at him, and was sure that he was about to die.

'Sanda, fight or will all die!' Medved screamed at her from behind the wall.

Despite her misgivings, Osmond dropped into a crouch position, took a deep breath and started firing, two rounds at a time, just like Windsor had taught her to do. Biratu and Meek followed her lead, letting loose with their handguns. The two guards had no chance and were felled by a hail of bullets.

Medved again led the charge, taking them towards the centre of the compound. He'd killed or wounded four guards before turning briefly to check on the others. He was looking back over his left shoulder when a round smashed through his right cheek bone sending shards of splintered bone deep into his brain. He was dead before his body hit the ground, causing Osmond, Meek, and Biratu to freeze where they had been standing.

Urah! Urah! Urah!' shouted Voronin, forcing them on.

Then they saw it, a hut right where Medved had said it would be, right at the heart of the compound.

'Everyone down!' shouted Voronin before throwing two grenades at the hut, one crashed through a window, whilst the other bounced off the door. He was the first to his feet after the grenades exploded but was immediately cut to pieces by a hail of bullets, his face and head disintegrating into a mist of blood, skin, and bone.

Only Zhukhov's Troika, consisting of Osmond, Biratu, and Meek, remained now. The three of them were on their own, with nobody to fight their battles for them.

The trio were only ten metres from the hut, and even though they'd been told that they couldn't be killed, they were too scared to move. Then as bullet after bullet flew harmlessly passed them, they finally started to believe that they might just be protected by enigmatic forces. But the sense of superiority they'd all started feeling, evaporated the instant they heard the sound of the now familiar, but dreaded, rocket-propelled net launchers.

'Hit the deck!' shouted Biratu as the man traps flew safely over their heads.

The mercenaries facing them had had time to don heavy body armour, but that didn't deter Osmond, who finally accepted the necessity of killing to achieve her goal, from taking head shots, hitting several of the mercenaries full in the face. That forced the rest of the guards to pull back, allowing the three of them to gain access to the hut.

Osmond was first inside and shot two guards, whom she thought might feigning injury, in the head. Remembering the C4 explosives, she ran outside and removed Voronin's backpack from what was left of his mutilated body, before running back inside.

'You two are going to have to provide cover fire whilst I find out what's at the bottom of the stairwell. It doesn't matter if you don't hit anything, they'll be sure to keep their distance as long as you both keep firing,' said Osmond before heading down the stairs.

Osmond had only descended two floors when she was confronted by a metal door that could only be opened from the other side. She removed two small packs of explosives from Voronin's rucksack and stuck them onto the door, close to where she hoped the bolts were. She set the timer for thirty seconds and ran back upstairs. Take cover, jam your fingers in your ears, and open your mouths!' she shouted. Biratu and Meek didn't need telling twice and the three of them curled-up into balls on the floor. Ten seconds later, they were surrounded by light, fire, and a shockwave. The danger over, they all ran down the stairs.

'Keep covering me, I'm going to see if we've got access to the service tunnel. I'll call up when I want you to come down,' said Osmond before kicking open what was left of the metal door, only to find another stairwell below it. She rushed down the stairs only to be confronted by another metal door. She was about to place explosive charges on the door when she heard footsteps from above.

'Where are you going?' she shouted up the stairs. 'There's another door that needs blowing, down here.'

'They've forced their way in,' said Biratu. 'We had to make a run for it. They'll grab hold of us if we go back up there.'

Osmond pulled out a pistol and aimed where she thought the bolts were, firing four bullets into each side of the metal door. She kicked it at it a few times but it wouldn't budge.

'Stand back,' said Biratu, before smashing the door down.

They were about to pass through the door when they noticed a sign, reading:

WARNING DANGER OF DEATH

ACCESS TO TUNNEL COMPLEX
PROHIBITED WHEN ALARM SOUNDS

Osmond checked her wristwatch; it was ten minutes to eight. She stopped and set an electronic countdown for twenty-nine minutes. Leaving only two minutes, after the alarm sounded, with which to save the world.

The three of them could hear footsteps on the stairs above them but were confident that none of the guards would dare to follow them down into the service tunnel, in view of the radiation risk. A few minutes later they were standing in front of a keyboard and a computer terminal.

Meek plugged-in a pen drive and got to work. It took him a few minutes to find the backdoor into the system and was soon able to create himself an account with full administrator privileges.

They were just starting to relax when the warning sirens started.

'Okay, Solomon, what are we looking for?' Meek asked Biratu.

'All programs waiting to run, in the job queue!'

'I could have guessed that myself. Is there anything else?'

'List programs in alphabetical order. I'll bet Abrahams named her program after something related to the apocalypse.'

'This has got to be it. A program named REV-ELA-TIO.N, is scheduled to start running in two minutes from now,' said Meek.

'Okay, William, kill the program!' shouted Biratu above the din.

Meek keyed-in a few commands but a number of error messages flashed up onto the screen.

'What's happening!' shouted Osmond.

'Nothing. The account doesn't have authority to terminate the program. They must have made a change to the operating system.'

'Can't you use another account?'

'No, it's this or nothing.'

'How about we forget about deleting the computer program and just blow a hole in the side of this monster?' suggested Biratu.

'That won't work. Natasha said that we'd need ten times the amount of explosives than we've got with us,' said Osmond.

The three of them were stood staring at the computer, sirens blaring in the background, when Osmond's attention was drawn to Meek's pen drive.

'This is the longest of long shots, but it might just work,' she said removing Meek's pen drive from the machine.

'What the fuck are you doing, Sanda?' asked Biratu, as he and Meek watched Osmond pull a small clear plastic bag out from her front jeans pocket, before plugging the green memory stick it contained into the terminal.

William, load and install the program stored on my pen drive,' she said, her expression radiating confidence.

ɷɷɷɷ

Maknov's replacement, Adarvan Buhaj, didn't hesitate to give Namdar the bad news.

'Mistress, an emergency exit shaft had been breached at the Collider,' he said.

'Where?' asked Namdar.

'At a town called town Meyrin, above the –'

'ATLAS detector,' interrupted Namdar. 'Can't anyone do anything right?'

'Many are dead, mistress.'

'I have placed so many obstacles in their path. Can they really stop me?' Namdar said out loud to nobody in particular.

'What was that, mistress?'

Namdar ignored Buhaj and looked west in the direction of the Atlantic Ocean. Towards North America and the solar eclipse. 'What time is it, Adarvan?'

'Four minutes past the hour,' he replied.

Namdar continued to look west. 'In sixteen minutes, the totality will consume Carbondale and it will be over,' she said before her eyes caught sight of a car racing along the A303. 'It seems that fate is on my side. The Maryland Witch Queen brings their doom!'

Three minutes later the Maryland Witch Queen passed Namdar two folded-up pieces of white paper. 'I'm sorry, mistress, but we found nothing belonging to the girl,' she said. 'Manning's people turned her London apartment upside down but found nothing there.'

'Two is more than enough to dismantle the Troika,' said Namdar, sensing for the very first time in hundreds of years, that nothing could stop her succeeding in her quest.

'You know what to do, mistress?' asked the Maryland Witch Queen.

The expression on Namdar's face answered the question. 'You must leave me now!' Namdar shouted, waving the Witch Queen and Buhaj away.

Namdar considered it a most undignified deed to have to take just prior to the end of her long life, but there was no other course of action open to her. So, without hesitation she squatted down and urinated over the open mouth of the Bellarmine jug. When she had finished, she replaced the jug's lid before throwing it onto one of the twenty-four fires burning on the periphery of the stone circle. Then she walked slowly back to the centre of the circle, retaking her seat on the Stone of Kings. She took a few deep breaths and steeled herself in anticipation of the coming pangs of death.

Biratu and Meek were sweating profusely.

'It must be the radiation,' said Biratu. 'The super conducting magnets must be pushing the miniature black holes into position.'

'But Zhukhov said we'd be immune to it,' said Meek.

'Maybe it's something else,' said Biratu. 'Maybe it's some form of magic. Whatever it is, Sanda isn't being affected by it.'

The sound of the word, Magic, prompted Osmond to start thinking of her happy place. The place where she retreated to in mind, if not in body, in times of trouble. She was about to encourage Solomon and William to do the same when they spontaneously combusted in front of her eyes, their bodies completely consumed by fire.

Osmond watched helplessly as the two men writhed in agony but was stirred into action by the sound of the timer on her wristwatch, telling her that twenty-nine minutes were up and that she only had about one minute to save the world. She kicked William's burning body away from the terminal and took his place in front of it. Fortunately, Meek had successfully loaded and installed Loki's program, so it was ready and waiting to delete any program of Osmond's choosing. She took what felt to her like an age to key-in the program's name, but it was the best she could do whilst remaining focused on her happy place.

Suddenly all went quiet. She checked the time on her wristwatch, it was eight twenty-two. Solomon and William were dead and she felt on the point of physical collapse, but all seemed good with the world. She staggered slowly up the staircase of the emergency exit shaft, half expecting somebody to attack or detain her, but the remaining guards chose to ignore her, concentrating on tending to their dead and wounded.

༄༄༄༄

What happened to Osmond after she exited the stairwell was a blur to her. She walked out of the compound without stopping to look at the bodies of Medved and Voronin.

An hour passed as she wandered the streets of Meyrin before she regained her senses. It was then that she checked the World news on her smartphone and was pleased to see that there were no breaking news stories about plagues, wars, floods, asteroids, or earthquakes. Although there was a story about an explosion at a Swiss recycling plant, thought to have resulted in some loss of life. She thought everything seemed unusually serene with the World.

A few hours later she checked into a four-star hotel close to Geneva airport, before showering and collapsing into bed.

༄ ༄ ༄ ༄

Dr Michaela Abrahams was all smiles. She'd been tempted to go into the office at CERN but thought better of it, thinking that days, like today, happened but once in a lifetime.

She had been packed and ready to leave her apartment for over an hour but hadn't been able to stop herself from donning her Witch Queen's leather miniskirt and garter belt. Her mind was so focused on that evening's celebratory black mass that she thought nothing of it, when there was a knock at her apartment door. Not thinking, for once in her life, she opened the door only to find Natasha Dokukin and Pyotr Volkov standing in the corridor in front of her.

Dokukin was onto Abrahams in a flash, getting her in a choke hold before and dragging her to ground. Leaving Volkov to calmly walk through the open door, locking it behind him.

Abrahams regained consciousness to the sound of Mozart playing in the background. It didn't take her long to determine that she was tied to a chair, with a gag in her mouth, her hands and forearms glued to an oak table. She also couldn't help but notice that her hands were splayed, with each finger spread out from the other.

'Yes, Dr. Abrahams, there is a reason why you are still alive and why we went to the trouble of separating your fingers and thumbs flat on the table. Can you guess what it is?' asked Dokukin rhetorically whilst unsheathing a razor-sharp knife. 'You see, we need to retrieve any, and all, copies of a particular computer program that you have coded. Might you know which one I am referring to?'

Abrahams tried to pull her limbs off the table, but they didn't budge a fraction of a centimeter.

'We have a problem. You see, I would much rather have interrogated you somewhere more private. Unfortunately, we had little choice other than to do this here, in your apartment. I'm not going to offer you false hope. You see, you are going to die here, today. All you can influence is how slowly, and how painfully, the process will be,' said Dokukin as she placed a small caliber pistol on the table next to the knife. 'You will be tempted to scream or call out for help. Trust me, you must resist the urge to do that - it will be so much better for you in the long run. Do we understand each other?'

Abrahams nodded.

'Good. First of all. Am I to take from your regalia that you are what they call a Witch Queen?'

'I would have thought that that much was obvious,' replied Abrahams, her tone brimming with scorn.

'I was told, but didn't believe, that you Witch Queens are in fact men. Now there can be no disputing that what I was told, is true.'

'What difference does that make to your mission?'

'None, I suppose.'

'Then can we please get on with whatever it is that you intend to do?'

'Very well. I won't draw this out any longer than is absolutely necessary,' said Dokukin, who was impressed by Abrahams's gutsy performance. 'I want you to tell us how many copies of your World Ending computer program exist, and where you've stored them,' said Dokukin as Volkov picked-up the knife.

'I don't understand your obsession with the computer program. Surely, since you are clearly aware of its existence, you are also aware of where the original is?'

'It is loaded on the computer system serving CERN's Large Hadron Collider. I haven't received verification yet, but if all went to plan, the program will have been safely neutralized by now.'

'That's the problem with you fanatics. You all have an inflated sense of self. You see, we know that you are few in number, and lack both manpower and the resources to break into CERN. There was no possibility of the Greyfriars stopping the program running and the Gateway from opening. The Mistress covered every eventuality.'

'Except for maybe this one,' said a grinning Dokukin. 'All that I care about is ensuring that there can be no possibility of a similar event happening at some unknown future date. Which is why you must die, and all copies of your program destroyed with you.'

'Prophesy states that the opening of the Gateway is a one-time event. Either my program ran successfully, or it didn't. If it did, then life, for you, will be short, painful, and brutal. If it didn't… we'll my fate rests in your hands. But surely, if you are a true believer, you understand that the window of time for my program has passed?'

'What do you mean by this?' asked Volkov.

'Doesn't the prophecy state that there can only be one start date, and one end date, for the seven-year Tribulation?

If my program successfully opened the gateway, the mistress's followers will spend the next seven years living in luxury, whereas you, and your kind, will live in utter misery.'

'Strangely, you don't seem at all concerned about your own fate,' said Volkov.

'Why should I be? If the Dark Lord is indeed free, I don't believe that you will be allowed to kill me.'

'You are either very brave or very stupid,' said Volkov. 'You are completely at our mercy. Nothing on God's earth can change that.'

'Prophecy says that one day, the Dark Lord will successfully escape the pit. Nothing that you or I do can change that. Either the Tribulation starts tonight, or it will commence at some other predetermined date that neither you, nor I, will likely ever be aware of. Nobody will really know whether or not we were successful until Monday 8th April 2024 – when the shadow of the full moon next passes over the town of Carbondale. Why don't you free me and go enjoy the next seven years of your lives? What's done, is done. Ultimately, you have wasted years of your short lives for nothing.'

A smiling Dokukin clapped her hands. 'Bravo, you gave us a fine speech. And you know what? I believe you. Time on this earth is short, but one day Pyotr and I should be welcomed into Heaven. I have no wish to jeopardize that by murdering you. I'm going to let you go, regardless of whether you give us what we came for.'

'What are you doing, Captain? Have you lost your senses!' interrupted Volkov, not believing his eyes and ears.

'No, Pyotr, she is right. Either the time is now, or it isn't. Her death serves no purpose in the grand scheme of things.' said Dokukin raising her right hand, indicating that he shouldn't interrupt her again. 'Give me all copies of the computer program and we will be on our way. I give you my word of honour.'

'And what of the word of your subordinate? How can

I trust him?'

'Our General is dead, and I do as my Captain commands. You have my word of honour that I won't harm you,' said Volkov.

At that moment, both the Russian's smartphones beeped, indicating that they had each received an encrypted text message. Its words read:

> Solomon, William, Milan, and Andrei, are dead. I think that we deleted the program in time but am not sure. It was a close-run thing.
>
> God willing, we will speak tomorrow.
>
> Sanda

Dokukin smiled. Methinks your Dark Lord might just be keeping you safe. If I'd read this message before giving you my word of honour, you'd be dead now. But what's done, is done. I won't go back on what I said.'

An hour passed before they left Abrahams's apartment, with the hard drives of her computers inside a navy blue attache case. It was a strange parting, as neither Abrahams, Dokukin, nor Volkov had any feeling for which, if either of their sides, had won what they hoped was their final battle.

Dokukin and Volkov then did as Osmond had done. They booked themselves into separate rooms in a four-star Geneva hotel, showered, and checked all news channels for any global disasters, before falling into their respective beds and getting themselves some much needed sleep.

SIXTY

Osmond's phone rang at seven a.m. It was Dokukin. 'Where are you, Sanda? Pyotr and I would like to meet you for breakfast.

'I booked myself in to a Geneva hotel on the Avenue Wendt, it's called the –'

'Geneva City,' said Dokukin finishing Osmond's sentence. 'That's bloody spooky. Pyotr and I are also booked into this hotel. Can you meet us in the lobby in ten minutes?'

'Yes, I'm almost ready to go. Ten minutes it is then,' said Osmond hanging up the call. *They are here, I can't believe it,* said the voice in her head. *Surely, this is the best of signs.*

Ten minutes later the three survivors were hugging each other with tears in their eyes.

'Do you think we won, Natasha?' asked a relieved looking Volkov.

'Why not? The three of us are alive and nothing bad has happened in the World. Might we three be the General's Troika?'

'All I know is that this has been the most insane month of my entire life,' said Osmond. 'I can't wait to get back with my family and try to get myself grounded back into reality.'

'The others, what happened to them, Sanda?' asked Dokukin.

'Milan and Andrei were shot to death. But without them we would never have made it into the tunnel.'

'I'm sorry but have to ask you this. Did *you* kill anybody?'

'Yes, I had no other choice. I shot several of the guards to death before Milan, and Andrei died.'

'What happened in the tunnel?'

'I'm not sure. One second Solomon and William

looked fine; the next, they both burst into flames in front of my eyes.'

'But you successfully killed Solomon's computer program before it ran, yes?' asked Volkov.

'It was a very close-run thing. In all honesty, I don't know if we were in time.'

'We've all seen the news. Nothing of significance has happened. I know that it's very early in the start of a new day, but you'd have thought we would have seen a sign, if something bad had happened,' said Dokukin, her face looking years younger than Osmond remembered it. 'Come on, you two, let's see if they will serve us some vodka with our breakfasts?'

Then their eyes caught sight of a TV screen. There was a breaking news story; live from Stonehenge, Wiltshire, England. It concerned the body of a middle-aged woman, found earlier that morning, sitting on the stolen Stone of Kings, at centre of the famous stone circle. All three of their heads dropped as they realised that Solomon Biratu's computer program, the Key to the Devil's Pit, might have run long enough to allow the Dark Lord, and his fallen angels, to escape back into the World, just as Namdar's life-force was sucked from her thousands-of-years-old body.

The three of them knew that they would only really know if Tuesday 22nd August 2017 was the start of the Tribulation, if, over the coming weeks, months, and years: the people of the world start falling victim to global plagues; religious leaders started corrupting their churches; wildfires seemingly set the world ablaze; the prospect of global war were to raise its ugly head again; and people started to be blocked by governments and corporations from earning a living, being denied access to employment and their bank accounts.

Osmond saw the strain return to Dokukin's face, making her look years older again. She couldn't believe that everything that they had been through, had been for nothing. It made her think of her years of blogging and her website.

'Don't look so sad, Sanda. We tried, and that is all that counts in this life,' said Dokukin.

'I'm sorry. It's just that we have all devoted our lives to this moment in one way or another. You and Pyotr have been fighting a real war, whilst I've tried to do my bit by blogging. I, like you, have devoted the last few years of my life to trying to save the planet. I just can't bring myself to accept that it might all have been nothing. The strapline on my website reads, "*People are fragile… the planet can look after itself*". I'm thinking now that I had it all wrong, and that people really are fragile, and that our leaders shouldn't have devoted so much time and resources to trying to save the planet.'

'Today is not a day to worry about such things, ladies,' said Volkov, his eyes smiling but his expression tinged with sadness. 'I will insist on having vodka with our breakfasts. As today, truly is the start of the rest of our lives.'

'Who knows, Pyotr? Maybe you and I will be married someday,' said Dokukin, before kissing Volkov gently on the mouth. 'Come, let us celebrate friendship between all peoples and nations.'

And with that, the three of them linked hands and strode towards the restaurant.

At that exact moment on the Giza Plateau. A young Egyptian boy watched, awestruck, as a tall masculine looking woman walked out of the Great Pyramid. Camels grunted loudly and donkey's kicked-out and squealed whilst the hairs on back of the boy's neck stood on end. The woman stopped to look him, her gaze seemingly penetrating into his very soul. Then she smiled, what he thought was a most terrifying smile, before winking at him and vanishing into the heat of the late morning sunshine.

THE KEY TO THE PIT

ABOUT THE AUTHOR

JOSEPH BUSA was educated at Royal Holloway College, University of London, where he took a BSc in Chemistry before going on to study a PGCE in the teaching of science at the University of Southampton. He has had a variety of jobs but hopes that in the writing of books he has found his true vocation in life. He was born and lives in London.